THE CLOUDS
BENEATH THE SUN

TF176564

Awarded for excellence in public service
Dumfries and Galloway
Libraries, Information and Archives

Dumfries and Galloway
L I B R A R I E S
Information and Archives

Central Support Unit: Catherine Street Dumfries DG1 1JB
tel: 01387 253820 fax: 01387 260294 e-mail: libs&i@dumgal.gov.uk

24 HOUR LOAN RENEWAL BY PHONE AT LO-CALL RATE - 0845 2748080
OR ON OUR WEBSITE - WWW.DUMGAL.GOV.UK/LIA

THE CLOUDS BENEATH THE SUN

Kenya, 1961. As a small plane carrying Natalie Nelson lands at a remote airstrip in the Serengeti, Natalie knows she's run just about as far as she can from home. Trained as an archaeologist, she has fought hard to be included in a team excavating ancient remains in Kenya, but before she can find her bearings, the dig is surrounded by controversy and murder. As a growing attraction to famed colleague Jack Deacon becomes a passionate, reckless affair, Natalie must give evidence in a trial that could spark violence and turmoil, and destroy everything she hoped for...

The Clouds Beneath The Sun

by

Mackenzie Ford

Magna Large Print Books
Long Preston, North Yorkshire,
BD23 4ND, England.

British Library Cataloguing in Publication Data.

Ford, Mackenzie
    The clouds beneath the sun.

        A catalogue record of this book is
        available from the British Library

        ISBN   978-0-7505-3353-9

First published in Great Britain in 2009 by Sphere

Copyright © Mackenzie Ford 2009

Cover illustration © Max Owen by arrangement with Arcangel Images

The moral right of the author has been asserted

Published in Large Print 2011 by arrangement with
Little, Brown Book Group Limited

Magna Large Print is an imprint of Library Magna Books Ltd.

Printed and bound in Great Britain by
T.J. (International) Ltd., Cornwall, PL28 8RW

For Sarah, Mark, Isabelle,
Sienna and Henry.
In gratitude for endless hours
of happiness in the Karoo.

This book is a novel.
The plot has been invented,
the characters are fictional.
But it is inspired by a true incident.

Contents

The Kenya/Tanganyika Border
September, 1961

The Apology

The Land Rover juddered to a halt. Natalie Nelson jolted her head on the side window and was shaken awake. 'What's the matter, Mutevu? Why are you stopping? Watch out for that termite mound! Have we got a flat tyre? What's wrong?'

Natalie was weary – no, she was drained, exhausted, *spent* and this delay was too much. She'd been travelling without sleep now for more than twenty-three hours, since she had left Cambridge some time yesterday, and she was anxious, longing, desperate to reach Kihara camp. However primitive the beds might be, however much a relic of Empire, however scratchy the horse-hair mattresses, she'd be asleep in no time – just try stopping her. A two-hour train ride from Cambridge to London; two hours across London to Heathrow; two hours *at* Heathrow, waiting; thirteen hours in the air, including a two-hour stopover in Cairo; two hours at Nairobi International and more waiting; and then two hours in the smallest, noisiest, bone-shaking single-engined contraption she had ever seen, which had dropped her out of the sky at the red-clay Kihara airstrip not forty-five minutes ago. Twice already she had nodded off in the Land Rover and that took some doing when you were driving over the corrugated volcanic ash that the Serengeti boasted in places.

'Elephants,' muttered Mutevu Ndekei.

Natalie frowned. For as far as the eye could see,

all around them, smooth bone-coloured rocks caught the African sun, making the landscape resemble a vast graveyard where ungainly dinosaurs had met their end. Here and there clumps of flat-topped acacia trees threw patches of shade across the shimmering gold-green of the savannah grass that swayed in the breeze. Gazelles grazed in the distance, now and then raising their heads to look for trouble.

But right in front of the car, near a massive fig tree, was a small herd of elephants.

She frowned again. 'Yes, I can see that but ... they're not dangerous are they, elephants? Why don't we just drive round them?'

This was Natalie's first dig as a fully fledged member of an archaeological team – she had just turned twenty-eight and her Ph.D. was barely six months old. But she had worked in South Africa as a student and so was not a complete novice in the bush.

'One of them is flat on the ground – he or she may be dead.'

They both watched as the other elephants moved in closer to the animal that had fallen.

'I don't understand, Mutevu. What does it matter if–?'

'*Shsh*. Elephants can sometimes be difficult if an animal dies,' he whispered, pointing to a large she-elephant looping her trunk around a tree and pulling at the branches.

Mutevu, who had been the only person at the strip to meet Natalie – the rest of the team were in Kihara Gorge, excavating – was as soft-spoken as he was huge, a strapping six-foot-three Maasai, black as night, with tribal cut-marks gouged out of his cheeks. He had told her his main job was as camp cook, but he also helped out with the driving.

His enormous fingers found the diminutive ignition key and killed the engine.

'Elephants seem to understand death – not as much as humans do: they don't bury their dead in graves, nothing so elaborate – but they're not like other animals, either, who show no signs of loss.'

Now Mutevu pointed at an old male elephant standing by the fallen animal.

'They appear to have a form of grief and will remain by a dead body for days on end, almost as if they are offering comfort or holding ready to help if the fallen animal should move or show signs of life.'

They both watched in silence as most of the herd stood still, stopped eating and just looked on as the large female this time broke off an entire tree branch, thick with leaves, and carried it in her trunk towards the collapsed beast. Then she dropped the branch on the elephant, so that the creature was partially covered.

'That's amazing,' said Natalie under her breath.

'Are they burying the animal or covering it, to keep it warm? No one knows,' said Mutevu softly. 'But it's clearly an emotional time, and to drive through or near a herd when they are in this mood can be dangerous. We'll just wait.'

Natalie reached for her camera.

For the best part of an hour they watched as the elephants completed what Natalie had to concede looked very like a ritual. Four or five other animals followed the lead of the she-elephant and tore off branches of trees and covered the dead elephant. Then, one by one, they moved off, leaving just the solitary male still standing by the corpse.

The only sound was the wind, gently rocking the Land Rover.

When the main herd had all but disappeared across the plain, and the old male was left by itself, Mutevu's fingers reached for the ignition key. He switched on the engine and the Land Rover rolled forward.

Natalie's mind was in a whirl. If elephants experienced grief, did they have any conception of an afterlife? Did that mean they had the rudiments of religion?

She rubbed her eyes with her fingers. She was too tired to face that kind of question just now. But it was the kind of question Natalie liked, the kind of question she had come to Africa for. As an expert on extinct forms of life, she was hoping to make her fair share of discoveries in the coming months. The excavation Natalie was about to join was the most prestigious in her chosen field, and the invitation to become part of the team was a big feather in her cap. So long as she didn't make a fool of herself, and published one or two good papers, a fellowship of her college was now a distinct possibility.

Mutevu slowed the Land Rover to negotiate some dried ruts where a herd of something had churned up the ground. He stretched out his arm and pointed: 'Bat-eared foxes.'

Natalie yawned, smothered it with her hand and grinned sheepishly. She looked to where Mutevu was indicating, but she couldn't see anything. Though she had worked in South Africa, her 'bush eyes' were very underdeveloped. The foxes' camouflage was just too good for her.

Mutevu accelerated as they cleared the ruts. The sun was high now and hardly any shadows could be seen across the plain. Natalie marvelled at the landscape: the shimmering grass, the lush greens of the fig and acacia trees, the rust-red rocks, the wide sky. This was one of the reasons she had chosen Africa; it was so far – and so different in every way – from Cambridge.

Cambridge. She'd had to get away and the invitation to Kihara couldn't have come at a better time. Until recently she'd never have imagined she would ever want to escape the university but then she had never imagined Dominic would do what he had done, and in the way that he had done it.

She was beyond tears now, but the skin on her throat still broke out in a sweat when she thought of... It had been this way since, since that day four – no, five – months ago, when he had told her he was going on a long tour and that, well, he didn't want to see her again. Just like that, a 'guillotine' as her mother would have said, drawing a finger across her throat: a bolt from the blue.

Natalie hadn't suspected that anything so dramatic, so final, so *terminal*, was in the wind when Dominic had suggested coming up to Cambridge from London for the day. It had happened scores of times before. But, she supposed, she had been naïve. In her experience some people were born naïve, just as some people were born knowing and others were born wise. It wasn't true in her case, however, that she was born naïve. She knew now that she had had a very naïve upbringing.

'That's the gorge there,' said Mutevu, pointing.

Natalie lifted her drowsy head and nodded. A great red-brown quartzite gash slashed through the plain ahead of them and off to their right. She'd heard so much about Kihara Gorge and the great discoveries throwing light on early mankind that had been found there. Soon she would be part of this landscape herself.

She yawned again, returning to her thoughts, unable to stop herself despite the sheer grandeur of the surroundings. She had met some very different women at Cambridge when she arrived there as an undergraduate; they were far more sophisticated and even cynical but before too much of it rubbed off on her she had fallen for Dominic. She knew she was physically attractive to men but when she arrived at university she was totally inexperienced. However, because of her father's involvement with church music, as the organist at Gainsborough Cathedral in Lincolnshire, and because her mother taught music as well as French and still sang in the choir there, Natalie had been much more knowledgeable than her undergraduate contemporaries about composers, opera and musical theory. That, as much as her looks, had set her apart at the lunch where Dominic had been the guest of honour. Someone had fallen ill and withdrawn from the dinner being given for him after his cello recital in

24

King's College Chapel a day later, and he had himself invited her to make up the numbers.

All her upbringing had warned her against becoming involved with a married man – a fact which Dominic had made no attempt to conceal. But – she could admit it now, when she was all alone, many months afterwards and thousands of miles away in Africa – she had been just a little bored with herself as a Lincolnshire provincial and had thought that a risqué affair with a man who was becoming famous would complete her Cambridge education. She had secretly envied some of the more sophisticated women she had met at university, who were much more casual in their liaisons than she was, who lived with men without marrying them – a growing trend that disconcerted Natalie and shocked her parents – women who seemed to know all manner of clever and fascinating older souls in London, in the theatre, in journalism or the new world of television.

To begin with, several of these women had surprised her, telling her she was 'mad' to fall for 'someone like Dominic', whatever that meant. But, as time went by, and the affair had lasted more than a term, she had become the object of envy on the part of these very women who, it turned out, were *not* as enamoured with their own lifestyles as it appeared.

Mutevu slowed the Land Rover as they came to the lip of the gorge, and changed gears as the vehicle began to slither down the slope. There seemed to be thorn bushes everywhere and Natalie pulled in her elbows where they stuck out

25

of the window, to stop her skin being scored.

Dominic had been impressed when Natalie got a first and, when she had stayed on in Cambridge to work for her doctorate, when most of her undergraduate friends disappeared to London, her relationship with him had been a source of nourishment in what was for her, for a year or so, a more solitary existence. Her parents, pleased by her exam results and by the fact that she was staying on in Cambridge to complete her Ph.D., had probed gently about any 'relationships' she might have. But it had taken her nearly two years to admit to her affair with Dominic and the revelation that he was married had devastated her mother, who hadn't really adjusted by the time she died.

The Land Rover crested the lip of the gorge on the south side and the camp came into view: a constellation of tents in various shades of dark green, surrounded by a huge fence of spiky thorns. Mutevu drove in through an opening in the fence and reversed the vehicle into a space reserved between two large, flat-topped acacia trees. He killed the engine again.

'No one will be back from the gorge for another hour or so – lunch is late here, about two. You've been allocated that tent there, at the far end of the row. I'll help you with your–'

Suddenly he let out a loud gasp and shouted, 'Leopards! Not *again!* That's the second time this month. They come for the goats when everybody else is in the gorge, working.'

He blasted the horn, and, seeing and smelling the Land Rover, the leopards – there were two of them – began to slink away, edging along the row of tents and scampering out of the entrance.

Mutevu watched them go. 'Leopards are rare, Miss Natalie. I bet you haven't seen one that close before – eh?'

Getting no reply, he looked across to the passenger seat and smiled.

She had seen nothing, nothing at all. She was fast asleep.

Shadows cast by the hurricane lamps played across the refectory table. The tang from the flames hung in everyone's nostrils. The refectory tent was open down one side, where it gave on to the nearby campfire, around which chairs were arranged in a rough circle. After dinner, some of the team liked to sit chatting. At night temperatures cooled in the bush.

Mutevu Ndekei, now back in his chief role as the camp cook, shuffled around the table holding a large serving plate with strips of roast kudu, the local deer. His white T-shirt stretched tightly across his massive chest and he shuffled because he was wearing a pair of green rubber wellington boots given to him by a British archaeologist years before. Mutevu was very proud of them, was never seen without them – he cooked better with his boots on, he said – but they were slightly too big for him. He leaned forward so that Natalie Nelson could take her share of meat. As she helped herself, she listened to Eleanor Deacon. As did everyone else.

A white Kenyan by birth, Eleanor Deacon was probably the most well-known palaeontologist in the world. She had been excavating in and around the Kihara Gorge for nearly forty years, first with her husband Jock and, since his death six years ago, leading the digs herself, though her sons Christopher and Jack were following in their parents' footsteps. Thin, tall and bony, Eleanor Deacon's silver – almost white – hair, brushed back as always in a chignon, gave her a remarkably sophisticated air, especially stuck out here in the bush. But she was formidable too, and ran her excavations with an iron rod, which she used on herself as much as on others. She wore no jewellery but tonight she was dressed in a crisp white shirt above khaki trousers, with a bright yellow scarf tied around her throat. A pair of gold-rimmed half-moon spectacles glittered on her nose. Natalie thought the director looked more French than Kenyan.

Eleanor sat at the end of the long table, where she was always served last. She took a few strips of kudu then leaned back so that Mutevu could withdraw the serving plate. Leaning forward again, she picked up her knife and tapped her champagne glass with it. The chatter around the table died.

She smiled at all the others, one by one, and held up some envelopes. 'Post. Russell, there's one for you, one for Kees and *three* for Richard.' She handed them around. 'Nothing for you, Arnold, I'm afraid.'

'None of my wives missing me? Oh dear.' He made a face, before grinning.

Natalie was sitting next to Arnold Pryce, a botanist, and had already learned that he had been married four times. And as often divorced. Though small and round, he was in his way a bit of a dandy. Tonight he was wearing a cravat at his throat, with a college design on it: shields and unicorns. She was also aware of some pungent aftershave.

Beyond him was Kees van Schelde, a Dutch geologist, probably in his twenties, and Jonas Jefferson, a specialist in human anatomy and the camp doctor. So far as Natalie could see, he was more or less Eleanor's age.

Christopher Deacon, Eleanor's son, sat at the far end of the table. Among other things, Natalie had learned that he was the excavation's photographer.

'As I think you all know, Natalie Nelson – who picked up the post for us in Nairobi – is the latest addition to our team.' Eleanor nodded to Natalie. 'Natalie is a zoologist, a specialist on extinct forms of life, who did her Ph.D. under Frank Whittard. I expect she's going to flake out at any minute because she came directly from Cambridge in one day, but I want to welcome her formally to Kihara and to tell her that her timing couldn't be better ... because I also want to offer a toast to Daniel.' She raised her glass. 'Daniel, what *would* we do without you – Daniel, the lion of the gorge!'

Around the table, glasses were raised.

'Daniel!' they chorused. Someone did an imitation of a lion's roar and they all laughed.

For his part, Daniel Mutumbu didn't touch his drink. He was the only black palaeontologist on the team and didn't really like champagne, or alcohol in general come to that. But he smiled back at them.

Eleanor turned to Natalie. 'Normally, my dear, alcohol isn't allowed here in Kihara.' She smiled. 'But I suppose everyone knows I keep a few bottles of champagne handy for when we have something to celebrate – and we certainly have something to celebrate tonight.'

She waited for the hubbub to die down. Two bottles between ten didn't go very far but it was enough to loosen tongues.

'Daniel and Richard here – Richard Sutton, who you will get to know and Russell, Russell North ... well, they made a discovery in the gorge today, an important discovery, a *spectacular* discovery – at least, we think it is. They found a knee-joint, a tibia and a femur: two leg bones of a hominid at a level which indicates that this early form of mankind walked upright here, right here in Kihara, two million years ago. Early man left the trees and raised himself up on two legs in this very gorge.'

'Yesss,' hissed Richard Sutton. He was thin, spare, fair-haired, handsome, Natalie thought. From what had been said earlier, as dinner was beginning, she knew he was a New Yorker, a full professor at Columbia University.

Mutevu Ndekei had reached Eleanor's place the second time round, with the vegetables. As she took some potatoes, she addressed herself to Richard Sutton and Russell North. North was Australian, Natalie had learned, though he lived in America too, as an associate professor at Berkeley in California.

'We'll check tomorrow,' Eleanor went on, 'but I agree the bones you found are hominid, human-like. On the small side, but you'd expect that. We'll confirm the level of excavation tomorrow. I take it you photographed everything, and marked the site?' She sliced her potato.

Richard coloured. 'Of course we did, Eleanor. We're not novices, for Christ's sake.'

'Watch your language, Richard, please. I was just making sure you had everything covered. If this is as important as you say it is – and the champagne tonight means I think I agree with you – we are going to come under intense scrutiny from other colleagues. Our methods must be above suspicion. Don't be so jumpy.'

Richard was draining his champagne glass and he wiped his lips with his napkin before replying. He shook his head. 'Don't worry, Eleanor. We made a sensational discovery, at the two million level. There's no doubt about the date, the excavation itself was clean and neat, everything has been properly recorded and photographed. We fenced off the site with thorny acacia branches. We can build a proper fence tomorrow. Relax.' And he launched himself on his dinner.

Eleanor nodded, watching him eat: his precise movements, his sharp features. One of the reasons she had selected Sutton for the dig was because he was a thorough, rigorous scientist, utterly competent, whose capacity for work matched her own. A New Yorker by birth, Sutton's father, she knew, was a Manhattan lawyer, the right-hand man to a real estate millionaire, who had not been entirely happy when his son had shown academic leanings. But, since he had, Richard Sutton Senior had done everything he could to ensure Richard Junior was the best palaeontologist in the business, providing his son with the finest education money could buy and then supporting important excavations financially so long as his son was part of the team. This did not make the Suttons friends with everyone, but most digs were so inadequately funded that many directors were only too happy to have Richard Junior along, if that meant the books would be balanced. And in any case, he did not really need his father's support any more; Richard Junior was an excellent excavator with a good mind. As Eleanor knew, he already had several discoveries under his belt, including a hominid skull dating to 150,000 years ago, and a species of extinct hippopotamus.

'The way that tibia and femur fit together strongly suggests an upright gait – are we agreed?' Eleanor set about her own dinner.

'That's the point,' said Russell North. 'It's a knee-joint like that which makes shopping and bowling possible.'

Eleanor grinned. She liked North. Whereas Sutton, though ferociously efficient, was a shade on the automatic side, North was a warm human soul with a sharp sense of humour. He had a temper, she knew, and he could be awkward – direct in the Australian way – but mostly he was fun on a dig, again with a number of discoveries to his name. And besides, no one was perfect. He was destined, she felt sure, for great things. He was a year or two younger than Sutton.

'The way the two bones fit together,' North

went on, 'implies that some form of hominid was walking upright two million years ago. That is much earlier than we thought, much earlier than anyone thought, much earlier than the textbooks say. Richard and I have discussed it and we think we should write a paper on this and rush it to *Nature.' Nature* was the weekly science magazine, published in London, where most major scientific discoveries were announced.

Eleanor nodded. She reached for the water jug and filled her own glass. Then she fixed her gaze on Natalie Nelson. 'Natalie, let's hear from you. You've just arrived; you have a fresh mind. How does the discovery strike you?'

Since the Nelson woman had arrived only that day, Eleanor had yet to form an opinion of her. The newly minted Dr. Nelson came highly recommended. Her specialism was a very useful expertise to have on a dig like the one Eleanor ran, but the director had not anticipated Dr. Nelson being so attractive. She was tall, almost as tall as Eleanor herself, had close-cropped dark hair which curled forward under her ears, a longish face with cheekbones that stood out and cast their own shadows, long tapered fingers and what the women's magazines, the last time she had looked, called a 'full figure'. Eleanor Deacon had already taken on board that both Russell North and her son Christopher had been immediately drawn to the newcomer and she hated that sort of emotion in the confined quarters of an excavation. Romance on a dig was not unknown: her own late husband had made a speciality of it, so she knew at first hand that it could make life very difficult.

Natalie swallowed some water. After a few hours' sleep she had unpacked, showered and changed into a blue shirt with khaki trousers. She wore no ring or necklace but had on a man's watch. Her eyes were as dark as the night outside the refectory tent.

'I'm sorry to be a wet blanket,' she said, setting down her glass. 'But I think you would be unwise to publish until you can check the tibia and femur you have found against a set of modern bones. If your dating is right they're two million years old, but you can't be certain they prove bipedalism without a close comparison and, well, you have probably thought of it, but if you get such a simple thing wrong ... it could be embarrassing.'

'No!' breathed Sutton. 'No – I won't have that!' He slapped the table and looked hard at Eleanor. 'How many digs has Natalie been on, how many hominid bones has Dr Nelson seen close up, in the field?' He paused. 'Very few, very few if any, that's my bet. This is her first day here, for pity's sake. What does *she* know? This creature was bipedal. It's a straightforward piece of anatomy. *I feel it!* I've been excavating in Africa for ten years. *Nature*, here we come!' He thrust his chin forward and glared hard at Natalie, staring her down, his lower lip stuck out beyond his upper lip, daring her to contradict him.

Natalie coloured. As he had reminded everyone, she was the least experienced of those present. But she still thought he was being *méchant,* as the French said: cruel.

Eleanor came to her defence. 'Don't be such a

34

bully, Richard. Natalie is right. We have to be careful.'

'But that means delay,' complained North, putting his knife and fork together. 'Richard and I are here only until Christmas. After that we disperse, back to the States to teach. It will take much longer to write this paper when Richard is back in New York, I'm in California and you are still here in Kenya, Eleanor.'

'I agree, Russell.' Eleanor smiled. She paused as a great barking of baboons broke out nearby. But it quietened down as quickly as it had started. She laid her hands on the table, palms down. 'But we are scientists, not journalists with a deadline to meet. Of course we need modern bones, to make the comparison Natalie suggests. I don't know why none of us thought of it – perhaps the champagne has gone to our heads, clouding our minds. Natalie, coming from the outside world, has brought us some fresh air.'

She sat back and transferred her gaze from Natalie to Richard, to Russell. 'I understand your sense of urgency – both of you – but you must curb it. Richard, what would your father think if you published prematurely and then got egg on your face – egg that might be plastered all over the *New York Times*?'

Sutton said nothing but he worried at his watch on his wrist. Eleanor's barb had hit home.

Mutevu Ndekei came round again, clearing the dinner plates. Richard and Russell exchanged glances.

'Look,' said Eleanor, modifying her tone. 'We'll assume that the bones tell us what we *think* they

35

tell us. We'll write up the paper, here, now, in camp, while we're all together, as if the comparison with modern bones has been done so that we are all ready to go into print as soon as the comparison has actually been made. That way the delay will be minimised.' She looked around the table. 'Don't worry. No one else is going to find bones like this – Arnold here is more likely to find another wife.' She grinned and the others laughed. 'You can afford to wait a few weeks. What Natalie suggests is a very simple piece of science craft, Richard. Very simple, but vital. And you know it in your heart.' She smiled at Natalie and then looked back to Richard. 'Think how convincing a photograph of your bones would be alongside some modern examples.' She rested her elbows on the table. 'You should thank our new arrival, Richard, not abuse her.'

She raised her glass. 'Now, enjoy what's left of your champagne. Who knows when we'll taste the next bottle?'

Natalie sat in the canvas chair outside her tent and looked out at the night. Everyone had their own quarters on Eleanor Deacon's digs, each tent big enough to stand up in, and Natalie was grateful for that. All tents, she had discovered, had their own bucket shower and latrine, too – another real luxury – and were spaced far enough apart for true privacy. No doubt because she had been the last to arrive, Natalie's was in fact at the end of the line. The tents were laid out in a large 'T' shape and hers was at the foot of the central stem, so she was doubly fortunate. This was the first excavation she had been on since she was a student, and where she had full responsibility for one particular aspect of affairs. She was already finding the experience very intense: everyone else was so much more experienced than she was, all were extremely highly motivated, as the exchanges at dinner showed, and took their responsibilities so very seriously. She didn't mind. That's how she liked it, in fact, but she was grateful, for tonight at least, that people hadn't lingered over the dinner table, so she could return to her tent, sit, wind down, smoke a cigarette and, her guilty secret, sip a late whisky. The flask was on the table in front of her now. She knew alcohol was banned but it wasn't as if she was an alcoholic – far from it. She liked one whisky a day, late at night, when the busy-ness was all over and she was by herself. She was ready for bed – more than ready – but one nip settled her; it did no harm.

She listened to the night. Barks from the baboons, shrieks from the chimpanzees. What did they find to shout about so much? There was also the odd roar from lions, who always seemed so much closer than they actually were. Or so she hoped. Across the camp she could see three of the men still sitting talking. They had moved from the refectory table to near the campfire: Richard, Russell and Christopher. Eleanor had already turned in for the night, as had the others. The kitchen tent and storeroom were also dark and silent: Mutevu was in bed too.

Natalie smelled the whisky she had poured into the small silver cap from her flask, and sipped the liquid. She had acquired the taste from her father, long before he had gone off into that private world he now inhabited alone since Violette, her mother, had died. Not surprisingly, being a choirmaster, Owen Nelson was a deeply religious man whose twin passions were the music of Bach – the greatest sacred composer in his view – and the single malts of the Scottish highlands, Scotland's great gift to the world, as he liked to say. In Natalie's early teens, immediately after the war, Owen had driven his wife and daughter, in his brand-new Hillman, on annual excursions to Scotland in search of distilleries he had yet to try. It was in the course of those holidays that Natalie had first encountered Loch Ness and looked out of the car window in vain for the fabled, long-necked monster. The very next day, at the Hunterian Museum in Glasgow, she had stood underneath the never-ending skeleton of a Diplodocus suspended from the ceiling of the museum's main gallery, and to her young mind it had seemed all too obvious that the dinosaur and the mysterious creature in Loch Ness were pretty much the same beast. The museum had sold a jigsaw of the dinosaur, which Natalie's mother hadn't been able to resist, and the young woman's interest in extinct forms of life was kindled.

She smelled the whisky again and rolled another drop around her tongue, felt the liquid slip down her throat as she swallowed. Curious how no one ever remarked on how sensuous whisky was. She again looked across the camp to where the men were talking. Christopher had gone, but Richard and Russell sat close together. The campfire was almost dead.

Although this was still her very first day in Kihara, she was aware of the effect she had produced in the camp. More than one of the younger men had looked at her in the way men looked at women they felt attracted to. She pulled on her cigarette. Even that carried a history, reminding her of the way her mother had met her end. Even so, a sense of well-being spread down through Natalie's shoulders and chest: the nicotine, plus the alcohol, working their magic. She was dimly aware of some new studies that had linked tobacco-smoking with lung cancer but, from what she knew about the design of the experiments, the evidence was far from conclusive. And, like her whisky, she so enjoyed a smoke at the end of the day. What harm could one cigarette do?

Richard Sutton Junior was, outwardly at least, the best-looking of the younger men in the camp. But he was also the most cocky, and Natalie hated his overconfidence. Russell North wasn't bad-looking, not as striking as Richard maybe but, judging by his performance at dinner, he was a damn site more fun to be around. Kees van Schelde was different again. The Dutchman was small – too small for her – with pointed features, a small nose and remarkably smooth skin, with hardly any beard showing. He was very tidy, *bien rangé*, economical in his manner and movements. Natalie was sure his tent would be immaculate.

Christopher Deacon was harder to read. He wasn't bad-looking either but there was something *unformed* about him, she felt. More than the others, he watched life from the sidelines; or he hadn't yet grown in confidence to be wholly his own man. Of course, it couldn't be easy with Eleanor around all the time, but then he *had* chosen to hold on to her apron strings. He had an elder brother, she had heard, called Jack, who was away in Nairobi or London – she wasn't sure which. Maybe Jack was more formed.

She took another sip of whisky. She was still smarting from the way Richard had snapped at her over dinner. Natalie had been making a simple point, one that was obvious to any scientist who reflected carefully about the situation they found themselves in. And she had been grateful for Eleanor's support. Eleanor, she knew, regarded her not with suspicion exactly, because Natalie was more than enough qualified for the job. No, it was a more personal reaction, having to do with the fact that she was a young woman surrounded by four young men. Well, that couldn't be helped.

She watched as Richard and Russell got to their feet and moved away from the dying fire. There would be an early start tomorrow, following up today's momentous discovery, and she would for the very first time be able to explore the fabled gorge for herself. The two men dispersed and walked slowly back to their respective tents. The camp was dead for the night and it was not yet nine-thirty.

Natalie looked up. The stars were so bright down here in Africa: they seemed so close. Amazing that there was a man-made satellite up there with them now and talk of sending men to the moon. She doubted it would ever happen.

Another burst of barking shattered the peace out to her right, and she wondered if a fight had broken out among the baboons, or if a young animal had been snatched away by a predator. The skies looked so peaceful compared with life on earth. She was tired but she didn't think about bed. However tired she was, these days sleep wouldn't come. It wasn't just that Dominic refused to go away, that he clogged her mind – like the way she had heard anaesthetic could bide in the small vessels of the brain for months after an operation. She had left Cambridge without saying goodbye to her father and that had been hard. Natalie's parents had been – her father still was – unsophisticated, unworldly and in its way that's where the problem lay.

It had something to do with being an only child. It wasn't just that she was overprotected as a young girl – though that was true enough – but her parents too had been very naïve, inexperienced, unworldly. Her father had met her mother when he was a student at the Guildhall School of Music in London and she was a member of a French choir that had come to London for a competition. Owen Nelson spoke some French; Violette Royere spoke rather more English, so they had been able to explore London together. He knew where the best church choirs sang, where the best music shops were to be found. Violette came from a small town called Moirans-en-Montagne – Moirans in the mountains – west of Geneva. It could not have been more different from the pancake-flat fens of Lincolnshire, and when Owen had visited Violette a few weeks later he had loved the landscape almost as much as he had fallen for her. They had been married soon

41

after and Violette had moved to Gainsborough early in 1932, Natalie being born just over a year later.

In Gainsborough, music had been Owen and Violette's life – a beautiful life, Natalie thought, a pure, straightforward, innocent, clear, clean life but *closed*. Music, she now knew, could be so fulfilling that it drowned out everything else. It hadn't with Dominic but it had with her parents. They had remained married, and happily so – Owen Nelson the organist and choirmaster, Violette teaching music and her native French in a local school – until Natalie's mother had died just ten months before when, on a camping holiday, she had fallen asleep in her tent with a lit cigarette in her hand. The tent had caught fire and Violette had been first asphyxiated and then burned.

With Natalie's father being so much a part of the church and her mother a teacher, in provincial England, serving others, they had led relatively simple lives. Yes, her mother had stood out in Gainsborough, thanks to the fact that she smoked those strong-smelling French Gitanes cigarettes, which she had to order specially, and because she knew more about wine and make-up than the average Lincolnshire mother. Her haircuts, too, could be ... well, daring. But, Natalie guessed, the most flamboyant thing Violette had ever done was marry a Protestant. It had caused a major rupture in the very Catholic Royere family, so Natalie had learned, but Owen and Violette had found that their passion for music was more than doubled when they were together, and they had never looked back.

Then had come the war. Natalie's father had spent most of the Second World War playing the piano, as accompanist to a well-known opera singer who had toured the troops. Owen had suffered a slight shrapnel wound when one concert had been shelled, but he had carried on playing and received a medal in 1946. But all that meant he was away for months at a time. During the war years, when Natalie was reaching her early teens, she saw her father on barely three occasions and mother and daughter became very close.

Moirans-en-Montagne was famous for its traditional toy-making industry. Violette had worked there as a toy-maker before she had met Owen and, when she arrived in Gainsborough, she had brought with her a number of beautiful, hand-carved wooden jigsaws and a wooden toy theatre, with equally wonderful carved puppets. Just before France was invaded in 1940, Violette's sister sent her two daughters to England for safety and so, during the war, the Nelson household in Gainsborough was mostly French and entirely female. By the time peace came, Natalie was virtually bilingual and had acquired a passion for jigsaws and the theatre.

Violette's accident had ended her life but started something else. Owen Nelson had been propelled into his shell. He had thrown himself into his work, embraced the church and his faith ever more closely and turned his back on Natalie. She reminded him too much of Violette, he said.

Then had come the blow with Dominic, and

Natalie had been doubly plunged into despair, bereaved twice over within the space of a few months. The worst of it was that she suspected Dominic had found her naïvety attractive to begin with but that it had eventually palled. In the middle of her wretchedness, the letter from Eleanor Deacon had arrived, inviting her to Kihara. On other digs, during her work for her Ph.D., Natalie had impressed her seniors, who had spread the word. So the roller coaster of Natalie's emotions was still on the rails, just.

'Mind if I join you?'

She flinched. She recognised Russell North's voice but hadn't heard him approach. She had thought everyone was in bed. Natalie turned and looked up at him. 'You've found me out,' she whispered, raising the cap of her whisky flask. 'Drinking in secret.'

He sat down in the other canvas chair, on the far side of the small writing table they each had. 'Your secret is safe with me. It's not a silly rule to ban booze on digs, but a late-night nip can't do any harm.'

He pulled at the sleeve of his shirt where it had been caught up with his watch. He was wearing a khaki shirt and jeans and a pair of what she now knew Americans (and Australians who lived in America) called loafers. No socks. Hair showed on his chest above where his shirt was unbuttoned.

Russell looked at her for a moment without speaking, absently rubbing a finger down a crease in his cheek. At length he said, softly, 'I came to apologise, Natalie. Dick shouldn't have yelled at you like he did tonight. He was out of line, way

44

out. But we are both so fired up. This find is big – *big*. We've got to get into print as soon as we possibly can. Dick and I are working on that, but he was over the top in going for you like a baboon on heat. I'm sorry. Really.'

A wind stirred. The stunted calls of bats, overhead, punctuated the silence.

'Are we forgiven?'

What did Russell mean, that Dick and he were working on how they could go into print quickly? But she was relieved he had come to apologise, even if it was really Richard who should be sitting here. So all she said was, 'Thank you. Of course I forgive you. It is an important find and I'm glad I was here when it happened.' She held out the cup of whisky.

'Can you spare it?' Instinctively, he looked across to Eleanor's tent, which was in darkness. 'I'd love one.'

'Only on condition that you don't betray me to the authorities.'

He made a mock salute. 'Deal.'

Natalie handed him the cup she was drinking from, which formed the lid of the flask which contained the whisky.

'Ahhh,' Russell said softly, downing the scotch. 'That hits the spot.'

They sat together in a companionable silence.

'Listen to the baboons,' he said after a moment, as a burst of screaming could be heard. 'They're worse than we are.' He looked about him and went on, 'You can tell this is a woman's tent.'

'What do you mean?'

'Little touches. This is your very first day here

but that photograph there, the little vase of flowers, above all the smell. Is it perfume or talcum powder, or what?'

'The photograph is of my parents. The flowers were a gift, put there by Mgina – you know, the woman who cleans the tents. The smell, if there *is* a smell, can only be soap. Who would bring perfume on a dig?' The minute she said it, she smiled. 'Arnold Pryce!'

Russell grinned back. 'Well, no one ever puts flowers in *my* tent. All my tent smells of is sweat and dust. You must come visit.' He grinned again, stood up and so did Natalie. For a brief moment they stood very close together, so close she could smell him. He was wearing some sort of aftershave, not as strong as Arnold Pryce's but not just sweat and dust.

He said nothing but looked down at her, breathing hard. The shadows slid over his throat as he swallowed and his Adam's apple moved.

'Goodnight.' Russell turned, ducked under the guy ropes that held up the tent and was gone.

Natalie hid away the whisky flask and tidied a few things that didn't need tidying. She was glad Russell had apologised. He was a not unattractive man. Not in the Dominic class, of course–

She checked herself. She must stop making these comparisons. Dom was gone, *gone.*

She moved around the tent for a few minutes – changing into her pyjamas, brushing her hair, and teeth – until she could be certain Russell was back in his own quarters. Then she took another cigarette and returned to the seat she had been sitting in. She lit the cigarette, breathed in slowly, and then out slowly. She thought briefly of her mother in her final moments as the nicotine infiltrated her system.

Natalie looked up at the stars, feeling tired but content. Here she was, at last, at long last, on a dig in the warm night of Africa, thousands of miles from Cambridge. She turned off her hurricane lamp and darkness – save for the stars and the crimson glow of the campfire logs – closed in around her.

Now, with any luck, she could have a few moments to herself.

'Oh yes,' said Eleanor Deacon. 'That's the two-million level all right.' She stood, legs apart, shoulders thrown back, head held erect in the morning sun, the skin on her cheeks sweating slightly. She stared down at the wall of the gorge. She was wearing a knee-length gabardine skirt, leather boots, the same white shirt of the evening before and her hair was covered in a large white bandana. Her eyes were ablaze with excitement.

They had all come out to the gorge early this morning, using three of the Land Rovers assigned to the dig. Christopher Deacon was already hard at it, and had been for hours: his tripod in place, an umbrella on a pole behind him, shielding him and the camera from the sun. He'd brought a guard who stood some way off. They also had other equipment necessary for proper publication of the discovery – measuring sticks divided into yards and inches, to show scale; white paint to mark off the area where the bones had been found; soil bores to take samples of the earth and

47

rock around the find-spot; better fencing to keep out wild animals; and plenty of buckets in which to store the soil-sand that had been dislodged during the digging and which, in days to come, would be scrutinised and inspected and scrutinised all over again, to make sure nothing had been missed. Arnold Pryce was just beginning the painstaking task of sifting through the soil-sand for ancient pollen. He too had a big yellow beach parasol, to keep off the sun. From a distance the excavation resembled a stylish picnic.

So this was the famous Kihara Gorge, Natalie reflected, as her eyes raked the landscape. This was the centre of her attention for the next few months – two rocky red walls, thirty yards apart, occupied by spiky thorn bushes, thin trees, dead wood, dust and, if the smell was anything to go by, various vintages of dung. It was a long way from Jesus Lane in Cambridge.

Eleanor turned to Daniel. She swept her arm in an arc around the find-spot. 'I want an area thirty feet either side of the discovery and thirty feet in front sealed off. Build a proper fence, five feet high. Anyone going inside the fence must wear lightweight shoes, not boots. There's a good chance that the rest of the skeleton is around here somewhere, so let's create a little haven of safety.'

Daniel nodded. 'The Maasai won't like it. Any fence we build they might pull down.'

The Maasai were the local tribe in the area around Kihara. They lived by herding goats, sheep and cows and regarded all land in this part of the Serengeti as theirs.

'Take them a gift then, Daniel. A bolt of cloth

maybe. We have some in the stores. Tell the elders what we are doing. Say that the fence will be temporary. Will you do that?'

Daniel nodded. He was a Luo himself, a tribe with its homeland some miles to the north-west. They were traditional enemies of the Maasai but for the moment at least, and in recent memory, intertribal relations were good.

Eleanor spent some time showing Daniel and a few of the other local helpers where she wanted the fence built. Above them the sun rose in the sky and shade disappeared. Baboons peered over the lip of the gorge, then ran away. A few deer ventured between the wild thorn bushes on the far side, then they too disappeared.

Around one o'clock, Eleanor called a halt. It was too hot for any physical work and the light was too bright for photography. They drove back in high spirits, the Land Rovers racing one another across the flat plain of the Serengeti, churning up great red-brown dust clouds behind them. Giraffe looked on, then lolloped away.

Back at the camp, most of them took a shower. It was always dusty in the gorge and, with water limited, a shower at this time of day was much more useful than first thing or in the early evening.

Mgina, the slender Maasai woman Natalie had mentioned to Russell North, brought Natalie's shower water in two galvanised iron buckets. Although she was uneducated, Mgina had picked up some stilted English in the few years she had been working at the camp and, despite her cheeks being stippled by tribal cut-marks, she was pretty,

49

Natalie thought, and had a natural, slow-moving, languid grace. She was slight but still wiry enough to carry the water with which she filled the canvas shower cistern. Natalie had established that Mgina came from a village about five hours' walk from the camp, where she had numerous sisters and brothers.

While Natalie took a shower, letting the hot water chase the sand and grit out of her eyelids and ears and sluice down the back of her neck, while she lathered her arms and thighs and let the smell of the soap, which she had brought with her from Gainsborough, remind her of the rainy Lincolnshire fens, Mgina collected up her used shirt and trousers and underwear, and set out fresh ones on the bed.

When she had used all the available hot water, Natalie half-dried herself so she didn't drip water everywhere, but then she let the remains of the water evaporate on her skin as she sat on her towel on the chair of her dressing table, combing her hair. Evaporation was deliciously cooling.

She had always had a thing about her hair, ever since she was a girl. She never felt properly dressed unless her hair was brushed and brushed and brushed again. Her fellow undergraduates at Cambridge had teased her about it but she hadn't minded. And they had given up in the end, and accepted her for what she was. In the gorge, she realised, brushing her hair was even more important: with water strictly rationed, brushing kept the dust to a minimum and she needed to feel that her hair was as clean as could be.

Mgina watched as Natalie did this, as fascinated by her straight hair as Natalie was with Mgina's close-cropped curls.

'What is your comb made of, Miss Natalie?'

'Tortoiseshell.'

'It is very beautiful.'

Natalie nodded her head. 'Yes, it was my mother's – she gave it to me.'

'Does she have hair like you?'

'She did. She's dead now. She was killed, in an accident.'

'I am sorry for you. They go fast, these cars.'

'They do, yes.' Natalie put down the comb. 'And your family, Mgina? How are they, they are well?'

Mgina made a face. 'Not the little one, Odnate. He has the 'flu, I think, but also spots under his tongue.'

'Oh,' said Natalie, quietly. 'Oh dear.' She frowned and stopped brushing her hair. 'When did this 'flu start, Mgina?'

'The day before yesterday. There was a feast the day before that and it was the first time Odnate had been old enough to attend. The next day he was ill – it was too much for him.'

Natalie had stood up and was towelling herself dry. 'What did you eat at this feast?'

'Corn, berries, meat of course. Fruit. What is it, Miss Natalie?'

Natalie had thrown the towel on the bed. 'Just wait there, Mgina, while I get dressed.'

In front of the other woman, Natalie stepped into her underwear, put on her fresh set of trousers and shirt, and laced her boots. She fastened the cuffs of her shirt at her wrists, so her arms were

51

protected from the sun. Then, 'Come with me. Leave the laundry on the bed. Quickly now.'

Frowning herself, Mgina did as she was told. Natalie led the way along the row of tents to where she knew Jonas Jefferson was billeted.

'Jonas!' she half-shouted when they reached his tent. 'Are you there?'

A short pause, then the flap was pulled back. 'Yes – what is it?'

Natalie turned to Mgina, then back to Jonas. 'Mgina's brother has 'flu, she thinks. But he also has spots under his tongue.'

Jonas looked from Natalie to Mgina and back again. 'Anthrax?'

'He woke up with it the day before yesterday, after a big feast. The meat could have been contaminated.'

Jonas nodded. 'You could be right. How do you know about anthrax?'

'I saw it on a dig in Israel two years ago. Do we have any penicillin?'

'Yes, of course, but it's precious. Where does Mgina's family live?'

'The village doesn't have a name, but it's five hours' walk away – ten to twelve miles.'

'Okay. I'll get the antibiotics; meet me at the Land Rovers in ten minutes.'

'Anthrax?' said Eleanor, helping herself to water from the jug as Mutevu Ndekei began serving dinner lamb chops. 'That can be serious, right?'

'Oh, yes,' said Jonas. 'If you don't catch it in the first couple of days, the patient can be dead inside a week.'

52

'Nasty,' said Eleanor with a shudder. 'And how do you catch such a disease?'

'It varies. Through an open wound, from someone else who has it. In this case by eating contaminated meat.'

'And penicillin cures it?'

Jefferson nodded. 'I'll be driving over to see the boy again tomorrow.' He looked across to Natalie and smiled.

'You saved the boy's life,' said Eleanor, addressing Natalie. 'How do you know so much about disease?'

Natalie was helping herself to chops. 'As I told Jonas, I was on a dig in Israel, with Ira Ben-Osman, two years ago. There was an outbreak among the local Palestinians. Three died but we managed to save another fifteen. They had all eaten contaminated meat.'

The business with Mgina and Mgina's brother had been quite an episode. Natalie didn't feel as though she had saved someone's life but the boy – when they had reached him – obviously didn't have 'flu. He was vomiting blood, had severe abdominal pains and a fever. It was right that they had gone when they had. Mgina's family had clearly been worried – their traditional herbal remedies were not working. Of course, the penicillin hadn't produced any immediate effect, so the family had still been anxious when Jonas and Natalie had left. They had done their best to reassure Odnate's parents but had not wholly succeeded. Hopefully, tomorrow would bring better news.

The lamb had reached Eleanor. She inspected

53

it doubtfully. 'How can you tell if meat is dangerous?'

'It's not easy,' said Jonas. 'Animals that have
anthrax collapse. They mustn't be used for food,
which is probably what happened in this case. If
the spores are dense enough, you can see them
with the naked eye – they are grey-white and
resemble ground glass.'

Eleanor picked up the chop in her fingers and
turned it over. 'Hmmn. Did anyone else in the
village contract the disease?'

'Not so far as I could see,' replied Jonas. 'Odnate
was the youngest at the feast, with the least resistance. If the animal they were eating was not badly
infected and well roasted he was just unlucky.'

Eleanor nodded. 'So is the boy out of the
woods?'

'Not necessarily. His family must be disciplined
and give him the full course of antibiotics.'

'Is that going to leave us short? You know, in
case we have an accident here?'

Jonas shook his head. 'We're fine, unless we
have our own epidemic. But next time anyone
goes to Nairobi, they should top up our supplies.'

Eleanor nodded again. 'If I talk to Jack, I'll mention it. I'm not sure when he's planning to come.
He's on some political committee in Nairobi.'

She sat up and her gaze took in Natalie and
Jonas. 'Well, I'm glad you two could help. Anything that brings blacks and whites closer is
important right now. I'm told there's been more
oath-taking up north in Nakura, where a
thousand Kikuyu were gathered in the bush for a
blood-letting ceremony where they vowed to kill

54

anyone who gets in the way of Independence. And it's the third time in the past two months. A curfew has been imposed and two newspapers closed for publishing coded notices, telling people where the oath-taking would take place. It's going to be like this in the run-up to the independence conference in London in February, I am afraid.'

There was a brief gloomy silence, until she suddenly turned in her seat. 'Mutevu, what's the matter? There's something different about you tonight I can't put my finger on it.'

He grinned sheepishly. 'Some monkeys got into the camp, ma'am. They stole one of my boots–'

'That's it!' cried Eleanor. 'Of *course!* You're not shuffling.' She peered round the edge of the table and inspected his footwear. 'So your beloved wellingtons have gone missing, eh? You're reduced to plimsolls, I see.'

'Just one boot was taken, Miss Eleanor.'

'We can fix that, I'm sure. Don't worry. I'll have Jack buy some in Nairobi.' She smiled.

'Thank you, Miss Eleanor, but the old ones were a gift from Sir Philip Sisley. He signed them. Don't bother Mr Jack. He's busy, I'm sure.' And Mutevu was gone.

Eleanor smiled as he left the room. 'I should have guessed the boots had sentimental value ... because they don't fit.' Her grin took in the whole table. 'Now, where was I? Yes, well done, Natalie, that was quick thinking, about the anthrax I mean. But if this episode looks like it has a happy ending, we can get back to–'

'Yes, yes, this paper on the knee-joint needn't

55

be very long, isn't that so?' interrupted Richard Sutton somewhat awkwardly. 'And if you insist we need modern bones for a comparison, maybe I should go to Nairobi, or New York, find some bones, in a hospital or a morgue, and then come back.' He swigged his Coke from the bottle.

'Don't be silly, Richard.' Eleanor pushed her shirt more firmly into the top of her gabardine skirt. 'No one wastes digging time like that. Just because you've made one discovery doesn't mean you – or Russell here, or Christopher, or any of us – will not find something even more important in the days ahead.' She took off her spectacles and waved them at him. 'Don't be so impatient. No one's going to "scoop" you on a thing like this.'

'How can you be so sure?' Sutton banged his Coke bottle down on the table. 'This is a big breakthrough, Eleanor. Front-page news. The biggest coup of my career, and of Russell's. Daniel's greatest find. And it won't do your reputation any harm, either. The Deacon legend will be glossier than ever. We should move fast. I feel it in my bones.' He looked around the table, from one face to another, daring them to disagree.

Natalie met his gaze.

He looked away first.

Eleanor, who had been chewing one of the wires of her spectacles, enfolded them in her hand. 'Richard, please. *Please.* I have been excavating in Africa for nearly forty years, and running digs for half that time. They are collective affairs, as you well know. Now, I agree that you all have made an important discovery. Front-page news, as you put it. Or so we think. But what if Natalie here is right, and a comparison with modern bones does *not* support your theory? If you go rushing off to Nairobi, or New York, or somewhere else, you'll have wasted days of valuable digging time – time that I have organised, raised money for, negotiated permissions for with the government and the local tribes. That's not been easy.'

She leaned back as Mutevu Ndekei reappeared to remove the plates.

'I won't have it, Richard. No one is standing in the way of publication, or censoring what you have discovered. For pity's sake, I, we, are just asking you to see sense, make a simple comparison first, and delay for a few weeks. It is perfectly normal behaviour that happens all the time.' She reached up and removed the bandana from her head, folded it neatly and laid it on the table next to her napkin. 'And you are surely overlooking the fact that, if we have found a tibia and femur in this part of the gorge, there is an excellent chance that we will find some other pieces of the same skeleton, perhaps even a skull. That would be even more momentous than what we have already.'

Richard went to say something but she waved him down, slapping the table with the open palm of her hand, and rattling the cutlery.

'You force me to say this, Richard, by your … your refusal to back off, see sense, acknowledge that you are part of a team. But if you leave now, I'm warning you – officially warning you – that you can't come back.' She took a deep breath. 'We have achieved what we have on our digs by

57

discipline. Not by being authoritarian, I'm not an ogre as you well know, but by having a few rules, for the benefit of all, and sticking to them.'

She swallowed some water. No one else around the table was about to say anything. Most of them kept their eyes fixed firmly in front of them.

'Now look,' Eleanor went on, more amenably, 'let's not argue. I want this paper to be published as quickly as possible, just like you do. Maybe we should write *two* papers; one on the discoveries, one on the implications. But I have other responsibilities and you, in my view, are being unreasonable.'

Richard said nothing. But only with great difficulty.

'Is there anything else like this in the world?' Natalie asked. 'It's extraordinary.' She held her camera to her eye and took more photographs.

'I don't know if it's unique,' replied Christopher, 'but it's certainly very unusual. You can see why the local Maasai, who are theoretically Christians, still worship these sands.'

Natalie, Christopher and Kees van Schelde were standing in front of a small sand dune on the Serengeti plain, about eight miles or so from the camp. It was not far off dusk and Christopher had brought them here to show them one of the 'local sights', as he put it, Natalie and Kees being the two newest members of the dig.

Kees was also taking photographs. 'Explain it to me again, will you? I'm still not sure I understand completely.' Kees was the youngest of the team, a twenty-five-year-old Dutchman from the

University of Amsterdam, who had yet to complete his Ph.D., but he had already been on several digs, making him considerably more experienced than Natalie – if less qualified, formally speaking.

'Sure,' said Christopher. He leaned against the bonnet of the Land Rover. 'This being a flat plain, the winds can be quite strong with very little to impede them. Notice that the edge of the dune that is facing the wind is fairly steep, whereas the trailing edge – on the lee side, if you like – is quite shallow. When the wind blows, what happens is that grains of sand on the leading edge, the steep edge, are blown up into the air, and then fall, and settle on the trailing edge. When the wind is *very* strong, like it is now, that process is magnified, it happens much more quickly, with the result that, over a matter of days, the entire sand dune can move, maybe as much as five feet a day. Over the months, the dune can move miles – and then, when the wind changes, move back again. Because it moves so much, the local Maasai think the dune is mysteriously alive, which is why they worship it.'

He slid into the driving seat of the Land Rover. The others finished taking their photos and then Natalie got in alongside him and Kees climbed in the back.

The light was fading fast as they headed home. They looked about them as the animals began to appear.

'Have you ever been to Italy?' Kees asked.

Christopher shook his head.

'No,' said Natalie. 'I'd love to go, but why do

you ask?'

'They have this thing called a *passeggiata* when, in the early evening, everyone walks up and down the main street of town, looking at everyone else, who they are with, what they are wearing. It's just like that here in the bush. The animals come out and are on a sort of parade.'

'Hmmn,' growled Christopher. 'With one big difference. Here, one half of the animals are trying to eat the other half.'

'Do you miss Amsterdam, Kees?' said Natalie. 'I've only been once. I loved it. The trees, the canals, the narrow houses.'

Kees smiled. 'I don't miss it because I know I'm going back. If I couldn't go back I'd be very unhappy. The best thing about Amsterdam are the bicycles. Because of all the canals, the streets are narrow, so the traffic is slow and everyone uses bicycles. The city is small so nowhere is more than fifteen minutes' ride from anywhere else. That means you see more of your friends in Amsterdam than in other major cities. And because of that you *have* more friends than in other major cities.' He leaned forward and tapped Natalie on the shoulder. 'Were you on holiday when you visited?'

'Yes and no. My parents were singing in a choir, in a choir competition, and they had reached the final. I was just a girl and was taken along. Their choir lost but I loved the city. The contest was part of a flower festival.'

Kees nodded. 'Yes, I was going to say that, after the bicycles, the next best thing about Amsterdam are the flowers. There are endless flower

60

festivals of one sort or another, and flower-sellers at every corner. Do you sing, now you're older?'

Natalie made a face. 'Sore point. I *do* sing, yes, and not badly. My parents wanted me to have a musical career but I preferred science. We fought like mad about that, but they eventually gave way when I got my place at Cambridge.'

'I went to a geological conference in Cambridge. Lots of bicycles there too. Do you live in college?'

'Yes, I do. You?'

'We don't have colleges. I share one of those narrow houses you admired, with someone else who teaches at the university. He teaches music, as it happens, and plays the cello.'

Natalie coloured. It was silly. Kees couldn't know about her complicated relationship with the cello, but she couldn't help herself. Would she ever be able to hear the cello again without thinking of Dominic, without rapidly re-running the entire course of the affair, itself not unlike a piece of music, with a rousing opening, a serene middle and a sad coda. How she fought with herself to prevent that loop in her brain from springing to life, like a wild animal disturbed in its sleep.

And must all conversation, from now on, carry a hidden menace, that it would always lead, as this one had, in directions she would rather avoid? How long would she be a prisoner?

Thankfully, the camp came into view across the gorge. Christopher slowed, the vehicle giving off a succession of creaks and groans as they descended the bank, scattering a troop of monkeys with the vehicle's headlights.

'Which are the bigger nuisance in the camp,' said Kees, 'monkeys or baboons?'

'Oh, monkeys,' said Christopher, 'baboons are–'

'Stop!' cried Natalie. 'Christopher, stop! Look!' And she pointed.

'Where? At what?' he replied, braking hard, so that the Land Rover's engine shuddered and stalled.

'Sorry,' breathed Natalie. 'I didn't mean to sound so excitable but isn't that ... doesn't that look to you like a wellington boot?'

Christopher leaned forward and peered to where she was pointing. 'You know, I think you could be right,' he said slowly. 'Do you want to get it?'

Natalie got down, while Christopher restarted the engine. She retrieved the boot and carried it back to the Land Rover. 'It looks like it's torn, ripped near the ankle,' she said, getting back in. 'But it can be repaired.'

'Well done,' said Christopher. 'We have to keep Mutevu sweet. He's a good cook, but a bit temperamental.'

Darkness was now settling all around them as they traversed the gorge, climbed the bank opposite and entered the camp. Natalie got down and, taking her camera and the wellington with her, returned to her tent. There were a couple of hours before dinner and she knew what she wanted to do. She had done some camping as a girl when she had always had with her a bicycle tyre repair kit, for repairing tears to the inflatable mattresses inevitably used in camps. She had brought the repair kit to Africa, not knowing what sort of beds were used on Eleanor Deacon's digs.

She took the repair kit out now and, after cleaning the wellington, applied gum around the tear and fixed a rubber patch that covered it more than adequately. She wedged the boot where she had stuck the patch under the foot of the bed, and sat there reading for half an hour. She judged that by then the patch would be stuck firmly to the boot.

It was now not much more than an hour to dinner and she knew that Mutevu would be in the kitchen. But he wasn't. Maybe he was in the storeroom, she thought, and went on through to the other side. As she came round the door, the first thing she saw was the gleam of his white T-shirt.

'Mutevu,' she said, 'look what I – oh,' she breathed as she stepped further into the room. 'Richard, sorry, I didn't see you there.'

Richard Sutton was also in the storeroom, standing next to Mutevu.

'Natalie, hi,' he said. 'Give me a minute, will you? I've a touch of indigestion and Mutevu was giving me some bicarbonate of soda to treat it.' He stepped back. Mutevu turned and went to a cupboard where he took down a white box. 'Two teaspoonfuls,' he said, opening it to reveal the powder. 'No more.'

'Thanks,' said Richard, patting his stomach. 'This should do the trick.' He looked at Natalie. 'Have you got there what I think you have?'

Natalie held up the boot and Mutevu suddenly beamed. 'Miss Natalie! Where did you find it?'

'In the gorge. We scattered some monkeys playing with it.' She showed him the patch. 'It was torn, so I repaired it.'

Mutevu took the boot as she passed it across. 'What is your favourite food, Miss Natalie? You must tell me. I must repay you this kindness.' He found the other wellington, which he had kept in the storeroom, slipped off his plimsolls and changed immediately.

'Oh, don't worry, Mutevu. I'm just pleased we found it. Now, I'll let you get on. Dinner isn't far away.'

'And a good dinner it will be, Miss Natalie.' He grinned. 'I cook much better with my boots on.'

The Burial Ground

Mutevu Ndekei leaned forward so that Eleanor Deacon, as always the last to be served, could be given her chops. Lunch, three days later. Lamb chops and chicken were the staple foods at the camp and that was fine by Natalie. The local deer meat she found too heavy, too dense; the fish – brought in frozen from Lake Victoria – too watery, too lacking in flavour. Not that she had voiced these views. Like a good team player she ate whatever was put in front of her.

Outside the refectory area, the sun bleached the ground, the dead wood of the spiky acacia branches that enclosed the camp, the washing which was stretched on lines between the tents, like flags. The Land Rovers, cooling under the trees, gave off mysterious metallic clicks and cracks.

Natalie was feeling famished today. While the rest of the crew had been in the gorge, Jonas and she had visited Mgina's brother Odnate again. They had found him much improved. He had stopped vomiting, his temperature was down and the ulcers under his tongue were atrophying. He hadn't regained his appetite yet but there was no doubt he had turned a corner. Natalie had been very cheered by what she had seen.

'Mutevu!' said Eleanor forcefully all of a sudden. 'Can you please explain something to me?'

Everyone stopped eating and Mutevu stood up straight, holding the big serving plate. 'Yes,

Miss Eleanor?'

'Why is it ... why is it that each of us is given two chops, while Natalie here is given *three*? This is not the first time I have noted your – what shall we call it? – *generosity* in her direction. I know she's new, I know she's pretty, but is there some other reason for it? I'd just like to know, that's all.'

Natalie blushed. She had begged Mutevu not to single her out but he wasn't deterred; he kept piling her plate high. Mutevu stood back from the table.

'Miss Natalie found my boot three days ago, Miss Eleanor.' He lifted his leg, to show her. 'And she repair it where the monkeys tear it.'

Eleanor Deacon smiled. 'So *that's* it.' She nodded at Natalie. 'Well done, my dear. I can't complain, I suppose.' And she smiled at Mutevu. 'And I have to say the food has been exceptionally good these past few days. You did say that you cooked better with your boots on, and it seems to be true.'

Smiling to herself, she went back to her own food. 'Now,' she said, slicing into her chicken. 'Although we need to be as thorough as possible, I feel we should finish surveying JDK as soon as possible, by the end of the week, certainly.' JDK stood for 'Jock Deacon's Korongo', the name the local Maasai had given the cul-de-sac off the main gorge since digging started there years ago. 'There is still a chance that we will find the rest of the skeleton to which the tibia and femur belong but we have a lot to get through this season. Richard, Russell, how long do you think you'll need?'

Russell North sat across the table from Natalie.

Two evenings before, he had again joined her during her late-night smoke. They had again talked about their work and he had impressed her with his knowledge. And when she had produced the whisky, he had presented her with some chocolate. Twice during their conversation he had laid his hand on her arm. When he had taken his leave, he had once more stood very close, looking down at her.

And that was close enough, Natalie now knew. Some day, some day soon, she hoped, she could move beyond Dominic. But not with Russell, not here, not now. Physically, there was nothing wrong with him, but that wasn't enough. Russell was too raw, too straightforward even. That wasn't a bad thing in itself but Dominic had been so ... so playful when they had met, so full of allusion, so light in his touch, so ambiguous in a gentle, soft way. Russell was pulling her in too quickly. Or trying to.

He now looked from Natalie to Richard, to Eleanor, to Arnold Pryce, to Daniel, to Jonas, to Kees. Then he nodded at Richard, who got up from the table and walked away from the refectory area to his own tent.

'Eleanor,' said Russell softly. 'There's something we were going to tell you all tonight but, since you've raised the question of timing, we might as well discuss it now.'

'Oh yes?' said Eleanor. 'What is it?' She swallowed some water from a tumbler. Across the camp they all heard the radio stutter into life. It was kept in Eleanor's tent, which was bigger than the others. The pilots of small planes were swapping information about the weather, or talking to air traffic control at Kilimanjaro, the nearest proper airport.

Before going on, Russell turned in his seat. Richard was walking back from his tent carrying a towel wrapped around something. Back inside the refectory area, he approached the small serving sideboard across from the main table.

Russell got up and went to stand next to Richard as Richard unwrapped the towel. He was rather theatrical about it, pulling back first one flap, then another, then another. With a final flourish, he pulled back the remaining flap.

'*Voilà!*'

Revealed on the towel were two long, thin bones.

'What on earth–?' Eleanor put down her knife and fork with a clatter.

'A tibia and a femur,' said Russell North. 'A *modern* tibia and femur.'

'Proving,' chimed in Richard, 'that our find is as sensational as we thought.' He looked directly at Natalie. 'We've addressed Natalie's criticism, we can now say so in print, and can show that her objections, however proper they were, are unfounded.' He smiled down at Natalie to show that he wasn't bullying her this time. 'These are modern bones and although they are bigger than the ancient ones they have exactly the same configuration as those Daniel discovered in the gorge.'

All eyes were on the sideboard.

'And where, may I ask, did you find these bones?' Eleanor had pushed her plate away from her.

70

Richard went back to his place and sat down again. He lowered his voice. 'You know that tribal burial ground – it's about four miles from here, on a slope with lots of trees, where the goats play. We visited a grave last night. Very late.'

'You did *what?*' Eleanor ripped off her spectacles. She spoke in barely a whisper.

'Don't worry. We didn't do any damage. No one saw us.' Richard looked up at Russell and smiled. 'We replaced all the earth we had dug up and smoothed it over. Now we can send the report to *Nature* from here, as Russell said. It will be very dramatic. And it cuts the chances of anyone beating us to the punch.'

'The evidence is quite clear, Eleanor.' Russell had also returned to his place at the table, taking the tibia and the femur with him. He now held a bone in each hand and brought them slowly together. They interlocked neatly. 'The arrangement of the joint is virtually identical in the ancient specimen and in the modern specimen. Hominids walked upright two million years ago.'

There was silence around the table. All eyes were on Eleanor. She refitted her spectacles around her ears. Her own eyes flashed, the whites catching what light was left, her lenses magnifying the effect. The colour had quite gone from her face, the corners of her mouth were turned down, her jaw was set forward, straining the skin on her neck. When, at length, she did speak, her voice had an icy edge to it. 'Let me get this right: you stole some bones from a tribal burial ground. You sneaked into a sacred place, late at night, and just helped yourself to someone's ancestors?

71

You disturbed the peace of a tribal sanctuary that has been that way for generations?' She caught her breath. 'Are you ... are you *completely* mad? Do you not realise what you have done?'

Her eyes held Richard's. She didn't blink.

'Come on, Eleanor, don't exaggerate. Yes, it's a burial ground but think what we can now do: it won't take us more than a few days to complete the paper, and we can send it to London by the end of the week. We don't have to say exactly where we found the bones–'

'Shut up!' She snatched off her glasses again and all but mangled them in her fingers. 'I won't hear a word more of this and don't tell me I'm exaggerating.' Eleanor's mouth was a mere line across her face; her lips had all but disappeared. The skin on her throat was again stretched tight as her chin jutted forward. She still didn't blink. 'Don't show your ignorance like that, or your cockiness.' She breathed out through her nose. 'Do you know how *long* it has taken me to negotiate excavation rights in this area? You don't think I just need a government permit do you? I need the consent, the agreement, the *approval* of the local tribes: the Maasai, the Datoga, the Itesu. The Maasai are Mutevu Ndekei's tribe – how do you think they are going to take this? What do you think his standing in his tribe will be now? What if they find out? Did you think of that?'

She rubbed her fingers around her eyes. 'What gave you–? Who thought of–? No, I don't want to know.' She shook her head. 'I cannot believe that grown men, educated men – *professors* – could be

72

so foolish, so wrong-headed, so insensitive.' She shifted her gaze from Richard to Russell, then back to Richard. 'You are, you are...' A strand of hair had fallen from her chignon. She pushed it back up. 'Words fail me.'

'Now we know what we know,' said Richard, 'and after we have taken some photographs, we can put the bones back—'

'Don't you dare!' hissed Eleanor. She leaned forward and pointed at him with her glasses. 'Don't even *think* about setting foot in that burial ground again. Desecrate the site a second time? Now I know you're beyond the pale.' She put her spectacles back on. As she did so, they could all see that her hands were shaking. 'Look, this is a potential disaster.' She pointed at the tibia and femur. 'We'll hide those bones. Wrap them up and give them to me. Go on, hurry up.'

As Russell moved to do as she said, Eleanor shook her head again and groaned. 'I am beside myself with fury. Nothing like this has ever happened on one of my digs before. It's disgraceful, barbaric. I feel sick.'

'Eleanor, come on. You're over-reacting,' said Richard. He was lounging in his chair. One leg was crossed over the other and he gripped one ankle with his hand.

'No, no. No! I am *not* over-reacting.' Eleanor still didn't raise her voice but her tone was vehement. She slapped the table with the flat of her hand. 'What you have done is unforgivable. Sacrilegious, arrogant and crass. If the Maasai find out about this, I hate to think what will happen. The dig might even be cancelled. It was a condition of the government permit that we obtain the agreement of local tribes. How are the chiefs going to feel when they find out that their sacred burial ground has been interfered with?' She took the bundle of bones from Russell and pushed him away. 'My God, I have never been so angry.'

She stood up and held her head high, so that the full length of her long neck was exposed. 'You are both very foolish men,' she said. 'Monumentally foolish.' She took a deep breath. 'I would make sure your careers were ruined but for the fact that our only hope now is to hush this up.' She picked up a spoon and pointed it at all the others, one by one. 'This information, this ... *crime*, goes no further than this table. It is not to be mentioned again. Ever. You will not talk about it even among yourselves. You will carry on as if nothing has happened. Is that clear?' She looked from one to the other. 'I said, is that clear?'

One by one they nodded, signalling their agreement.

Eleanor lowered her voice to a whisper. 'The paper will not now be published until we have all left here, until we have found another modern tibia and femur with which to make the comparison, and can say so. We must put this behind us and we must cover up.' She glared at Richard Sutton. 'This is the worst example of vandalism I have ever encountered. You had better make as many discoveries as you can on this dig, Professor Sutton, because I will not have you or Professor North back again. If, that is, we are allowed to work here in the future.'

She took the towel with the bones in it and

74

scraped back her chair. She addressed herself to Richard and to Russell. 'You have both made a serious error of judgement. Wholly unacceptable. In MY eyes, you can never recover from this act of gross stupidity and insensitivity. The only way you can even begin to make amends is never to mention your foolishness, your insensitivity, your sacrilege, your sheer racial arrogance again, to stay as far away from the burial ground as possible, and to make another important discovery that will take everyone's mind off this one.'

Eleanor stood absolutely still, erect, her eyes on fire. Even her fingernails seemed to shine in the gloom.

She turned and stalked off, back to her own tent.

In the deep distance a lion roared. Natalie, seated within the glow of her hurricane lamp, turned towards the sound. This, she decided, would be her abiding memory of Africa. Sitting by herself, in the dark, late at night, gazing up at the velvet sky and the stars and hearing a lion roar – oh, miles away.

Other sounds of the night, less distinctive, formed a backdrop to the lion. The stutter of a nightjar, elephants breaking wood as they sucked bark from nearby trees, the cackle of a hyena.

The warmth and the dryness were part of the experience for her, too. Lincolnshire, in contrast, was wet, very wet. Not that that bothered her too much either. She treasured the memory of an afternoon with her father on the beach near Chapel St. Leonards, on the Lincolnshire coast, when she had been eight or nine. It was during the war, one of the few times he had been home, and they were bathing when it had come on to rain. Everyone else had cleared the beach but not Owen, who had carried on swimming. He enjoyed rain, he said, just as much as he enjoyed sunshine. If you lived in Lincolnshire, he said, it helped. If you didn't enjoy rain, life on England's East Coast could get pretty miserable. Natalie knew what he meant, even if she didn't agree totally. Ever since, she had associated rain with her father.

Both were a long way away now.

Would her father ever come back from the locked-away place he now inhabited? She knew he still went through the motions as organist and choirmaster at Gainsborough. In fact, she had heard from the bishop that Owen Nelson 'poured' himself into his playing: his grief at his wife's death coloured every note, modulated every key his fingers touched. But when he stepped away from the organ, when choir practices or performances were concluded, the shutters came down and, as Natalie knew all too well, her father grew smaller. Did he imagine Violette still in the choir, did he still hear her mezzo-soprano above all the others?

He had rebuffed all attempts by Natalie to approach him, and she was secretly fearful that she knew exactly why. Natalie could barely put her fears into words but, when the sweat broke out on the skin over her throat, what went through her mind was the dreadful possibility that her mother's death was no accident, that she had deliberately set fire to her campbed because her daughter was having an affair with a married man and Owen Nelson *knew it.* Her father blamed Natalie for the death of his wife. How terrible was that? That was why he stayed in his locked-away world, locked away from his daughter in particular, and that was one reason why she had had to get away, to leave it all behind.

She had hoped that, being so distant and in such different surroundings, she would have thought about her father – and her dead mother – less, but the sweats on her throat kept coming.

'Natalie?' It was Russell.

She was expecting him. He slipped into the other chair as he had done before.

The flask of whisky and its cup were where they always were at this time of night, on the small table, next to the ashtray Natalie used. She pushed the whisky across and he took it.

'Not a good day,' he said eventually.

She didn't look at him. 'No.'

Another pause. Insects buzzed at the glass of the hurricane lamp.

'Are you as mad at us as Eleanor is?'

She rubbed her tongue along her lips. 'I'm upset, yes. How could you be so ... so *crude?* Blundering into a burial ground, robbing graves. I don't know whether it's juvenile or like something out of a nineteenth-century horror story.'

He slid the whisky cup across the table and massaged the back of his neck with his hand.

'We didn't think it was such a big deal.' He turned his gaze towards her. 'Is it really? The tribal goats are always grazing on that burial ground, kicking up the soil with their hooves and snouts. With any luck, no one will notice.'

She inhaled her cigarette once, twice.

Go slow, she told herself.

'Are your parents alive or dead, Russell?'

'My mother's dead.'

'Buried or cremated?'

'Cremated.'

'Well, my mother is buried in Lincolnshire. In the local churchyard, next to the church where my father learned to play the organ. He is a very religious man, Russell. How do you think he would feel if someone dug up his wife's bones, just to prove or disprove some *theory*, something that could be settled in a few weeks anyway without ... without doing that sort of damage?'

'I know, I know. It was wrong.' He rubbed his neck again. 'But Richard was so persuasive. He's terrified someone else will beat us to the punch. He convinced me it was no big deal–'

'Don't hide behind him, Russell. You played your part. If you didn't feel as strongly, you should have stopped him.'

'I know, I keep saying that. I'm not hiding. I'm doubly in the wrong, yes. I should have stopped Richard and I didn't. I shouldn't have gone, but I did.'

They sat for a long time without speaking. Natalie finished her cigarette. The whisky – that night's ration, anyway – was gone. The noises of the bush carried on around them.

After a while, Russell said, 'All you hear is animals. You never hear the people of the bush, do you?'

'That doesn't mean they're not there,' replied Natalie.

Another long silence.

Russell stood up. Natalie remained seated. He stood behind her chair, leaned down and kissed the top of her head. 'I've been wanting to do that since the moment I first saw you.'

She didn't move or respond. He put his hands on her shoulders but at this she squirmed free and stood up.

They faced each other.

He moved forward.

'Good night, Russell,' she said firmly.

'Water?'

Natalie straightened up, pressed her hands into her back, then wiped her forehead with her sleeve. It was four mornings later and every able-bodied member of the dig was in the korongo, trying to fulfil Eleanor Deacon's aim of finishing this part of the excavation by the end of the week. This morning, at least, there was a wind getting up. Warm, but it helped ease things a little.

Natalie took the bottle from Christopher Deacon. 'Thank you.'

In front of them the wall of the gorge, all around where the tibia and femur had been found, was being attacked. The soil-sand, newly exposed, was darker than the surrounding surface, which had long been bleached by the sun. Everyone who was able to was picking away at the soil. Arnold Pryce was sifting soil through a sieve. A little further along, Kees and Jonas were stooped over another stretch of gorge. Today there were a few clouds beneath the sun, which occasionally provided shade. So far, however, there had been no new discoveries.

'How are you settling in?' Christopher had hitherto kept his distance from Natalie. He was normally polite but – not formal exactly – reserved. He had a slightly clipped accent, almost but not quite South African.

'I'm loving it,' replied Natalie. 'I didn't enjoy all the excitement about the burial ground, of course. I hadn't anticipated such high drama. At Cambridge when you study archaeology you also study anthropology. No one who's studied anthropology could have done what Richard and Russell did.' She sighed. 'But the discovery's exciting, isn't it?'

'Very. What a pity it had to be marred by that silly prank. Though prank is hardly the word.'

Natalie handed back the water bottle. 'We'll all get over it, I suppose. Especially if there's another major discovery.'

'It's not us I'm worried about,' said Christopher. 'As you say, *we'll* get over it. Meals will be a bit sticky for a few more days but as we unearth other bones, if we do, we'll gradually put this behind us.' He looked down the gorge, shielding his eyes from the sun with his hand.

'What are you worried about, then?'

He breathed out. 'The Maasai. They are very proud, very fierce when they want to be. Richard and Russell may think they covered their tracks but it was dark when they raided the burial ground, so how they can be one hundred per cent certain of that I don't know. We can't go back and inspect, that would just draw attention to the matter. My mother's spent so long making friends with the Maasai – arranging medical help, educational scholarships, employing some of them, like Mutevu Ndekei – she's very sensitive on their behalf.'

'Maybe that will help, if the tribe is upset.'

'Maybe. But they can be tricky, the Maasai. They're supposed to be converts to Christianity but many of the men still worship their traditional gods – the fig trees – and the women give sacrifices at those local sand dunes that I showed you.' He turned towards her. 'See what I mean? The Maasai are the Maasai. I wouldn't like to predict how they will respond to this incident.'

She had never known Christopher say so much.

'What's that noise?' she said, after a pause.

'That moaning sound, you mean?'

She nodded.

'It's the whistling thorn.'

When she frowned, he added, 'Come on, I'll show you.' He waved to the guard, Aldwai, to show that he was making a move, and stepped over to some acacia bushes. He pointed. 'Whistling thorn, Latin name *Acacia drepanolobium*. Look, see these spikes growing out of the branches? They are two to three inches long and very sharp. But look also at the bulbous bases.'

He pointed to a brown-red bulb about the size of a golf ball, also with a thorn growing out of it. 'In themselves these are quite succulent, but watch.' He pressed the narrow neck of the water bottle he was holding against one of the bulbs. After a very short delay, swarms of ants emerged from a series of holes in the skin of the bulb.

'Uggh!' breathed Natalie.

'Yes,' said Christopher with a chuckle. 'Whistling thorn is a perfect example of symbiosis, which is why the Maasai revere it so much. The plant allows these biting ants – and believe me they *are* biting ants – to live in its bulbs because when herbivores, giraffes especially, feed on the bulbs, in next to no time they get a mouthful of biting ants, and then they don't come back. The thorn provides a home for the ants and the ants provide protection for the thorn.'

They watched as the ants disappeared back inside the bulb.

'When the ants burrow into the bulbs, they make tiny holes in the skin. Then, when a wind gets up, the holes make a moaning sound. As the wind gets stronger, they produce a higher-pitched whistle. Which is how they get their name, "whistling thorns".'

He drank some water.

'Then there's the fact that this thorn wood is very hard and resistant to termites. That makes it useful for spear handles, tool handles and building. It makes good charcoal and its sap can be used as a gum. Very useful, whistling thorn.'

He poured water into the palm of his hand, then slapped it on the back of his neck. A cooling manoeuvre.

'Turn round,' he said.

She did as she was told and again, using his hand, Christopher slapped water on her neck.

'Mmm. Thank you,' she whispered. 'What a treat.' Having Christopher do what he was doing reminded her that Mgina had failed to bring her

82

shower water yesterday. In fact, she hadn't seen her all day now she thought of it. Not more trouble at home, she hoped.

'Jack will be here soon. Maybe he will be able to help out with the Maasai situation.'

'What do you mean? What does Jack have that you don't?'

'He's an honorary Maasai. He's a bit older than me and when he was growing up, there were some Maasai boys in the camp and he and they became firm friends: he speaks Maasai as well as Swahili, and as well as he speaks English. One of the boys he grew up with was Marongo, who is now head of the local village, Ndekei's village. Jack used to stay with Marongo and his family, in their hut, and took part in a celebrated battle when another tribe tried to steal their cattle. That's when they made him an honorary Maasai.' Christopher pointed to his own forehead. 'Jack has a famous scar where he was hit by a lion cub. He was lucky not to be blinded.'

'Where is this hero now?'

'Nairobi. He's always been more politically involved than either my mother or me. There's a lot of pre-independence manoeuvring going on, a lot of black–white tension, as you can imagine and he's – look!' he cried. 'Richard is waving. They seem to have found something.'

Natalie followed the line of Christopher's out-stretched arm. Sure enough, about a hundred yards away, Richard was waving, beckoning them. Natalie set off towards him. Her shirt was just as stained with sweat as everyone else's. Christopher went with her.

As they approached, they could see Russell and Daniel gently lowering an animal skull on to a sheet on the ground.

'This is just up your street, Natalie,' said Richard warmly. 'Do you recognise it? I think it's some sort of horse, or zebra.' He smiled.

She knelt down. Russell and Daniel crowded round. A cloud obscured the sun and, temporarily, the temperature eased.

'Richard, you're right,' she breathed after a moment. What they had was almost half the skull of a horse-type creature, even containing a few teeth.

'I'll have to check, back at camp,' she said eventually. 'But it looks to me like a skull of *Equus plicatus*, an early form of zebra.'

'So it's not new?' Richard sounded disappointed. 'What's the level here?'

'Same as the tibia and femur. Two mill.'

'Then if I'm right it is nice confirmation of what we think we know, which is that the zebra moved into Africa from India about two million years ago and then went extinct in India. We're not talking hominids here, but this is an important discovery. A letter to *Nature* maybe.' She stood up and smiled at Richard and Russell. 'Well done.'

'I told you I have an eye.' Russell turned. 'And Dick here has the hands. Look at how beautifully he carved that out of the rock. And what a pity it isn't new.' He smiled at her and put his hand on her shoulder. 'If it had been, Dick suggested we name it after you: *Equus nelsoniensis*. It's big, isn't it?'

84

She nodded, wiping her brow with her sleeve. 'You're right again and that's an interesting theoretical issue. We now know extinct species of hippo, of giraffe, of pig, of horse, of zebra and of elephant. They all have one thing in common: the extinct forms are larger than the modern forms. Why should that be? What evolutionary significance does that have? And why is the opposite true for hominids? Modern man is larger than the extinct forms. It doesn't make sense.'

'It doesn't make sense to discuss such a heavy issue in the baking sun,' said Russell. 'But let's explore that at lunch. It will help break the ice with Eleanor. We can include that in our theoretical paper. Maybe you'd like to draft that part, Natalie?'

'Yes,' said Richard. 'Good idea.'

Natalie was flattered. Then, again, she checked herself. What did a prehistoric zebra have to do with an early form of man? And why should it be named after her? Was she being dragooned on to their side, and against Eleanor? Were Russell and Richard still intent on publishing their paper quickly, despite all that had happened? She couldn't believe it.

She looked at Christopher but couldn't read his expression.

'I can make a draft,' she said. 'Of course I can, and I'd be pleased to. But there are other books I'd need to check, back in Cambridge I mean, before I could go into print. And other colleagues I'd like to consult.'

Richard looked at her and nodded.

What did that mean? she wondered. Did it

85

mean anything? Why was everything to do with this dig, even important discoveries, now complicated by layers and layers of speculation? She had never anticipated this.

'Let's take it one step at a time,' she said in a measured way. 'I do have a few books back at camp. I'll give you a more considered response at dinner. How's that?'

'Fine,' said Richard, 'just fine.'

When Natalie got back to her tent there was still no sign of Mgina. The bed had been made but, from the different way the fresh towels had been folded and laid out, someone else had done the cleaning that morning. So she just dumped her hat and sleeveless waistcoat, in which she kept her bits and pieces, and left her tent, aiming for the area of the camp behind the refectory, near the storeroom, where the laundry was done. What had happened? One of the cleaning staff should know.

She was halfway across the clearing when she saw Jonas Jefferson getting down from a Land Rover. Jonas saw Natalie at the same time as she saw him and immediately set off towards her. As he drew close, he took of his hat and growled, 'Odnate's dead.'

'What? No, please *no!*'

He wiped a hand across his face. 'The family stopped giving him the pills.'

She stared at him. The skin on her throat was damp with sweat.

'I've come across this before. Even in Britain, people don't always complete the course of antibiotics. Some of the time, if you've a bad dose of 'flu, say, it may not matter, it delays recovery but that's all. With more serious diseases, however, it matters very much.' Jonas put his hand on her shoulder. 'What you saw in Palestine wasn't Africa. Palestinians are generally highly educated, relatively speaking, but here ... here, traditional ways are still very powerful and they can, and do, reassert themselves. Once Odnate was feeling better, he got up, started playing, looking after the goats, and stopped taking his antibiotics. The family let him. Then, as soon as the symptoms reappeared, his parents concluded that western medicine was no better than their own remedies, they resorted to their herbal cures, and didn't bother to tell us – it was their affair. The poor boy died yesterday.'

Natalie couldn't think what to say. It was as if there was a big, empty space in her brain. It had happened before, when her mother died. 'When is the funeral?'

Jonas stared at her. 'He wasn't a chief or a warrior: he was a child.' He passed his hand over his face again. 'I'm sorry Natalie, but his body was left out in the bush last night, to be eaten by predators and scavengers. There's nothing left of him to be buried. It's the tradition here.'

Natalie felt out of breath. This was a bad business and it had just got worse. 'Did you see Mgina?'

He nodded. 'She's upset but it's a large family. I'm not saying the Maasai don't feel grief the way we do because they do, keenly, and he was a lovely boy. But mortality is high in the bush.

That's not supposed to comfort you, but it is a fact. Mgina says she'll be back in a day or so.'

He took his hand off her shoulder. 'I'm sorry. I have some sedatives if you'd like one.'

Natalie still felt winded, but she shook her head. 'No, no thanks. I'll just lie on my bed for a bit. It's so ... so *disappointing.*'

He nodded. 'That's the right word. It's one of the first things you learn when you qualify as a doctor: that there are some people you can't save, even though – according to the book, according to the rules – they should survive. It's harder here because local traditions are so strong, and so different from ours. You're not a doctor, so it's hit you harder. Pity there's no hard liquor on this dig – otherwise, I could prescribe a shot of brandy for you.'

He smiled.

Witness

Natalie looked at the packet of cigarettes she held in her hand. The moonlight was so bright tonight that she could read the writing without the aid of the hurricane lamp. The campfire was alight – just – but its crimson glow was dim. She took a cigarette from the pack and slipped it into her mouth. Flicking open her lighter, the flame jumped up and caught the tobacco. She didn't know which she liked more, the first taste of her first cigarette of the day, or the first sip of whisky at night.

She put the cigarette pack in the breast pocket of her shirt and leaned forward to light the hurricane lamp. After it had caught, she turned the flame down low and savoured the tang of paraffin in her nostrils. In the distance she could just make out the skyline of the Amboseli mountain, its smooth shoulders sinking into the maroon gloom of the plain.

Natalie knew that as soon as Russell saw the glow of her lamp he would be over. Tonight, she definitely needed company. Odnate's death had upset her. Having, as she had thought, rescued him she felt as if part of herself had died with him. Natalie felt partly cheated and partly foolish, for thinking that it was so easy to save a life, and she also felt naïve, that she had been so ignorant of those local customs that, in the end, had won out.

Naïvety. It was the curse of her life. It was her naïvety that had got her involved with Dominic and had, in the end, been responsible for his moving on, moving on without her. For the umpteenth time Natalie relived that last afternoon, by the river in Cambridge, against the backdrop of Trinity and King's College Chapel. By Cambridge standards it had been a sunny day, gloriously warm but with clouds too, blotting out the sun from time to time. They were walking but both wheeling bicycles, planning to ride into the countryside, as they sometimes did. She still wasn't sure whether what had come next was sophisticated or cruel, or both.

Dominic would often hum or softly whistle tunes and it had become their private game for Natalie to guess what he was humming or whistling. If she couldn't guess the tune, she would try for the composer.

'Oh, I know that,' she had said enthusiastically that day. 'It's from that new musical. What's it called? That's it, *West Side Story*. Leonard Bernstein, that's the composer.'

'Well done, and the tune?'

'*America.*' She sang the words, 'I-want-to-be-in-Ame-ri-ca. Okay-by-me-in-Ame-ri-ca...'

Dominic had smiled and said, 'Bernstein's asked me to play with him.'

Natalie had stopped in her tracks. 'Dom! That's wonderful! When? Where?'

'New York. Just before Christmas.' He had stopped too. 'It's part of a tour I'm going on. A year on the road: Canada, Mexico, twenty-seven of the United States.'

'A year?'

'Uhuh.'

92

'Starting when?'

'I leave for Vancouver next week.'

A cloud passed beneath the sun.

'How long have you been planning this?'

'A few months.'

It was a warm day and the skin on Natalie's throat was clammy. But she had shivered. This was the first she had heard of any tour.

'Vancouver couldn't be further away.'

He had nodded. 'I like it that way. I'll be there a month, rehearsing and giving masterclasses, before moving on. A fresh city every three or four days, for months on end. A complete break.'

The last three words were spoken as the clouds cleared the sun and his face was suddenly on fire. But she could see that it wasn't just the sunshine.

'A complete break?' she had repeated.

He nodded. 'Susan and I are getting divorced. I need to devote myself to music for a year, at least.' He pointed to the bicycles. 'This was always ... you'll be Dr. Nelson soon, moving on.' He wiped his lips with his hand. 'It's time, Natalie. I can't take you with me.'

Just then, they heard – very faintly – the choir in King's College Chapel. It was the middle of the afternoon, on a weekday, so it must have been a rehearsal. But the voices reached them, clear enough to be heard but faint enough that she couldn't make out what was being sung.

'I am sorry, Tally,' he had whispered, using the name her family and friends had used since Natalie was a girl. Dom had leaned across the bicycles and kissed her cheek. 'Music comes first for me, you know that. You've always known that.

More than marriage, more than children.' He took her hand where it rested on the bicycle handlebars. 'More than this.'

He had kissed her hand. More had been said, much more, but Natalie wouldn't plead, so they had talked around the subject. One of the things she had always loved about Dominic was his voice – mellifluous, milky, melodic – and even that afternoon, amid her anguish, she had loved the sound of him speaking. But all Natalie had achieved, really, was to delay his departure. She knew that couldn't be delayed for ever and she let him kiss her on her cheek a second time, before turning, mounting his bicycle and riding off.

Natalie had remained where she was, the sound of the choir still clear, still faint.

She had never discussed divorce with Dominic, never pressured him in that way. But she had imagined it – oh, how she had imagined it.

Her distress that afternoon had soon given way to anger. Anger was never far away for her, as she realised all too well. And she knew where it came from. While Owen Nelson had been away in the war, Violette had had an affair. It had lasted for months but Violette had assumed that Natalie was too young to understand, or even to notice. But Natalie was not too young, and she *had* noticed. The man was an RAF pilot stationed near Gainsborough and the affair had ended long before Owen returned, slightly wounded. But that wasn't the point. Natalie had always been angry at her mother's betrayal, angry that she knew she couldn't tell her father without wounding him still further, and doubly angry, triply angry, that Violette had taken her daughter's affair so badly, so much to heart, when she had done the same thing herself only worse, because she had been already married herself. That was one of the reasons Natalie had followed a scientific career and not a musical one: to get back at her mother, to spite her. The fact that her mother's death was a mystery angered her too. Was her mother having the last word? In coming to Africa, Natalie hoped she was escaping her anger.

Eleanor had mentioned a fresh mystery at dinner. A small plane had crashed near Mutonguni, east of Nairobi, killing the pilot and two passengers, who were senior members of KANU, the Kenya African Nationalist Union. Although the crash had been blamed on the fact that the plane had been refilled with the wrong kind of fuel – jet fuel not propeller-type Avgas – and was therefore an accident, the possibility remained that the switch had been deliberate, and politically motivated. With independence not far off, almost any event now threatened to have political overtones. If Richard and Russell's invasion of the burial ground should be discovered...

Natalie pulled on her cigarette and observed Russell's outline as he moved silently across the ground between his tent and hers. He was wearing his usual white shirt and jeans. He slumped into his usual chair.

He sat for a few moments without speaking, until his breathing became more regular.

Natalie had already laid out the whisky and what remained of the chocolate on the writing

95

table. Russell snapped off a piece and slid it into his mouth.

Chewing, he said softly, 'A better day today.'

Natalie said nothing. Russell almost certainly didn't know about Odnate and if he did his priorities were elsewhere. The discovery of the ancient zebra skull had brought about a lively discussion at lunch, and then again at dinner. There had been no mention of the tibia and femur, or of the burial ground, and to an extent the unpleasantness of a few days before, if not forgotten, had been put aside.

At dinner there had also been some light relief. Arnold Pryce and Eleanor had been into the nearby town of Karatu earlier in the day, to refill one of the Land Rovers with diesel and top up the spare cans, and they had found a week-old copy of the London *Times* which they had bought second-hand from a local white farmer they had met at the filling station. Richard Sutton had observed Arnold reading the paper and snatched it from him. At dinner he had asked, 'How can you have a newspaper that only has adverts on the front page? Adverts for schoolteachers, for tickets to the opera, for second-hand Rolls-Royces, for pity's sake? Is that what the British think is the most important news?'

'It's meant to calm you down,' replied Arnold testily. 'Most news is bad news and that only upsets people.'

'And there's a half-page devoted to dances. Why are the British so interested in dancing?'

'That's the "season",' said Arnold. 'Mothers give dances for their eighteen-year-old daughters, so they can meet the best young men in London. It's an ancient tradition.'

'Sounds like anthropological gobbledegook to me,' said Richard. 'No wonder you Brits have lost an empire.'

'For traditions to *be* traditions,' insisted Arnold, 'to last, they must be successful at some level. But then we know you are not a great respecter of tradition, Richard.'

That had closed the conversation.

Today's discoveries also showed that, so far as Natalie was personally concerned, she was now much more a part of the team. At the table, Eleanor had deferred to her superior knowledge on extinct forms of life and the others too had heard her out in respectful silence when she was explaining about ancient forms of horse and zebra. Natalie had felt good about that.

In her tent, she passed the whisky across.

Russell just wet his lips. 'Eleanor is warming to you.'

Eleanor had been ice cold where Richard and he were concerned.

Natalie said nothing. It wasn't her fight and she wanted to keep it that way.

He wet his lips with whisky a second time. 'I saw you talking to Christopher in the gorge today. He seemed very animated.'

She let a long pause elapse, to emphasise that her privacy was her own affair. 'He explained the noise the thorn bushes make, and was telling me about his brother, Jack. That's all.'

Russell suddenly reached down between his legs, picked up some sheets of paper he had brought with him, and handed them across. 'Here.'

'What is it?' Natalie asked, not taking them, but guessing what the papers were.

'It's the first draft of the article. Richard's typing, with my corrections in blue. We thought you'd like to see it. He's going over it again, right now.'

'Article? You're going against Eleanor's wishes?' The skin under her chin, on her throat, felt clammy with sweat.

'No. Well, not entirely. We're going to wait a bit, for her anger to subside, then try again. Once she sees the paper's written, she'll be excited, as excited as we are.'

And by showing it to her, now, before Eleanor saw it, Russell was trying to stampede Natalie into being an ally, a co-conspirator.

She took back the whisky cup with one hand and dabbed at her damp neck with a hand-kerchief in her other. 'No, Russell. I don't want to look. Not yet. You're trying to ... it's as if you're trying to solicit my support, coerce me, make me take your side. I don't want you to do that. Leave me out of this, please.' She took a deep breath. 'Christopher was telling me this morning that the Maasai are a very proud people, fierce even. He's worried what they might do–'

'Another reason for publishing quickly.' Russell laid the papers next to the chocolate. 'As soon as they see how important the site is, they'll see the point of our raid.'

'The *point*? Russell!' Natalie let out a loud exasperated sigh. 'Even now, you don't seem bothered by what you did. It's ... it's awful!' She banged the flask on the table. 'Here, have another drink. Let's break our one-nip-a-night rule and talk about something more pleasant. This conspiracy talk upsets me.' She poured a second nip of scotch and handed it to him.

As he took it, he held her hand and brushed her fingers with his lips.

She snatched them away.

They were both breathing heavily.

'Don't be so locked away,' he whispered, after a while. 'Loosen up.'

She was surprised, shocked even, by his choice of phrase, exactly the words she had used herself to describe her father. Is that the impression she gave?

'I ... I'm not locked away,' she faltered. 'I've only been here a few days. I ... I'm not ready.'

She knew it was inadequate as she said it. But it was, in a sense, true enough. Her very presence in this camp, among this elite team, might be a feather in her cap academically speaking, but she was here too because of some weird psychological arithmetic, a form of emotional calculus that began with Dominic Fielding, took in her mother's death, her father's grief, the anger that she rode with difficulty, and ended with her late-night winding down sessions, when she faced her demons, alone, as she knew she had to, and tossed and turned in bed until oblivion overcame her.

That was more than enough emotion for now.

'You're not ready? That sounds like a long story, with a bad ending.'

He waited but she didn't respond.

He nodded. 'Let's not fight, Natalie. That's not what I want.' He paused. 'What I want, what I would really like is–'

'Russell–!'

He stood up and raised his hand. 'Okay, okay, enough for tonight. Let's sleep on it.'

He went to brush her cheek with his fingers but she moved her head away. He turned, walked back down the line of tents, and disappeared.

The moon had moved on in the sky and Natalie turned her chair so she could sit facing it. She lit another cigarette and picked up the whisky. Russell had hardly touched the second nip. She held it to her nose, smelling the liquid. Natalie wasn't a drinker but she did like her nightcap. Russell's visits just pushed back these quiet moments that she loved.

How different he was from Dominic. Dominic had been fulfilled by his music and that had given him an inner certainty that she had loved, as if he knew some great big secret about life: about how to enjoy what life had to offer, about how to slow it down as it went by. That was the effect Dominic had had on her. When she was with him life slowed down, its details were magnified, it was like living in a novel. Dominic had even made love slowly, knowing they would get there eventually, that it was worth the wait.

How she missed those moments, that change of pace.

Natalie had snatched her hand away from Russell without thinking twice. His gesture had been flattering, but she didn't want flattery. She wanted to be less angry and she wanted ... she wanted what she couldn't have. She wanted Dominic and her father back in her life. She couldn't have Dominic, and she couldn't have her mother, but was her father lost to her for ever?

Getting her father back would help her loosen up. Russell was right about that: she needed to.

Natalie wiped her lips with the back of her hand, turned and extinguished the hurricane lamp. There was so much light from the moon, she didn't need it. The moon was almost a perfect circle, a silver-white disc that made the sky around it appear blue.

Barks and screams from the trees broke into the silence. She saw the light in Russell's tent go out. Natalie looked up at the moon again, letting the whisky past her lips and trickle down her throat. There it was again, that sensuous feeling. That was the one shortcoming of life in the bush, which otherwise for her was near-perfect. There was no sensuality in Kihara. Dominic had awakened that side in her and, oh, how surprising and wonderful that awakening had been. A fire ran along her skin even now, just thinking about some of the times they had first made love. Sex with Dominic had been quite different from the sex described in a new book by that Russian author, Vladimir someone, about a young girl called Lolita, and which had been published only after a change in the law.

She ran her tongue around her lips, feeling the fire of the whisky fade. She must put Dominic behind her.

A wisp of cloud drifted in front of the gleaming silver disc and immediately vanished. A movement caught her eye, a figure in white. It was Mutevu Ndekei. He walked – or rather he shuffled – carefully, his silhouette passing by the dim glow of the campfire, clearly trying to make as little noise as possible. But she would know that shuffle anywhere.

Natalie smiled. Mutevu was doing what Russell North had done: visiting someone in their tent, no doubt one of the women who helped out as cleaners or assistant cooks, or who ironed the khaki shirts that had to be washed every day.

Mutevu disappeared. She wondered with another inward smile whether he would have more success with whoever he was visiting than Russell had had with her. Natalie crushed out her cigarette and poured what remained of the whisky back into the flask.

Once in bed, sleep wouldn't come. As usual. She had slept well the first night because she had been exhausted after the long journey, but then her usual sleep pattern – or non-sleep pattern – had reasserted itself. Tonight, as well as the usual barriers to oblivion, there was the added distress of Odnate.

What a waste. Why was life so untidy? Why could people not see where their best interests lay? But where did *her* best interests lie? Was she always going to be a scientist? And just a scientist? She had never dwelled on having children – Dominic had two and, he said, that was quite enough. But Odnate had been so cute. To lose a son: how Odnate's mother must be feeling tonight. And here Natalie was, worrying about getting to sleep.

The noises off – the baboons and chimpanzees and the occasional hyena – accompanied her thoughts like a Greek chorus, keeping a respectful silence one minute, generous in their vocal support the next. Somehow, amid the theatre of the night, she drifted off to sleep.

Natalie was awake at dawn. That was nothing new. In Cambridge, she was used to getting up when the rest of the college was still asleep, walking by the river with only the mist for company, watching a milky sunrise over the roofs of this college or that: the yellow-white light striking the ornate stone fretwork of King's College Chapel where Dominic had given his recital.

She lay on her bed, listening to the African day getting going – the unceasing, seemingly urgent gossip of the nightjars and lapwings, the early morning coughs and complaints of the baboons, the deeper snort of a water buffalo.

Natalie raised her hand and touched the roof of her tent. It was warm, the sun already baking the canvas. She looked at her watch: just before six. She swung her feet out of bed but looked down before she let them rest on the floor. You never knew when you might get a visit from a snake or something equally unpleasant. But the floor was disfigured by nothing more dangerous than dust.

She stepped across to the front of her tent, untied the opening and looked out. The sun was already fiercely bright but the heat hadn't built up yet. There was a faint smell of dung in the air.

A herd of something herbivorous had passed by the gorge during the night.

Natalie got dressed. She didn't wash or clean her teeth but she did run a brush through her hair. Lacing up her boots, she stepped outside and tied the tent flaps closed behind her. She made her way to the refectory. She wasn't sure what time the kitchen staff started, but Natalie knew how to turn on the gas and where the water bottles were stored. She could make her own coffee.

As she passed the fire, she paused to kick soil-sand over a log-ember that still glowed red. As she did this, and looked up, she saw a monkey running out from one of the tents along the top right arm of the 'T'. It was carrying something, something black but shiny. It looked to Natalie like a camera.

No! Whose tent had the monkey been in? They were a perennial problem, these monkeys, and a camera was a valuable object, in both a financial and a scientific sense. She knew that Arnold, Jonas and Richard occupied the tents in that arm of the camp. One of them was obviously up early and had left his tent flaps open: something they were all warned against, something that invited trouble.

Natalie set off towards the tent which she had seen the monkey leave. There was no point in giving chase – the creature had already slipped through a diminutive gap in the thorn fence and disappeared, taking the camera with it.

The tent was four along, last but one in the row. Sure enough, as Natalie approached, she could see that the flaps were open, swaying idly in the light breeze. Keeping the tents closed against the animals of the Serengeti, especially at night when the camp was quiet, was such a basic piece of bush-craft that Natalie, as she neared the tent, was immediately apprehensive. Whose tent was this? Who had made this basic mistake? And why?

She stood in front of the tent.

Now she noticed that the tapes, which were used to close up the tent, were in fact still tied in knots. The flaps hadn't been left open, they had been cut – sliced, slashed. *Entaillé,* involuntarily the word came to her in French.

She called out softly, 'Hello? Hello?'

No answer.

She called out again.

Silence, but for the sound of the breeze. A warthog or a hyena made a grunting sound in the distance.

The back of her neck was sweating now.

Natalie stepped forwards and bent down. She pulled back the flap and at the same time took a half a step further inside.

It was dark inside the tent and it took a moment for her eyes to adjust. What she first noticed, before her eyes had accommodated fully to the gloom, was a buzzing sound.

Flies.

And then she saw them: a small black cloud zzzing back and forth above the bed. There must have been hundreds of them, thousands, zig-zagging, circling, hovering.

It took her another moment to register that, this

105

side of the cloud, was a body, a torso: arms, legs wearing undershorts, an abdomen with hair over the chest. It was very still, utterly motionless.

Flies were moving in on her now, bombarding her cheeks and chin.

Natalie swallowed to keep down the vomit that was rising in her throat as she took in – beyond the cloud of swarming, swirling, *seething* insects – the parted lips and nose and open eyes of Richard Sutton.

There were flies buzzing in and out of his mouth, invading his nostrils, crawling around the rim of his eyelids. They were feeding on him. They burrowed in his hair, lodged between his toes, were laying eggs in his ears.

She threw up.

And again.

The bulk of the flies – a cloud, a grinding, growling cloud – was gorging on Richard's throat, picking at the blood that had sprouted where his windpipe, as she could now see, had been cut, and then congealed when his heart had surrendered.

Black blood was wrapped around his throat, on either side of his neck, like a surgical collar. Flies bustled each other out of the way in their eagerness to gorge.

Her stomach heaved again but it had nothing more to give. Natalie retched but had only spittle to show for it.

She looked around the tent. It had been ransacked; there were papers everywhere, a table overturned, clothes pulled out of drawers, the water jug was on the floor, books appeared to have been chewed. Was that all the monkey's doing? Natalie took in the smell of what she assumed was urine. That must be the monkey's also.

The dull drone of the flies drilled through the tent, filling it with sound. The cloud was – if anything – getting bigger, and Richard's mouth had all but disappeared. It was as if he were spewing flies.

Her eyes watered and she turned to escape the horror, half-stumbling and half-falling out of the tent, chewing savagely at the fresh air, now warmed by the clear, clean sunshine.

Natalie remained for a moment on all fours, her abdomen continuing to heave, swallowing huge chunks of air, breathing out in a series of gasps, letting her stomach regain its equilibrium, the spittle she had retched drying on her chin. Then she wiped her eyes with the back of her hand and clambered to her feet. She had to get away from the insistent drone of those flies, that menacing black cloud of unstoppable carnivores.

Natalie stood, still gnawing the air, her eyes still watering as her stomach continued to swell and subside in an involuntary staccato arrhythmia. The hair at her temples was damp with sweat.

She had to raise the alarm. At the very moment she thought this, she noticed three monkeys appear through the thorn fence and just sit, watching her. As soon as she moved away from the tent, she knew, they would invade. The flies didn't bother them.

It couldn't be helped. She wiped her nose with her hand, wiped her eyes and the spittle on her chin with the sleeve of her shirt, and then half-ran and half-stumbled toward the Land Rovers, parked under the acacia trees. Reaching the first one, she snatched open the glove compartment, fumbled where she knew the keys were hidden. She found the ignition and switched on.

Natalie looked back and saw the three monkeys edging towards Richard's tent.

She forced the palm of her hand against the steering wheel of the Land Rover and blared the horn again and again and again.

'Drink that,' said Jonas Jefferson, handing Natalie a steaming cup of coffee. 'If I had any brandy I would give you that, too. You've had a shock.'

Natalie sat at the refectory table. Her blasts of the Land Rover horn had wakened the entire camp, as she had intended. Christopher had been the first to appear, then Russell. She had told them what she knew, what she had seen.

At first disbelieving, and then uncomprehending, they had approached Richard's tent together, warily, until they had seen yet another monkey gambol out between the tent flaps carrying a photo frame, which it dropped when it saw them, and hurried off toward the acacia fence. Then Christopher had lost no time in entering Richard's tent, with Russell following him.

Natalie had watched from a distance. Now that her ordeal was over, for the time being at least, shock had set in. She had begun shaking. The only dead body she had seen before this was her mother's and that, she was now convinced, had been a mistake. She couldn't remember her mother as she had been in life: standing behind her father at the piano, singing together the songs of Hugo Wolf, now and then reaching across for her beloved Gitanes. Instead, the image Natalie couldn't rid herself of was Violette Nelson's charred limbs, the blackened crust of her skin, the faint smell of singed hair.

It was the same now with Richard Sutton. As she swallowed her coffee in great, greedy gulps, the zzzing of those flies, that seething black cloud, the sound of an electric drill feeding on the red-black chasm that was Richard's throat, kept rising in her mind, the flies crawling in and out of his nostrils, picking at his eyelids.

A fly had entered the refectory tent and its buzzing brought her out in a sweat all over again.

The coffee helped, but not much.

Eleanor had appeared not long after Christopher and Russell. She had taken in the scene and, as Natalie was interested to observe, when the older woman came out of Richard's tent she looked as angry as she was shocked. She asked Christopher and Russell to cordon off the area around Richard's quarters, to mount a guard to stop any more interference by monkeys, and then retreated to the radio-telephone to contact the police and the coroner in Nairobi.

By then the ancillary staff had begun to gather in small groups and Jonas had appeared. After inspecting the body, and seeing there was nothing he could do, his first thought had been for Natalie. She had refused a sedative but the coffee was more than welcome.

From where she sat she watched as Jonas took a sheet from the laundry area and carried it to

Richard's tent, no doubt to cover the body and shield it from yet more flies. Then all three men converged back on the refectory tent. Eleanor did the same.

There was by now a large jug of steaming coffee on the main table. One by one they helped themselves, then swallowed in silence, until Eleanor murmured, 'The police are on their way, plus Dr Ndome, the coroner. It's an hour and a half's flight from Nairobi, as you know, so they should be here inside three.' She turned to Jonas. 'You've covered the body?'

He nodded. 'That wound, it looks like a machete was used.'

Eleanor nodded over her coffee.

Kees and Arnold Pryce appeared and were told what had happened.

Silence as they all reflected on Richard's final moments.

Natalie finished her coffee and wiped her lips. 'I ... I may have seen the killer.'

All eyes turned to her.

'I was sitting smoking last night, as I always do. But I'd switched off the lamp, because the moon was so bright. I was winding down, listening to the animals, when I suddenly saw someone. It was Mutevu Ndekei.'

'You're sure?' Eleanor looked fierce. She was wearing a khaki-green shirt this morning, and sand-coloured chinos.

'Oh yes, I think so. He was wearing those rubber boots he always wears. I could tell it was him by the way he shuffled.'

'And he was headed towards Richard's tent?'

110

Natalie thought for a moment. 'He was going that way, yes. I saw him move past the campfire.'

'Was he carrying anything?'

'Not that I could see. I thought he was maybe visiting a woman, or coming back from a meeting.'

'You'll have to tell this to the police.' Eleanor threw the dregs of her coffee into the remains of the fire. 'What with your evidence, and the fact that Mutevu's missing, there's no mystery about the culprit.'

'Or the motive,' breathed Christopher.

'No,' sighed Eleanor, very quietly.

'You think – you think this is a revenge attack?' said Russell quietly. He had gone very pale.

'I do,' said Eleanor, setting down her mug on the table. 'I wish it weren't true but I fear that it is. Mutevu is a Maasai. He was around the table when Richard and you let slip what you had been doing in the burial ground. He may have overheard and told the elders who authorised him to ... to do what he's done.'

'I don't believe it,' Russell said, still whispering. 'If you're right, it's crazy, mad, sick. All we did was steal a few bones. You don't slit someone's throat for that.'

'Not in California perhaps,' replied Eleanor tartly. 'Though there have been some pretty sick murders there, as I seem to recall.' She thrust her chin forward. 'But let's not run ahead of ourselves too much. The police will be here this morning. I must let the next of kin know, and the foundation that is sponsoring the dig. And I'll call Jack; he'll have some thoughts about this.

There'll be no work today, of course, but we'll meet later, when it's quieter and the shock has worn off, to decide what to do.'

She looked at her watch. 'Natalie: Christopher and Russell can cope here, I should say. I think you should go back to your tent and write an account of what you saw last night. Sign it and date it and I will then witness it. A fast, contemporary account will be much more impressive as evidence. Do you understand?'

Natalie nodded. She had been up for barely an hour and already she felt exhausted.

'Good.' Eleanor looked from Natalie to Christopher, her gaze lingering on Russell. 'There's a lot more I could say, but now is not the time.'

Eleanor, Natalie, Christopher and Russell stood halfway down the Kihara airstrip and waved as the Piper picked up speed, lurched forward and began to raise a cloud of red-yellow dust behind it. The noise grew, the plane's tail lifted and, just as it drew level with the waiting group, its wheels left the ground. A few eland antelope grazing near the strip ran away from the noise.

Eleanor led the waving as Dr Ndome, the coroner, waved back from the pilot's seat. The plane gained height, banked and turned off, away from the sun, on a bearing for Nairobi. The foursome on the ground climbed into the Land Rover for the drive back to camp.

'Three planes in one day,' said Christopher. 'I can't remember the strip being so busy.'

It was true enough. The police and the coroner had been followed by another small plane carry-

112

ing three journalists. Aggressive, sceptical men who had smoked too much, brought their own beer and had poked around for a few hours, then flown back to Nairobi to file their stories. No one had bothered to see them off. And, shortly after lunch, the air ambulance had arrived. The ambulance men had remained on the ground barely an hour before they had flown back to Nairobi with the body.

During the day everybody in the camp had been interviewed by the police, exact measurements had been made of the scene, a plaster cast made of a footprint of a wellington boot found outside Richard Sutton's tent, and endless photographs taken. The police had taken away Natalie's written statement, though she had also been questioned closely by the most senior of the three police officers who had accompanied the coroner, and he had made a careful record of her answers. To cap it all, one of the other police officers had found a small piece of cloth snagged on one of the dead thorn bushes that formed the fence of the camp near Richard Sutton's tent. It was part of Mutevu Ndekei's apron.

For most of the way back to camp they drove in silence, each alone with his or her thoughts. But then Eleanor said, 'I've informed the next of kin.' She rubbed her eyes. 'That's not something I've ever had to do before or want to do again. And I've told the foundation. I expect we'll get reactions over the next few days. Maybe a visit.'

'It's a pity we can't release the news about the discoveries,' said Russell. 'I mean, it's something positive.'

Christopher, in the front passenger seat, next to his mother, turned swiftly to him in the back seat. 'How can you say that? What have you got in your veins, Russell – ice?' He lowered his voice. 'Someone's just died, horribly. Choked on his own blood. It's not a question of one press release or another.'

Natalie stared at him. She had never known Christopher display so much emotion over anything.

'I'm sorry,' breathed Russell to the others after a pause. 'I didn't mean it in that way. Come on. I'm as upset as anyone. After all, I'm at risk too.'

'Yes,' said Eleanor, hissing the word. 'I've been thinking about that. How do you feel, Russell? I mean, if this crime was committed for the reason we think it was, there is no question but that your life is also in danger. How do you want to manage the sleeping arrangements tonight?'

Russell craned forward. 'What do you mean?'

They had almost reached the fence of acacia and sisal thorns that surrounded the camp.

'You have a handgun, I believe. But I think I should give you a better weapon for tonight. I'm not sure who else on the staff is Maasai. Also, I'll make a show of handing over the gun at dinner, so everyone will know you've got it. That might make it safer. Do you know how to use a shot-gun?'

He smiled nervously. 'I guess. It's a while since I used one.'

'Hmmn.' Eleanor cast her eye over the fencing as she drove into the camp through the gate. She was responsible for everything. 'Here's what we'll do,' she said, reversing the Land Rover into its space. 'I'll show you how to fire it, and you can loose off a couple of rounds. The noise will be a warning too.' She switched off the engine and opened the door. 'Natalie, you'd better sleep with me.'

'What? Why? What on earth for?' Natalie's heart sank. What would happen to her late-night winding-down sessions?

'Security. Mutevu is still at large, so far as we know, and you are the only witness. I suppose you could be at risk, too.'

'No! Eleanor, you're over-reacting, surely?'

'It's your first time here, Natalie. Trust my judgement. I know this part of the world and with independence not far off these are unsettled times. There's been trouble even at a nurses' training college, where they require their nurses to become nuns. Local Kenyans say that's inappropriate now. Independence is affecting everything. No, you'd better sleep with me. For tonight anyway, until I work something out.'

Natalie looked across to Christopher for help but he just shrugged and banged shut his door. His mother was boss.

A woman ran forwards. She was dressed in the same white overall that all the kitchen staff wore.

'Yes, Naiva, what is it?' said Eleanor, putting the keys of the vehicle in the glove compartment where the monkeys wouldn't find them. 'Has Mutevu been arrested?'

'No ma'am. But one of his rubber boots has been found. Masera was in Elephant Korongo this afternoon and he saw some baboons playing with it.' She paused, looking frightened. 'It's covered with blood.'

'Do you mind if we have a second nip?' Russell North lifted the whisky flask off the small table in front of him. 'What a day! I don't want to live through a day like that again, not any time soon.'

Natalie sat across the small table, as usual. The usual noises came from the jungle, quarrels and moans; the usual stars flickered silently overhead.

'No, go ahead. We broke our one-nip-a-night rule last night. Today certainly counts as a two-nip day.' She flashed a brief smile at Russell.

Dinner tonight had been a stilted affair. Eleanor, as Natalie could see only too well, was angry inside – a swamp of swirling, searing, curdling emotions. In decades of digging, nothing like this had ever happened to Eleanor Deacon, or her excavations, and despite the shock, despite the over-reaction of Mutevu, and/or the Maasai, despite the horrors of blood and coroners and air ambulances and cynical, prying journalists, Eleanor's main feeling was regret, regret that the killing had happened, rather than sympathy with Richard Sutton, who had done something very foolish in her view. That much was plain.

Natalie found Eleanor's reaction understandable, but she did not agree with it. Richard and Russell had behaved badly – yes, very badly. They had been wilful, crass, egocentric beyond, well, beyond all understanding. But theirs was not a capital offence, not in her book, not by a long chalk. Grossly insensitive, yes; insulting, yes; disrespectful, yes. All that. Their behaviour made her

116

breathless just thinking about it. But the crime, surely, did not merit the punishment, which was also beyond understanding, and barbaric. Those flies on Richard's throat, in his nostrils, the pungent acrid smell of urine ... she shuddered all over again.

Russell poured a second cup of whisky and handed it across to Natalie. She shook her head. 'You first.'

He gulped the liquid. 'What a mess.'

'Not what I imagined for my first real dig.' She took the cup. Natalie hadn't changed all day. No one had bothered with showers. She felt dirty and wretched.

'Is that the first dead person you've seen, Russell?'

He shook his head. 'No. But don't ask any more. I grew up in the Outback, remember. I don't want to talk about it, not tonight. Okay?'

'I'll change the subject, then. Since I'm going to be spending the night with her, tell me what you know about Eleanor.'

Russell took back the whisky cup and drank from it, smacking his lips as he did so. He rubbed the back of his neck with his hand. He hadn't shaved and the stubble on his chin was longer than ever. Russell looked a bit wretched too.

'A difficult woman, but then she's had a difficult time. She was old Jock Deacon's second wife. Jock, born in South Africa, was a dedicated palaeontologist – also very good – but he had one flaw, and it was a big one.' Russell stroked the crease on his cheek. 'Women, younger women, a succession of them. He divorced his first wife – a bad career move in those days, which cost him a full professorship in your very own university, Cambridge, as it was still very strait-laced in the years before the war. Denied that avenue, he allowed himself to expand in other directions.' Russell rubbed the stubble on his jaw, passing his fingers back and forth, seeming to notice it for the first time. 'Jock ran the first and the finest digs in the Kihara Gorge and although he married Eleanor two years after his divorce from his first wife he was soon philandering. One young researcher after another turned up here; he gave them projects, and took them to bed.'

'Didn't she mind? And how do you know all this?'

Monkey screams came from the gorge. Natalie and Russell grinned at each other.

'I'll answer the second question first.' He wet his lips with more whisky. 'I know all this because everyone in palaeontology knows it, but also because one of the women – Lizbet Kondal, a Swede – worked in my department at Berkeley, and she told me first-hand.' Russell played with what was left of the chocolate packet that Natalie had placed on the table. 'Did Eleanor mind? If she did, she never let on. Jock was a bit of a showman on the side. He knew he had to be: had to make palaeontology sexy to the foundations in order to get them to part with their money. Therefore it didn't hurt if he was a little larger than life – and the press lapped it up. But Eleanor was always more interested in the science, and she was the better scientist in any case. She let Jock go round the world lecturing, raising funds, charming foundations and young women in more or less equal measure. Meanwhile, she got on with the hard slog of recording all the finds, putting them in order, writing them up.'

Natalie lit a cigarette.

'They must have loved each other in the early days; after that the arrangement suited both of them. Then, finally, it got very competitive and that was not so nice to watch. Towards the end of Jock's life, he realised that Eleanor had overtaken him. She knew more, had published far more – and far better – papers.'

He sighed, passing his fingers through his hair. 'Finally, she was offered the Cambridge professorship he had always been denied, that and a Fellowship of the Royal Society, the first and only palaeontologist to be honoured in such a way. Some say his envy at her success killed him, but in fact Eleanor is always generous about Jock. She could never have done what she did without the funds he raised, that's what she always says.'

'Did she never, you know, break out?' Natalie was longing for a shower and, above all, a clean bra.

He shook his head. 'I've never seen it. Lizbet told me Eleanor did once have an affair, with some government lawyer from Nairobi, but if she did she was far more discreet than Jock. Few details leaked out.'

Russell fell silent and for a moment neither spoke. There were more clouds tonight and much less moonlight. The yellow glow from the hurricane lamp made the shadows deep. Russell's eyes were blacker than ever.

He leaned over, and reached for her hand.

She took it away, as she had done before.

He shook his head. 'You still can't loosen up then?'

'Russell! Think what's happened today. I'm still in shock at what I saw, what I discovered. Your life might be at risk, you've got a gun – *two* guns – to keep away who knows what. Now isn't the time–'

'But that's not why ... that's not why you did what you did, is it?'

Natalie didn't reply immediately. She wanted to slow down. Pauses, silences, could mean as much as words. 'I told you, I'm not ready.'

Russell looked at her, holding the whisky cup to his lips. 'If you say so.'

If he didn't believe her, she thought, well, that couldn't be helped, and it was perhaps better that way. It shouldn't always be necessary to spell things out. Russell wasn't ... damn Dominic.

The silence lengthened. Strong animal smells wafted in from somewhere.

Eventually, Russell said much more quietly, 'I'm sorry.' He sighed. 'I seem to have spent the last few days being in the wrong.' He looked across at her. 'But I'm not wrong in how I feel about you, Natalie. I've fallen for women before but not ... not ... to tell you the truth, when I'm with you I feel even better than I did when we made our discovery. Ten times better. Better than sunshine, whisky and discovery all added together.'

She shook her head. How blatant did she need to be?

But not tonight. They'd all been through too

much in the last hours. So she inspected her watch. 'I'd better go. Wish me luck.' She lifted what was left of the whisky and held it out for Russell.

He shook his head. 'You drink it. For Dutch courage.'

They both smiled and Natalie swigged back what was left of the second nip.

'See you at breakfast.'

Eleanor Deacon's tent was bigger than anyone else's, much bigger. That made sense, because it comprised an office in the front, with a bedroom beyond a big flap that was always kept closed. Eleanor stored all the files in the office part, paperwork in connection with both the palaeontology and the administration. Against one wall of the outer tent was a table with the radio-telephone, which intermittently barked into life. Next to it was the first-aid box, for use if Jonas wasn't around.

When Natalie arrived, Eleanor was sitting at her desk and writing in her journal by the light of a hurricane lamp. Everyone knew that Eleanor kept a journal, which she compiled at the end of every day, though no one had ever seen what she wrote. Most of them assumed that she was going to publish her diaries sooner or later, or possibly posthumously.

As Natalie ducked into the tent, Eleanor stopped writing, looked up and smiled. Natalie was surprised to see that Eleanor was already changed for bed – she was wearing a pair of men's pyjamas that were much too big for her. They were

121

coloured yellow, with a brown check.

Seeing Natalie's eyes roaming over her frame, Eleanor looked down at herself and said, 'These were Jock's. I've never bothered to get a new pair.'

Natalie nodded. 'You'll be setting a new fashion.'

Eleanor was about to allow herself a smile at this, but suddenly looked up sharply. 'Do I smell whisky on your breath, Natalie?'

Natalie coloured. She knew she had coloured, too, so there was no point in denying the allegation. She nodded.

Eleanor stood up. She was flustered, irritated more than angry. 'I have strict rules about alcohol. And I know those rules were among the papers you were sent in Cambridge, on your appointment. Has Russell North got a secret supply?' Eleanor put down her pen and took off her spectacles.

'No, no. It's mine.' Natalie brushed the hair off her face. 'I'm not an alcoholic, Eleanor. I have a small flask with me and every evening, after dinner, I like to sit alone, under the stars, having one last cigarette and a few sips of whisky. It's not a crime and it doesn't affect my work. Like you write your journal, I relax in my own way. That's what I was doing when I saw ... when I saw Mutevu Ndekei.' She knew she was trembling but forced herself to keep looking steadily at Eleanor.

Eleanor had closed up her journal and was putting it away in one of the filing cabinets, which she kept locked. 'Where is this flask now?' she said.

'In my tent.'

'You can give it to me tomorrow.' Eleanor picked up her spectacles from the writing table. 'I'm sorry, it may seem excessively zealous to you but I have my rules. I don't for one minute think that a nip of whisky will affect your work, my dear, but if any of the Africans found out, your flask would be stolen in no time and one or more of them would be drunk in no time plus ten minutes. Do you understand?'

Natalie nodded, deflated. 'I suppose so.'

Eleanor turned away, towards the flap that led to the bedroom. 'I'll keep it under lock and key, until you go home. With the champagne, in case we find something really important.' She smiled. 'Now, come through and I'll show you where you are sleeping.'

She led the way, carrying the hurricane lamp with her. Natalie followed. She had never been in here before and was amazed by what she saw. Apart from two single beds – laid out like in a hotel room, side-by-side with a small table between them – the room was dominated by photographs. Photographs on tables, photographs hanging on tent poles, on a small bookshelf. Photographs of Eleanor, of Jock, and of one celebrity or another: Jomo Kenyatta, leader of the Kikuyu tribe; Solly Zuckermann, who she knew was Britain's chief scientist; Sir Evelyn Baring, the Governor of Kenya; Haile Selassie, Emperor of Ethiopia. There were also photographs of hand axes, fossil bones, skulls of early man and other primates, photographs taken at conferences: the whole world of palaeontology in one form or

123

another. And there were a number of blow-ups of Kenyan stamps showing ancient skulls Eleanor and Jock had found.

As Natalie worked her way around the photographs, Eleanor sat on her bed, kicked off her shoes, let her hair down and began to brush it. She let Natalie finish her tour of inspection before saying, 'You get into bed first, then we'll talk.'

Natalie unbuttoned her shirt, unlaced her boots, stepped out of her trousers, folded them and laid them on a chair next to the bed. She slipped off her bra and put on her own pyjamas, blue cotton. She slid between the sheets. The bed was firmer than the one in her own tent.

Once she could see Natalie was settled, Eleanor took the hurricane lamp and left it in the office outside. Coming back in, she said, 'There's enough fuel for the lamp to last through till morning. The light might deter any late-night prowlers.'

Some light from the office leaked into the bedroom, enough for Natalie to see Eleanor get into bed. There was obviously going to be no chance to read, or smoke. Both women lay on their backs.

Natalie stared up at the sloping canvas roof and let her eyes adjust to the gloom. She listened to the night. A wind had got up and was playing in the webbing of the tent supports. The thorn was moaning softly. She heard the low grunt-cough of a warthog. She had gone the whole day without a shower, something she hoped wouldn't happen too often in the future.

'I really do think it's safer for you to sleep here

until Mutevu is caught.' Eleanor broke in on her thoughts unceremoniously. 'But I wanted a chat anyway, my dear. I know so little about you, in a personal sense, of course. I've read your research, and I know you were with Tom Little in Blombos Cave in South Africa.' Eleanor turned on her side to look at Natalie. 'You're very beautiful – I've seen the way both Russell and Christopher look at you – but you don't get much post from Britain. Is there no man in your life?'

So Russell wasn't the only blunderbuss, thought Natalie. Not for the first time tonight, she blushed. Thankfully, once again, in the gloom no one could see. But she was trapped. 'No, not any more. I was ... there was a man back home, for nearly three years. He was a musician, a cellist, always travelling and always married. I spent weeks, months, waiting. Waiting for him to come back from a tour, waiting for him to get a few days free from his wife, waiting for him to come down to Cambridge, waiting on platforms for the train to London.'

'What happened?'

Natalie told Eleanor about that last afternoon, with the bicycles by the river, and the faint singing of the choir. She couldn't look at Eleanor as she said all this. 'I was so surprised, so winded, that I didn't put up any resistance. I mean, you can't fight for someone, can you? I've never believed that. When you read it in books, I mean. Part of the experience of loving is ... is of being loved in return, and that has to be freely given...'

She tailed off. This was too much intimacy too quickly. That was one effect of life in the bush.

Eleanor lay back on the bed again, staring up at the slope of the canvas. She let a period of silence elapse, before saying, 'Great literature can be very misleading, my dear.' She had a jar of skin moisturiser and had begun applying it to her cheeks. 'Great literature is always about grand passion – meaning great love affairs. Have you ever noticed how almost no one in the *real* world lives like that? Not any more and maybe not ever. Oh, I grant you it's what a lot of people say they want, or think they want. But is it really?' She slipped off her watch and placed it on the table between the beds. 'Jock taught me a lot – I'm sure you've heard he was a great womaniser, always chasing after younger women. All true, but less than the truth, a good deal less. Jock knew one thing and he taught it to me, and he taught it well. It is that in modern life – and by modern life he meant life with all the risk taken out, the risk of illness, the risk of starvation, the risk of war – that enduring passion, fulfilment, is to be found most of all in intellectual pursuit. Sexual passion, being in love, fades. Everyone over a certain age knows that but few admit it or accept it as Jock accepted it.'

She continued rubbing moisturiser into her cheeks.

'Jock and I had a very passionate marriage for a few years, and we had two lovely girls and two boys. But he always insisted that the passion would pass, and that I was not to be surprised or regretful when it did. And he was right: it did pass. On both sides.' She lifted her watch, to look at the time. 'What Jock did before it faded, how-

126

ever, was see to it that I was properly launched on my career. I don't mean he found me jobs but that he enthused me with a love – yes, a passion – for all that you see around you, here in Kihara. It was the same with his affairs. They weren't casual, the way some affairs are. Yes, he went to bed with a succession of young women, but all of them – each and every one – went on to have a passion for some aspect of archaeolgy, anthropology, zoology or palaeontology. All of them, just like me, were infused with a passion by Jock. He had quite a gift; maybe the greatest gift one person can give another, outside children. You could say he impregnated a succession of women with a particular intellectual imagination.'

She changed her tone, the first time Natalie had heard it, almost a whisper, intimate. 'And these are passions that last a lifetime, Natalie. Unlike people, intellectual passions are constant.'

Natalie didn't run with the conversation straight away. When she did, she softened her own tone, because her point was fairly sharp. 'Weren't you hurt by Jock's affairs, Eleanor? And don't you get lonely, now, not having someone to share all this with any more?'

It was Eleanor's turn to pause. She lay, breathing steadily, a faint wheeze emanating from her throat. 'Yes, I suppose I was hurt, the first time. But Jock didn't change towards me in any other way; he went on sharing the gorge with me, sharing discoveries, his thinking. He was such a generous man, so open, so un-jealous. He had realised early on the importance of the gorge, that he had to devote his life to it and what it had to offer, and he helped show me that I should follow his example and share that grand passion. He showed me that we were both incredibly lucky to have such an opportunity.'

The wind pulled at the flaps on the tent. The thorn had quietened down.

'Do I get lonely? No man has ever asked me that question. The answer is no. Three of the children are involved in the gorge – I can share the life with them.'

Natalie wasn't sure she believed Eleanor. This conversation had turned intimate pretty quickly, as if she had been waiting for the opportunity.

But Eleanor hadn't finished. 'Do you have any brothers or sisters? Are your parents alive?'

'I'm an only child; my mother was killed in an accident a few months ago.'

'So you are close to your father?'

Natalie didn't reply immediately, weighing her answer. 'No.' What was she going to add? She wasn't sure she was as ready to be as intimate as Eleanor felt able. 'After my mother was killed, my father ... he retreated into himself. He's the organist and choirmaster at Gainsborough Cathedral and music is his life, just as it was my mother's. He surrounds himself with music. They both did.'

'And you are locked out?'

'Yes.'

A pause. 'And why, do you think, does your father take it out on you?'

'I'm not sure that he does.'

'You are an only child and he spurns you? Come, come, my dear, there's something you are not telling me.'

'But Eleanor, even if that's true – and I'm not saying it is – what business is it of yours? I hardly know you, you hardly know me. My family life is my own affair. Why do you want to know?'

'In case it affects your work – isn't that obvious?'

'Like the whisky, do you mean?' Natalie didn't want an argument, which this showed signs of becoming, but she sensed it was important, right now, to make a stand, not to give way. 'People must come into the gorge with all sorts of family backgrounds – and, yes, problems. Who knows what goes on inside Arnold Pryce, or Kees van Schelde, but that doesn't stop them being good at what they do. Why should I be any different?'

'Oh, I know what makes Arnold tick. Oh yes.' Eleanor put more moisturiser on her cheeks. And I also know that if your father has turned against you after your mother's accident, there's something you're not telling me.'

'And *I'm* saying it's a private matter, Eleanor. I don't want to fight with you, of course I don't. I've only been here a few days, a few days in which a wonderful discovery has been made and now an appalling murder has occurred. But I don't see why my estrangement from my father–'

'Was your mother's death an accident – or something else?'

Thank God for the gloom, Natalie thought. Though she said nothing, her body language provided a clear enough answer. She blushed, the skin on her throat was damp with sweat, she swallowed and swallowed again.

Still she said nothing. And that, she realised, was an answer of sorts.

Eleanor was still rubbing moisturiser into her forehead. 'I'm not sure you know this, but my own father was a missionary. He was sent out her to convert the "natives", as they were called in those days, and he had some success. But his daughter grew up to marry Jock Deacon and together they explored this gorge and helped devise a new explanation for man's origins, very different from what it says in the Bible.' She paused. 'My father took what we found out here very seriously; he was convinced by the discoveries in the gorge and it shook his faith in the scriptures.' She finished rubbing cream into her cheeks and screwed the lid back on the jar. 'One day, nearly ten years ago now, he was cleaning a gun and it went off. We never knew – and don't know to this day – whether it was an accident or suicide.'

She pulled her bedclothes higher up the bed.

'Is that what you're going through? Is that, perhaps, why your father has done what he has done? Was your mother's death really an accident?'

Natalie was still not angry exactly, but irked.

Dammit, yes, she was angry. 'I still don't see why–'

'If you ran away from England, from Cambridge, if you came down here nursing a wound – imaginary or otherwise – *I want to know*. The camp is a small, closed world, feelings can run high, high and hot. If you are running away, you might ... you might do something with Russell or

Christopher, or the other men here, that you – and I – could soon regret.'

Eleanor picked up her watch again and inspected it.

'I'm sorry if you think I'm prying, interfering, poking my nose where it doesn't belong. All that. But heading off trouble before it arrives is one of my jobs.' She lay back down again. 'So tell me, are you hiding, are you running away?'

Natalie tried to relax herself. Yes, maybe digs like Kihara could be emotional swamps but did so much attention need to be given to prevention? Why not just tackle these problems when they arose, *if* they arose?

'I don't know if my mother's death was an accident, Eleanor, or if it was something else. She was a moderately heavy smoker, she and my father were on a climbing holiday in the Lake District but, unusually for them, she had had a drink with lunch. She had gone for an afternoon nap – not something she normally did – while my father went hiking. Did she fall asleep smoking? Was she temporarily depressed by the alcohol? How can we ever know?'

Natalie gazed up at the roof of the tent, rippling in the breeze. An image of her mother's charred remains was replaced in her mind by one of the cloud of flies over the open chasm where Richard Sutton's throat should have been.

'There was nothing to suggest anything other than an accident except that it happened a few weeks after I had told my parents about my affair with the married man. They had both been upset, my father more angry than anything, but my mother was shocked, devastated and, yes, disappointed.' Natalie took a deep breath. 'I never thought disappointment could so ravage someone until I saw how my mother reacted. I realised then what aspirations she had for me and how important those aspirations were for her.' Natalie closed her eyes and opened them again. She wasn't going to talk about her mother's affair, the reason for her anger. 'People say that it is wrong for parents to live through their children, and I agree with that. But I also half-think it's natural – not *un*natural, anyway – and in any case for the parent concerned, and whether it's wrong or right, living through your child can *feel* real enough. When I told my mother about the affair, it was like she had been punctured, as if all the air had been let out of her. All those aspirations for me disappeared in an instant.'

Her mother had had no right to feel that, Natalie felt, after her own betrayal of Owen.

Natalie shook her head in the gloom. 'It was terrible. She wouldn't look me in the eye, she wouldn't phone back when I rang her up. I know she prayed for me in church. She had always sent me little notes to Cambridge, about pieces of music she had heard, or French fashion tips, or enclosing reviews of new plays in the news-papers, and she stopped doing that. She used to take the train down to Cambridge every two weeks to have lunch with me, or see one of the theatrical productions I was involved in – I used to find or make props for the dramatic society. But those visits stopped too. I hated it but there was nothing I could do.

132

'After the ... after she died, I stayed at home for a couple of weeks to be with my father, but he was never there. He was either taking choir practice, or practising the organ, or praying in the cathedral, or at my mother's grave. When he did come home, he went straight to his room – their room – and had his dinner sent up.'

Natalie turned on her side. Eleanor was just a shape in the gloom.

'I was growing angry with him. He was grief-stricken – we both were – but he was behaving unnaturally. I was about to tackle him when he suddenly said he wanted me to leave. He held in front of me a sheaf of papers.' She paused. 'They were life insurance policies. He said that, a few days before she died, my mother had confided something like, "If anything should happen to me, don't forget the polices in the drawer." She meant the drawer where their marriage certificate was kept, where my birth certificate was kept, and my degree.' Natalie wiped her lips with her tongue. 'My father thought that, not only did my mother commit suicide – a cardinal sin for a Catholic – but that she did so in a way that made it look like an accident, so the policies would pay out. That's what she'd meant when she had re-minded him where they were kept.'

Natalie lay back down and stared up again at the sloping tent ceiling.

'I haven't spoken to my father since that day. Then Dominic, my cellist lover, ditched me. Your invitation to Kihara saved my sanity. You don't need to worry about me, Eleanor. I'm not about to do anything rash or rushed.' Was that true? she

133

asked herself. Her anger had been known to explode into recklessness, if only in small ways. She had resigned from the drama society in Cambridge over a prop that had got lost, and she had regretted that. Once, shopping in London, she had encountered a difficult assistant and sworn at him in French, assuming he wouldn't understand. But he had.

'I've told you far more than I ever intended, Eleanor, so I hope you won't broadcast this generally. I don't want to be thought of as the walking wounded. I'm basically fine.'

Neither spoke for a while. Natalie could again hear the wind playing with the rigging of the tent.

'I can understand that being estranged from your father must be hurtful,' said Eleanor eventually, in almost a whisper. 'Especially as you have lost your mother and the man you were seeing. But I agree with you: Kihara may help with the scars.' She turned, puffed up her pillow, and lay back again. 'If it is any comfort, I have always found the companionship and sociability of family life to be in large measure an illusion. Children are fine when they are young, as toys. It is intellectually interesting to watch them grow, see their personalities develop. Take Jack and Christopher, for instance. They have the same parents and grew up together, yet they could not be more different. Jack is outgoing, self-confident, what-you-see-is-what-you-get. Christopher is diffident, inward and – I hate to say this – just a little jealous of Jack, or Jack's self-confidence. The girls are different again.'

She paused.

'Where does Christopher's jealousy come from and why isn't he jealous of his sisters?' She pulled the blankets higher up the bed. 'Have you never noticed how a person's family life is a poor guide to how he or she performs in the rest of life?' She coughed. 'T.S. Eliot, that American poet, said one aim in life is to *escape* our families, our childhood, not to be conditioned by them, and I agree. Real independence is the name of the game, and intellectual work the real high point of life for people with a scientific curiosity like us. Research – discovery – is the highest calling, the enduring passion. In a world without God, without salvation, the only fulfilment is to be had from the respect of others.'

Natalie wasn't sure how to respond. Eleanor was not at all like Natalie's own mother but she was giving her something to aim for amid her distress. She heard a buffalo baying far off. Maybe he was alone, too, separated from his herd. 'This murder must be heart-breaking for you.'

'Yes. But what's happened has happened. I appreciate it's a personal tragedy for Sutton, and his parents, and to some extent for Russell, but the main thing now is to move on. Richard's death doesn't change the excitement or the passion. We must keep a sense of proportion. A death is a death, a terrible thing. But when I'm ready I'm going to move things forward. The needs of the gorge must come first.'

'Oh? What are you going to do?' To her surprise, Natalie was feeling sleepy. But then it had been a wearing day.

'I can't say yet. There are ways to do these

things. Just remember our chat, my dear. I've enjoyed it. You'll find me hard at times ... well, not hard, I hope, but strong, tough. And I'm tough on myself too. All I ask is that you remember what's underneath.' She pulled up the covers and turned her back on Natalie. 'Now, I bid you goodnight.'

'Goodnight.' Natalie closed her eyes. She could smell the paraffin from the hurricane lamp outside. The buffalo moaned again in the distance.

Natalie poured her second cup of coffee from the enamel breakfast jug, and helped herself to another slice of toast. In her first few days on the dig, she had lost her appetite. The coffee seemed too strong, Mutevu's bread too doughy, she could never get used to powdered milk. But she had adjusted now and looked forward to breakfast as soon as she awoke. The more so today as breakfast had been skipped in yesterday's high drama.

It was just before seven, so the sun was not too hot. Natalie had been up nearly an hour but even so Eleanor had beaten her to it. In fact, it had been Eleanor's voice on the radio-telephone that had wakened Natalie. Hot water had been provided in the washbasin at the side of the tent, as normal, so Natalie had at least cleaned her face and neck. Did that mean Mgina was back? Natalie wouldn't feel really fresh until she'd showered, but a wash was better than nothing.

Kees van Schelde, Christopher Deacon and Arnold Pryce were already at breakfast.

Pryce was a finicky eater, who invariably cut what he was eating into neat little squares. 'Who is that rather pretty girl who helps you in the dark room, Christopher?'

'Why? Are you thinking of getting married again?' Christopher grinned. 'And don't let her hear you calling her a girl,' he added. 'She's twenty-one, and a mother twice over. She's a *woman.*'

'Is she a Maasai?' growled Pryce. 'Is she one of her husband's *many* wives?'

'You should have been a Maasai,' said Kees. 'Then you wouldn't have to keep getting divorced.'

'It's a civilised civilisation, in some ways, I agree.' Pryce spooned cereal into his mouth. 'But not all Maasai habits are equally agreeable, eh?'

No one said anything for a moment. Natalie buttered her toast.

'No,' Christopher said at length, almost in a whisper. 'And there's something you don't know.'

Everyone looked at him.

'Some of you may have been there a few days ago when my mother asked Daniel to send the Maasai a bolt of cloth, as a softener because we have fenced off that korongo.' He paused. 'It was left outside the gate to the camp during the night.'

'They *returned* it!' Pryce was astonished. He put his fingers to his lips. 'Oh, my.'

Christopher nodded.

Natalie put down her cup. 'And that means what, exactly?' But the way her heart was rocking about in her chest told her that she already had some idea.

'Well, it's hardly good news, is it?' Christopher cupped his hands around his coffee mug.

'They're not happy – but then we knew that.'

'What else do you read into their behaviour?' Kees put down his knife.

'Well,' said Christopher, adopting a deliberate tone. 'I'd say it's a measured response, a warning.' He looked at Natalie. 'When we are here, digging, we pay the Maasai to keep away. We pay in cows – it's their main form of wealth.'

'Cows? How many cows?' This was all news to Natalie.

'Oh, half a dozen. They're not very expensive for us, but they mean a lot to the Maasai.' He swallowed some coffee. 'Anyway, the gift of cattle is always popular – and they get another six at the end of the digging season. So ... they don't want to drive us away.' He helped himself to an apple. '*So*, the fact that they returned the bolt of cloth means two things.'

No one else said anything. All eyes were on him. He was his mother's son.

'It means we are not out of the woods, yet. That the Maasai are still grieving about the invasion of their burial ground. And it means they reserve the right to take back the korongo, destroy our sites and stop what we are doing here–'

'No!' said Kees and Natalie at the same time.

'Unless ... unless, well, you can probably work it out for yourselves.' Christopher looked down, avoiding eye contact.

Natalie turned over what Christopher had said in her mind. No, she couldn't work out what he was getting at.

Naiva, the young woman who had met them on their return from the airstrip the day before, who

138

had for the time being taken Mutevu Ndekei's place, was busy putting out some fried eggs on the side table. She refreshed the coffee jug and brought more butter.

Suddenly, before Natalie could grill Christopher on what he meant, Russell North strode into the tent. He nodded to Natalie as he swung one leg over the bench where she sat and whispered, grinning, 'How did it go? Get any sleep?' He helped himself to coffee, and reached for a banana.

'It was quite a night,' replied Natalie, quietly. 'I'll tell you the details later. You?'

'Not good.' He bit his lip. 'I suppose the shock of what happened only kicked in when the exertions of the day were over. Anyways, I couldn't stop thinking of Dick: Dick in life, Dick in death.' He shook his head. 'Did you hear that buffalo moaning? Like he or she was in labour or mourning.' He gulped at some coffee. 'No sound of any assassins but I didn't drop off till about four. I meant what I said last night. Did–?'

Natalie saw Eleanor leaving her tent, and head their way. She put her hand on Russell's arm to stop him saying anything he might regret.

Christopher didn't hear or see any of this, or if he did he didn't show any signs of doing so, seemingly absorbed in his thoughts.

'Good morning,' said Eleanor briskly to the refectory area in general, smiling a tight smile and sitting in her usual place. She took some coffee and said, 'I was just on the phone with the Commissioner of Police in Nairobi.'

The others looked at her. Christopher was

fiddling with a camera.

'Mutevu has been captured and arrested, I am relieved to say. He was found in Langata and charged with murder.' She looked towards Natalie. 'There's no need for us to share tonight, my dear.'

Her mouth in her coffee mug, Natalie nodded.

'Do you want the gun back?' said Russell.

'Yes, I do. But I have some bad news for you, I'm afraid.'

'Oh? What? The night passed off without incident. You say Mutevu's been arrested. I would have thought that's good news.' He was unpeeling his banana.

'It is, it is – so far as it goes.' Eleanor set down her coffee cup and laid the palms of both hands flat on the table. 'But you have heard about the bolt of cloth that has been returned?'

Natalie nodded but Russell frowned and said, 'What bolt of cloth? What's going on?'

Christopher seemed stung into life and repeated what he had already told everyone else.

'It's a warning,' said Eleanor. 'Quite civilised, I'm bound to say.' She paused. 'It tells us someone else will come for you, Russell.'

'Then we'd better send to Nairobi for more guns, or some security–'

'*No!*'

It was said vehemently, harshly, coldly. Her tone pinned everyone to their seat.

'No,' she said it again, more calmly. 'You can't run a dig like that, like it's under siege, and I won't.' Eleanor sat upright. Her fingers gripped a fork, her knuckles were white. 'I'm sorry, Russell, but you're going to have to leave.'

Everyone around the table sat very still.

Naiva, standing nearby, held her breath.

Russell said very quietly, 'What did you say?'

'I've been thinking about this, hard. You must leave.'

'No. I refuse.' Russell still remained calm, almost immobile.

To Natalie, it was much more impressive – much more menacing – than if he had shouted and lost his temper. He had shaved this morning and, despite his lack of sleep, looked much less ravaged than last night.

'You can't refuse,' replied Eleanor. 'My authority on this dig is absolute.'

'Eleanor, I repeat: I refuse to go.' He reached for another banana. 'I was with Daniel and Richard when we discovered the tibia and–'

'It's for your own protection. We can't have–'

'Bullshit!' Russell spat out the word but he still kept calm, unpeeling the banana.

'Russell! Are you crazy?' Eleanor leaned towards him. She hadn't touched her coffee. 'The Maasai are a clever people and proud, very proud. I know what I'm talking about. And while we're at it, fish out my letter of invitation to you to join this dig. There was an attachment. Maybe you didn't read it.'

'I read it!'

'Then you know that you agreed to accept my authority.'

'Yes, but no one ever imagined something like this–'

'For once I agree with you. But whose fault is

141

that?' She looked from Russell to Natalie.

Natalie returned her look. She didn't like what was happening but she still marvelled at Eleanor's inner strength. The intimacy of last night had vanished completely.

'I was part of the team that found the knee-joint.' Russell looked around the table, for support. 'It's my project now, now that Richard's dead. You can't just throw me–'

'Yes, I can. I don't pretend I like doing it, and I fully acknowledge your scientific right to take the lead in regard to the knee-joint. But science is only science. I can't risk another death.'

'There won't *be* another–'

'Russell!' Eleanor threw out her chin again, so that the skin on her throat was stretched tight. 'The police commissioner in Nairobi is a friend of mine. I have already spoken to him this morning, after Mutevu was arrested. He's as worried about your safety as I am. When I told him about the bolt of cloth being returned, he was even more alarmed. He agrees that you must leave, that it is the very least we can do.' She nodded to Naiva to bring her an egg. 'Now, I am going to send for a plane for you, to pick you up tomorrow morning. That gives you today to wind up here. Either you go freely, of your own accord, or I will ask for two policemen to come in the plane. The Commissioner has already told me he's willing to send them. You will be flown to Nairobi under police escort and a seat found for you on a flight to London.'

Russell shook his head as he chewed his fruit. 'You'd do all that?'

'I would. I will. This is not a joke, Russell. This is a crisis. I may be saving your life.' She signalled to Naiva to bring her some bread. The worst of the ordeal was over.

'And the dig?'

'The dig means everything to me, Russell, as you know. But saving your life comes first. I should have seen the risk straight away. But even if I had, I doubt I could have persuaded Richard and you to leave.' She smiled grimly. 'Now that in one sense it's too late, I insist. Half the milk's been spilled, but I can still save some. The dig may survive one killing; it certainly couldn't survive two.'

There was a silence around the table.

Naiva took the opportunity to leave.

Russell looked at Natalie. For the briefest of moments his expression softened into a smile.

Natalie's heart was back on its roller coaster. Was Russell going to use her as another reason for wanting to stay? Was he going to make more of what had happened between them, as ammunition?

Then his smiled vanished and his expression hardened again. 'If you do this,' he said, glaring at Eleanor and stabbing on the table with a knife, 'I reserve the right to say what I think, to write what I feel, wherever and whenever I want.'

'That too is against the conditions of your invitation here. But I don't suppose I'm going to chase you through the courts if you disobey. Just be careful, Russell. Attitudes are changing in Africa, all over the world. You may not have everybody's sympathy.'

With the blade of the knife, he rubbed the crease on his cheek. 'Attitudes *are* changing, Eleanor, yes. You can't run digs in such a high-handed way any more.'

'I'm sixty-five, Russell. I've got another five years in me. I don't intend to change.'

They sat staring at each other for a moment. Naiva came back in with some warm fresh bread.

Russell looked at Natalie again. Did he want her to speak up on his behalf? She couldn't. That assumed too much. She said nothing.

Then Eleanor asked, 'Well, do I send for the police? Or will you go in a civilised manner?'

All colour had drained from Russell's face. His breathing was heavy. 'I'll go, Eleanor. There's no need for the boys in blue. But I'm not going quietly. The world is going to hear about this. Our own little world, and the wider world too.'

Eleanor got up. She nodded to Russell. 'Thank you. I'll go and phone for a plane.'

Mgina laid some laundry on the bed – shirts, handkerchiefs, cotton socks. Natalie stopped reading and looked up.

'*There* you are, Mgina. I've missed you.'

The woman stepped back out of the tent, into the glow of the hurricane lamp. She moved deftly, silently, like many local Africans.

Mgina smiled. 'I had to stay at home, Miss Natalie. My mother... Odnate was the youngest.'

Natalie nodded. 'Is your mother a strong person, Mgina? How many of you are there?'

'I have three sisters and two brothers.' Mgina checked the level of paraffin in the hurricane lamp.

144

'My mother is strong but...' She shook her head.

Even in her unhappiness, she was graceful, thought Natalie. 'What is it, Mgina? Is something else wrong?'

The other woman gave a small nod. 'Odnate would not have been the youngest for long.'

Natalie caught her breath. 'You mother was pregnant again?'

Another brief nod.

Natalie bit her lip. 'And – and she lost the baby?'

Mgina looked at the ground. When she looked up there was a tear in her eye.

Natalie didn't speak. What was the other woman thinking? That if Natalie and Jonas hadn't interfered, Odnate would still have died but in a quicker, more natural, less traumatic way? And that her mother would not have lost the child she was carrying?

Or was that Natalie's conscience talking?

She strained to find something positive to say, to provide the conversation with a lift. 'You did right to stay with your mother. She has never needed you more.'

Mgina produced a shy grin through her tears. 'What happened to Odnate was very bad. What happened to my mother was very bad too. The rains come all at once, out of season, as we say. The clouds are hiding the sun. But not only bad things have happened.' Her grin widened to a smile: 'I am going to be married.'

Natalie felt dizzy. Had she heard right? Mgina's smile – amid her tears – told her she had. But who became engaged in the middle of mourning, amid the tides of grief?

She reprimanded herself. Who was she to judge? For all she knew, among the Maasai, having a daughter become engaged was the best antidote to grief there was. Come to that, it might work anywhere else also. Come to that, and despite herself, she felt her own heart lift; she found that she too was smiling.

'But that's wonderful! When? Who is the lucky man?'

Mgina wiped her eyes and gave Natalie another shy grin. 'In a few weeks. Endole Makacha. He's the son of one of the elders. I'm lucky – I'll be the third wife.'

Natalie's stomach churned. Although she had told Christopher Deacon she had studied anthropology as well as archaeology at Cambridge, and although she had no real faith herself, she had been raised a Christian and she found the polygamy of Africa difficult to accept. She was about to say something sharp when again she stopped herself. Mgina didn't think that her situation, as someone's third wife, was odd so why criticise? Natalie fought with herself for a few moments before asking, 'Will you not be having a Christian wedding?'

The other woman still held a bundle of someone else's washing, which she hugged to her bosom as she shook her head. 'A traditional wedding, Miss Natalie.'

Natalie's face puckered into an expression that was half-smile and half-frown. 'But aren't you a Christian, Mgina? Hasn't your village been converted?'

Mgina grinned again and looked at her feet.

'And you are happy being a *third* wife?'

Mgina was still concentrating on her feet. 'My mother says it is better to be married than not to be married. And she says I must not be ... jealous? You say jealous, is that a word?'

Natalie nodded.

'My mother, she says jealousy is like termites in timber, they weaken even the strongest wood.'

'Your mother is very wise, Mgina.'

'Natalie?' The voice broke in unannounced. It was Russell.

'Just a minute.' She had guessed he would come.

Natalie stood up and crossed to her dressing table. She picked up the tortoiseshell comb Mgina had always admired. 'It's for you,' she said softly, turning to the other woman. 'Congratulations.'

Another big grin from Mgina, as she took the comb. She nodded to Russell and then hurried off, carrying her bundle into the gloom.

Natalie turned back to Russell and held up the whisky flask. 'Last night Eleanor noticed whisky on my breath. I promised to surrender this today but so much has happened, I forgot and so did she. This is our last chance.'

'You see! She's worse than the Gestapo.' He raised his arm in a mock-Nazi salute.

'Stop it, Russell, stop it! Your life is in danger. Forcing you to leave may hurt, but it's for the best.'

'For the best?' He was dressed in jeans and a khaki shirt. He took one step back, half turned and pointed in the direction of the gorge. 'I'm part of a group that makes the most important fossil discovery in years, one of maybe the five most important palaeontological discoveries of all time, she wants to throw me off the team and you say my expulsion is for the best!' He took a deep breath. 'Now Richard is dead, I'm the one who's going to have to write the all-important paper – Daniel hates that sort of stuff – and *I'm* the one who should be taking these bones to our colleagues and potential critics, so they can see for themselves.'

His fists had clenched and his coal-black eyes flashed in the light of the hurricane lamp. 'I'll never get another chance like this. There will be other bones near where we found the knee-joint, even a skull maybe. You must see that, even if Dr Himmler won't.'

'That's unworthy, Russell. Ignore what she says. If the Commissioner of Police in Nairobi thinks your life's at risk, it's no joke.'

Across the gorge, trees cracked and crunched as some elephants went through.

'What if I changed my mind – and stayed?'

'You gave your word.'

'Stuff that! The fossils are here. *You* are here. Maybe you don't feel about me the way I feel about you, but give it time, give *me* time. I know we Australians can be direct, awkward even. But you've only seen me in the gorge. Come to California where everyone is more relaxed, softer, gentler.' He shook his head. 'If I refuse to go tomorrow there'll be another scrap, but maybe after it's over she'll change her mind.' He clenched and unclenched his fists, took another deep breath. 'I haven't put up enough of a fight.'

'You know Eleanor much better than I do.' Natalie bent down and fiddled with the hurricane lamp, to make the flame bigger. 'But I know one thing: she won't change her mind.'

Russell leaned forward. He shook his head again. 'I'm going to miss you.'

Natalie shook her head. 'I told you – the whisky parties are over.'

She handed him the cup and he took it, smiling. 'I'll never be able to drink whisky again without thinking of you. Have you got a photo I can take with me?'

Oh dear. It wasn't in her nature to be cold but she couldn't let Russell leave thinking there was more between them than there was.

'One good thing comes out of this.'

'Oh yes? What might that be?'

'You're free now to find some modern bones, that either match or don't match the ones you found in the gorge. Your paper will be published more quickly than it otherwise would have done.'

He nodded. 'I guess. But what if you or Jonas, or Eleanor, God forbid, discovers a skull? Our findings will be overshadowed–'

'But that's a big "if". You know that. Don't be so ... so *confrontational* all the time. You've made a great discovery – enjoy it. Well, maybe it's hard to enjoy it, given what's happened to Richard, but savour it, if you can.' After a moment, she added, 'I'll savour everyone in Cambridge knowing I'm a colleague of yours.' That put a distance between them, the use of such a neutral word as 'colleague'.

'I had hoped we'd be more than colleagues, Natalie.'

She sipped some whisky and handed the cup back to him. She let the silence lengthen.

She let the silence speak.

It was kinder that way.

Smoke from the campfire wafted over them.

'Have you had a chance to think about what you are going to do – immediately, I mean?'

Russell shrugged. His fists were still clenched. His breath still came in short bursts, his chest rising and falling, rising and falling. 'Get to New York as soon as possible. See Richard's parents. Then back to Berkeley, find those modern bones you've been banging on about.' He didn't smile. 'Then, all being well, send a paper into *Nature*. The paper is already half-written, as I showed you a few nights ago.' He chewed a knuckle. 'Then we'll have to see. I'm the wronged party here, Natalie. I know you don't see it quite like I do, but that's how it seems from where I sit. So I'll take advice from colleagues, discuss it with Richard's father, talk to my lawyer–'

'Lawyer!'

'Sure. Why not? I may be leaving in the morning, but that doesn't mean I'm rolling over.' He ran a finger down the crease on his cheek. 'I have some claim here. There are a lot more discoveries to be made in Kihara and I'll be back, some day – you can bet on it.' He leaned forward. The stubble on his chin was beginning to show itself again. 'I don't want this business to come between us, Natalie. I can't help the way I feel

150

about you, and I won't hide it – it's not in my nature. If you don't, or can't, reciprocate it's a pity but maybe you'll change. Anyway, so far as you are concerned, I'll be as civil as I can while I'm here, but I won't hide from you the fact that I intend to raise the most almighty stink when I get back to the US. Everyone's going to hear about this and Eleanor Deacon's name will be trawled through the mud.' He gave a curt nod. 'You can count on it.'

Natalie rubbed her eyes, the wood smoke from the fire was beginning to make them sore. 'And will we all be dragged through the mud with her? Is that dignified, Russell?'

He handed back the whisky. 'Of course, I won't drag you through it. You're not part of it, so you can trust me on that score. As for dignity – well, fuck dignity. I'm being kicked out tomorrow, my goddamn tail between my legs. Retired, hurt.' He brandished a clenched fist. 'Well, I can hurt back.'

Natalie took the cup but shook her head. 'My first dig as a fully qualified scientist, and it will become famous for all the wrong reasons: murder, bad blood, recriminations, a slanging match. The discoveries, the achievements, will be over-shadowed. Whatever you say or don't say, Russell, I'll be tainted. Always.'

He lowered his voice. 'You're asking me to do *nothing?*' He shook his head. 'This has gone too far.' Now he nodded. 'But I'll keep you out of this, you'll see. My quarrel is with Eleanor, not you–'

'And I'm telling you that you're being naïve!'

151

Natalie was nearly shouting. 'You're so upset, your pride has been hurt, you haven't thought it through. The world isn't interested in niceties, in details like that.' She left her chair and tied up her tent, to stop insects getting in. 'If you go ahead and do what you say you're going to do, we can all wave goodbye to any academic ambitions we ever had. You'll turn this into a soap opera!'

'So what are you saying? That I should just ignore this? Give up the chance of a follow-through, kiss off the opportunity to rewrite history?' His voice had been rising but he lowered it again. 'No way, Natalie. No-fucking-way.'

For a long while there was just the sound of them breathing. Neither looked at the other. By the sound of it, other quarrels were taking place nearby, among the baboons.

Natalie wished they could just enjoy the night, listening to the sounds of the bush, as she and Dom had lain together, listening to music, not feeling the urge to talk all the time, their skin touching.

As she sat down again, Russell leaned forward. 'I'm sorry, Natalie, real sorry. The last thing I want is to screw up your career, or for us to part ... well, like this. I haven't hidden my feelings for you, and they haven't changed – if anything, they're stronger now than ever–'

'No! Russell, stop!' She fought to keep her voice low. 'I don't want any special treatment from you. We're colleagues, that's all. Friends, yes, I suppose, though I hardly know you and you hardly know me. But that's all.' She wiped her lips with her tongue. 'I have been trying to tell you, but you haven't been listening. Don't go back to America, to Berkeley, thinking there is more between us than there is.' She softened her tone: she found it hard to do what she was doing but her instincts told her she must clear the air with Russell before he left.

'You're a clever man, and I like you but...' she faltered, and then regained her momentum. 'But when I finally come out of the shadows I'm living under, when I'm ready to move on...' She looked him hard in the eye and let out a deep breath. 'I'm sorry. I'm happy to be your co-worker, colleague, friend. But don't leave with any other idea.'

Russell stood up. 'I'm sorry, too, Natalie, very sorry.' He looked down at her and nodded. 'And I wonder which of us, at the end of the day, is going to be sorrier?'

He turned and walked off towards his tent.

Special Delivery

Natalie, crouched on all fours, brushed the sand-soil from a thin splinter of fossil bone poking out from between two large stones in the wall of the gorge. There were no clouds today to offer respite from the shimmering heat and she could feel her wet shirt sticking to her back. Sweat dropped down inside her collar in great globules. The French word for sweat, *sueur*, was much less unpleasant, Natalie thought. Strands of her hair were plastered to her temples. This afternoon's shower couldn't come soon enough.

Natalie re-examined the position of the bone splinter. Sweat dripped into her eye and she removed it with her knuckle. It was time for a rest. She stood up.

Four days had gone by since Russell's ill-tempered departure and, during that time, the tension in the camp had risen and fallen more than once. With Russell gone, there was no longer any sense of confrontation, but then Daniel had reported that Mutevu Ndekei – now in custody in Nairobi – had refused to see him in Kiambu prison: a bad sign. Eleanor had arranged for the bones which Richard and Russell had stolen to be returned to the Maasai. These had been accepted but her request for a meeting with the elders of the tribe had been turned down, for the time being. 'These were not propitious days,' she had been told.

Like everyone else on the dig, Natalie kept a

small towel hanging half-in and half-out of the back pocket of her trousers. She pulled it free and wiped her neck. On the lip of the gorge right opposite where she was working, the lines of the albizia and croton trees formed a dark lacework against the sky.

She tried not to think of Russell. How he must miss just being here.

She focused her attention again on the splinter of fossil bone that she had found. Either side of it, she now noticed, there was a large stone, about the size of a head or a melon, almost big enough to be called a boulder. Next to them were two others and she stepped back to get a better look.

A bead of sweat ran from the skin on her throat down her chest and between her breasts. That sometimes happened when she was suddenly surprised or excited.

A childhood spent making and doing jigsaws had given Natalie not an obsession exactly, but a taste, a *fascination* with patterns, with regularity and randomness. She was forever counting things – railings, paving stones, window panes, the seats and rows in theatres – to check out their regularity, their design.

Now, as she stared at the boulders in the gorge wall in front of her, she asked herself if they amounted to a pattern, if they were regular or random?

'Water?'

Natalie turned. She hadn't heard Christopher approaching. He was almost unrecognisable in his floppy hat and sunglasses. She took the bottle he offered. 'Thanks.'

As she drank, he stood next to her, his gaze following hers as once again it swept the gorge. 'You know all this used to be a huge lake, don't you?'

'I read the basic stuff, yes, of course, but how big?'

'About fifty square miles. Roughly the size of London.'

She handed back the bottle. 'This is a better land use.'

He took off his glasses, grinning. 'I agree. But it's also why this area is so flat, and so rich in fossils. The early hominids – and all the others animals – liked to live near the lake for the fresh water. Then, about two and a half million years ago, one of those mountains over there, which is a volcano, erupted. Millions of tons of ash were deposited on the lake. People, animals and plants were buried under about four hundred feet of hot molten lava. Imagine. Makes our problems seem trivial. Then, in the intervening years, flash floods have caused fissures and gorges. Kihara is the biggest and the most productive – from a fossil point of view, I mean.'

Christopher put the empty bottle away in his pocket. 'Look, there's a lake about three hours' drive from here, where you see all sorts of animals and rock art. I'm learning to fly so one day I can take you by plane. But for now, what do you say? We could drive up one weekend, overnight in a convenient cave I know, wake up at dawn and watch the show, drive back later that Sunday.'

Natalie looked at him.

'When I say "overnight", I simply mean ... what

I mean is...'

He fell silent. He had already said quite a lot for him.

Natalie decided to help him out. 'I did a rock art course at Cambridge. I'd love to see some *in situ*.'

He smiled, in relief. 'Good. Where were we?'

'See that there?' She pointed at the bone in the gorge wall. 'I think it's a femur from an extinct buffalo.' She reached out and held his shoulder. 'But before you bend down for a closer look, take in those stones. Does anything suggest itself to you?'

Christopher looked sharply at her, then at the stones, then back at her. He shook his head.

'Don't they seem regular to you? Regularly spaced, I mean. Arranged.'

He inspected the stones again. Then took a step back for a better look. 'What are you getting at?'

Natalie slipped the towel back into the pocket of her trousers. 'I'm not sure yet. They just seem too regular to be natural. It set me wondering.' She bent down again. 'Anyway, look at this.'

Christopher crouched alongside her as she placed the tip of her finger at the end of the fossil bone splinter. 'If this little creature is what I think it is, it's a first – not a spectacular first, but important.'

'Go on,' Christopher said, immediately attentive. He peered closer to the splinter. She could smell his aftershave.

'Actually, it's not so little, is it? It's a buffalo-type creature called *Pelorovis*. It went extinct about 800,000 years ago, and its claim to fame is

160

that it had turned-down tusks.'

Christopher looked doubtful. His skin was shiny with sweat.

'Oh, yes. Every other animal with horns near its mouth – elephants, mammoth, rhinos, pigs and boars – has horns or tusks that turn up. Why did those on *Pelorovis* turn down? What was their function and was it associated with why they became extinct?' Natalie felt more sweat drip inside her shirt. 'It's one of the great mysteries in my speciality and the beast has never been found as early as this, two million years ago, not in sub-Saharan Africa anyway. So the discovery will be well worth a paper for *Nature.*'

He put his hand on her shoulder. 'Well done. Your first discovery. We should celebrate.'

'It's hardly earth-shattering.'

'No, but it's important. That will go down well with my mother. She might not get out the champagne but you've made your bones, as they say in the mafia. How are you getting on with her, by the way?'

Natalie nodded. 'We had an interesting talk the night I shared her tent with her, but ... but...'

Christopher raised his hands. 'Hold on! She's done something to irritate you. Or you have, to irritate her. It can't have been important or she would have told me. What is it? What's bothering you?' A smile was beginning to appear around the edges of his mouth.

Natalie massaged her temples with her fingers. 'It's nothing in itself. Nothing. But, well, every night after dinner, after we've discussed whatever we've been discussing, I like to sit outside my tent and wind down. I love the skies down here, the night sounds of the bush – the animals bantering, like it's market day. Or killing each other in a shower of screams. And I have one cigarette – I'm not a big smoker, just one. And a tiny nip of whisky. Tiny, but it relaxes me.'

Natalie faltered. Christopher was Eleanor's son, after all. She wasn't sure she should have started this. But she had, and he had asked. 'The night after the ... incident, as I arrived to sleep in your mother's tent, she smelled whisky on my breath. It was ... she made me feel like a lush. And she made me hand over my flask. She said alcohol wasn't allowed on the digs here, except when she chose to celebrate some discovery or other, and that if the locals found the flask they would get drunk.'

'She has a point, Natalie.' Christopher wiped his forehead with the sleeve of his shirt.

'Has she? *Has she?* I've been thinking about what she said, and watching. Half the black Africans who work here are Muslims and would never touch a drop of drink. The others, if they were drink-crazy, could easily steal the sugar we have and brew their own concoction. They don't, but that's not the point. I'm an adult, Christopher. Totally responsible, totally sane, someone who loves her job.'

Natalie was getting worked up. It was much too hot for that. She forced herself to breathe more slowly. 'I am perfectly capable of having one cigarette and one nip of whisky a night without letting it interfere with my work, without sinking into a haze of alcohol fumes and dancing naked through the camp. Your mother ought to acknowledge that.' Natalie looked down at the ground and inspected the dust on her boots. 'I've said more than I intended.'

'No, no,' he replied, putting his hand on her arm. 'It's not the first time people have used me as a kind of Trojan horse into my mother.' He grinned. 'And I know what you mean. She can be fierce. For her, there's only the dig, and I have to remind her that there are other things in life.'

Christopher wiped his forehead. 'Take Virginia, my sister, who's a doctor in Palestine. As a girl she was very close to our grandfather – we all were in our own way, but she particularly adored him. However, they turned out to be ships in the night, in one way at least. As he lost his faith, so she grew more and more interested in the Bible. That's why she's in Palestine, not only to help the Palestinians but because she's fascinated by the Holy Land. I think my mother's ferocity so far as the gorge is concerned, although it fired Jack, Beth and me, put Virginia off. She's quasi-religious and part of it is because she's anxious to show there are other things than the gorge.'

Natalie nodded. 'I understand but that's not what I'm getting at. I don't mind a bit if, while we are all here, the dig comes first, dominates everything else. It's such a privilege to be in Kihara that I wouldn't query that. My only point is simple: we are not all the same, but that doesn't mean that those of us who aren't Eleanor Deacon are drunks and liars and cheats who are intent on putting the whole excavation at risk.' She felt the wet shirt on her back. She had made herself hot all over again. 'I'd better stop. I'm making it sound more of a problem than it is.'

He looked at her for a moment without speaking, then examined his watch. 'We've only another hour before we stop. I promised Daniel and Arnold I'd help them out today. Finish the area they're in.'

He made to move when they both heard the metallic drone of an airplane engine. There was no mistaking that sound, throaty and high-pitched at the same time. They each turned through 180 degrees, to watch as it came out of the sun towards them.

'He's low,' said Natalie as the airplane approached. She might still be the newest person in camp but, by now, she had seen more than a dozen planes 'buzz' the gorge prior to landing and none of them had flown so low – this one was barely two hundred feet above them.

Natalie and Christopher both shielded their eyes as the noise from the aircraft grew in intensity and it swept up the gorge directly overhead. The noise from its engines swelled till it was deafening.

Suddenly, not fifty feet from where they were standing, something hit the ground with a thump and a cloud of soil-sand billowed towards them.

'What on earth?' Natalie was mystified. 'Have we just been bombed?'

But Christopher was running towards the cloud.

She watched his silhouette as, half-hidden by dust, he looked around him, then he stooped and picked up a bundle.

'Newspapers,' he said, coming out of the cloud and smiling. 'It's Jack.'

'Newspapers?' said Natalie.

Christopher nodded. 'When we were boys, living in Cambridge during the war, Jack did a newspaper round. He hated it – it was the tamest thing he ever did, so he's always said. It's his way of letting us know he's arriving, spicing up newspaper delivery. These are the Nairobi papers. Come on, let's get back. He'll have all the latest political gossip.'

Natalie stared at the scarlet embers of the campfire. The smoke stung her eyes slightly and scratched at her nostrils. She barely noticed. Above the crackle of the flames, which curled fondly around the logs, there rose the warm chords of Elgar's cello concerto.

How different the camp was tonight. Eleanor, unless Natalie was mistaken, had embellished her mouth with lipstick. Daniel had on a crisp shirt she hadn't seen before. Even Naiva wore a fresh uniform. Clearly, Jack Deacon wasn't just anybody.

When they had returned to camp earlier that day, after their morning's digging in the gorge, Jack was already in the camp, unloading the two Land Rovers that had met him at the airstrip. He had his own plane and flew it himself, as Christopher had said. It had crossed Natalie's mind that his arrival was a bit like that of Father Christmas – he had brought with him all manner of gifts: film for Christopher, penicillin for Jonas, wooden fencing for Aldwai, a case of champagne, batteries for this and that.

But his most precious possession was all his own: a wind-up record player and a couple of dozen records. 'All I could fit into the Comanche,' he said.

Everyone was sitting around the logs now, listening to the Elgar as the flames of the fire began to subside. It had been weeks since any of them had the chance to hear music and everyone sat very still, just listening, each locked in their own thoughts and memories. Wherever Jack went, apparently his music went with him.

'Who's the film star?' he had said to Christopher when Natalie had got down from the vehicle that had driven back from the gorge.

Jack was surrounded by equipment – buckets, shovels, bolts of cloth, even a few books.

'Careful,' said Christopher. 'This is Natalie Nelson, *Doctor* Natalie Nelson. She's had her Ph.D. for all of six months. Today she made her first discovery.'

'Six months?' said Jack Deacon, holding out his hand. 'That's two months longer than me. I'm Doctor Jack Deacon, Doctor Nelson. Have you got used to the title yet? I haven't. Doctor Deacon sounds like a fairground quack to me, someone who cures–' He grinned. 'You fill in the rest.' He nodded. 'Doctor Nelson isn't bad. It sounds efficient, clinical, it sounds as though you know what you are doing.' He grinned again.

In truth, Natalie thought, Jack Deacon was a bit like a film star himself. Who did he remind her of? He had full, dark eyebrows, hair that rose up from his forehead in a wave, very slightly buck teeth and prominent cheekbones. Who was it? Who was it? It was a film about American soldiers in the Second World War that she was thinking about; she had seen it in Cambridge. Not Marlon Brando, though he had been in the film, too.

A log fell and a shower of crimson sparks rose into the air.

Yes, she had it. *The Young Lions*, that was the film. Starring Marion Brando and ... and Montgomery Clift – the name came to her: that was who Jack reminded her of.

Her mind went back to the Elgar. She knew it well. It was one of the pieces Dominic adored. Where was he now? she wondered. How often did he think of her? Did he think of her at all? She was thinking about him a little less each day, wasn't she? She changed the subject inside her head. The conversation at dinner had been different from usual, too: politics. Eleanor had set that particular ball rolling.

'What are people saying in Nairobi, Jack? How soon will independence come?'

He wore a pale blue shirt with a plain gold ring on the little finger of one hand. Natalie thought he looked tired around the eyes.

'Most people are pushing for next year, but I think it will be further away than that. If I were a betting man, I'd put money on mid-sixty-three.'

'Who, exactly, do you mean when you say "people"?' said Christopher.

There wasn't much family resemblance between him and Jack, Natalie thought. Jack was a couple of inches taller, more muscular. There were one or two wisps of grey hair near his ears. He must be – what? – thirty-three-ish. A bit old to have just got his Ph.D.

'I mean the leading figures in KANU and KADU – Kenyatta, Nzoia, Nambale.'

'These are men you know?' Eleanor had leaned forward so that her face came into the direct light of one of the hurricane lamps hanging from the roof of the refectory tent. That was when Natalie had noticed she was wearing lipstick.

'Yes, of course I know them – Nairobi's not a big place. I'm a member of KANU, I'm on one of their committees. That's why I couldn't get here any sooner. I came as quickly as I could, after I heard about the murder.'

'Which committee is that?' said Arnold Pryce. 'How many committees do they have?'

Jack extended the thumb of one hand. 'A constitutional committee.' He put up his index finger. 'A land reform committee, a foreign policy committee, a finance and tax committee, a labour law committee, an education committee – that's the one I'm on–'

'Oh? Why is that?' Eleanor played with her spectacles.

Jack pushed back his chair. 'Think about it. We white people are going to have a tricky time when independence comes. This is a black country. Black people, black politicians, will want to see immediate change. So we are going to see a rapid evolution in patterns of land ownership, in the ownership of the big industrial companies and the commercial outfits, like car dealerships, breweries, cinemas, bus companies.' He swivelled the

168

ring on his little finger. 'But there are two areas especially where they will need the whites, where white people who were born and raised here can be a big help – the banks and education. Most of the banks here are owned by whites, because most of the money originates in London or Johannesburg or New York. I know nothing about money but I *do* know about education and they – I'm talking about people like Kenyatta and Nzoia – know that they are going to need the help of educated people, white people with the right contacts, in universities in Britain, South Africa, America, to train schoolteachers, university professors, doctors, above all the bureaucracy that will run Kenya in the future. If Kenya is to be truly multi-racial after independence, the best hope is that we – the whites – can help shape the country via its educational institutions.'

'And *will* it be multi-racial?' Kees rested his chin on the fist of one hand. 'Those newspapers you brought with you suggest there's quite a bit of anti-white feeling building up.'

Jack tugged at one ear with his fingers. 'Yes. Some chimpanzees, en route from Nairobi to the Medical Research Council laboratory in Britain, arrived dead. It seems they may have been poisoned, as a protest against what some people see as scientific colonialism. The spectre of independence is infecting everything just now.'

He shifted in his seat. 'There are two things of particular importance that are happening. KANU and KADU are jostling for position and – with independence so very real all of a sudden, with a constitutional conference in London next February – old, traditional grievances are beginning to resurface, tribal memories and resentments, which may well come to a head after independence, if the various tribes don't get what they want. And of course underneath it all, everyone knows that the more trouble there is, the quicker the British will want to leave.'

There had been a silence around the table then for quite some time.

Until Christopher had said, 'What's in it for you, Jack?'

Jack frowned. 'What do you mean?'

'Oh, come on. People *say* they go into politics for this or that idealistic reason but there's always a personal – a selfish – motive, isn't there? What can a white person hope to achieve in a black country? You must have some secret aim: money, power, position.'

Silence around the table.

Jack stared hard at Christopher. This was a Christopher Natalie had never seen before.

The silence lengthened. Then Jack lifted his glass to his lips and drank some water. 'I'll ignore that.'

That was when Eleanor had changed the subject, and said to Natalie, 'I understand you found a femur of a Pelorovis this morning. What can you tell us?' She removed her spectacles and rubbed her eyes.

Natalie fingered her watch. Above them, four hurricane lamps swayed in the breeze, casting a warm yellow glow over everything. 'I'll have to check in the books I have with me, but I'm fairly certain it's never been found so early down here.

We had thought Pelorovis evolved about one and a half million years ago, then went extinct 800,000 years ago – quite a short lifespan for a species, which generally last at least two million years. So this extends the lifespan and makes it an important find. Of interest to specialists only, I would say, but, yes, well worth drawing attention to.' She brushed hair off her face. 'Among zoologists it's famous for having these down-turned tusks – very weird.'

'What are the theories?' Arnold Pryce, in a dark green shirt, had lit up his pipe. The smell was not unpleasant.

'About why its tusks were turned down?' Natalie was longing for a cigarette herself but she preferred to smoke alone. 'One theory is that Pelorovis fed on small mammals and used its tusks to spear them. Another is that it fed on mammals that live underground like voles – and used the tusks to break through the soil.'

'Were they never used for defence?' Christopher rested his elbows on the table and looked levelly at Natalie. He was wearing a crisp white shirt that made his skin look darker. It suited him, she thought.

'I don't see how they could have been, do you?' She held her hand out and curved her fingers down. 'In order for the tusks to point forward, the buffalo would have to lift back its head. Very uncomfortable and not a strong posture for fighting.'

'Were its tusks ivory, like elephants, or hair, like rhinos?' Kees wore a button-down American-style shirt. He was the most fastidious dresser of all.

'Oh, ivory. Pelorovis was not related to the rhino in any way, and never was.'

'So, a short paper for *Nature*, yes?' Eleanor replaced her spectacles.

'If you agree, yes. Just a letter to the editor, describing what we've found. A few hundred words. Nothing more.'

'Never mind. It's important in its way, scientifically, and every little thing adds up. It's positive.' Eleanor looked around the table but no one said anything. She glanced at Christopher and then back to Natalie.

'Christopher tells me you have a theory about some stones you have encountered, some boulders. Is now a good time to discuss it?'

Natalie wiped her lips with her napkin. 'I think "theory" is a rather grand word for what is really just an idea, a hunch.' Her glance took in Christopher. She hadn't thought he had paid much attention in the gorge when she had pointed out the boulders. But he hadn't missed a thing.

'But go on anyway.' Eleanor's gaze raked the table and she smiled. 'No one's going anywhere. I think we can all drink coffee and listen at the same time.' This was a signal to Naiva to bring in the tray of coffee mugs.

Natalie reached for another banana. 'Well, all right, here goes. My idea is this. When we excavate the gorge, we are looking essentially for three things: fossil bones, stone hand-axes, plant remains. Fine. But what if early man already had a culture – and don't jump down my throat, yet. I don't mean symphony orchestras or film studios. What about the rudiments of a shelter?'

172

She paused, to give others the chance to object, but no one said anything.

Naiva began handing round the coffees. A jug of milk was placed on the table, and some sugar.

'What gave me the idea is this. As we've just been discussing, there are some remains of Pelorovis in the gorge. This adds to all the other bones already discovered there.' She helped herself to milk and, though she shouldn't, one spoonful of sugar. 'These buffalo remains were found in conjunction with a number of stone axes – nothing unusual there. Almost certainly, the axes were used to butcher the buffalo and slice the flesh off the bones. There are few human or hominid remains in the area, so this was a killing and eating area, maybe, but not a living area.' She stirred her coffee and drank some.

'However,' she added deliberately, 'and this is my main point: however; on one side of these remains – and *only* on one side – there are a lot of large stones, small boulders about the size of a skull. They are nine or ten boulders high and they extend into the gorge again, nine or ten boulders thick.' She looked hard at Eleanor and took a deep breath. 'Now, this is as far as we've gone, so I can't say that the evidence is any stronger than what I've just told you but it seems to me that, given the fact that these boulders are only on one side of the animal remains, and that the layout of the boulders is not random but is obviously artificial, I am wondering whether what we have here is a wall, man's earliest wall. Perhaps built as a windbreak, something that would have offered some shelter from the elements while early man

173

was having a meal. The prevailing wind is from the west, and the animal remains are all to the east of the stones.'

Another gulp of coffee. 'And so, what I am saying is this: instead of excavating in a vertical direction at this point, we need to excavate very carefully – in a horizontal direction *into* the wall of the gorge, and record the position not just of bones and axes and fossil plants, but of ordinary large stones as well. We could be overlooking important evidence.' She cupped her hands around the coffee mug. 'That's it. That's all.'

All eyes now turned to Eleanor. She had been listening intently, her chin resting on the ball of her hand. For a moment she said nothing.

Natalie's heart was beating fast. Eleanor, she well knew, was famous for her caution, for never over-interpreting evidence, and she could be very caustic – vitriolic with those who did.

Natalie glanced at Jack. He smiled and winked.

At length, Eleanor spoke. 'Have you by any chance made a drawing or diagram of this "wall", so-called?'

Natalie nodded.

'May we see it?'

Natalie rose. 'I'll get it.'

She stood up and hurried to her quarters. She had left the drawing on her writing table and was soon back in her place in the refectory tent.

'Here you are,' she said, sliding the drawing across.

Eleanor stared at the drawing for what seemed an age. Tonight she was wearing a bright blue shirt, the sleeves rolled up to reveal her wrists and forearms. Her hair shone in the yellow light.

In the silence they could hear nightjars worrying in the trees of the camp.

Finally, Eleanor looked up and across at Natalie. 'I don't think your case is proved, my dear – not yet. But I commend you on your observation.'

She tapped the drawing with her spectacles. 'This could be nothing or it could be the most exciting find in, oh, I don't know how long. Clearly, we must follow it up.' She put her spectacles back on and smiled warmly at Natalie. 'I have to tell you, Christopher was the one who brought you on this dig – I felt we needed another anatomist. Well, Christopher was right and I was wrong.' She handed back the drawing. 'Don't lose that. Make a copy. We'll act on your hunch first thing tomorrow.'

It was then that she had suggested listening to some music, a proposal that everyone had accepted enthusiastically. There were no flames in the fire now, just the crimson glow of the crisp embers and the occasional crackle as the wood snapped under the heat.

Elgar's concerto, Natalie knew, because Dominic had told her, had been composed at his house in Sussex, England, from where he had been able to hear the rumble of artillery across the Channel in France, in the First World War. He had hummed the main themes on his deathbed, suggesting that it was, perhaps, his favourite composition. The concerto, as she also knew, this time from hearing it so often, was Elgar's response to the war, an expression of his disillusionment.

What music did her father play these days, late at night? she wondered. He had always adored Bach, and had a copy of the famous portrait by Elias Haussmann in his study at home, gazing down at the piano. Would she ever see that room again, hear her father play, turn the music for him as he did so, as she had done so often when she was a girl? Without her father, she had no home. Her room in Cambridge was cosy, especially in winter time, when the gas fire was lit and she toasted tea cakes on it. But it wasn't home. The camp at Kihara was fine as far as it went, and she felt at ease here most of the time, but it wasn't home either. What *was* going to happen? Dominic wasn't coming back, but did her father have it in him to forgive her for what he thought she had done to her mother? Should she write to him? But if Natalie did, and he didn't reply, they would be further apart than ever.

The record was reaching the end: the sad, painful, slow coda not quite filling the night as, every so often, the shrieks of the baboons, or the cackle of hyenas drowned out the cello. Can anyone have heard this music in such weird surroundings? she thought.

Then she corrected herself. These surroundings weren't weird. This campfire, this gorge, this plain, and this music, all together, and however much the animals might add their voice, was wonderful.

Natalie laid out the small table by the entrance to her tent, and placed on it a pack of cigarettes, an ashtray and a notebook. She was still very jealous of her late-night moments but three changes had been introduced in the light of Richard's murder. She now sat looking the other way, across the camp towards the hills rather than in the direction where she had seen Mutevu in his wellingtons, sneaking through the night. She had with her a notebook. Since the discoveries had begun to occur, she now felt the need to record her reactions and to write up some of the details: much better to get them down straight away when they were fresh than to revisit them later when all sorts of things might be forgotten. And of course, there was no whisky.

She settled in her chair, reached for the cigarettes and looked up at the sky. No moon tonight but the shimmer of the stars was not a bad alternative. She heard a zebra snort nearby. She was learning to identify more and more bush noises. And smells.

Pulling on her cigarette, letting her frame settle, she picked up her notebook and began to scribble some lines. She described how the idea that there was a rock shelter in the gorge had come to her. That was the kind of question not tackled in scientific papers, but which people like journalists would want to know.

Next she turned to some thoughts about the prevailing winds in the Kihara Gorge. From what she now knew about them, did it make sense for the rock shelter to be orientated in the way that it was? Eleanor, who was herself growing increasingly excited about the 'shelter', as they were calling it, had spotted that its layout was semi-circular, not straight. That made it more interesting as a structure. Natalie closed her eyes and tried to imagine life as it might have been two million years ago.

'Mind if I join you for a moment?'

Natalie's eyes jerked open. She looked up, to see Eleanor. 'Not at all. Let me get you a chair.'

'No, no. Don't worry, and don't move. I'm not staying – I know how you love these late nights to yourself. I came to give you this.' And she put down on the table Natalie's whisky flask. Natalie looked from the flask to Eleanor but said nothing.

Eleanor was carrying her own notebook in one hand. With the other she took off her spectacles. 'I was wrong. Christopher convinced me. I was wrong about one or two things, my dear. I stand by my belief that a dig has to be run strictly, otherwise it falls apart. But, as Christopher said, I should get used to judging people individually, not putting everyone in the same boat.' She pointed to the flask. 'It's not a security risk, or a major corrupting influence. I'm sorry I was so strict about it. Please forgive me.'

Natalie, astonished by what she was hearing, nevertheless waved away the need to apologise. 'Would you like to share one with me? See what all the fuss is about?'

'No, thank you. I don't have a head for spirits. In any case, I fancy you'll want to be more on your own than ever tonight.' She held up two envelopes. 'Post. I completely forgot to give it to you at dinner. Something else I need to apologise for.'

She put the letters on the table, next to the

flask. 'Good night, Natalie.'

Eleanor disappeared into the gloom.

Abstractedly, Natalie muttered 'Good night' and picked up the letters. Both had a New York postmark. One, she could see, was from Russell. Radio silence had been broken.

She inserted her finger under the flap. There was just one handwritten sheet inside, in black biro, plus some typed pages. The resident nightjar was in full voice.

The letter began:

Dear Natalie,

I hope you receive this without it being first opened by her ladyship...

Not a good start.

I haven't got back to Berkeley yet. I stopped off in New York and saw Richard's parents. As you can imagine they are devastated – crushed. No, that's not quite right. Devastated, yes, but not crushed. Richard's father, Richard Sr., is quite a man and he is, if anything, angry, very angry. Spitting bile, fire and brimstone. Not with you, of course (I'll come back to that), but with the Deacons in general and Eleanor in particular. Richard's body has now been released after the inquest and is being flown back to Manhattan as I write. As soon as the funeral is over (I'm staying), Richard Sr. is planning his own trip to Nairobi and the gorge and then we shall see what we shall see. All I can say is this: expect fireworks.

I enclose a draft of the paper for <u>Nature</u> on the knee-joint (I found some modern bones in a Manhattan

179

hospital!) Daniel's name comes first, then Richard's, then mine. All of you are included. Please show it around, so everyone can endorse it before it appears. I can't bring myself to write direct to her ladyship.

I'm sorry our relationship had to begin – and end? – in the way that it did. But perhaps it's not the final word. I hope that this season's digging is – for you – a great success. After that – well, let's see. I already look back on our late-night whisky sessions with great fondness and nostalgia. I repeat that you'll find me a much more relaxed figure in California. Come see.

Russell.

She re-read the letter. He was still very raw, that much was clear. His rawness was a form of energy, one of the things that she liked about him. But, now that he was away from the camp, his bitter side seemed to be overtaking him. And she wasn't available to defuse his anger. And how much of a threat was Richard Sutton Sr.? Russell's tone sounded ominous.

She poured herself half a cup of whisky, raised it to her lips, smelled the liquid, and felt the familiar, comforting burn as it sank down and spread its warmth across her chest. Men were a little like whisky, she reflected. They could warm you and they could scald you. Russell was no different from Dominic on that score. Was she unlucky with men? she wondered. Or did she invite trouble? She had agreed to spend the night in a cave with Christopher: was that wise? She really did want to see the rock art Christopher had mentioned, and she sensed she could handle him.

She rubbed her tongue along her lips, feeling the scorch of the whisky fade. Then she slid her finger under the flap of the second envelope and took out the sheet inside.

Dear Dr Nelson,

I have been given your name by Professor Russell North, a colleague of yours, though of course I already had your address because my son, Professor Richard Sutton, was until recently also a member of your excavation team.

You will anticipate the reason for this letter. Russell has told my wife and me that you were a witness to the recent dreadful events that resulted in the tragic death of our son, and will be giving evidence at the trial. Tragedy is tragedy, but this one was made worse by the very great distance between Kenya and New York, where we live, and by the fact that business/legal commitments unavoidably keep me here when my instinct – our instinct – is to leave immediately for Kihara.

And so I am writing this letter, and sending it by special delivery. At the moment, as I say, I am detained in New York on business matters that cannot be put to one side. But, as soon as we are able, my wife and I shall be travelling to Kihara to see for ourselves the location where this awful crime took place. We are counting on you to see that justice is done and that the cruel killing of our son is matched by the conviction of his murderer, who we understand is in custody. This is probably not a situation where money makes any difference but please be assured that I am a wealthy man and that I am willing to spend whatever it takes to achieve justice.

181

Since I do not know you, Dr Nelson, and because I do not know even Professor North that well, I am unsure how exactly to pitch the tone of this letter. My wife and I are devastated by our son's death. Nothing can bring him back but we very much hope – on the basis of what Professor North has told us – that your testimony will give us some satisfaction. I understand that in Kenya murderers, if convicted, are hanged. That would provide some small comfort for my wife and me.

We look forward to meeting you in the not-too-distant future.

Sincerely yours
Richard Sutton (Senior)

Natalie looked out at the inky darkness and lit another cigarette.

She re-read Richard Sutton Senior's letter, especially the part where he said he would spend 'whatever it takes' to avenge his son's death. What did he mean and how did money come into it? Was the lateness of the hour getting to her or was there just a hint of menace in that wording?

'Look at these, Natalie. Aren't they beautiful?' Kees van Schelde stood over her, his hand outstretched.

Natalie, crouching by the wall of the korongo, stood up and wiped her forehead with the sleeve of her shirt.

'My god, Kees, yes. What are those?'

'It's obsidian, volcanic glass. You find it all over the ancient world – North America, Central America, Scotland, Indonesia, Greece, here in

182

Africa. Go on, feel them, touch them.'

She took the slivers in her hands. They were cool to the touch, with sharp edges.

'I've heard about obsidian,' Natalie said. 'But I've never seen it in the wild, so to speak. Where did you find it?'

He pointed. 'Upstream of the knee-joint but at a slightly more recent level.'

'Are they hand-axes?'

'They could be, but if they were they would have been ceremonial. Obsidian is both soft and yet brittle, too weak to be used for proper tools.'

Natalie thought for a moment. 'So early man had a ceremonial life?'

Kees tugged at an ear with his fingers. 'Too soon to say. It could be. But obsidian has one other property – other than the fact that it is shiny and sharp, and could have been polished to serve as mirrors or jewellery – and that is the fact that its chemical make-up varies quite a bit from area to area.' He took back the slivers and put them in the breast pocket of his shirt. 'There are three or four sources of obsidian known in Kenya and I should be able to check if these came from any of those sources. They are all some way off and may tell us about early man's trading patterns.'

Natalie put her hand on Kees' shoulder. 'Brilliant. But if it came from far off, what would early man have traded it *for*, what did he have to barter?'

'Good question – and the answer is: we don't know. Rare wild plants maybe, with medicinal properties? Hand-axes made of local rock that were super-sharp or super-hard? We just keep looking.'

Natalie took a water bottle from her bag, lying at the foot of the korongo wall, and offered some to Kees. 'Do the Maasai use obsidian as jewellery?'

'I don't think so. From what I've seen they use bloodstone and Korobo powdered glass.'

'Maybe it would be a good move to offer them some. After what's happened.'

Kees nodded. 'If I find any more I'll certainly suggest it. These two pieces are precious, though. I need them for analysis.'

He drank more water, wiped his lips with his hand and passed back the water bottle. 'What do you make of all the recent ... goings on?'

Natalie took the bottle and shook her head. 'I can see that from Eleanor's point of view these are uncharted waters, and potentially disastrous. But a murder has been committed and that's not a small thing, not at all. Ndekei could hang.'

'Are you in favour of the death penalty?'

'I think I am, yes. There's a lot of talk in Britain, right now, of abolishing it, and the arguments on both sides are compelling.' She drank some water. 'How do you see it?'

'Well, the death penalty was abolished in Holland a long time ago, in 1870 I think–'

'What! As early as that?'

He nodded. 'Yes. It was reintroduced at the end of the war because the government was worried people would take the law into their own hands and assassinate collaborators. Under the reinstated law, about forty collaborators were executed

184

legally, but no one since 1952.' He looked at her. 'It was the right thing to do, in post-war circumstances, but not any more. I agree with that. The law should be more ready to move with the times and take into account wider circumstances and someone's background, how they are brought up – any of those things can be mitigating factors.' He paused before adding, 'I do sympathise a little bit with Eleanor, that Richard and Russell brought it on themselves.'

'But not to the point of being killed, surely?'

Kees shrugged. 'It seems harsh, yes. And a machete is a messy, bloody way of going about it. On the other hand, the machete is a traditional weapon here and only emphasises that we are guests, outsiders, who should show some respect for Maasai ways.'

Natalie was sweating. Was it Kees' argument which got under her skin or was it the still, hot air of the gorge?

He wouldn't give up. 'Maybe you could say that you will only give evidence if the prosecution doesn't ask for the death penalty. That would bring justice, but save a life.'

'I'm not sure that's allowed.'

'And that's my point. We accept the rules too easily.'

'The rules have evolved, Kees, changed gradually over a long time and for a reason, just as there's a reason for human evolution beginning here in this place. I'm sorry you feel the way you do,' she said, sighing. 'But I can't change my view. It's my background, how *I* was brought up.' She placed her water bottle in her bag. 'You don't seem to find that a mitigating factor where I am concerned.'

'You choose.' Jack Deacon held out a stack of records. 'My mother says you come from a musical family. You can decide what we listen to tonight.'

Dinner was over and Natalie had just settled into her chair near the fire. She loved watching the flames dance among the logs and listening to the cracking and occasional hissing sounds they gave off.

So Eleanor had told Jack about her background. What else had she told him? On the one evening the two women had shared a tent, Natalie had revealed quite a few intimate details about herself. About Dominic. About her mother's death, about her estrangement from her father. She had asked Eleanor not to broadcast these – not failings, exactly, but *blemishes* – aspects of her life that she wasn't eager to have known more generally. She didn't want people feeling sorry for her: pity, condescension, making allowances. She had already found a Pelorovis skull, an ancient wall – if she was right about those boulders – and she was beginning to make her mark. That's what counted now. Her anger flared for a moment.

Jack was sitting in the canvas chair next to Natalie with a pile of brown wrappers on his knee, each with a record inside. Every wrapper had a hole in the centre, so the record label could be read.

'Go on,' said Jack. 'Other people can choose other nights. Here.'

He passed the stack of records across.

She began to sort through them: Bruch's violin concerto, Brahms's third symphony, Schubert's *Death and the Maiden*, Prokofiev's symphony number four, Barber's adagio, Satie's *Gnossiene Number One*, Liszt's *Sospiro*.

She handed him the Barber.

'You like sad music, then?'

'They're *your* records, Dr Deacon.' She met his direct gaze. 'I usually find beautiful music sad.'

'Oh, really? Even Mozart, or Haydn, at their most jolly?'

She nodded. 'Yes, I agree, Mozart can be jolly. But music is so mysterious, and so many composers had unhappy lives – Beethoven, Schubert, Schumann, Mahler, Schönberg. Don't you think that's the underlying attraction of music for most people – that it is consoling? That implies sadness, wouldn't you say?'

He took back the records. 'Do you have a Ph.D. in music as well, Dr Nelson? You chose something I find very sad-sounding. Does that say something about you, I wonder?' Without waiting for an answer, he cranked the machine, put the record on the turntable and lowered the needle to the outer edge.

The slow string sounds of the adagio slipped into the night, the deeper register of the cellos and basses gradually winning out, slowing down and keeping in check the more sinewy, lighter strains of the violins and violas which threatened to break out and soar high above the campfire. For a moment equilibrium was attained, a sound that for Natalie reminded her of the sea swelling and rolling, swelling and rolling, as calm as the deep ocean ever gets. Then the tones turned darker, slower still, the initial motif repeated in a lower register, as if to mark a burial at sea. So it seemed to Natalie.

As the final sounds died away, a rumpus could be heard across the gorge. A fight had broken out among some animals and it took a while to resolve itself.

Natalie smiled at Jack, who smiled back. 'Doesn't sound as though the baboons care for Samuel Barber. Shall I play it again?'

She grinned and nodded.

He lifted the arm, cranked the machine again and carefully laid the needle on the edge of the record. For a big man he was surprisingly gentle with the needle, she thought. The ring on his little finger caught the light from the flames of the fire.

As the strains of the adagio spread through the night for a second time, Natalie looked around her. Arnold Pryce had his eyes closed and his head was thrown back. Jonas stared into the fire, its shadows moving across his face. Kees also stared into the fire and for some reason looked cross. Christopher was talking to his mother but she had her hand on his arm, as if to quieten him. Once or twice he glanced across to Natalie.

Their trip to the cave at Ndutu the previous Sunday had been as engrossing as Christopher had promised. The lake had been much like she had imagined Eden to be when she was a girl, with hundreds of different species of animal, all drinking side-by-side as if the struggle for

188

existence had been put on hold for a couple of hours. The rock art had been very vivid – with large, mysterious figures fighting smaller ones. Christopher had explained that no one – not the archaeologists, not the locals – knew whether they were Zulus, not normally found in this part of Africa, or gods. There had been mild excitement when, as it seemed to Natalie, a lion had roared its head off right near the cave, but Christopher had reassured her it was a lioness separated from its pride and only trying to locate them. Once or twice he had stood very close to Natalie but each time she had moved smoothly away.

The adagio was over for the second time. Jack lifted the needle, gripped the record and slid it back into its sleeve. Again, she noticed how gentle his movements were.

'Got any jazz?' shouted Arnold Pryce, breaking the mood entirely.

'Basie and Biederbeck, will they do?' Jack shouted back.

'They're my choice, when it's my turn,' said Pryce, getting up from his chair and heading for his tent. He waved goodnight.

Jonas was still staring at the fire, his thoughts far, far away by the looks of it.

Kees got up and waved goodnight.

'I hear you went to the rock shelter with Christopher.'

'Yes, it was wonderful. You've been?'

'Of course. I showed it to him in the first place. The Maasai showed me, when I was a boy. You spent the night there?'

'Isn't that the point? So you can see the animals

189

early the next morning, when they visit the water?'

He nodded. 'See any lions?'

'No, but we heard some, just as we were going to sleep.'

'Did that frighten you?'

She nodded. 'To begin with, but Christopher explained what was happening – a lioness had got separated from her pride. She called out, they answered, she went off to join them.'

'It all sounds very cosy.'

'It was. We built a fire, Christopher cooked. He says you used to call him "Christine", when you were boys, because of his cooking. Brothers can be a bit cruel, yes?'

Jack looked at her, a slight smile along his lips. 'Did he tell you what he called me?'

She shook her head. 'What was it?'

He didn't reply directly but said, 'Do you have brothers or sisters?'

'No.' Obviously, Eleanor hadn't told him much. She had kept the confidence Natalie had asked her to.

Jack stifled a yawn. 'Christopher and I have rarely seen eye-to-eye. We rub along for our mother's sake, for the sake of the gorge, but we flare up from time to time. We're like a couple of water buffalo who square up to each other now and then but don't do too much damage, not these days. But it's not nice to be near, when it does happen.'

She shrugged. 'I'm tough enough. Don't worry about me. Being an only child doesn't mean I'm soft.'

'Did I say you were soft? No – and I wasn't thinking it. I think there's something sad about you, and you are certainly not as tough as my mother, not by a long way, not yet anyway. But, you're not soft, no. In fact, so far, Dr. Nelson, I'm impressed.'

'Sad? Why do you say that? Because I chose the adagio?'

He looked at her. 'I'm not going to argue with you but, for what it's worth, your eyes, your face – your very beautiful face, I have to say – is like a shield. You smile, you don't smile, but whatever you do your eyes don't change. I've watched them, around the dinner table. They're like an eland's eyes, or a kudu's, when they lift their heads to look for predators. Have you been preyed on?'

He leaned forward and kicked the fire, so that the logs burned better.

'I hope your brand-new doctorate wasn't in psychology – because if it was, you didn't deserve it. You are way off.'

'Am I?' He pulled his chair closer. *'Am I?* Is it the trial? Is it getting to you? Or is it something else?' He leaned forward; their knees were nearly touching.

Oh dear, thought Natalie. First, Russell, then Eleanor, now Jack. Did she give off some subliminal chemical – what was the word? pheromone – that encouraged people, newcomers, people who didn't know her, to charge in where her private life was concerned?

'Whatever you think you see, whatever fanciful theory you are developing, based on what I think of one eight-minute adagio, forget it. Just

191

because we are stuck out here in the bush, with no one but each other for company, just because I made some off-the-cuff remark about music that you have made more of than I ever intended, that doesn't mean ... that doesn't mean ... you remind me of Montgomery Clift, that film star, but you're behaving like Anthony Perkins in *Psycho*.'

'Didn't see it,' said Jack. 'Was it bad?'

'Scary.'

He leaned back and grinned. 'Have it your way. But I'm telling you, Natalie Nelson, *Doctor* Natalie Nelson, you're getting over someone or something. You're holding yourself in. There's anger there, as well as sadness. If you had brothers or sisters you'd have to share it, you couldn't help it. And the burden would be eased. That makes me think that it's not the trial, that it's something you arrived here with.'

She stared into the fire. She didn't like what she was hearing. He was right, of course, damn him, but she wasn't for the life of her going to say so. Natalie hadn't realised she was so obvious. Was she? No one else had said what he had said. Not Christopher in the cave, when he had all night to talk, not anyone. Was Jack so much more observant than anyone else, or just less discreet? Had all the others observed what he had, but failed to say anything? How embarrassing, if true.

'Your silence tells me quite a lot,' he said softly when she didn't reply, but she gave him such a glare that he quickly added, 'Okay, okay, let's drop it. I'm told you like a late-night smoke, so I won't go on. Just one housekeeping point. My

192

mother's had word from the court in Nairobi. They want you there some time in the next week, to make a deposition.'

'A what?'

'A deposition, a statement about what you–'

'I've already done that!' Natalie hated what she was hearing now, too. The effect of the music had quite worn off.

'I know, I know, but you have to do it again, in front of the prosecution and the defence counsel, in the presence of the court stenographer. They may want to ask you questions, decide how exactly the trial will proceed.'

She just looked at him.

'I'm sorry,' he said, leaning forward again. 'It's me who's telling you all this, instead of my mother, because I'm flying up to Nairobi myself, the day after tomorrow. I have things to do, political things, and supplies to buy. You can come with me if you wish. It will save you a very long drive in a Land Rover – hours.'

Natalie stared again into the fire. She didn't know what to say. Her experience of Nairobi was confined to changing planes at the airport there.

'Look,' said Jack quietly. 'Don't be so ... don't think of Nairobi as a problem. It's very different from the gorge but it's just as much a part of Kenya as this place is. You'll see things in Nairobi that you'll hate, you'll meet the barrister who will cross-examine you at the trial, you might see some political demonstrations. Better to find out now how you respond to all that than at the trial, and have everything thrown at you at once.'

She still didn't respond.

'All right, then, what else? Oh, yes. I'll show you around, be your guide. We'll stay at a good hotel, you can have a proper bath for once, we'll have dinner in a real restaurant, you can get out of your jungle gear and into a frock. You can wash your hair properly. Maybe we can buy some more records. You will get to see me in a blazer – think how exciting that could be.'

He kicked the fire again. The flames flared up.

'Come on,' he said, in barely above a whisper. 'What do you say? Get it over with.'

She was still staring at the few remaining flames of the dying fire.

'You'll be able to phone your father.'

She transferred her gaze from the fire to Jack. He obviously didn't know what he'd said. It was her father's birthday in a few days. Under normal circumstances a phone call would be a real treat. But now, what reception would she get?

At least, if she went to Nairobi, she'd have the option of placing a phone call.

'We need to finalise this now.' Eleanor sat very upright in the refectory tent. 'Jack and Natalie are flying to Nairobi tomorrow and they can post these papers from there. It will save days.'

Dinner was a good two hours away but everyone was ranged around the dining table. Eleanor had called a publication meeting.

'First, have you all read the paper Russell sent in via Natalie? Highly improper etiquette, but there we are. Any comments?' She looked around.

Jonas leaned forward. 'He found some modern bones through a doctor friend in New York, I see.

194

Are we happy to trust him on that?'

'Oh, I think so,' said Eleanor. 'He may be a difficult man, but he's a good scientist.'

'I thought there were going to be *two* papers,' said Arnold Pryce. 'One on the discovery, another on what it all means.'

Eleanor nodded. 'Yes, that was the original idea. But, given what's happened, and that Russell *still* thinks he'll be "scooped", I'm inclined to let him announce the discovery and write up the implications later.'

Silence around the table.

'So we tell Russell to go ahead?' Eleanor looked from one to the other.

No one said anything.

'Then we are agreed.' She took off her spectacles and rubbed her eyes. 'Now, Natalie's shelter. Has everyone read her paper? Any comments?'

'I think the tone is a little too bullish,' said Kees. 'Take the title, for instance. "An ancient shelter in the Kihara Gorge" is too – well, it assumes too much, it begs all sorts of questions. And it will antagonise potential critics.'

'What would you prefer instead?' said Eleanor.

'Something with a question mark in the title or something bland, like – oh, I don't know– "A provocative arrangement of stones in the Kihara Gorge". Or, instead of "provocative", maybe "intriguing". Something like that.'

'Natalie?' Eleanor looked across the table and smiled.

Natalie shrugged. 'I don't mind. If Kees is happier with his title, I'll go along with it.'

Christopher nodded. 'I agree with Kees.'

'Well, I don't!' interjected Jack.

Christopher reddened and looked briefly at Natalie.

'I'd fall asleep before I read to the end of Kees's title.' Jack hunched forward. 'Look, by all means have a question mark to get yourselves off the hook, but Natalie has pushed our investigation into a totally new area and titles are there to catch people's attention, to show them we are breaking new ground.' He doodled with a pen on the paper in front of him. 'How about, something like, "The origins of architecture?", with a question mark, of course.'

'No! No!' chorused several people at the same time.

'Too sensationalist,' cried Kees.

'Too glib,' said Christopher.

Now it was Jack's turn to fix his brother with a glare. 'There you are – it got you all going. That's my point, that's what a title should do.'

'In journalism, maybe,' said Eleanor, shaking her head. 'I'm with Christopher and Kees on this one, Jack.' She turned to the others. 'But surely we can think of something that will keep Jack awake *and* not be sensationalist.'

Silence around the table. Several of them were scribbling draft titles on sheets of paper, then crossing them out.

'Try this,' said Arnold Pryce at length. '"Ancient Man's first building?", with a question mark.'

'Strictly speaking, you don't need the word "ancient", and whatever it is, it's not a building,' said Natalie.

'"Man's first structure?" then. How about

that?' Pryce looked around the table.

Eleanor glanced at Jack. 'Would that keep you awake?'

'If it's a structure it's a building. It's better than "A provocative arrangement of ... whatever".'

'Christopher?' Eleanor leaned towards him.

'I still think we risk being accused of reading too much into the evidence.'

'Kees?'

'Well, it's either a structure or it isn't. I think Arnold's title is justified so long as it has a question mark.'

'And so do I,' said Eleanor. 'Let's agree on that.' She looked around the table again, from person to person. No one spoke. Christopher looked angry, Natalie thought.

'Kees, how are you getting on with your obsidian analysis?'

'I need more time. I've narrowed the source down to Rongai or Kebrigo but the pieces of glass I broke off to use are too small for the tests to distinguish. I did that so as not to destroy the original discoveries. But I definitely need larger pieces so I'll have to cut them again. It will take me a few days more.'

'Don't worry. Better to get it right than to hurry and make mistakes.'

'Either way, though,' said Kees, 'either way, these sites are a good hundred miles from the gorge. Early man was trading far and wide.'

Eleanor nodded. 'So we keep a look-out for what early man might have been trading with.'

She looked about her. 'I think that's all. Well, except that ... except that you should know that I have asked again for a meeting with the Maasai elders, to discuss the whole Ndekei business, but they still say the times are not propitious. Jack, can't you help out here?' She fixed him with a look.

'I'm an honorary Maasai, mother, not an elder.'

'But they'll listen to you. You helped them once.'

'And being even an honorary Maasai means I have to behave with *their* interests in mind, not anyone else's. They're not fools. They know what you want to see them about, what you will try to achieve, and the more you ask, the louder their denials will be, because that makes their position all the stronger.'

'So what do you suggest, if anything?' Christopher got in before his mother could.

Jack shook his head. 'I have one thought, but it's half-formed. There are one or two people I need to see when Natalie and I are in Nairobi. Let's get through that, and then we'll see.' He smiled at Natalie.

'Make sure you bring her back in one piece,' said Christopher.

The Judge

Belching exhaust fumes from buses and lorries filled the street with acrid soot. Rust-red dust from the roads caked the windows of the vehicles, grouted the faces of the pavement traders. The smell of burning corn, cattle dung and coffee filled the morning air. Shouting on all sides. Horns honked, a loudspeaker broadcast a call to prayer, radios played in the open air. Sharp sunshine that hurt the eyes broke into splinters of light on the chrome-work of cars. Downtown Nairobi.

The flight up from the gorge had been as enjoyable as Jack had promised. He seemed to Natalie an accomplished pilot, who had been thorough in his pre-flight routine before they took off: checking the wings, the wheels, the fuel, all the gauges on the aircraft dashboard, concentrating hard. She felt safe. The small Comanche had flown low, at barely two thousand feet, and Natalie had looked down on herds of elephants, a long line of wildebeest, a score of hippos lurking in a sand-coloured river, coffee groves, opencast mines, villages galore. The tiny plane had landed on the huge main runway of Nairobi airport, Jack and Natalie listening in to the radio conversations between other pilots and air traffic control. After using a pitifully small amount of airstrip, the Comanche had turned off into the private terminal of Nairobi International.

Jack left his plane near a couple of private jets. 'I

park here so I can get a good look at them,' he said to Natalie, grinning. 'You never know, maybe one day.'

They were now in a taxi, a battered black Peugeot with green writing on the bodywork. There was no air-conditioning and the rear window on Natalie's side had broken halfway down and refused to budge. There was a smell of diesel in the car, as if the carburettor was leaking. Their exhaust billowed out as black as everyone else's.

'The courthouse is just along here,' said Jack, sensing her discomfort. 'Not far.'

The traffic was inching along, the street jammed with cars and buses and lorries and little three-wheelers carrying light goods. People walked their bicycles along the pavements, ringing the bells to warn pedestrians of the change in the rules.

This was a street of shops. Hardware shops with bright silver-looking galvanised buckets and enamel washbasins hanging outside, white string-headed mops and bright saffron-coloured sponges, wooden stools and ginger-tinted coco-nuts mats. There were chemist shops with green crosses above their doors and windows lined in yellow cellophane against the sun. There were shoe shops with plimsolls hung in bunches, like white bananas; uniform shops with nurses' out-fits, grey and white, in the window, khaki shirts, Sam Brown belts, and long socks. Diffident Indian shopkeepers, in chocolate-coloured overalls, watched the world go by.

'See, there's the square ahead, the courthouse is set back.' Jack pointed past some thin trees in the middle of the expanse, to where an elegant neo-classical white mansion was coming into view. 'It'll be cooler in there.'

The road opened out into the square, but it made no difference to the speed of the traffic. Now the vehicles were choked seven abreast rather than four. Natalie noticed a dead fountain among the straggly trees, where some emaciated dogs were sniffing each other and playing. Old men were sleeping on the dried mud – the grass had obviously given up long ago. A white police box, for directing traffic, was directly ahead, raised on a dais. It was abandoned.

Outside the courthouse was a tall flagpole, supporting two flags: the Union Jack and, beneath it, the black, red and green flag that, come independence, would represent Kenya. The taxi dropped them, they grabbed their overnight bags from the boot and Jack paid the driver.

Inside, as he had said, it was cooler. It was also very busy. People clustered in knots, one or more of their number nervously awaiting cases to begin. Tall black policemen in white pith helmets contrasted with the occasional white barrister, incongruous in short wigs and black gowns. Jack scrutinised a directory on a wall.

'Room 208,' he murmured. 'Follow me.'

He led the way up a wide staircase of polished wood, which doubled back on itself, leading to the top floor. Turning right, Jack found 208, knocked and went through. A tall, good-looking man with iron-grey hair, wearing a waistcoat, white court tabs at his throat but no jacket, stood behind a massive mahogany desk. The office was a huge, light, airy room with three broad windows that gave on to the square. A portrait of the young queen hung above the desk.

'Jack,' the man boomed, 'How *are* you? How's Eleanor and that lovely sister of yours?' He came round the desk and shook hands with Jack, not letting go of his hand.

'Max, you're looking well,' said Jack. 'My mother sends her love. Beth would probably have some fighting talk for you if I'd spoken to her lately but I haven't. She's still in Boston, finishing her Ph.D.' He half-turned. 'Sir Maxwell Sandys, this is Doctor Natalie Nelson. Natalie, this is Max, deputy attorney general and the man who taught me to fly.'

Outside in the square Natalie could hear a band playing. Military music, if she wasn't mistaken. Some political event or other? She'd been so obsessed recently by her discoveries in the gorge, and so removed from civilisation at least in its modern manifestation, that she had hardly kept up with the country's countdown to independence.

Sandys stepped forward and took Natalie's hand. His skin was very soft.

'So you are our star witness, eh?' He had cornflower-blue eyes, unblinking. 'No one told me you were so beautiful, Dr. Nelson. No wonder Jack keeps you hidden away in that bloody gorge of his.' He showed her to a seat. 'How are you settling in?'

Sandys' cologne wafted over her. How much did he put on?

'Apart from the reason I'm here in this office,

204

Sir Maxwell, I'd say my time in Kihara has been spectacularly wonderful. Jack and Eleanor don't keep me hidden. All the wild animals in the Serengeti couldn't drag me away.'

He let go her hand. 'Splendid. You're a Cambridge graduate, right? Me too. Corpus Christi. Which college were you at?'

'Jesus.' Natalie hated this sort of Little England conversation.

Sandys took out the watch in his waistcoat. 'How do you think the Colonial Secretary's visit went?'

'I think he got what he came for,' said Jack. 'He saw enough trouble to realise independence has to come sooner rather than later, and that KANU have far more support – and far more *impressive* support – than KADU. They can create real trouble if they don't get their way. That helps him know who to invite to the independence conference in London in February. Do you see it any differently?'

Sandys shook his head. 'Not really. There'll be major land reform, of course, and the white farmers are not going to like it. But the white-collar people – the lawyers, doctors and teachers – will still look to Britain; that influence will remain strong. I remember you said that the last time we talked. Are you still involved with KANU?'

Jack nodded. 'I'm still on their education committee, yes. We have our hotheads, people who want to switch allegiance to the Russians, or the Soviets as the Americans now call them. But even the hotheads can see that Western medicine is better than the Russian, and as for law, Russia isn't exactly known for its justice system. You probably read that they've just introduced the death penalty for stealing state property, and they shoot forgers. So yes, I still think education is the key, to keep Kenya in the fold and to help it find its feet.'

Sandys nodded. 'Good, good.' He looked at his watch again. 'Before we begin the deposition, I have some big news for you.' He had their attention.

'Ndekei hasn't changed his plea, or anything fundamental like that, but instead what he *has* done is more provocative, more newsworthy, more racially sensitive, more potentially catastrophic and possibly much more dangerous. He is going to run a defence – a defence that is beyond him, intellectually speaking, a defence that has been concocted by the political sophisticates among his tribal elders – to say that he was acting under tribal law and that, according to Maasai tradition, what he did was perfectly legal.'

'Jeeesus!' whispered Jack, looking at Natalie.

Sandys nodded. 'It won't work, of course, not in law. But that's not the point; the point is it makes the trial a political trial straight off. It pits black against white, colonialists against the tribes, the past against the future. It will have all the trappings of a show trial, a circus, which Natalie here will be caught slap in the middle of.'

He fixed her with his eyes. 'I will explain the details after the deposition, over lunch. You need to understand just what you are taking on, what the risks are.' He smiled. 'Those risks are not negligible, but I'm sure you'll be just fine and that Jack will help.'

Sandys turned to Jack. 'Maybe we could have a drink later?'

'I don't see why not,' replied Jack. 'At the club?'

Sandys nodded. 'Say six? Now, if you'll excuse me, I must get on with the deposition.'

He led the others out into the anteroom and then across to the corridor on the other side of the staircase, into a long conference chamber with a table and chairs, where two other men, one black, one white, were waiting.

'This is Hilary Hall, who will be leading the defence of Ndekei, and his junior counsel, Tombe Nshone, who comes from the same tribe as the accused.'

Hall had a pock-marked, rather red face, whereas Nshone was a tall, very handsome man, whose skin was made to seem all the blacker by his being dressed in a navy-blue pinstripe suit and brilliant white shirt.

At a smaller table, to one side, sat a short woman wearing a dark blue dress. She had one of the new bottle-blonde hairstyles. In front of her was what looked like a small typewriter.

'This is Adele Compton, Dr. Nelson.' Sandys took a jug of water and some glasses from a sideboard and placed them on the main table. 'She is the court stenographer and will record our conversation this morning.'

Both women exchanged nods.

'Would you like to sit there?' said Sandys, indicating a seat at the end of the table. 'Hilary will sit one side and I the other. Jack, are you staying?'

'I don't think so. You don't need me, do you?'

'Not at all. In fact, it's better if you're not here.'

'How long will you be?'

'Two, two-and-a-half hours. At the most.'

Jack made a face. 'I don't think I can get back before lunch – can you look after Natalie?'

'You're going to risk leaving this beautiful woman with me?' Sandys smiled. 'Don't blame me if you don't see her again.'

Jack chewed his lip with his teeth. 'Dr. Nelson has been in the bush for some weeks, Max. Don't blame me if you get your fingers burned.'

Natalie coloured. Was she in the room or not?

Jack held out his hand, to take her bag. 'I'll stop by at the hotel, and leave our luggage with the concierge.'

She handed her bag to him. Jack made for the door. As he did so, Nshone said, 'Dr. Deacon, I'll come with you. There's something I must discuss with you. Hilary doesn't need me any more than Max needs you.' They went out together.

And so, for the next two hours, Natalie answered Sandys' questions. The rival counsels – obviously old friends – were courteous with one another, with her and with Mrs Compton. No fresh information was revealed by these exchanges, and at about five to one, Sandys looked at his watch, rubbed his face with his hand and said, 'I think that about wraps it up. Hilary?'

Hall nodded, screwed the top on his pen and leaned back in his chair. 'Thank you, Dr. Nelson,' he said, smiling down at her. 'That's all very clear, I think. Max's office will send you a transcript, for you to read and sign. We need trouble you no further.' He turned back to Sandys. 'A good morning's work, Max. I think that by the end of the week we should be ready to go to the judge and ask for a date. Agreed?'

'Absolutely.' Sandys had also been using a fountain pen, which he now slipped inside his jacket. 'No need to delay more than is necessary, especially in the current climate.'

'My thinking exactly.' The camaraderie continued. Hall gathered his papers, stood up and went out.

Sandys waited until he had disappeared. A commotion could be heard in the square outside.

'Now, that wasn't so bad, was it?'

She shook her head. 'I still wish I'd never seen Mutevu.' She turned in her seat. 'Tell me one thing, because I'm confused. If Mutevu is going to argue that he was acting according to Maasai custom, then isn't he admitting that he killed Richard and if so why does my testimony matter? It seems to me that it doesn't matter if I saw his face or just his shuffle, not if he is going to admit the killing.'

Sandys played with his tie. 'Ah, yes, but the law doesn't work like that. Or I should say court procedure and court practice don't work like that. No one wants this trial to degenerate into a racial, black–white issue. So, given what became plain today, what will happen in the trial is this: at the very beginning, Ndekei will have the charge read to him and asked how he pleads. He will plead "not guilty" but at that stage he doesn't have to give his defence, his argument, just that he pleads not guilty. In law, he doesn't have to reveal the nature of his defence until the prosecution's case has been put. Then, after his plea, we – as the prosecution – will present our case, with you as the main witness. When our case has been put, and before Ndekei's arguments are even heard, Hilary will almost certainly ask the judge to dismiss the charges, saying that since you never saw Ndekei's face there is not enough evidence to convict him. If the judge agrees, then Ndekei will be released, on the grounds of insufficient evidence, and the temperature – the political temperature – will be kept low.'

'And will that work? Is that what this morning was all about? Are you preparing to lose the case?'

'Not at all, not at all. I'm just explaining the system. It would be just the same if we were in London. We don't know yet who the judge will be but we saw this morning that you will be an excellent witness so the trial will proceed and only after we have put our case will Ndekei have to reveal his defence: that he was acting according to Maasai tradition. That will be explosive but by then, we will have spirited you away.'

Natalie looked over to the window. Where she was, she couldn't see out. 'If I'd just kept my mouth shut...'

Sandys leaned over and patted her knee. 'You'll be fine.'

She stood up to look out of the window, to see where the noise was coming from all of a sudden. She saw several people with placards; it was a small demonstration.

'What do the posters say?' asked Natalie. 'Why are they screaming? *What* are they screaming?'

'They're nationalists, and Marxists,' replied Sandys. 'Mainly from tribes who feel they were dispossessed of their land by the white man, usually long ago in the nineteenth century. They feel that, after independence, they'll get their land back. But they're only part of the problem. There is another group made up of Muslims. They loathe the Marxists and want a more ... a tighter Islamic law. You know: no drink, your hand cut off if you are convicted of theft, three wives for everyone.'

Natalie looked out at the demonstrators. Many of them were children, no more than twelve or thirteen. 'Is there going to be trouble at independence?'

'There's bound to be some. There already *is* some. But things are moving fast enough towards independence to head off the worst excesses, I think. It shouldn't be too bad, if the governor keeps his head.'

Sandys was silent for a moment. Then he looked over his shoulder, to make sure no one had come back into the room.

'Natalie, given the statements you have made, to the police and today in your deposition ... well, under the law, we can compel you to give evidence. But of course we would rather you gave evidence willingly, of your own free will.' He fingered the tabs at his throat. 'What I mean is – knowing the risks, the glare of publicity that you may well attract, the hostility, the pressure, the media glare – we need to know, as soon as possible, whether you are likely to change your mind. If you *are* going to have second thoughts about your testimony better to have them now, than on the eve of the trial. Am I being clear enough for you?'

Natalie looked out of the window again at the placards. 'Sir Maxwell, I can't pretend that I like being caught up in this ... this mess. Yes, part of me thinks that Richard and Russell brought this trouble on themselves. Yes, I understand that Mutevu Ndekei was only obeying local traditions. But did Richard Sutton deserve to *die?* No, I don't think so. I am British, brought up in a Christian household. I saw what I saw. I can't go back on that and will tell it to the court. In the same way–'

He tried to interrupt but she waved him down.

'–in the same way, if I say I will give evidence, that is what I mean. I – will – give – evidence. I don't want to be the object of any demonstration, or smear campaigns in the press, or anywhere else for that matter, but I owe it to Richard, and to Russell, to give evidence, quite apart from my own conscience.' She smiled. 'Am *I* being clear enough for *you?*'

Sandys nodded and stood up himself. 'Yes, yes it is. Thank you. I wish all witnesses were like you, my dear. No wonder Jack is so taken with you. All being well, Ndekei will hang before Easter. Lunch?'

Natalie stared at her face in the mirror. She had good skin, she knew that. People were always telling her. But the shadows under her eyes, so prominent in the wake of Dominic's defection, hadn't quite gone. What colour were they? They weren't brown – that was too strong a word. They weren't grey either – that was too weak. They were nothing like bruises, so purple and yellow were out. Whatever colour they were, they gave her face a washed-out, vulnerable look. As though she spent her nights crying. True enough in its way. She wished they would disappear and added a little powder, as camouflage. It worked, up to a point.

She tried some brownish lipstick. That suited her colouring. A smidgeon of red-brown rouge on her cheeks, just under her cheekbones, and she was more or less done. She stepped into her dress – the only one she had brought and which had been hanging over a hot bath for the past three hours, in the hope that the steam would help at least some of the creases fall out. It was white, with green and yellow flowers printed on it. Short sleeves. She clipped on a gold bracelet her mother had given her. Shoes with wedge heels. The only heels she had with her in Africa.

Natalie was ten minutes away from dinner with Jack and sat now in a wicker chair on the balcony of her room in the hotel, overlooking the pool where she'd eaten lunch. Beyond the lobby area was an arcade of shops – selling newspapers and magazines, traditional clothes, European jewellery – and then a covered walkway alongside the pool, where one area was set aside as a restaurant. She looked around. All the people seated at the tables in the restaurant were white, all the staff black. There were at most half a dozen bodies in the pool, but they were all white, too, as were those lounging on the long chairs covered with towels. But the man cleaning the pool was black, and the man handing out towels. It was no more than what she had expected but, after her experience of the demonstration and what Sandys had to say about Mutevu's defence, she couldn't help but notice.

She had spent the afternoon touring Nairobi in Maxwell Sandys' car, with Mbante, the driver, pointing out the sights in his not-very-good English: the governor's house, the National Assembly, the market, the train station, the main mosque – an ugly affair, she thought, in blue concrete with hardly any windows. They had driven past the racecourse, with its thin grass and rotting railings, which had once been white. And along embassy row, with its flagpoles, security gates, barking dogs and hidden tennis courts. Mbante hadn't specifically meant to show her but she had seen anyway the shanty town on the edge of the capital, the chaotic bus station – for blacks only, it seemed – and a local hospital, with bin upon bin of surgical waste overflowing into the car park. The National Museum had been closed, as had the National Library. Temporarily, or permanently, she couldn't tell. She had seen two other much smaller demonstrations, but on each occasion Mbante had turned the car quickly away.

When she had got back to her room she still had a couple of hours to kill before dinner and so there was more than enough time for a debate with herself over whether to call her father. It was a risk and she alternated between anger at him and a longing to hear his voice. When she had received the invitation to Kihara from Eleanor Deacon she had written to her father, to tell him she would be going abroad, and for some months. She had allowed time for the letter to reach him, then phoned. His housekeeper, Mrs Bailey, had answered. She had gone in search of Natalie's father but had returned to say he was practising at the piano and was not to be disturbed. Owen Nelson practised at all hours and was simply being distant, deliberately so. Natalie had left for Africa without saying goodbye.

If she phoned now, would it be any different? Her mother had always wanted to come to Africa, to see the great animal migrations she had read about. Would that make her father more amenable to a phone call from Nairobi, or less?

Natalie didn't know but it was his birthday in a few days and so, crossing her fingers, she placed a call with the hotel operator. She didn't know when she would get another chance. But the operator hadn't rung back yet.

Having tried on her shoes, she quickly slipped them off again as she affixed first one, then the other, earring. Single pearls: her mother's, naturally. They were lovely – plain, simple – and matched Natalie's skin colour perfectly. But every time she put them on, she experienced a twinge of guilt. She only had them because her mother was dead.

Natalie realised with a start that she had nothing with her that Dominic had given her.

She had found Maxwell Sandys' conversation after the deposition disconcerting. Had he really been trying to find out if she would back down,

215

if the going got tough? Or was he – she hesitated to think this – actually *inviting* her to change her testimony? She hoped not. That was against all she had been brought up to believe, and it certainly wasn't fair to Richard, or his parents – or even fair to Russell, who hadn't lost his life but had lost so much else personally. Where was Russell now? she thought. Was he back in Berkeley yet? At his desk, stirring up trouble?

She would ask Jack. He would know what Sandys had meant by his questions. Come to that, though, what had Max meant by his remark *about* Jack: that he was 'taken' with her? She knew what he meant at one level, of course. She understood the words, as spoken. But Jack, though considerate, had certainly never given her cause to think of him ... they had met only days before.

Her earrings were fixed. She stood and again slipped her feet one by one into her shoes and stood in front of the mirror. Yes, the earrings, half-hidden behind her hair, caught the light. She hadn't put on too much lipstick and those shadows under her eyes ... were still there.

Natalie picked up a small bag and put her lipstick and a small handkerchief inside. She stared at the room phone as if that would make it ring, conjuring up her father, thousands of miles away. Nothing happened and she grabbed her room key and went out.

A buzz of conversation – of people drinking, talking and eating – swept up to greet her. The rooms were gathered around the top of the lobby, off a gallery which looked down. She could see Jack sitting at the bar, by himself. He was wearing a sand-coloured lightweight linen jacket, dark blue cotton trousers and a pale blue shirt, no tie.

She descended the stairs. Her heels sounded on the wooden planks and, when Jack heard them, he turned to look. He rose from the bar stool and walked towards her.

'You should wear a dress more often. You look wonderful.'

'Thank you.' She touched the lapel of his jacket. 'You look good, too. Very handsome. But I was promised a blazer.'

There was a moment's awkwardness between them. Then Jack smiled and said, 'Drink? Gin and tonic, wine, martini?' They moved back towards the bar.

Natalie followed. 'No, I'd like a whisky, on the rocks.'

'Of course, silly me. My mother told me.'

He turned. 'A whisky for Rita Hayworth,' he called across to the barman.

He was drinking what looked like a gin and tonic. They clinked glasses and sipped their drinks.

'How was your afternoon?' Jack helped himself to nuts.

Natalie had decided to delay her questions about Maxwell Sandys until their dinner proper. She was perfectly content to enjoy the atmosphere of the bar, a little casual conversation in civilised surroundings. This time tomorrow they would be back in the gorge.

'Nairobi is pretty much as I expected. The French have this new term, *le Tiers Monde* – the Third World – and Nairobi is a perfect example. All the trappings of modernity, a great deal of which doesn't work, and eagerness for independence, whether they are ready or not.'

'No one is ever ready for independence, Natalie, not if you listen to the people who are about to lose power. I had a drink earlier with Max. I asked him what his office is doing to bring on black lawyers and he got quite shirty – he said it was none of my business. He was covering his tracks. He should be doing more, and he knows it.'

'You talked about "hotheads" this morning, in Max's office. Are you being a bit of a hothead yourself?'

'Is that what you think?' Jack looked worried, then grinned. 'I just think that if white people – white *Kenyans*, never forget – are to have any role in the new country, play any part politically, we have to make our voices heard now, and we have to play to our strengths. Helping to bring on black talent is one of the best ways of showing, well, of showing our goodwill.'

'And not everyone has goodwill?'

'No. Not at all, and on both sides. There are still plenty of out-and-out racists, and many more like Max, reluctant to embrace change. And there are plenty of black racists too, of course, who think that the only good white is one with a plane ticket back to Britain.'

'How many whites think like you?'

'Not enough.'

Natalie hesitated. 'Have you made many enemies?'

He drank some gin and swallowed hard. 'A few, yes. People who know change is coming, has to

218

come, but will do nothing themselves to bring it about. Most of them never say what they really think but their silence, their sheer inaction, can't be disguised. Have you never noticed that hatred and silence go together? Hatred and sulking. Hatred is always ashamed of itself.'

Natalie was turning this over in her mind when he added, 'That's the head waiter, Stanley. I think they're ready for us.'

Natalie glanced over in the direction Jack was looking. An elderly white man, bald and dressed in wing collar and tails, was standing next to the entrance to what looked like a serious dining room. For some reason, Natalie had assumed they would be eating by the pool.

'Come on,' said Jack, getting up. 'I don't know about you but I'm famished.'

The dining room was decorated in the same style as the bar, as if it were a safari lodge, with slatted blinds, much greenery, zebra hides on the walls, cream-coloured linen. Half of the room was covered, half open to the sky. There was a staccato rasp of crickets in the bushes.

As they sat down at the table, the head waiter who had shown them in lit a small candle, lost between the glasses. Two menus were brought.

'Another whisky?' said Jack, pointing at her almost-empty glass.

'Why not?' She put her small bag on the floor by her feet.

They both picked up the menus.

Jack grunted. 'This place can't make up its mind whether it's in Africa or Sussex.' He smiled. 'Look – roast beef and Yorkshire pudding, shepherd's pie and below that, ostrich steak. They could probably find some warm beer, if we asked.'

'Do you miss Britain, Jack? You were born here, weren't you?'

'Yes to your second question. No to your first. I may *look* British but I'm African through and through.' He set the menu down. 'Who could live in Britain once he – or she – has lived here? I know it's not perfect, but don't you feel something every time you go out to dig in the gorge? Could you live surrounded by all those little houses, little gardens, little roads? All that rain?' He shook his head. 'I couldn't.'

'I'll have to, I suppose. Cambridge isn't quite as bad as you say. Small – yes, but very beautiful, and open to the sky, like Africa.'

'You've only been here a few weeks. There's plenty of time to let the landscape get under your skin.' Jack's hair was flopping forward and he pushed it back in an unselfconscious way that she liked. 'I've watched you, smoking late at night, outside your tent – no, I wasn't prying.' He put his hand over his heart. 'I was checking the fence one evening, when we thought a fox had got in. I told you the other night, the time we were listening to the adagio, that your face is a shield. Outside your tent, you look ... composed, self-contained, complete. No one's complete, of course, ever. But you do your best to look it. You give off this aura of being very self-composed – I wish I had it.' He took a roll from a small basket at the edge of the table.

'Everyone seems concerned about my composure,' replied Natalie tartly. She swallowed some whisky. 'That's all Maxwell Sandys could talk about in that courthouse: whether I will make a good witness. I'm here as a scientist, Jack.'

Before he could interrupt, she waved him down. 'I *love* Kihara, the nights as much as the days and, Richard's death apart, I've had the most amazing start to my time here. Better than I could have hoped for scientifically, much better.' She broke off a piece of bread from a roll. 'But I daren't think ahead. From what Max was saying, with these independence talks coming up, the trial may be seen as political in some way – and create a huge fuss. I don't want that and I'm sure you don't. The only publications I want my name in are academic journals.'

Natalie stopped. The waiter had reappeared to take their orders. She chose sea bass – who knew when she would see fresh fish again? Jack had the beef. She opted to stay on whisky and he preferred beer. The waiter went away again.

His eyes held hers. 'I understand that. There is, however, something you don't know. Something that my mother doesn't know and something that not even Maxwell Sandys knew when you were with him.'

Another short silence, until she murmured, 'Go on.'

Jack took a sip of water, to ease the dryness in his throat. 'That lawyer, Tombe Nshone, who left the room with me ... we went for a walk in the grounds of the courthouse. He had a message.' Jack leaned forwards and lowered his voice. 'He made his point by saying that he's from the same tribe as Ndekei. He has law degrees from London and Toronto but he is a Maasai. His message was from the elders – they're called *loibone*.' He paused. 'As you know, the Maasai regard the gorge as their land, to do with as they please.'

He paused again. Natalie searched his face for some clue as to what was coming. There was a solid lump of foreboding in her stomach.

'Ndekei will plead not guilty. We knew that. But...' He looked around. The dining room was filling up though so far there was no one at the tables next to them.

'But,' he went on, 'if Mutevu is convicted, the Maasai will exercise their right to reoccupy the gorge. Only they won't just occupy it. They will destroy it.' Jack's hair had flopped forward again, but this time he left it where it was. 'They say that Kihara is the root of the problem. They say we white people are more interested in bones that are millions of years old, that have turned to stone, that belong to no one with a name, than we are in their recent ancestors. They say that if they destroy the gorge, if they hack into the walls and occupy the area with their goats and cattle, we will go away and there will be no repeat of this problem. Their burial ground will be safe.'

He fell silent, knowing the effect this would be having on Natalie.

'I know there's a lot of racial thinking in Britain, Natalie, but I tell you this: these people are not stupid or politically naïve. They know that, with independence in the offing, this case pits modern thinking against traditional practices and will receive a lot of attention. So their threat is not a feint. It plays into the hands of both the Marxists and the Muslims.'

He sat back as the food arrived.

Natalie said nothing while the plates were laid before them. Her distraught features said all that needed saying. Jack continued as though he hadn't noticed the food.

'It turns out that the actual grave which Richard and Russell looted wasn't just anyone's. It belonged to a great warrior, one the Maasai have remembered and revered for generations.' He pushed back his hair at last. 'Years ago – I mean in the nineteenth century – the Maasai never buried their dead. They left them in the bush, wrapped in their favourite cloaks, to be eaten by scavengers – hyenas, lions, vultures. It sounds grisly to us but it makes sense in a hot country with wild, savage animals who might dig up corpses.' He finally noticed his food and sprinkled salt and pepper on it. 'Then, at the turn of the century, the Maasai were converted to Christianity – or some of them were. They started to bury their dead, but not everyone, only the chiefs and warriors and their wives, their great ancestors. They built a fence around a small but important burial ground to keep the animals out, although their goats feed there because, for obvious reasons, the burial ground is fertile and bushes and trees do well there.'

He cut into his food.

'But ordinary people are still disposed of in the traditional way. The Maasai are now this weird mixture of Christian and pagan–'

'Yes, I know,' Natalie cut in. She told him about

Mgina's brother, Odnate, and what had happened, her visit with Christopher and Kees to the sand dune.

'There you are,' said Jack. 'Exactly my point. And the defence will make a lot of that.' He rubbed the scar over his eye. 'I don't want to lay it on too thick, Natalie, but the defence will allege that you were having an affair with Richard, that Russell was jealous, that that is the real reason Richard was killed, and Ndekei was set up, Russell being sent away to cover up. And that therefore you are almost as much to blame as they were, that you are part of a conspiracy and made up your evidence–'

'But you know that's not true!'

'I know it, yes. And Ndekei knows it. But they've obviously heard from someone within the camp, or Ndekei himself, about your late-night whisky sessions with Russell. They're going to make this a racial thing, a tribal thing – modern Western law against traditional custom. You are the only witness and you will be caught in the middle. With these independence talks in the background, it could get unpleasant.'

The solid mass of foreboding in Natalie's stomach had grown denser and expanded. 'Tombe told you all that?'

Jack nodded, let a pause go by, then said, 'Okay, okay. Enough. Let's change the subject. We can't take this further tonight in any case.' He paused, to chew some beef. He signalled the waiter for another round of drinks. His previous order seemed to have been overlooked.

She didn't stop him.

224

They ate in silence for a while.

Another plane went by overhead. From the straining sound it was taking off, not landing, probably bound for Europe, maybe London. What had happened to her call to her father?

Eventually, Jack said, 'I saw the CV you sent my mother, so I know about your schooling and your degrees, I know you're a Gainsborough girl and that your father is a choirmaster, but what else? Never been married? Never sung in a rock band? Never swum the Channel?' He smiled, doing his best to relax her. 'All right, I'll make a guess that you have never swum the Channel. But what about marriage – ever been close?'

'Why don't we start with you, instead?' Natalie wasn't calm yet, but she tried to appear so, resting her chin on her fist. 'You go first. I haven't even seen your CV, so we need to even things up a bit.'

The fresh drinks arrived. She tried her fish again. The ball of foreboding still clogged her stomach. Jack seemed to have an appetite for both of them. He chewed his beef with gusto, washing it down with the new glass of beer.

'I was brought up here,' he said when he could. 'In Africa. The local schools were pretty primitive, so for the first few years my parents taught me at home. I have two sisters, one four years younger, the other six years younger. I was allowed to dig very early on and both my parents spoke fluent Swahili, as well as English, so I did too, when I was fairly young. I know a good bit about wildlife as well – growing up in the bush – but just before war broke out, in 1939, the family moved to England. My father had an appointment at Cambridge and for the next seven years we lived there. After a childhood in the bush, I found Cambridge irksome. I liked the fens well enough, and the coast – watching out for German planes and submarines, the way boys imagine these things. But it can get pretty cold in Cambridge, as you must know, and I hated things like the Boy Scouts and doing a newspaper round and, once the war was over, I couldn't wait to get back to Africa.'

Jack ran his fingers around the rim of his glass. 'We returned in 1946, when I was eighteen, so I never went to university, not then anyway. I came back to the gorge, started digging again, learned to fly, travelled a bit – America, with my father, who was fundraising, met a Canadian woman, a doctor, but she didn't fancy the idea of coming to live in Africa. I finally went to university in 1952, when I was twenty-four. Columbia in New York. Then my father died, just before I finished my Ph.D. and I zoomed back to support my mother. I stayed a couple of years and only finished my doctorate, as I told you, about the time you did.' Absently, he touched a scar above his eye.

Natalie hadn't noticed it before. 'And you never played in a rock band?'

He grinned. 'No, but as it happens I *can* sing. That's how I met my Canadian medic – we both sang in the same church choir in Manhattan. I had sung in one of the college choirs at Cambridge as a boy and when I asked they gave me an introduction to the American Choral Society in New York, who directed me to Riverside Church, which is the church attached to Columbia.'

Natalie had given up on her fish. Truth to tell, she rather fancied some of Jack's beef but it didn't look as though there was going to be any left. 'Bit odd, isn't it – a palaeontologist spending so much time in a church?'

The restaurant was filling up. All the diners were white.

'I'm not religious, not in the slightest. You're right there. But the music ... it's not just beautiful, but *stirring*, don't you think?' He rubbed his chin where his beard was beginning to show. 'I remember once being in South Africa, swimming on the east coast, the Indian Ocean. Late one afternoon, a shoal or whatever you call about three hundred dolphins came by. They saw us, came over and played with us, breaking the surface of the water, arcing through the air, surfing on the waves, brushing against us underwater but never in a threatening way. Everybody loved it, children and adults.' He took his hand away from his chin. 'A dose of dolphin makes you feel so *good*, in an uncomplicated way. Church music is a bit the same.'

She tipped the ice from her dead whisky glass into the one that had just been brought. 'You're right about the effect it has. It's like a mental shower – it wakes you up and cleans you inside all at the same time.'

Jack finished his dinner. All the beef had gone. He finished chewing. 'Do you know Luitfrid Marfurt's *Music in Africa*?'

'No, no I don't.'

'He compares African choral music with the European tradition. African music – African songs

– are much more about farming, bravery and the land than straightforward religion. And technically, African songs are more about singing and response. His argument is that African music is much more sophisticated than white people think.'

Jack was a baritone, she guessed. He had a mellifluous voice that she enjoyed listening to. And his conversation didn't travel in straight lines either, didn't follow obvious routes. He had a self-confidence but wasn't knowing or pushy. He talked like he flew, with authority, without fuss, like he knew what he was doing. Dare she say it, he was a bit like Dominic.

Jack was doing his best to make Natalie warm to him. But the truth was that tonight, during this dinner, nothing – not even the sudden arrival in the restaurant of Dom, or her father, or three hundred dolphins – could have taken her mind off the trial and what Jack had just told her. He made all the running in the conversation, talking about music, concerts he'd been to, operas he had seen, choirs he had heard, and when it came to her turn she uttered a few sentences and then faltered into silence, like an engine running out of diesel.

She refused dessert and cheese. And coffee. Jack paid the bill and then, on the way out of the restaurant, asked her if she'd like a nightcap at the bar. She nodded but as soon as he had ordered she made him cancel it.

'I've had enough whisky,' she almost growled. 'What I really need is a walk.'

He was perched on a bar stool and got down off it.

'A walk? Under the stars, like your late-night sessions in the gorge? Would you like to be alone?'

Briefly, Natalie nodded. She had the fist of foreboding in her stomach – that was more than enough company.

At least Jack was sensitive to that.

She went out through the main door. Jack made no attempt to follow her.

Natalie turned left out of the hotel. It was still warm despite the lateness of the hour. The road itself was dusty but she crossed to the far side because there was more light: the shop windows were lit, showing women's fashions, rather outmoded fashions as far as she could tell – long skirts, wedge heels, hair styles piled up in a way that Eleanor Deacon would not have looked twice at, and suggested the war was still on.

The pavement on this side of the street was raised high and made of wood. The wood magnified the sounds her footsteps made. The shop windows now showed furniture – sofas, wardrobes, beds made of what looked like laminated plastic.

Natalie turned and looked back the way she had come. No sign of Jack Deacon.

She was interested that he was so involved in politics. Politics had never interested her but she could concede that it was a dimension of life that put the rest into context, forced someone to sort out his or her priorities. Jack Deacon had set her thinking.

Natalie thought back to the conversation she had had with Sandys earlier in the day. She had put on a good show, she thought. She hadn't thought twice about giving evidence. It was the tradition she had been brought up in. But was she being fair on herself? After all, she hadn't seen Mutevu's face, just his strapping frame and his characteristic shuffle. She was as certain as could be that it was him – it *was* him – but would a court see it her way and was it worth putting herself in the limelight?

There was a red neon sign a few yards ahead. What looked like a bar. There was the sound of music.

Eleanor had made plain her views and so had Jack. He said that neither he nor his mother wanted – or expected – Natalie to change her testimony but she wasn't sure she bought that argument entirely.

Jack. She had enjoyed their dinner. She was pleased they had flown up together from the gorge in his small plane. Funny how something like that could affect the impression one got. The Comanche seemed Jack's natural habitat, an extension of him. It was only the second time she had flown in a small plane, or any kind of plane come to that, but it had felt natural; she had felt – yes – at home almost. It was as if her life had suddenly acquired another dimension. Jack and his plane had enlarged her life.

She was just approaching the bar. The heavy sounds of the music sent reverberations along the wooden boards of the pavement.

The call to her father still hadn't come through. So she was still on edge about that, whether he would agree to talk or not–

230

Two men – two black men – almost fell out of the bar as she came abreast of the door. Two heavily made-up women followed them, dressed in long, African-style, multicoloured skirts and headbands.

Natalie stepped off the pavement out of their way but one of the men shouted something in her direction, in a language she didn't understand.

The other man joined in. They were grinning, obviously drunk, and sweating. The two women were watching this exchange but talking to a third man, who seemed to be guarding the door to the bar.

Natalie tried to move beyond the two drunken men and resume her walk on the pavement, but they had followed her, still shouting words she didn't understand, and forced her to remain in the road. More people had drifted out of the bar. All of them were black, all of them were looking in her direction, and several of them were shouting.

The skin on Natalie's throat had itself begun to sweat and she decided to cut her losses and head back to the hotel. She turned, crossed the road and sprang on to the pavement. But now half a dozen of the revellers, all obviously the worse for wear, were crossing the street, moving towards her.

She sensed it would be a mistake to run but she couldn't avoid quickening her pace. The hotel was two hundred yards away. She had brought a wrap, draped around her shoulders, but now she lifted it and covered her head.

The group – seven or eight of them – were

heading her off. Natalie would be trapped unless she ran. But something stopped her. It would, she knew, be a defeat. It would spark something. But she was getting angry.

Suddenly, above the shouts in Kikuyu, or Swahili, or whatever language was being spoken, she heard a voice in English. 'Hey, whitey lady, you looking for black sex? You want king-size liquorice? Whitey men no good?'

The others cackled and she saw two of the men make lewd gestures.

'Hey whitey, whitey lady, you want ebony stick?' More laughter.

And now the men were blocking the pavement. The women were standing in the road. They were humming, and swaying in time to the song.

But the men weren't singing. Four of them blocked the pavement. Two just stood still, looking serious. A third man, she could see, held a walking stick, a carved ebony stick with an animal head – a lion? – at one end. He held the stick in one hand and beat the animal head repeatedly into the palm of his other hand. The fourth man had extended his arm and was leaning against the window of the shop where this was all taking place. He was gulping in air in big breaths.

The stench of alcohol-tinged sweat passed over her in waves. Her own sweat dripped down the sides of her cheeks, down her throat and between her breasts, inside her dress from under her arms.

The man with the stick pointed it at her. 'You looking for trouble, whitey lady? You want Nairobi night life?' He cackled. 'You found it!'

He moved towards her, still brandishing his stick.

As he did so, one of the other men said something in the language Natalie didn't recognise but it was obviously aimed at her because the man with the stick laughed and half-turned his head to acknowledge what had been said.

Quickly, Natalie leaned forward and snatched the stick from his hand.

Surprised by the suddenness of her movement, he couldn't prevent her taking it.

Natalie raised the stick. She held it so that the animal head was at the far end.

The man looked at her. He had stopped smiling. The other two men stood next to him.

It was a stand-off and there was nowhere she could go. She was surrounded.

Sweat again ran down her cheeks, between her breasts. Her anger was on the rise.

The man reached down, unbuckled the belt of his trousers and unthreaded it from the loops that held it in place. He wrapped part around his hand and let the buckle hang free.

He took a step forward and raised his arm.

Suddenly, the fourth man, leaning against the shop window, collapsed to the ground and vomited all at the same time. He retched again.

The man with the belt turned his head. One of the other men said something. One of the women called out. The man with the belt bent down next to the man retching. The woman called out again and she too moved forward and knelt next to him. All eyes had now turned to the sick man.

Natalie guessed he was choking on his own

vomit and was too drunk to realise what was happening.

She was still surrounded.

But she was on fire with anger and she was *itching* to act. Without warning, she took half a step forward and leaped over the sick man's body. Her foot slipped on his vomit and her ankle complained. But not badly and she cleared his form, her shoulder bouncing off the shop window. She winced and gasped loudly but kept going.

Someone called out but she didn't know who and she didn't stop. She threw the ebony stick into the road and kept going. Thank God she had wedge heels, she thought, and not stilettos.

Was anyone giving chase? She was breathing so heavily she couldn't hear. The hotel entrance was a hundred yards away. She kept going. Her wrap had come off her head and was hanging down her back. If anyone was chasing her, they could grab it. But she was ready to let it go, even though her mother had given it to her.

She kept running.

Then she noticed a figure was moving towards her. Black or white? It was too dark to see. She was ashamed of herself for thinking on those terms but now wasn't the time to ... was he going to stop her?

The figure was blocking the pavement.

Natalie leapt into the road.

The figure moved off the pavement, towards her. If only she'd kept the ebony stick.

She summoned a spurt of energy, of anger, and ran faster. The hotel was sixty yards away.

'Natalie?'

It took her a moment to realise that the figure was Jack.

She stopped, breathing heavily, turned, and leaned into him. There was a pain in her side. Sweat shone on her skin. 'Am I glad to see *you*.'

He put his arm around her. 'What happened? I saw a group of people, heard shouting. I saw you jump.' He reached round her and rearranged her wrap. 'You're shaking.'

She turned again. A figure, about thirty yards away, was scurrying back to the group by the shop window. Someone *had* given chase but hadn't caught her, and had given up when Jack appeared. Her anger began to subside. Her breathing came more easily.

Natalie was still shaking as Jack steered her towards the hotel and again put his arm around her shoulders.

Between sucking in huge gulps of air, she told him what had happened.

He nodded and said, 'I blame myself.'

They had reached the hotel.

'I had assumed you'd turn right, out of the hotel. *I* know, all the regulars know, that turning right leads to the main street and the bright lights, the cafés, lots of people. The other way, left, the way you went, leads to – well, Nairobi's red-light area. It's safe enough in the day, but not at night and I should have warned you. I'm sorry, it's my fault. That's why I came looking ... I suddenly realised that I hadn't warned you and that, maybe, you had turned left. Natalie, I'm very sorry.'

He held the hotel door open for her. 'How about a late-night whisky, to help settle your nerves?'

She nodded eagerly. She was still shaking.

At the bar Jack ordered her a scotch and asked the barman to leave the bottle with them. 'Knock back the first shot in one go, then sip the second. I find that always helps after a shock or bad news.'

Natalie did as she was told. The first one certainly had an effect. Her heart showed some signs of coming under control.

'There was a lot of talk in a language I didn't recognise. Was it all about sex, do you think, or race?'

'They had come out of a bar, right?'

She nodded.

'A bit of both, I would say. The men were with women so they were on their way to have sex with them when they encountered you. But, the black–white thing, it's always there, isn't it? There's a story in the papers today about Tanzanian troops training in Russia, and inviting the Russians back to train more of their troops. The idea is to teach Tanzanian soldiers to act behind enemy lines – in this case South Africa – to make trouble. The blacks in Africa are getting more assertive every day. That is as it should be, with independence coming up, but it does mean that there's friction everywhere.'

Natalie sipped her second scotch. 'Lucky for me you decided to come looking. Whoever was chasing me might have caught me.'

He shook his head. 'I did nothing. You saved

yourself. The way you leapt over that body of the man on the ground – it was like watching a wildebeest jump in the bush.' He swallowed some of his own whisky. 'I shouldn't say this, given the circumstances, but I don't think I've ever seen anything so lithe, so beautiful.'

'Fifteen shillings? *Fifteen?* You must be joking. Eleven, I'll give you eleven.' Jack slapped the money on the counter and pushed it towards the shop assistant.

The assistant, an old, bent, nut-brown wizened woman with irregular teeth and a wicked grin, pushed the money back again. 'Fifteen, master.'

It was the following morning, just coming up to noon and Natalie and Jack had spent the previous three hours shopping for supplies. After she had left Jack the evening before, after the excitement in the street and the whiskies in the bar, Natalie had returned to her room, to find a book propped against her door. It was *Music in Africa*, the book Jack had referred to earlier. And there was a note attached to it: 'In case you can't sleep tonight.' He had left it there before he had had second thoughts about where Natalie might go walking.

But she had lain in bed, wide awake, too restless to sleep and too disturbed to read, reliving her ordeal, recalling the smell of the sweet alcohol, sweat and vomit in the street, re-running her deposition in her head and trying to imagine the hostile questions she would receive in court.

And revisiting Jack's remarks about her lithe movements. It was a judicious remark, she

237

thought. He knew she had been shaken by her ordeal. He was making her feel better about herself but not making too much of it. Natalie liked that. She had found she was looking forward to spending the day with him tomorrow. It must have gone three before she had finally dropped off.

They'd checked out of the Rhodes hotel around nine, packed their bags into the boot of the car that Maxwell Sandys had lent Jack, and visited a variety of shops: a pharmacist, a vet, a garage, a bank and a liquor store where Natalie topped up on whisky. They were now in a shop that sold radio-telephones and other technical gear, where Jack was negotiating to buy a spare battery for his mother's radio.

He took back the eleven shillings, carefully put the ten-shilling note into his wallet, and turned to Natalie. 'Okay, let's go. We'll try that other shop, near the railway station.' He took from Natalie the bag she was holding and led the way out.

'Thirteen shillings,' shouted the old crone after him.

He stopped, and turned. 'Twelve and six.'

The woman cackled. They had a deal.

Natalie grinned and gasped at the same time. This was a side to Jack that she had not seen before and had never imagined existed. In each of the shops they had visited today he had haggled. And haggled successfully. To Natalie he was totally convincing when bluffing, though she reminded herself she might be being naïve. He drove the traders down, but they drove him up.

238

She was too inexperienced, really, to know if he got the best price. But she had enjoyed watching him.

Outside the shop Jack put the bags in the car and shepherded Natalie in after them. It was as hot as ever, dust and flies milling around, the smells and the heat acting in concert.

Jack got in the car alongside Mbante. 'The Karibu Club,' he said. Turning back to Natalie, he added, 'We're all done. So, lunch first – then we can head for the airport.'

Away from the centre of town the streets grew quieter, wider. There were more children, many of them shoeless. Trees appeared, a school with a field where children in uniform played in the sun. They reached a vast roundabout with a straggle of hibiscus. They passed by a stall selling flowers and cold drinks and reached a dual-carriageway where the traffic thinned. Here there were billboards advertising the new airlines, Land Rovers, cream to straighten the hair.

Mbante turned off the dual-carriageway into a lane lined with eucalyptus trees. Behind the trees, Natalie glimpsed large houses set back behind English-style lawns and vast bushes, rhododendrons at a guess. After a few hundred yards, they turned off the lane into a drive with a hedge down one side and a close-cropped lawn on the other. This, as Natalie soon realised, was the edge of a golf course.

'This is the Karibu Club,' said Jack softly. 'Karibu means "Welcome".'

They rounded a bend and the drive stretched before them, leading to the main clubhouse, mainly white, with blue shutters and a roof of terracotta tiles. Beyond the clubhouse was a polo field where a couple of riders – white – were practising, galloping their mounts and hitting balls towards some goal posts. Their sunglasses caught the sun. The contrast with downtown Nairobi was marked.

Mbante pulled up in front of the main club entrance, an ebony-wood porch with a thatched roof. A black man in a green blazer came forward to open the car door.

Natalie got out and smiled at the man. He vaguely reminded her of Ndekei. Jack hadn't mentioned the case today, or her ordeal, or the book he'd left outside her room. Sensitive again.

He led the way inside the club.

Broad planks of dark shiny wood lined the floor of the large reception hall. There was a smell of polish and tobacco smoke. A tall man, also in a green blazer, beamed at Jack.

'Welcome back, Dr. Deacon. How is your mother?'

'She's well, Bukawa, thank you. I'll tell her you were asking. How are the children?'

The receptionist grinned. 'We're all fine, sir. Thank you.'

'Say a special hello to Samara, eh? She's my favourite.'

Another big grin, as the receptionist took out a form for Jack to sign, so that Natalie, as a visitor, could enter the club. 'Fathers aren't allowed favourites, Dr. Deacon. But she'll be pleased you said hello.'

Jack handed back the form, turning to Natalie.

240

'Bukawa is a lucky man; he has *four* daughters.' He turned back. 'I'm looking for Frank Villiers, Bukawa. Has he been in today?'

The receptionist nodded. 'Try the bar or the library. It's too early for bridge.'

'Thanks.' Jack turned. 'This way, Natalie.'

Their footsteps made a clatter on the boards as he led the way down a corridor. Off to one side was a small courtyard, with tubs of flowers and tables and chairs set out under umbrellas. It was all very English, she thought, or what she imagined Brighton to look like. When they came to the library the smell of tobacco smoke intensified. Jack peered his head round the door while Natalie waited in the corridor. He nodded to people he knew and exchanged a few words. But, evidently, Frank Villiers was not in the library.

As Jack stepped back into the corridor, Natalie said, 'I didn't have you as the clubbable type.'

'You're right, I'm not.' He looked down out her. His hair flopped forward. 'My father was a member and he proposed me before I was too old to resist. In his day this is where a lot of work got done – the colonial government relaxed here when it was off-duty. So this is where my father negotiated licences to excavate, raised loans to help with his digs and entertained the academics out from Britain or the US. I need to see this Villiers chap, that's why we're here.'

'Why?'

'You'll see, come on.' He marched off again, further down the corridor, until it reached a corner to the left. At the right-angle there was a large double door, wide open. The shiny wooden floor continued beyond but the room was dominated by two huge ceiling fans, one over the bar itself – a long, carved, mahogany counter, gleaming with polish – and the other near a large full-length window, which gave on to a terrace beyond which was the polo field. Natalie could make out about half a dozen people sitting at some tables. She heard the low buzz of conversation.

Jack waved to the barman but made directly for the terrace. He stopped, half in and half out of the room, with Natalie at his shoulder. He nodded to one or two people, then grunted: 'There's Frank.'

He moved towards a small, silver-haired man in a dark suit and wearing a striped tie, who was reading an English newspaper next to a glass of what looked like gin.

Villiers looked up as they approached. He nodded to Jack and put down his paper, but he didn't smile.

'Frank, good morning. I'm sorry to disturb you. This is Natalie Nelson.'

The other man's expression softened slightly in her direction.

'Frank is clerk to the court here in Nairobi,' said Jack by way of explanation. 'I'm hoping he will be able to tell us if a judge has been assigned yet to the Ndekei case.' He turned back to the other man. 'Any news, Frank?'

Villiers was sipping his gin. 'Nothing certain, because the prosecution only applied for a date this morning. But if the trial is set for the week I expect, it will be John Tudor.'

'No!' hissed Jack softly. 'Please God, no.'

'What's wrong?' whispered Natalie.

Jack looked very put out. 'About three months ago, Tudor was the judge in the trial of a white security guard in a motor showroom, who had killed a burglar, shot him as the man – one of three – tried to steal a vehicle. The burglars were only boys but, because the shooting took place in the course of a robbery, which no one denied, Tudor judged there was no case to answer, and the white security guard went free. He's one of the most controversial figures in Kenya and exactly the kind of person we *don't* want to try this case.' He stared down at Villiers. 'What on earth possessed you to assign Tudor?'

Villiers primly folded his newspaper. 'Cases are assigned strictly by rotation, Jack. It was Tudor's turn.' He got up. 'I'm going in to lunch.' And he nodded to Natalie.

They both watched him leave.

'So Tudor's bad news,' Natalie said, still in a whisper, as Villiers disappeared through the bar.

'Terrible,' breathed Jack. 'He's been known to make racist comments from the bench. The governor even tried to have him recalled to London but Tudor has powerful friends in Whitehall and, I'm told, the palace itself.'

He brushed the hair off his face. 'Look, I'm afraid there'll have to be a change of plan, I need to see Maxwell Sandys again.'

'Why? What for? How can a judge be that important?'

'Trust me.' Jack was hardly listening to her. Instead, as she could see from his abstracted expression, he was busy thinking. 'Mbante will run

243

you back to the hotel – think you can amuse yourself for the afternoon?'

'Yes, of course, but–'

'Good. Check us both in again. There'll be no problem, the hotel isn't busy. I'll see you at dinner. Same time, same drinks, same table as last night, I should think. We'll catch up then. I'm just going to tackle Villiers one more time, see what else I can worm out of him, then I'll get a taxi to Max's office. Can you remember the way back to reception?'

'Of course–'

But Jack had gone.

'What's that French phrase that applies to us?' Jack held the chair for Natalie to sit in. They were about to begin dinner.

'What do you mean?' Natalie sat down and put what was left of her pre-dinner whisky on the table in front of her.

'Déjà vu, that's it. Same time, same restaurant, same table as last night, same drinks, you in the same dress and shoes, me in the same shirt and jacket.' He grinned as he sat down opposite her.

'But not the same conversation. Come on now, you wouldn't discuss it at the bar, you said we had to wait for dinner. What have you been doing all afternoon, why did we have to stay on, what's the real problem with this Tudor man?'

Jack sat back as their first courses were served, a chilled soup. They had ordered at the bar.

'I hate saying this, Natalie, but John Tudor is a racist. There are quite a few whites like him left here in Kenya who don't think the Africans are

244

up to modern life, who think tribal loyalties interfere with democracy, that tribes are the basis for
corruption and backwardness and that the South
African system – apartheid – is the right way
forward. Most of the time, however, Tudor can't
do much damage, travelling the countryside and
officiating at black-on-black crime.' Jack tried his
soup. 'What occurred to me, when I was talking
to Frank Villiers, is that, contrary to what he said,
Tudor was chosen deliberately for this trial,
chosen *because* of his views, *because* he's a vicious
white supremacist.'

'But why? Who chooses the judges, anyway?'

'Normally, as Villiers told us, they are selected
by rotation. But not always, not in big cases, not
in sensitive cases, not in politically relevant
cases.'

'So who did you see this afternoon, and what
did you find out?'

He wiped his lips with his napkin. 'Maxwell
Sandys, as I said. He was busy, he *is* deputy attorney general after all. But I hung around outside
his office for an hour and a half and, finally, he
had a spare twenty minutes.'

'And?'

Jack shook his head. 'I've never known anything
like it. Max is a very old friend of my mother.
Some say they were more than friends but I've
never had the guts to ask and she has never vol-
unteered anything. He's the godfather to my
sister, Beth, and has always been very friendly to
me – I sometimes stay with him when I overnight
in Nairobi, that's how well I know him. I had a
drink with him last night as you know and he was

affable enough.'

Jack raised his glass to his lips, then lowered it again without drinking. 'But today, today he was not so much cold as distant ... if I didn't know better I'd say he was positively shifty. He wouldn't meet my eye, kept drinking from a glass of water, as if his throat were dry, *but* – and this is what really bothered me – he wouldn't discuss Tudor's appointment at all, kept saying it was none of my business, that it was improper even for me to ask.'

'Didn't he have a point?'

Jack sat back in his chair and let out a sigh. 'If this were Britain, maybe. But it isn't. For the moment, at any rate, it's colonial Kenya and in Nairobi everyone who's anyone knows everyone who's anyone.'

Natalie had finished her soup. 'So what are you saying?'

'I'm saying something's going on, something secretive, something *manipulative.*' He wiped his lips with his napkin again. 'Something political.'

For a moment neither of them spoke. The waiter arrived and took away the soup plates.

Natalie said, 'What can be done? Is there anyone else you can see, anyone else whose advice you can ask?'

Jack shook his head. 'I told you – Nairobi is a small place. The judiciary are a small elite, responsible only to themselves and to London.'

'You think London has a hand in this?'

He bit his lip. 'I don't know. I can't think why London should get involved, but nothing would surprise me.' He shook his head again. 'I just don't know, but I don't like it.' Another pause, then he looked round. 'Well, maybe I do know. They've met you now. That's what this deposition business was partly about, not just to get your evidence down but to see what sort of a person you are, what sort of witness you will make. Now they've met you, they know you're strong-willed, very much *not* a racist and determined to give evidence. That's point one.' Jack gripped the stem of his water glass. 'Point two is this: London doesn't want this trial. The only way it won't go ahead is if you withdraw your evidence. So they select the most racist judge in the hope that you will be so appalled and disgusted that you will refuse to play your part.' He drank some water.

'That's what I think. London doesn't want this trial because the racial element may divert attention from the independence conference, may overshadow it. My mother doesn't want the trial for the effect it will have on the gorge. And you ... you are determined. It's quite a scenario.'

Natalie eyed Jack. He looked a bit flustered tonight. His hair was awry, his face was more flushed as he had angered himself in telling his story, his shirt looked as though it had been worn before, which was true enough. But it suited him, she thought. Jack wasn't the city type, he wasn't – what did the Americans call it? – clean-cut, that was it. He was more rough-and-ready. The shadow on his chin looked as though he hadn't shaved today. Natalie didn't mind.

In angering himself, he had angered her. All she had done was sit in her chair in camp and watch the night. And now the British government wanted the trial scrapped because it might spoil a conference. Just thinking about it made her heart race.

Neither of them spoke for a moment. Then Jack added, 'Here are the main courses, let's change the subject.'

They both sat back to allow the food to be served. He rubbed the scar above his eyebrow.

'How did you get that mark you are scratching? What happened?'

He shook his head. 'Nothing romantic or heroic, I'm afraid. We had some orphaned lion cubs when we were children – orphaned cubs are more common than you might think. They were great fun to begin with, very cuddly, but they grew up quicker than we did, quicker than we thought, in fact. I was playing with one of them one day, one of the cubs we called Kili, when she suddenly went for me and her claws were out when she cuffed me round the head. There was a lot of blood, though I was lucky, really. She could have caught my eye. But we had to release them into the wild after that.'

Jack's beer was finished and he signalled to the waiter to bring more drinks. While they waited, Jack talked and Natalie sat back and listened to him. She found she enjoyed just listening, where he was concerned. He talked about his sisters, his airplane, about KANU, all in an unselfconscious way, with lots of gestures he seemed unaware of – he pushed back his hair when it flopped forwards with a movement that she liked – his voice was easy on the ear – on *her* ear at any rate – and, all in all, he didn't seem in any way impressed with himself. He made Natalie forget the trial.

But the evening had not started at all well. Whereas the previous night she had heard nothing from the international operator about the phone call to her father, this evening it had come through straight away. She had been nervous all over again as the housekeeper had answered.

'Mrs Bailey? It's Natalie here, calling from Africa, from Nairobi in Kenya. How are you?'

'Oh, you know, fine. Same old aches and pains.'

'Sorry to hear that. Is my father there?'

'Hold on, I'll see. Where did you say you are?'

'Nairobi, in Kenya.'

Mrs Bailey put the phone down and Natalie had heard her walk along the hall. She was gone an age. When Natalie next heard footsteps approaching the phone, she tried to assess whether they were Mrs Bailey's or her father's.

'Are you there?' It was Mrs Bailey's voice.

The skin on Natalie's throat had begun to sweat.

'He can't come to the phone.'

'Did he say why?'

'He said to say he had someone with him.'

'And does he?'

'That's what he told me to say, Miss Natalie. And I've told you. Now you look after yourself.' And she had put the phone down.

Natalie had gulped her first whisky in the bar. She needed it. What would have happened, she had often wondered, if she had told her father about his wife's wartime betrayal? How well she remembered, even now, the afternoon she had heard noises from the upstairs bedroom, when she was supposed to have been at a picnic with friends, but had felt unwell, coming down with what would turn out to be chicken pox. Although she hadn't really understood what her mother and the pilot were doing with each other in the bed, when she had seen them through the open door from across the upstairs landing, the very fact that her mother had been too preoccupied to notice she was there told her a lot. And the noises her mother made had puzzled her for years, but not any more.

Thank God for Jack. He had been on hand last night when she had needed him and he was definitely helping tonight. A couple of whiskies and an hour or so with Jack and the unpleasant-ness with her father was undoubtedly eased.

She leaned forward. 'I might be prying again but you talk much more, and much more fondly, about your sisters than about Christopher. Why do you and he not get on? I noticed a certain *fire* between you two at the publications meeting.'

He looked at her, holding his glass to his lips but not drinking.

'We get by,' he said at length. 'We didn't get on as children – I'm surprised it still shows but if you've noticed it, others will have too.'

She said nothing.

'I am the oldest, the most wizened of the Deacon gang.' He grinned. 'So, as we grew up I was the first to have a bike, for example, the first to be able to fire a gun, ride a pony, I was the first to cross all those growing-up benchmarks. My sisters took it in their stride – they laughed when I fell off my bike and grazed my knee, or when my pony threw me and I broke a collarbone.' He wiped his lips with his napkin. 'But not Christopher. Christopher was always an angry child, certainly where I was concerned. He hated being number four, the smallest, the slowest, the weakest.' Jack hunched forward in his seat. 'When the rest of us climbed trees, for instance, and he was simply too small to do it, he would scream and yell and cry his eyes out. That only made the rest of us tease him, of course, and that in turn made him even more miserable. As he grew up, he grew out of it, but he always retained a competitive streak – and, I have to say, a jealous streak.'

He drank more water. 'There was a time when we used to fight a lot, and he would play not-very-funny practical jokes on me, like loosening the wheel of my bicycle, or cutting part-way through the strap of a stirrup.' Jack folded his napkin and set it to one side. 'The worst was when I was about fifteen, and he was twelve, and we'd had a fight. I can't remember what it was about but I can remember we were on holiday at Lake Naivasha – that's a stretch of fresh water about forty or fifty miles north of Nairobi. I think we may have argued about whether the Kikuyu were better long-distance runners than the Luo – it doesn't matter but it was one of those things that boys take seriously. Anyway, we were both sent to our rooms.

'Next day we were going fishing with Matoga, well into his sixties, who had been with the family for years. Christopher had been up early but said he wasn't feeling well and decided not to come.

'Matoga and I set off, but only after lunch, and

we took the skiff to Kangoni Point. It's a trip of about an hour but that's where the best fishing is. Once you are there, however, you have to be careful because it's quite near to a place where the hippos like to bathe.' Now he did sip some beer. 'The prevailing winds take the boat towards the hippos and every so often you need to start the engine and putter back to the point and start fishing again from there.'

He put his glass down.

'Everything went well for about an hour. We fished and regrouped twice or three times, and we caught some decent perch. But then, the next time we came to start the engine it wouldn't fire; it was completely dead. Worse, only then did we notice that the fall-back oars weren't in the bottom of the boat as they were supposed to be, in just such a case of engine failure. Someone had removed them and, in our eagerness to get out on the water, we hadn't noticed.'

He leaned forward. 'And so, there we were, just as the sun was setting, drifting helplessly towards Hippo Point. I don't know if you are aware of this but more people are killed every year in Africa by hippos attacking small boats than by any other animal. Lions or snakes or elephants or buffalo don't kill anywhere near as many. Hippos are the most dangerous animals on the continent.'

'What happened?' Natalie fingered one of the earrings her mother had given her. 'You're here to tell the story. And what does this all have to do with Christopher?'

'Matoga saved my life. Just south of Hippo Point, where we could see three or four hippos basking in the shallow water, about sixty or seventy yards away, a rock broke the surface of the lake. It was itself fifty yards or so offshore. Matoga used his rod and cast his line at the rock. Time and again he tried as we drifted closer and closer to the hippos, until the hook finally caught on the jagged edges of the stone. The fish you catch on Naivasha – Nile Perch – are big so the breaking strain of the line was quite strong.'

He shook his head slowly. 'Even so, Matoga told me to sit quite still. Any sudden movement could have rapidly increased the strain on the line and it would have broken, when there would not have been enough time to fix another hook before we were among the hippos.'

He drained his beer glass. 'Anyway, we sat very still and clung on to the rock, via the fishing line, as the darkness closed in around us. We were both very frightened – terrified – but we knew that, by then, my parents would have realised that something must have happened and would come looking for us. Even so, it took them about a couple of hours to find us, by which time Matoga, poor man, was exhausted from hanging on, resisting the effect of the wind.'

Jack passed a hand over his face. 'What does this have to do with Christopher? Next morning, Matoga and I took the boat's engine apart. There was dirt – soil, earth – in the carburettor, that's what clogged the engine and stopped it working. How did it get there?'

'Couldn't it have been an accident?'

'Yes, but unlikely, and Christopher chose not to come on the trip. He said he didn't feel well but he had been up early and by all accounts he ate a hearty dinner while we were clinging to the rock and no one had yet realised we were in trouble.'

'You think he tried to kill you?'

Jack shrugged. 'I'm not sure what he intended. I'm not sure he knew himself. I can't really believe that he tried to kill me – us – but he *did* have that anger in him then. And he knew where we were going and what would happen if the engine gave out. Why were there no oars in the boat? I should have spotted that, and so should Matoga, so we were partly at fault ourselves, as my parents reminded us in rather blunt terms.'

'What did they say – or do – about Christopher?'

'They never knew what we had discovered. I decided that it would look as though I was trying to blame him for my own incompetence.'

He reached for his napkin again and wiped his lips. 'But he and I have never ... something snapped between us that day. Christopher knew what he had done, how close he had come to... He's a lot calmer now, lost a lot of his anger, but things have not really been the same between us since then.'

Natalie wasn't sure what to make of Jack's story. It didn't sound like the Christopher who had taken her to the rock shelter above the lake, who sluiced water down her neck to cool her, who persuaded his mother to give her back her whisky flask. At the same time, on the night of the publications meeting, there had definitely been friction between the two brothers. She needed time to digest what she had just been told.

Natalie was an angry person herself, at times,

and it could make her reckless. She had never seen recklessness in Christopher.

She moved the conversation forward. 'I understand you lived in a Maasai village as a boy and were involved in resisting a raid. What was all that like?'

He was sipping his coffee and replaced the cup in its saucer before replying. 'Living in the village was revealing, I think that's the word. Boys are much more favoured in the Maasai way of life than in the world of white people. Boys play while the girls work – and they really do work: washing, cleaning, carrying. Boys sometimes run errands but if a boy takes hours to do it, all day, no one worries. If it's urgent they send the girls.'

He refolded his napkin. 'The raid was scary. It happened at night, in the darkness of early morning, and there was suddenly the sound of shouting and scuffling. At night, the Maasai bring the cattle in, inside two ring fences each made of whistling thorns, and the raiders had forced their way inside the outer ring. Our job, as boys, as I soon learned, was to hold on to the legs of the invaders, preventing them moving, while our warriors stabbed them with their spears.'

'That sounds highly dangerous. Was anyone killed?'

'Oh yes. Seven on their side, three on ours. One boy.' He smiled grimly. 'But we won. They retreated and we didn't lose any cattle.'

'You must have been terrified.'

'Yes, I suppose so, but it all happened so quickly and when you are a young boy you worry about pain but you haven't thought a lot about death, and so you are not frightened the way an adult would be frightened. At least that's how it seemed to me.'

'And as a result you became an honorary Maasai?'

He nodded. 'No one had any sleep that night, as you can imagine. When dawn came, not too long after the raid was over, we took the bodies of their dead warriors and left them on some rocks where their tribe could find them, or the vultures or hyenas. Marongo, my friend, and I were covered in blood, and they have a ceremony, following a raid, where the chief's wives must wash away the blood of the enemy, all the while singing traditional songs. Then they paint any scratches or wounds with a sacred paint, so you will recover quickly and your skin will be purified.'

He finished his beer. 'Then, as a reward I was given a cow, which I gave back to the village – I knew that was expected. And I was given a Maasai warrior's name.'

'Which was?'

'Ollantashante.'

'Does it have a meaning?'

'It is the name of a famous Maasai warrior, long dead.' He lowered his voice. 'In fact, it was the warrior whose bones Richard and Russell stole from the burial ground.'

Natalie stared at him. She had known, seconds before he uttered the words, what he was going to say.

'All roads lead back to the murder,' she whispered in turn. 'I had almost forgotten it, listening to your adventures.' She wiped her lips with her napkin and folded it next to her coffee cup. 'Do you still remain friends with – what was his name?'

'Marongo? Oh yes. He's the chief now. He's quite sophisticated – very bright and not a little cunning. You need that as chief. He's a good leader, with wider political ambitions. I fly him up to Nairobi every so often.'

'You mother wants to see him, try to talk him round. He's not playing ball.'

He nodded. 'Marongo's nobody's fool.'

Involuntarily, Natalie yawned.

'Sleepy – or bored?' Jack said.

'I'm certainly not bored,' replied Natalie sharply. 'And I don't know why I should be sleepy. I've done very little all day.' She smiled and finished her coffee with one gulp.

So did he.

'Are we still in déjà vu? Are you going for a walk tonight?'

She made a face. 'Well, I *would* like some exercise.'

'You'll remember to turn right, not left?'

'I–' she hesitated.

'Would you like me to come with you?'

'Would you mind?'

'No, not at all.'

But when they reached the main door of the hotel, the doorman approached Jack and addressed him urgently in what Natalie took to be Swahili. There was a prolonged exchange and Jack began to frown and look serious. At length he turned to her.

'There's a demonstration in the main square,

which is just off the main street where I was intending to take you. About land reform after independence. I don't think it's wise for us to go walking tonight. It's late, some of them will have been drinking. There could be... Sorry. Shall we have another drink?'

'You have one. I'll just watch. I've had enough.'

They retreated to the bar. The barman was black, she noticed. Everyone else was white.

While Jack was getting his drink, she re-ran in her mind the conversation they had had about the judge and his racist views. When Jack joined her, she said, 'Can London really interfere in a trial here? We are always being told our judiciary is independent.'

He offered her a cigarette. Natalie shook her head. She preferred smoking out of doors.

'They wouldn't normally interfere, no. You appoint people to run a colony and let them get on with it. They are the people on the ground; they know best. But these are not normal times. Independence is coming, tempers are running high, old rivalries and grievances are resurfacing, race is the biggest issue of our day. Black people are convinced their time is coming, and for most of them it can't come soon enough.' He pulled on his cigarette and blew smoke into the room. 'I've seen you looking around you, in this very hotel. It's a white world, with black staff. That has to change. It will change.'

Jack blew more smoke into the room.

'But London's priority is a smooth transition. That's not a small thing. Look at some of the horrors and mistakes that have happened in

Algeria, Egypt, the Belgian Congo. Seen from the Colonial Secretary's desk in Whitehall, one murder in Kenya is small beer, small beer that puts at risk a wider picture that might – might – precipitate hundreds of deaths.'

Natalie shook her head. 'I can see that, of course I can. But I can't go along with it. If we took that view, we could excuse any crime.'

Jack crushed out his cigarette in an ashtray on the table between them. 'No. All crimes have wider context, I agree. But some trials spark sensitivities. This one threatens to snowball in a way London doesn't like. The demonstration tonight, a demonstration that stops you and me doing something as innocuous as taking a walk, simply proves the point. In the current climate, ordinary life is suspended from time to time.'

Natalie didn't like what she was hearing. 'May I have one of your cigarettes now, please?'

'Of course.'

She reached for his pack, on the table between them, and as she did so, he did too.

Jack's hand closed over hers and held it for a moment, squeezing just slightly.

Then he smiled and let go.

There was mild excitement as Jack's twin-engined Comanche bumped down on the red-earth landing strip at Kihara the next morning. Their first approach had been hampered by the presence of the family of cheetahs that seemed to regard the strip as their home: the mother and cubs sleeping slap in the middle of the runway. As the plane raced along, about twenty feet from the ground, the cheetahs lifted their heads, got to their feet and languidly scampered into the long grass.

Natalie loved every moment of it. It was something that, under different circumstances, she could put in a letter to her father.

Two of the ancillary staff had brought out a brace of Land Rovers to meet the plane and all the supplies Jack had bought in Nairobi were transferred from the Comanche. They parked the plane where it got what shade was going, covered the cockpit with sheets, to break the worst effects of the sun, locked the doors and ran ropes from hooks on the underside of the wings to metal spikes hammered into the ground. Then they heaped thorn bushes around the aircraft to keep inquisitive animals away.

As they drove into the camp, Eleanor came out of her tent to meet them. Jack and Natalie got down from the Land Rover and he kissed his mother. As the ancillary staff began unloading the supplies, Eleanor, Natalie and Jack stood to one side.

'Well?' said Eleanor, addressing herself to Natalie. She was wearing a white shirt and sand-coloured chinos today. 'Did Jack look after you?'

Natalie smiled and nodded. 'I ran into trouble with some drunken blacks on our first night away. Jack turned up on cue.'

Eleanor look concerned. 'He let you go walking by yourself, at night?'

She turned to her son but before he she could say anything Natalie got in first. 'No harm done, Eleanor. I'm still in one piece, as you can see.'

There had been no more bodily contact between Natalie and Jack, nothing other than the brief squeeze of his hand over hers, the evening before in the bar of the hotel. But, by mistake, she had this morning left undone one more button of her shirt than was normal and Jack had noticed, his eye straying more than once to where the swelling of her upper breasts was just visible. As soon as they were in the plane, and he was occupying himself with his pre-flight routine, she had surreptitiously fixed her shirt. She had been embarrassed when he had first looked at her so frankly, but she found she enjoyed it too. Nothing had been said.

Jack glanced at Natalie now, taking in that her shirt had been buttoned. Then he relayed to his mother what he'd been told by Frank Villiers and Maxwell Sandys in Nairobi.

Eleanor heard him out in silence, at least to begin with. But, as he went on, she drew herself up, made herself taller, held herself more erect, her body trembling with tension. As Jack finished his account, she transferred her gaze to Natalie. 'So, the situation gets worse and worse. We'll discuss it at dinner. You must both be dusty and sticky, and I want to fix that new battery for the radio. Have a shower and I'll see you later.'

At dinner Eleanor had put her hair up in a chignon. She wore a pale green shirt and her wraparound khaki skirt. Her stylish dressing, Natalie had decided, was a form of self-discipline. Eleanor, she understood, dressed with men in mind, even here in the gorge. It was an aspect of her self-respect which Natalie admired.

Naiva had prepared a simple roast chicken, roast potatoes and carrots. Plain water was a relief: Natalie had drunk too much whisky in Nairobi.

'Tell me again what Nshone told you,' said Eleanor once they were settled. She was seated between Arnold Pryce and Jonas. Natalie and Jack sat together, opposite her. Daniel was nowhere to be seen. Kees was there, Christopher too. He smiled.

Natalie still hadn't made up her mind what she thought about Jack's fishing/hippopotamus adventure.

Jack repeated his encounter for Eleanor's benefit, and the others', adding in details about Natalie's deposition, the choice of John Tudor as judge in the case, and Maxwell Sandys' curious behaviour. Eleanor listened in silence, chewing her chicken, sipping her water.

'What was Nshone's tone?'

'How do you mean?'

'Was he confident, cocky, was he opening a negotiation?'

'I'm not experienced enough to know. They are planning to call more than one Maasai chief as witnesses, to explain their laws—'

'Will that be allowed?' Natalie interjected.

'It doesn't matter,' snapped Eleanor. 'If the court refuses to hear the chiefs, that merely rubs in the Maasai argument.'

Natalie's anger flared briefly at Eleanor's tone.

Silence around the table.

'And you say Maxwell was acting ... shiftily?'

'That's how it seemed to me. I think a racist

judge has been chosen so as to make Natalie think twice about giving evidence.'

'If Beth were here, she might be able to get something out of her godfather.'

'Well, I couldn't, that's for sure. Why don't you have a go? You've known him far longer.'

Natalie noticed a flash of something pass across Eleanor's face, *un coup d'oeil* as the French said. What was it? An instant softening? A fond memory? Jack had raised the thought, the evening before, that Eleanor and Maxwell Sandys had once been lovers. As he had insisted, Nairobi was a small place, especially the society of whites. Was the idea so far-fetched?

But the flash of something, whatever it was, had melted away immediately, and Eleanor was growling, 'I can try, I suppose, but I doubt he'd say anything over the radio-telephone, where everyone can hear.'

She placed her knife and fork together with her food half-finished. 'I've no appetite tonight. I can't eat, I can't relax, I can't concentrate. What a mess this is.'

She cleared her throat.

'This has all the makings of a first-class catastrophe. The destruction of the gorge! Thirty years of work overturned in a few moments.' She fiddled with her hair and sighed. 'Here we are, on the verge of not one but two major discoveries, two epoch-making announcements that will put Kenya on the map internationally – and what happens? This site, this gorge, this marvel of nature and science, where it all takes place, which in a few years could become a major tourist

263

attraction and a major revenue earner, is to be destroyed, vandalised, any possibility of new discoveries thrown to the lions – literally.'

Eleanor was looking intently at Natalie as she said this, and Natalie felt herself colouring.

'The Maasai visit the gorge almost daily at the moment. And not children with goats, but warriors with spears. They just watch, but it's enough, for now.'

The skin on Natalie's throat had turned clammy.

'I ... I can understand your anger, or disappointment, Eleanor. But you're not suggesting I don't give evidence, surely?'

'It wouldn't work, anyway,' interjected Arnold Pryce. 'If Natalie withdrew her evidence, think what a fuss Russell, and Richard's parents would make.'

'But we'd get over it.' Eleanor thrust her chin forward, the skin on her throat stretched tight. 'Yes, there'd be a stink – a big, unpleasant explosion of self-righteousness – but, at the end of it all, there'd still be a gorge. The site would still exist. The discoveries would go on.'

The assembled group was silent.

Natalie looked at each of the other diners in turn. 'I saw what I saw, Eleanor. That's all. You told me to write it down immediately, which I did.' She hesitated. 'Richard did wrong – yes. But did he deserve to die? You can't believe that he did.' She took a deep breath. There was something she had to say. 'You all seem to be taking Richard's death very lightly. So lightly that, if you must know, I am shocked by your attitude. It's not right, it's not normal ... it's not human.'

Eleanor curled her fingers around her spectacles, mangling them out of shape. 'I was born in Africa, my dear. I'm an African. I live with African ways and I understand and sympathise with a lot of them. What is happening here in the gorge is, in my view, one of the most important intellectual activities in the entire continent. It is helping to make Africa more important, more interesting, more attractive, more a part of the wider world – and that far outweighs one death, however regrettable.'

She brushed a strand of hair off her face. 'Yes, I told you to write down what you had seen immediately. But I didn't know then what I know now: that this whole venture is at risk. I responded as anyone would have responded on hearing of Richard's death, and then learning what you had seen. But now, now the situation has changed – and my view has changed with it. To put the gorge at risk – all the discoveries that have been made and remain to be made – I shudder and despair at the idea. I repeat: intellectually, the gorge is at the heart of Africa, of the *world*. It is where man began, *all* mankind. Very little is more important than that–'

'Mother!' began Christopher.

'It's all right,' said Natalie quickly. 'I can defend myself.' She gripped her water glass tightly and hunched forward over the table. Her anger was rising and she fought to control it. 'Palaeontology is a Western idea,' she said at length, 'not an African custom. If Kihara is at the heart of Africa, of the world as you put it, then it's thanks as much to Western modern notions as to anything else.

The Maasai have grazed cattle in the gorge for generations but have shown not the slightest interest in the fossils here or the stratigraphy. So the very fact that the gorge is emerging as important is due to a mix – a marriage, a symbiosis – of African and modern realities. Eleanor, you are not an African in the sense that the Maasai are.' She gulped some water. 'I can't withdraw my evidence.'

'You mean you won't.'

'Won't, can't: it's the same thing. I saw what I saw. You want me to unsee that? What Richard and Russell did was foolhardy – and yes, wrong, very wrong. How many times do I have to say that? But what Mutevu did to Richard was much, much worse. And before you say anything, yes, I can see the Maasai point of view, I can even sympathise with it.' Her fingers touched her mother's single pearls at her ears. What she would give to talk this over with her father, or with Dom. They were both clear thinkers, with a well-developed sense of what they believed. They would surely agree with the stance she was taking.

Or would they? Dominic had a very strong practical, pragmatic streak. He was aware of how the world worked, the real world of give and take, of cutting your losses when it was impossible to do otherwise. Her father was more idealistic and, had what happened with her mother not happened, would surely take her side now. But Dominic? Now she thought of it, she couldn't be so sure.

Natalie cupped her hands around her water glass. 'I'm not sure there's anything new to say tonight. In Nairobi, Jack and Maxwell Sandys tried to dissuade me by saying I will be vilified by political militants. You appeal to a different aspect of my make-up.' Natalie sighed. 'I understand both arguments. I don't want to get involved in a political cause célèbre and I've grown to love the gorge. But,' she bit her lip, 'our tradition of independent witnesses, juries, rules of evidence, I mean ... it may be called modern but it's just as old as Maasai ways. *Their* traditions are no more than a few hundred years old, are they? Ours, in fact, are older.' She clenched her clammy fist. 'That doesn't make them any more right, but it doesn't make them any more wrong either.'

Natalie rubbed the palms of her hands on her trousers. 'So I'm sorry if you feel I am betraying you. That's not how I see it, and I hope you can too, in time.' She looked directly at Eleanor. 'You selected Richard. He, with Daniel and Russell, made a great discovery. Significant. Don't you feel you owe him something? The dig, Kihara ... we all benefit from Richard's work.'

'She's right, mother.' Jack offered his support before anyone else could speak.

But Eleanor was in no hurry to be heard. She rubbed the back of her neck with her hand, revealing a damp patch on her shirt under her arm.

'Natalie,' she said quietly after a moment, 'I'm sorry if you think I'm an ogre. Of course I'm grateful for what Richard – and Russell – have done for us, for the dig, for the gorge. I understand very well your feelings. I can see what a quandary it must be for you. I understand all that, believe me.' She helped herself to more

267

water. 'And you know, I think – I hope – that I am not a stubborn person.' She half-smiled. 'Remember what happened with the whisky flask?'

Eleanor ran a finger around the rim of her glass tumbler. 'So I'm trying not to be stubborn on this matter, either. Really, I'm not.' She pushed her plate from her. 'I also know that when contentious matters are argued over too much, people – and that includes me – can be driven into a corner, into a cul-de-sac, making change, and therefore agreement, even more impossible. So, I will just say three things, and then we can move on.'

She raised a thumb. 'First, I repeat my thinking that the situation has changed. We couldn't anticipate when Richard's body was first found how the Maasai would respond. They have responded cleverly, from their point of view, and have in effect outmanoeuvred and outthought us. I think that you should withdraw your evidence but if you can't, or won't, so be it.'

She raised her forefinger. 'Two, we must proceed with our digging, as if nothing were happening. Nothing is to be gained from calling a halt at this stage.'

Her index finger went up. 'Three, we shall make yet another approach to the elders of the Maasai, the *loibone*, to see if they can be prevailed upon to change their minds. I'm not hopeful it will work, but you never know. Maybe they have their elders who are not stubborn too.'

Eleanor looked around the table. 'I think we all know where Natalie and I stand. But we haven't heard from you, Kees, or Jonas, or Arnold. This

268

is not something we can put to a vote, but do any of you want to say something? Or you, Christopher?'

No one did.

Naiva noiselessly removed the plates from the table. A buffalo called out somewhere in the distance. Smoke from the fire drifted into the dining tent, casting fuzzy shadows. The crackle and spit of the logs filled the silence that remained.

Natalie lay in bed in the dark. She had so looked forward to her late-night smoke and whisky when she had been in Nairobi but tonight, after her tussle with Eleanor, she was too much on edge and she longed for the oblivion of sleep. Dinner had been finished quickly, after Eleanor's little speech, and Natalie had returned to her tent and undressed in no time. She'd hardly slept in Nairobi so she was tired enough but, even so, sleep wouldn't come.

Before her arrival at the gorge, she'd been nervous, unsure whether she would be up to the mark academically speaking. Oh, for that sort of problem now. Nothing could have prepared Natalie for the conundrum she was now facing – and facing, very largely, alone. The irony was she hadn't, actually, done anything. She had been sitting quietly, smoking, enjoying the night, hardly moving, totally silent, staring into the darkness, when she had seen Ndekei. She had been as passive, as un-proactive as it was possible to be. And yet her total inaction was the cause of all the trouble.

269

Natalie turned on her side. She smelled the canvas of the bed, the detergent the sheets had been washed in. She recalled her first nights at college in Cambridge, the first strange bed she had ever slept in. God, she had been innocent. She recalled Dom's smell. That had always troubled her in a minor way. The reason she always noticed Dom's smell was that she was never with him long enough to take it for granted. She supposed that happily married couples, or at least those who managed to stay married for any length of time or just lived together, as more and more people were doing, stopped noticing each other's smell.

Jack had his own smell, too, of course. He smelled ever so slightly of his airplane, the leather seats, kerosene, or Avgas, whatever airplane fuel was called.

Lying in bed, in her pyjamas, she put her hand on her chest where she had inadvertently left her shirt button undone. She hadn't really shown too much of herself, not at all. But the very fact of the button being undone made her think of the first time she had unbuttoned her shirt for Dominic. Natalie had been embarrassed then but excited too, the first real thrill of sexual antici-pation she had known. With Dominic she had peeled off her shirt, then her bra, to let her breasts hang free, loose – the first time she had known that physical freedom in the presence of a man, in front of a man. Dominic had groaned and buried his face in her flesh, kissing and licking and sucking her nipples. That was when she had discovered how sensitive her nipples were – how, when Dominic had bitten them between his lips, she had chewed in air and wrapped herself around him. There were tears in her eyes, spittle at the corners of her mouth from their kissing. Dominic had licked her nipples again. She had never expected she could feel so wet.

When Jack had looked at her undone button, the feelings she had couldn't be compared with that day in her rooms at Cambridge, with Dominic. But, along with her embarrassment, there had been excitement too. An excitement she hadn't known in months.

Natalie dragged her mind away from Dominic and Jack. Eleanor had said tonight that they must dig on, as if the situation were normal. Yes. Yes, please – but was that practical, given what was hanging over them all now?

She heard a noise outside the tent. Footsteps. Did she have a visitor? From the footfall, she sensed it might be Christopher. She held her breath.

The footsteps went away.

In Nairobi, she had thought about Christopher even less than she had thought about Dominic.

That told her something.

The Skull

'Look, vultures.' Jack stood over Natalie as she crouched in the gorge, teasing the rock with a small pickaxe.

She stopped what she was doing, sat back on her haunches and looked up, shielding her eyes from the sun with her gloved hand.

'Must be a buffalo that's got into trouble,' said Jack softly, handing her a water bottle. 'Like to go see?'

Natalie gulped at the water and then shook her head. 'I don't want to witness any more crimes, Jack.' She smiled grimly, handed back the bottle and wiped her forehead with her glove. 'Besides, I'm in the middle of something.' She pointed with her pickaxe. 'I think I may have some sort of jaw.'

Jack was immediately attentive. He put the bottle away and knelt down besides her.

It was already a week since their return from Nairobi. Life was normal, more or less. They spent their mornings digging, their afternoons following up with note-taking, reading or drawing, and their evenings discussing their discoveries, or the lack of them, over dinner.

Neither Christopher nor Jack had visited her in her tent. Part of her hoped that Jack would stop by but he seemed content with their normal exchanges during work and at meals, and left her alone in the evenings to be herself. As he had done that evening in Nairobi, behaviour that everyone else had criticised him for. But not her. He didn't crowd her and she liked that.

Leaning forward, Jack whistled. 'Yes, that looks like the line of a jaw-bone. It looks hominid too. Careful how you go. You should get to the teeth soon. If there are any left.'

She craned forward again.

'Clever of you to spot the sweep of that jaw, Natalie. You seem to have an eye.'

'Years of doing jigsaws as a girl,' she replied. 'It gives you a taste for patterns.'

'Hmmn. Maybe. But, look, you need better tools than the ones you've got. You'll never be a crack palaeontologist with shoddy tools – you need some wire brushes. *This* jigsaw is no toy.' Jack stood up. He had leaned his shotgun against the wall of the gorge and he reached for it. 'There's a troupe of baboons not far away, so the Land Rover's all locked up. I'll have to go and get the key from Daniel. I'll be as quick as I can. Okay?'

She nodded and carried on picking away at the lining of the gorge. Fossilised bone tended to be softer than the surrounding rock and, in general, that could be felt through the tools they all used. The bone she was picking away at now she had noticed about two hours before. It was the curve that had caught her eye, smooth and sweeping, like the keel of a model boat. Definitely not natural.

As she chipped, the rough rock fell away and revealed more of the smooth line of jaw. She took a regular small brush from her pocket and drew it over the bone. Small crumbs of rock still adhered to the jawbone and had not been dislodged by the brush – that's why she needed something stronger.

She took a scalpel from her pocket and pulled off the protective metal cap, shielding the blade. Now she scraped at the top edge of the jawbone. The rock broke up into smaller pieces and some crumbled away. As it did so, her heart leapt as she suddenly saw the glint of a brighter substance. Could it be? She was a novice still but were those the remains of some teeth? Her tongue felt dry. She looked over her shoulder. Jack was nowhere to be seen, just Aldwai, the guard with his gun. Natalie bent back to her work.

She dislodged more rock. Yet more teeth came into view, their shine catching the sun, so that she gave out a short, involuntary grunt. She could now make out not one but three teeth. She didn't know much about the shape of teeth – that was Eleanor's speciality. But, but... Natalie tried to stop herself from thinking that she was in the middle of a major discovery. Her job was to excavate properly, carefully, making notes as she went along, taking photos as often as she thought necessary, and making drawings where that helped.

The skin on her throat was damp with excitement.

Could this jawbone and teeth be *that* important? she asked herself. There were no rules about who made the discoveries, save that Daniel had made more than anyone else. She had already found the Pelorovis fossil and the 'wall', as she thought of it. If she really was in the middle of an important find and it was written up in the newspapers, would her father read it? Would Dominic read it? If they did, they would know that Africa was not just an escape for her, as they might have thought. The Ndekei business apart, she was being strengthened all the time by what she was turning up in the gorge. Once her articles had been published, she would be more than a newly minted Ph.D., of which there were any number, especially in a place like Cambridge. She would have her own *form* at last.

In her excitement she had forgotten the heat but the sweat oozing down her back, the wet hair at her temples, never went away for long. Natalie stopped scraping, sat back and wiped her face with her sleeve. She reached for her bag, which held the camera. Once she had that ready, she took the six-inch ruler from her jacket pocket and laid it below the jawbone, for scale. Then she took a dozen or so pictures, varying the view slightly each time and moving closer and then further away.

'These should do the trick.'

She hadn't heard Jack return. She put the cap back on the lens of the camera and pointed. 'Look. Teeth.'

Jack kneeled down and peered forward. For a full minute he held his gaze on the jawbone, then he whistled again. 'Jesus, Natalie,' he said at length. 'You could have a whole skull here.' He turned. 'Look, I think we need my mother in on this and Christopher – we need the best pictures we can manage. Do you mind?'

'No, no. Not at all. You think it's that important?'

'It could be. You've done a good job here, but this *is* your first jawbone. My mother has lots of experience with this sort of discovery – in particular where other fossil bones might be in relation to this one. Having that experience is almost a skill in its own right. We need to bring her in and you need to watch her. You'll still get the credit, for making the discovery, I mean. But Eleanor and Christopher, and Daniel of course, will know the best way to proceed from here on in.' Jack stood up. 'You wait here. Don't do any more excavating for the moment. I'll leave Aldwai with you, so you'll be safe, and go and get the others. You need to watch how my mother proceeds from here on in. She and Daniel have devised special excavation techniques so as not to destroy other evidence nearby. We're looking at another all-day session here. I'll bring you some water, a sandwich and some fruit.'

And he hurried off.

Natalie stared down at the jawbone. She supposed that Jack had acted properly, in bringing in the others. Eleanor and Daniel certainly had much more experience at excavating than she did, as Jack had reminded her. And that was what counted, that the excavation be properly completed. And yet she couldn't help but feel a little disappointed. If she hadn't told Jack about what she had found, he might never have noticed and she would have had this find to herself for a while longer. She might have found an entire skull all by herself, a discovery that might have made her famous throughout her profession. The skull might even be named after her. As it was, she

279

couldn't excavate any more on her own without going against the general ethos of Eleanor's dig.

Natalie told herself again that that was as it should be. But, dammit, yes, she was disappointed.

She heard a noise behind her and turned.

On the lip of the gorge, about a hundred yards to the east, stood four men, carrying spears and wrapped in dark red cloaks. They stared down at her.

Now the anger rose inside her again.

Maasai warriors.

'What a beauty! Or should I say four beauties. A jaw, and three exquisitely curved sections of skull. Once again the gorge has delivered the goods. Champagne tonight, mother?'

They were all gathered around the table outside Daniel's tent. It was two afternoons later. Careful excavation of the jaw and associated fossils had gone on throughout the previous days, until dusk had made further work dangerous. Aldwai and two other guards had spent two nights in the gorge to protect the site from animals and, maybe, the Maasai, since Natalie had told Eleanor about the warriors who had been watching her.

Orchestrated this time by Eleanor herself, they had finished dislodging the fossils just on lunchtime and had in fact foregone lunch. Eleanor had spent some considerable time showing Natalie how to excavate a jawbone and, Natalie had to admit, she had a lot to learn. They had used a contraption not unlike a toothbrush but with metal wires at the end. The main point was to proceed slowly, keeping an eye out, as Eleanor counselled, for curves. Curves indicated either jawbones or skull bones, equally invaluable.

And three more curves had turned up, three sections of skull bone, each not much bigger than a stamp. Natalie had to admit to herself, secretly, that had she not told Jack about the jawbone, and had he not brought in Daniel and his mother, she might have missed the skull bones.

They were now nibbling strips of dried kudu meat that Naiva had left out for them. The fossils were displayed on the table outside Daniel's tent, being photographed and measured in their new surroundings, so that other scientists would be able to judge for themselves when the pictures were published later.

'How far were these bones found from the knee-joint discovered by Daniel, Richard and Russell?' Eleanor spoke generally, addressing no one in particular.

'Fifteen feet,' replied Daniel.

'And at the same level?'

'Yes.'

Eleanor turned to Jonas. 'It's your turn in the spotlight now, Jonas – you're the anatomist. We need to know what the chances are that this jaw and cranium come from the same skeleton as the knee bones.'

Jonas nodded.

Eleanor nibbled the meat. 'When you've made up your mind, we'll have to tell Russell. That's only fair but if your opinion is "yes", he's not going to like it. He anticipated something like this might happen.' She sucked the end of one arm of her spectacles. 'Now that we have some teeth, that will help us decide what this creature ate. Arnold can help there. We have some skull bones, which will help us work out the size of his, or her, brain. Skulls are Jack's speciality. A knee-joint, some teeth and some skull bones are quite a lot in palaeontological terms, if it's all one skeleton. This looks like a new species among man's ancestors.' She looked around the table at each one of them. 'If true, that's big news.'

'*Homo nelsoniensis,* how does that sound?' Christopher looked at Natalie and smiled. 'You found it, so it's your right to name the thing.'

Natalie coloured. 'I think it's a bit soon to be thinking of that, don't you? In any case, how can you tell brain size from the few bones we have found?'

'By comparison with bones from the skulls of other discoveries, and which are more complete.' Eleanor put back her spectacles. 'I have the necessary books in my tent, so we can make a preliminary inspection tomorrow, once we've done all the measuring and photographing.'

She fixed Natalie with her glare. 'If this discovery turns out to be what we think it is, and if your shelter idea stands up, you are going to be an overnight sensation – in the profession, I mean. And to think I was against you joining the dig, Natalie.' Eleanor smiled. 'But surely you can see now how important the gorge is, how the situation is changing all the time. You've helped transform palaeontology, my dear, in just a few weeks. This gorge is as much yours now as anyone's.'

282

Eleanor's words were meant as a compliment but they cut into Natalie, as both women realised. Natalie's good fortune, in the discoveries she had unearthed, only made the threatened destruction of the gorge harder to bear.

'Shoo, Jack. Go away. I want to talk to Natalie.'

Dinner was over for the night, Jack had let Natalie choose some music and they had planned to sit by the campfire for a few minutes, listening to Schumann's *Carnaval*.

It had been Jack's idea. About three nights before, and knowing that Natalie liked her late nights to herself, he had suggested a post-dinner music session, when they talked music, ate chocolate, listened to whatever that evening's choice of entertainment was and then went their separate ways. Christopher watched these encounters from a distance but made no attempt to get involved. He hadn't approached Natalie in anything other than a professional manner since the evening she had been in bed and he had withdrawn in silence.

This evening, however, Eleanor made Jack move. 'Go on,' she insisted. 'Well away, please. I want to talk to Natalie – out of earshot, Jack.'

'Going, going,' he grumbled but grinned. 'Let me just put some logs on the fire.' Then he disappeared.

Eleanor sat down next to Natalie and for a moment neither spoke. They stared into the fire and listened to the Schumann until the end. One by one, the others drifted from the campfire, to their tents.

'I can't help but notice, Natalie,' said Eleanor softly, 'I can't help but notice that you still receive next to no post. I can't do anything about the man you split up with – a cellist, wasn't he? – but what about your father? Are you still estranged? Is it something I could help with perhaps? Would you like me to write to him, tell him what a success you are becoming here?'

Natalie didn't know what to say. These sudden lurches into intimacy on Eleanor's part were disconcerting, to say the least.

'*Am* I becoming a success, Eleanor? Yes, I've made some discoveries but the Mutevu business puts everything under threat.' She paused. 'I hope you are not suggesting a quid pro quo: that you will write to my father, if I change my mind over Mutevu?'

Eleanor pushed up a strand of her hair where it had fallen from her chignon. 'No, my dear, that's not my plan at all. I'm sure you are torn every day about whether to give evidence or not. I'm not raking over those old coals, not tonight anyway.'

She put her hand on Natalie's knee. 'But with your father I may have some real influence–'

'But what would you say, and why would you say it?'

'Oh, I would start by saying what a success you are, how you have made three important discoveries. How much we all enjoy having you in Kihara. But then I would say you have stumbled into a dilemma and that you need the support of your family, that your father, as a religious man, a man of the church community, must know forgiveness, redemption, that he must find space in his heart to move past his ordeal, that unless he does he will be trapped in a cage for ever.'

Natalie was shaking her head. 'But why would you do this for me? Because I am a woman; because I am new in the gorge, alone; because you *pity* me? Would you do it for Jonas or Kees or Arnold? For Daniel?'

'I've done things for Daniel, lots of times, yes. I don't know about the others. I don't think they need my help. They all get lots of letters, even Arnold, even though his are from *lawyers*.' She grinned.

Despite herself, Natalie grinned too. But she wasn't grinning inside. 'No, Eleanor, I don't like the way I am being singled out for help – for *charity*, that's what it feels like. I told you about my father, about his reaction to my mother's death, not ... not to elicit your sympathy, your pity, but because you asked.' She shook her head again. 'I don't want to be treated differently from anyone else, or like I am some sort of *invalide*. Please. I don't need...' She paused. 'I don't need a mother.'

Eleanor didn't say anything for a moment. When she did speak, it was to murmur, 'There's a big age difference between us Natalie so, yes, I could be your mother.' She kicked the fire to make the logs burn better. 'But you're forgetting that I lost my own father. I see us – you and me – much more as sisters. But I have learned to put the guilt behind me. I have learned to live with the ambiguity of my father's death. And that is what you must do, in regard to your mother:

what your father must do. I could tell him all that, in a letter.'

'No!' gasped Natalie. 'No, please, no!' She gazed into the fire. 'I just don't see why my personal life has to have anything to do with the gorge. I don't need the help you think I do. Please don't keep watching me, watching how many letters I do or don't receive, whether you think I have some great invisible wound that gnaws away at me.' She chewed some air. 'I may not have adjusted to the ambiguity – as you put it – yet, or as you have done, but I *can* compartmentalise my life. I know how to concentrate, to keep my mind clear to spot the man-made among the random in the gorge. Haven't I proved that?'

Eleanor patted her knee again. 'Yes, you have, Natalie. Better than I ever imagined. But as I have warmed to you – and I *have* warmed to you – I have grown more concerned. Yes, you are ferociously efficient as a scientist, very much in my own mould, if I may say so. But at other times – at the dinner table when we are not talking about our work, or around this fire, listening to Jack's music – you can look so sad, so twice-bereaved as you once described yourself to me. How can I not react to that? I see nothing like that on Jonas's face, or Kees's, or even Arnold's'

Yet again, Natalie was hating what she was hearing. At the same time, Eleanor had said one important thing. Natalie had not learned to live with ambiguity, not just the ambiguity over her mother's death, but the ambiguity over the situation in the gorge, where her view was so different from Eleanor's own, and all the others. She didn't want Eleanor to proceed with her plan, she knew that. She must change the subject.

'Is there ... Jack and Christopher, I see something between them: a fire, a friction. Does it bother you? Does it get in the way, here in the gorge?'

Eleanor looked annoyed for a moment or two.

'Are you sure?' she said at length. 'They were always fighting as boys. Christopher especially was unruly. But he quietened down a long time ago. I think I told you the night you slept in my tent that he used to be very jealous of Jack, but I'm not sure that's true any more. There was the whole business of Gisella, of course, that was rather unfortunate but–'

'I don't know what you mean. Who was Gisella?'

Eleanor was still smarting from Natalie's quick-fire change of subject, still adjusting to the fact that she was determined not to accept her offer of help, and she was obviously wary of saying too much about her sons, of being disloyal to one more than the other. Eleanor looked about her, to make sure both men were beyond earshot, and then she spoke carefully, deliberately.

'Two years ago, Christopher fell in love with a woman called Gisella. She was a wildlife artist and he met her when he was taken to the opening of one of her shows in Nairobi. They had a whirlwind romance and, I think, I'm sure, he had considered marrying her. Anyway, he brought her to the gorge where the whole thing fell flat, or at least it did on her part. She went back to the city after only a few days, leaving Christopher bemused and deflated and very upset.'

Eleanor kicked the fire again. 'But she was a decent girl – woman – she knew she had hurt Christopher and she wrote him a long letter.' She gently touched her hair where the strand had fallen down earlier. 'He never told me what was in the letter but I could see he was hurting and so, one day when he had gone to Nairobi, I found the letter among his things and read it.' She made a face. 'I shouldn't have done it but he was my son and I could see he was in turmoil, just as I can see that you are now in turmoil.'

She let a pause go by.

'Gisella had left, she said, because although she had arrived in the gorge as Christopher's girlfriend, she had very quickly fallen in love with Jack.'

Natalie turned involuntarily towards Eleanor and Eleanor nodded.

'Gisella made it clear in her letter that Jack wasn't aware of her feelings for him, that she had fallen for him "at a distance", as she put it, and nothing had gone on. But that was why she had left in such a hurry. She had no idea, she said, if Jack felt about her the way she felt about him but it was safer for her to leave before … before, as I remember she put it, she hurt Christopher more than she was hurting him already.'

Eleanor stared into the fire before going on. 'Imagine all that. Imagine the currents and cross-currents swirling around in that whirlpool of emotion. Was Jack really not aware of Gisella's feelings for him? These things have a way of revealing themselves after all. Was he therefore aware of the full extent of Christopher's obvious distress? Did Jack know he had – however inadvertently – been part of the cause of his brother's unhappiness? Deeper still, if Jack *didn't* know about Gisella's feelings, did she underneath it all want Christopher to *tell* Jack that she had fallen for him? Would Christopher have done that? And what did he feel about his brother? Gisella had said in her letter that Jack wasn't aware of the situation, and had done nothing to bring it about, but was that true? Who tells the complete truth in situations like that?'

Natalie felt the warmth of the fire play on her cheeks. 'Having read the letter, what did you do?'

Eleanor looked at her. 'What would you have done, my dear?'

'I'm not sure I would have read Gisella's letter in the first place.'

Eleanor nodded. 'You are not a mother yet, Natalie. I had one son hurting. I didn't know how deep the whole business went. Was Jack involved or not? If he really wasn't aware of Gisella's feelings, what would happen if and when he *did* become aware of them?'

She removed her spectacles and cleaned them with her handkerchief. 'I sent Christopher to a conference in Paris. While he was away, I told Jack, on one of the occasions he was in Nairobi, that I had been asked to write a book on the gorge and that the publishers wanted the illustrations to be paintings and drawings, not photographs. So I asked him to see Gisella and ask her if she was interested.'

'And?'

'And nothing. Whatever Gisella felt for Jack, and whether she felt the same after a few weeks had elapsed, Jack certainly didn't reciprocate the feeling – nothing happened. So I concluded that Gisella had been truthful in her letter. Jack didn't know about her feelings for him. Once or twice after Christopher came back from Paris, I introduced into the conversation the fact that Jack had seen Gisella, that nothing had come of the book project and there had been no subsequent contact between the two of them.'

'And you think that settled everything?'

'No, of course not. I'm not naïve. Of course it didn't settle everything. But, at the least, what I did showed Christopher that he had not been betrayed by his brother, rather by Gisella.'

'But ... but Jack had been the catalyst. Isn't that enough to stoke Christopher's jealousy?'

'Yes, maybe, but that had already happened. I could do nothing about it. You can't protect your children from everything, so you protect them where you can.'

Natalie stared into the dying fire. 'And what about if there *had* been something between Jack and Gisella?'

'Again, I'm realistic. If there had been something, better to have it out in the open. Jack is my son just as much as Christopher is. And being so obsessed by the gorge doesn't stop me wanting to be a grandmother some day, see the Deacon name perpetuated. That's more likely to happen with Jack than Christopher. Jack adores children.'

Natalie could still feel the glow of the campfire on her cheeks, but the heat was fading. 'So it all settled down, did it, after the Gisella episode? I mean the rivalry between Christopher and Jack.'

'As much as these things ever do. There will always be some rivalry between brothers.'

Was Eleanor quite as sensitive to her sons' rivalry as she thought? Natalie asked herself. Mothers couldn't always second-guess their own children. Look at what had happened in her own case.

Eleanor stood up, to indicate the conversation was over.

Natalie stood up too.

'I've said more than I ever intended.' Eleanor smiled but sternly. 'I take it you don't wish me to intervene with your father?'

Natalie shook her head.

'You're sure?'

Natalie stared into the remains of the fire. 'My father is my problem.'

Between her fingers, Natalie gripped a cigarette. Even its smell was comforting. Before her, on the small table, the flask of whisky was laid out where it usually was. The moon was not up yet and so the night, beyond the reach of the camp lights, was dark, inky dark, impenetrable.

It was the following evening and, after dinner tonight, they had listened to Massenet's *Manon*, about lovers and letters and misunderstandings. She had adored it but Arnold Pryce had complained again that Jack didn't have enough jazz.

Natalie put the cigarette to her lips and drew the smoke into her lungs. At moments like this she felt a long way from that courtroom in

Nairobi. She could tell herself that this was her life: the relative solitude of the bush. And that she had made a good start – she could look forward to decades of quiet evenings like this, after a productive day excavating.

But in that darkness ahead of her lay the gorge. Who knows how many Maasai warriors were out there, right now, and what mischief they were planning?

Dinner, for once, had been a light-hearted affair, the conversation a million miles from the excavation or the trial. Arnold Pryce had received a letter from his lawyer in London. His last wife had decided she was unhappy with the settlement that had been agreed and was threatening to go back to court to have their arrangement revoked.

'I may have to live here for ever, Eleanor,' he had complained, in mock seriousness. 'I can't afford to return to England.'

'What if she comes looking for you?' said Jack, grinning.

'Unlikely. It's too far from the hairdresser's.' His face shaped itself into a rueful smile. 'Or the shoe shops.'

'Tell us about your wives, Arnold,' Natalie had said. 'What's it like, being married four times?'

He had needed no second bidding. In fact, he seemed happy to get it all off his chest and, for three quarters of an hour, had regaled them with details of his four courtships, four weddings, four honeymoons, four betrayals and divorces, each of the latter seemingly more hostile than the last. Arnold Pryce, it was clear to Natalie at any rate, loved women but tired of them all too soon and invariably became convinced that the grass was greener. He didn't have Jock Deacon's ability to infuse his women with a passion that would last a lifetime, but he told his story with a self-deprecating wit that suggested to Natalie at least that his fourth wife wouldn't get very far.

Jonas had teased Kees. 'It's your turn next.'

Kees had coloured. 'I haven't been married once, let alone four times.'

'You can tell us all about Amsterdam's red-light district, then. It's famous.'

'What makes you—'

'Enough!' Eleanor had hissed, standing up, to indicate the end of dinner. She had again motioned Natalie to sit next to her at the campfire. Not more talk about her father, Natalie hoped.

When the two women were settled, Eleanor whispered, 'Russell's made his first move.'

Natalie wiped her clammy hands on her trousers. 'What do you mean?'

'Christopher went into Karatu this morning, to shop for supplies and collect the post. There was a copy of a solicitor's letter from Russell to the secretary general of the foundation that funds the dig, formally complaining about me and my allegedly "high-handed authoritarian behaviour" in insisting he leave the excavation after his "seminal" discovery. He sent me a copy and he sent the foundation a copy of the paper that has gone to *Nature*, on the knee-joint. A paper that, of course, ignores the whole burial-ground business.'

'What will the foundation do?'

'I don't know for sure but they won't like it.' She stopped and fixed Natalie with a stare. 'Russell writes to you. He seemed fond of you. He needs to be softened. Can you...?'

Natalie bit her lip. 'He's written me one letter, yes, but that's all. He's still as raw and as sore as the day he left. I can *try* to calm him down but I'm not sure it will have any effect.'

'Give it a go, please. I believe he will listen to you.' Eleanor gripped her spectacles in her fingers. 'I've also heard from the Maasai elders. Their next "propitious" date, when they feel able to see strangers, is ten days from now. The fact that they've agreed to see us is a good sign, but they are unpredictable.' She tapped her chin with her spectacles. 'You've never wavered, have you?'

'No.'

'And you're not going to waver now, even after all the new discoveries?'

Natalie shook her head and kept looking into the fire. 'I think I have right on my side, Eleanor, but there's something else too. In the war, my mother's family – who were French, as I think I told you – were part of the Resistance. One of them was betrayed – *trahit*, that's a French word I can't forget. He was killed. So my mother was always very patriotic, very anti *"collabo"*, as the French call it. That's why I'm the way I am, I suppose. Or one reason.' Natalie didn't mention the anger within her, where, as often as not now, the fire was directed *against* her mother.

That had all happened earlier. Now, sitting outside the tent, Natalie reached for her whisky. Had she told Eleanor too much? Was her

294

mother's influence too strong? What was the difference between resistance and stubbornness? Was there one? Once upon a time, Dominic would have helped her.

She heard a footfall, and half-turned. It was Jack.

'Don't worry,' he whispered, standing over her. 'I haven't come to disturb your precious late-night privacy. Or not for long anyway.'

Natalie smiled and held out the cigarette. 'But I'll bet you'd like to taste this.'

He took the cigarette from her and drew on it before handing it back. 'Can it be good for you, all that smoke in your lungs?'

She shrugged. 'It's very relaxing, don't you find?'

He nodded. 'Did you see that article in *Nature*? About the link between smoking and lung cancer?'

'Yes. But it hasn't been confirmed.'

'It has,' said Jack. 'In Germany and in America. But I agree – the experiments weren't very well designed.'

He pointed to the whisky on the table. 'I don't like to intrude on your evenings, but ... but, what I came to say is this: as it's Sunday tomorrow and my mother's going to Nairobi, and there's no digging, I wondered if you wanted to go flying. There's somewhere near here – a mystery destination that I'd like to show you. Interesting geology, masses of animals, perfect picnic spot.'

'Are there any hairdressers or shoe shops?'

'There's a lake where you could wash your hair. Other than that, no.'

'Then I'd love to.'

'Good. I'll say goodnight then.' Jack waved and was gone.

'That's the Bololedi river – it's like a dry ditch from up here.' Jack leant across Natalie and pointed. 'We're now just entering Tanganyika airspace, about sixty miles to go.'

'To where? Or is it still a secret?'

He nodded. 'You'll see why.'

Jack identified himself to air traffic control at Kilimanjaro Airport and, on their instructions, climbed the plane by a couple of thousand feet. 'I prefer to fly low,' he said. 'You get a much better view, but there are some Tanganyika air force planes in the vicinity. We have to keep out of their way.'

Natalie nodded. She liked flying, she had decided. It put everything into perspective, she thought. She had always been good at reading maps and she had one on her knee now. It was fascinating to see how the map related to the actual topography of the land.

'Over to the left!' Jack shouted, to make himself heard above the engine noise. 'Lake Natron. It looks pink because it's a soda lake.'

'Meaning?'

'There's no inflow of water, or outflow. So it tends to evaporate, and there's a build-up of sodium carbonate and that encourages a special bacteria, called halophilic bacteria, which are pink. It's that pink which gives flamingos their colour. Lesson over.' He grinned.

They crossed some low hills, the shadow of the

plane rising to meet them.

'Loliondo,' shouted Jack. 'Look out for elephant and the wildebeest migration route.'

But Natalie could see neither. She hadn't yet developed her 'bush eyes'.

They were now crossing a shallow valley between two sets of hills as Lake Natron curled round towards them. Jack kept looking over the instrument panel at the land ahead.

'Don't you navigate by instruments?' she said.

'No, by the seat of my pants,' he replied, looking across and grinning again. 'I know it round here, don't worry, we're not lost.'

'What are you looking for?'

'Telegraph poles alongside a road – ah, there they are.'

As Jack said this, he banked the plane to the left and began to climb again. 'As you have noticed, we use the latest navigational techniques on this aircraft, following the road for a bit until it disappears into the rainforest on the side of that mountain.'

Natalie looked down and could see a thin strip in the red-brown soil where, here and there, vehicles raised the dust. But then the road disappeared into the lush undergrowth.

The land was rising to meet them quite rapidly now. She could clearly make out distinct trees – what she knew as Kigelia, Euphorbia and more fever trees. Natalie still had complete faith in Jack as a pilot but the ground was now not at all far below them. She looked ahead and could see a skyline of bushes and trees – they were clearly approaching some sort of escarpment though she couldn't, as yet, see what was on the far side.

The ground rose and rose towards them; the treetops got closer and closer to their under-carriage. The shadow of the plane was almost as big as the real thing. The sounds of the engines changed as they echoed off the ground just below them.

'Now!' cried Jack as they crested the escarp-ment and the engine noise and the land fell away together.

Natalie stared ahead of her. She didn't speak. Ahead of her was one of the most extraordinary sights she had ever seen.

Ahead of her was a ring of mountains forming a complete – and an almost perfect – circle. The circle must have been ten miles in diameter, more, much more. Below, hundreds of feet below, thousands, was a plain and a lake, completely cut off from the outside world by the mountains – a vast, secret place.

'Ngorongoro Crater,' said Jack. 'A dead volcano but the biggest crater on earth – save for that one in Japan whose name I forget, and that doesn't have the wildlife that you are about to see.' He started to bring the plane down. 'I always follow the road here, because it gives someone new like you the best – the most dramatic – introduction. Are you knocked out?'

'I think it's... I'm speechless. How can some-thing so big be so secret?' Natalie shook her head. 'Can you get here by road?'

'Yes, of course, but it takes for ever and you're likely to meet elephants and that can be tricky. Flying in is the best way, and not normally

298

allowed. But I did one of the rangers here a favour some time back and he promised to turn a blind eye. The crater is over three thousand square miles, more or less the size of Crete.'

'Are we going to land?'

'Sure. Of course.'

'Where?'

'You'll see. There's no airport, not even a strip, but there's a stretch of road that runs by the lake. We'll land there.'

'Is it safe?'

Jack nodded. 'Provided there's no other traffic and the lions aren't sleeping there today. We'll buzz the place first, to make sure it's all clear.'

He leaned across her again. 'Look down there: lions – the black dots. With a herd of wildebeest nearby.'

Natalie looked down. 'And are those flamingos?'

'Yes. They make more noise than a trainload of children.' He brought the plane down still further, approaching the lake.

Natalie could see that, straight ahead, a gravel road ran alongside the lake, next to a beach of sorts.

Jack flew along the road, on the lake side, about a hundred feet from the ground. The road seemed clear and he banked the plane and began to go round again.

Their second approach was bumpier than the first but they landed safely enough.

'Landing's not the problem,' said Jack as they got down from the aircraft. 'If some lions come by and occupy the road now, how do we scare them away so we can take off again?'

Seeing her alarm, he grinned. 'Just teasing. The rattle of the engines is usually enough to send anyone running for cover.'

Jack went to the back of the plane. 'Help me with the picnic?'

She stood next to him.

'Arriving by plane is much more dramatic than coming in a Land Rover, but the drawback is that we have to picnic wherever we land. It's too dangerous to go walking – there are not just lions here, but wildebeest, water buffalo, rhino, elephants, hyenas: all the creatures you get out-side the crater but all a little bit different genetically, because they have been cut off for so long and have inbred. That makes some of the creatures here even more quirky and skittish than usual. If we had a Land Rover we could drive around the lake, but we're stuck.'

'I don't mind,' Natalie said, taking the basket from him. 'I don't think I'll ever forget that moment we crested the escarpment and I saw what was below. I thought the lake Christopher showed me from that cave in Ndutu was Eden, but this is even more so.'

Jack nodded but said nothing more. He took the basket from her and crossed to where the wing of the plane cast a large shadow on the ground. 'Useful things, wings,' he said. He had two folding chairs and a folding table and he laid them out in a line, so they were all in shadow. 'Only water, I am afraid. But chicken – I know it's your favourite.'

They sat down. 'You sit facing one way,' Jack

said. 'Me, the other. If you see anything dangerous, don't wait to holler. We leave the door of the plane open, for a quick get-in. Clear?'

Natalie nodded, swigging some water. Jack unwrapped the chicken legs, some whole tomatoes, some bread, two oranges, and that was that. As the breeze swept around them, Natalie became aware of a noise, a constant high-pitched hubbub. 'What's that?' she said.

He pointed. 'The flamingos – it's non-stop. That's why they're so thin: they expend all their energy talking, like–' He faltered.

'Like women? Were you going to say "like women", or like "fish-wives", you were, weren't you?'

He nodded. 'Guilty.'

She ate her chicken leg.

'Are you ... what do the Americans call them? A feminist?'

Natalie wiped her lips with her napkin. 'Yes and no. I don't make a fetish of it but, well, yes, I think it's about time women had a fair crack of the whip, a chance to do things they haven't had chance to do before.'

'This new pill thing, this contraceptive pill, that's going to change things a bit – yes?'

'I guess. Some things are already changing. A lot of my friends at Cambridge – well, girls in my year, girls I knew – some of them, when they graduated and left university, went to live with their men without getting married. The pill will make that sort of thing easier.'

'For the couple concerned, maybe. But what about if they have children?'

'I suppose the pill makes that less likely. Women will have more control now. That has to be good, don't you think?'

He shrugged. 'In one way, yes. Yes, of course. But say we start having fewer children as a result, is *that* a good thing?'

Natalie chewed on a chicken leg. 'The other night by the campfire, when your mother shooed you away–'

'Yes, I've been meaning to ask, what was all that about?'

'Some of it was private but she did say, at one point, that you are her best hope for giving her grandchildren, that you like children. Where does that come from?'

Jack shrugged again. 'I shouldn't have to explain that, surely. Doesn't everyone want children? Don't you?'

Natalie nodded. 'I suppose I do want children, yes, but I haven't thought much about it. I told you, I had an affair with a married man. I was very happy. He had two children, there was never any question of ... of me having a child with him. Children were never talked about.'

When he didn't say anything immediately, she went on, 'Your mother seems to think that neither Christopher nor your sisters is as likely to have children as you.'

Jack finished chewing some chicken. 'I suppose it's true that Christopher doesn't have the interest in children that I have. But Virginia is a doctor, doing good works in Palestine; she and her husband think that having children now would hamper their work, and they are right. But they'll have children at some point. And Beth ... she's impulsive, noisy: she's just as likely to get pregnant as she is to get married in Las Vegas.' He grinned, biting into his tomato. 'Our mother doesn't really understand Beth.'

'And she understands the rest of you?'

'She thinks she does.'

'Does she interfere much in your lives?'

'Why do you say that?'

'The night she shooed you away from the campfire, when she came to sit with me, she had a proposal – to intervene with my father. I thought it well-meaning but very... I didn't welcome it: it wasn't her place to do what she suggested doing.'

'Oh yes, that sounds like our mother all right. She's always matchmaking for us. When we were at school she was always writing to the head-master if we showed some gap in our learning that she found alarming. Our mother never sits back and lets life go past. She has definite views about shaping the future. Did she agree to do as you asked?'

'What do you mean?' Natalie, in the process of chewing her tomato, spilled some juice on her hand.

'I mean: if you asked her not to interfere, did she agree not to? If you left it ambiguous, she is quite capable of taking matters into her own hands and proceeding anyway.'

'Oh no. There was nothing ambiguous about my reaction. If she *has* intervened with my father after that I shall be ... you'll be able to hear my roar from very far away.'

They both sat in silence for a while, eating.

'See the elephants?' Jack said at length and pointing. 'Near those trees.'

Natalie nodded. Heat shimmered above the lake, making the reeds a green-grey mass of abstract lines. The hubbub of the flamingos was as loud as ever.

'Speaking of ambiguity,' said Natalie after another pause, 'your mother told me that she has learned to live with the ambiguity of your grandfather's death. Do you think that's true?'

Jack didn't reply straight away. When he did, it was to say, 'I'm not sure I follow what you mean. What was ambiguous about my grandfather's death?'

'Was it an accident or suicide? Come on, Jack, that's obvious.'

He thought for a moment. 'Okay,' he said then. 'Tell me first why you were talking about his death to begin with.'

Natalie wasn't sure she wanted to get into all that but she *had* started the conversation and Jack's question was reasonable.

'The night I spent with her, in her tent, the night after Richard was killed, we got talking and she asked me about myself and in particular why I received so few letters. I told her about Dominic but I also told her about the death of my own mother.' Natalie repeated to Jack what she had told Eleanor weeks earlier. 'And when I told her there was doubt about whether my mother had deliberately set fire to her bedclothes, she told me about the way your grandfather had died.'

Jack let a long silence elapse. The wind was

stiffening. Grains of sand were blown against the flesh of their legs.

'There was nothing ambiguous about my grandfather's death. It was suicide.'

Natalie looked at Jack. 'How can you know that? He was cleaning his gun, wasn't he?'

Jack drank some water. 'He left a message.'

'What? What kind of message? What did it say? Your mother never mentioned a note.'

He nodded. 'It wasn't a formal note, so she chose to ignore it.' He swallowed more water. 'He was a vicar, Natalie, remember that, and a missionary. Next to the body was a Bible. It had a ribbon attached to it, one of those ribbons that help you keep your place in books. When we opened the Bible at the place where the ribbon was, it was the Book of Ecclesiastes and five lines were underlined.' He turned his head to her. 'I have never forgotten them: *"He that increaseth knowledge increaseth sorrow... Therefore, I hated life; because the work that is wrought under the sun is grievous unto me... Better is the end of a thing than the beginning thereof."* I'd say that's pretty clear, wouldn't you?'

A long silence passed.

Jack looked out across the lake. 'I think my grandfather was holding the book when he died, and he was holding it because he had lost faith in it, lost confidence in the story it told, and he was hoping against hope that what he was doing would bring him some peace of mind, redemption. I think that when my mother talks of ambiguity, the only ambiguity was whether Gideon Taylor achieved the equanimity, the solace, the peace he sought, or whether he merely achieved oblivion. And I think she told you the lie that she did to help you, to make you feel less cold, less alone, less abandoned.'

Jack reached out and put his hand on Natalie's arm. 'And now I have robbed you of whatever comfort you derived from my mother's version of reality.'

He passed her some water. 'I can't tell whether you are shocked or bewildered or disappointed or angry, but I know I want to be the one to tell you. And it's fortunate we are here, in this magical but very cut-off place, where you can digest what I say before attacking my mother with all your guns for misleading you. Or attack me, for dis-abusing you. She was trying to help, but I've seen how strong you are, how resilient, self-reliant.' Jack smiled. 'And *lithe!*' He nodded. 'I know you prefer the truth, however unpleasant, and you'd probably have found out sooner or later about my mother's manipulation of reality, and maybe in a way that would have done a lot of damage.'

They sat on, the wind slightly rocking the small plane.

Natalie wrestled with her thoughts, with what Jack had said. He was right in his observation: her feelings veered from anger to shock to bewil-derment. Worst of all, she felt used by Eleanor and, yes, manipulated, *cheated*.

She drank more water; her shock and bewilder-ment were giving way to anger. 'When you have all these children you say you want, Jack, are you going to intervene in their lives like your mother interferes in yours?'

He put his hand on her arm again. 'Parents can't help but interfere in their children's lives. That's what being a parent *is*, it's how they show they care. And, much of the time, especially when children are young, parents *do* know better. I agree that, as they get older, children come to know their own minds–'

'But what gave your mother the right to–'

'Nothing did. It's not a question of rights, Natalie, it's a question of negotiating our way through whatever life throws in our path. My mother was trying to help you. I know you don't see it that way, for the moment anyway, but she was. And maybe she did help. Although there was no ambiguity over her father's death, it sounds as though there was over your mother's.'

'But she *pretended!*'

Jack looked at her and squeezed her arm. 'Don't we pretend all the time?' He smiled. 'When we flew back from Nairobi, both you and I pretended not to notice that you had left undone a button on your shirt that is usually done up. And the first chance you had to do it up, while I was distracted, you did. I noticed straight away but pretended not to.' He squeezed her arm again. 'I'm not saying all pretences are as important as others. I'm just asking you not to judge my mother too harshly. Not because she's my mother but because you are going through a bit of a roller coaster just now, and she was trying to help.'

Natalie unconsciously checked the button on her shirt, the one Jack had referred to. She noticed what she was doing and smiled at him sheepishly.

'All right, all right. I'll calm down. But can you please tell your mother to lay off, that I don't need help all the time, that I can be safely left alone to clean a gun, that I'm not going to set fire to my tent with a cigarette, that I can sort out my own problems myself.' She breathed out heavily. 'It should be obvious by now, from the discoveries I have been making, that whatever is happening inside me doesn't affect my concentration on our work.'

'We can all see that, Natalie. Relax. I've put the record straight. Let's go on from there.'

Jack was right, she told herself. He *had* cleared the air. She found herself feeling cleaner, clearer-headed, less entangled in her past. Was it what had been said, or simply his presence? Jack had that effect on her; she had noticed that before.

Changing her tone, she said, 'I find it faintly indecent that you pay so much attention to one of my shirt buttons.'

'Then you know nothing about men, or about some women,' he replied. 'I found it ... exciting is the wrong word. Erotic, that's it. For a while, I thought you'd done it deliberately—'

'What?'

'Watch out!' cried Jack, scrambling to his feet. 'Lions. Leave the plates. Get in the plane.'

Natalie quickly did as she was told. Without looking where the lions were, or how many they were, she climbed into the Comanche, Jack after her, with the picnic basket. He closed the door and they both watched as a pride of five lions – three females and two males – walked by. They sniffed at the plane, the table and chairs, licked the plates, and then walked on to some dunes about thirty yards away.

'Let's get some air in here,' Jack said and opened one of the side windows, which had a metal clip on its rear edge.

'The male's manes are black,' said Natalie after a pause.

'Yes, it's a local adaptation. The reeds by the lake here are very dark and the black manes help camouflage the lions when they are hunting.'

Three of the lions now appeared to be resting but one, a male, was sniffing around a female.

'This looks interesting,' said Jack. 'I think they are going to copulate.'

She stared at him. 'Do you *like* watching animals have sex? Sounds a bit off to me.'

'That's just your Christian upbringing getting in the way. My interest is purely scientific. Ah – here we go.'

They watched as the male lion mounted the female, gave a few thrusts, bared its teeth in what could have been a grimace or a grin, and then withdrew.

Jack looked at his watch. 'Eight seconds.'

'How romantic.'

'But the purpose has been achieved – impregnation. It makes sense, in the wild, with a lot of predators around, to get it over with quickly.'

'Do you think the lioness is happy with the arrangement?'

'She doesn't know any different, so I don't see why not. It's as risky for her as for him, so the quicker it's all over the safer they both are.'

The lions were moving on.

Natalie used the binoculars Jack kept in the plane to focus on the lions as they drifted off.

'I nearly married an only child.' He said this as he put his water bottle on the back seat.

'What happened?'

'She died.'

'I'm sorry.'

'Leukaemia.'

He peeled an orange and offered it to her. She took it. 'Are you over it? Over her?'

'It was nearly a decade ago, so yes.' He looked across to where the lions had all but disappeared. 'I've not been in a hurry.'

Natalie handed him back some slices of orange. 'Does that mean you are now?'

'No, but you can't always let life slip by. You have to *act*. I agree with my mother there. The next five years in Kenya are going to be taken up with the transition to independence. There'll be a lot of politics. By the end of that time I'll be nearly forty, on the late side to have children.'

'Do you think so?'

'I do, yes. I don't want to be sixty when my children are at university. Children matter to me.'

With his fingers he gripped the door handle.

Natalie leaned forward. 'So you *are* in a hurry. That could be dangerous. Are you feeling broody?'

Jack rubbed his fingers over his chin. 'Horrible word. Let's just say that time is at the back of my mind, and that I can foresee a turbulent era coming up.' He opened the door, got down and helped her out of the plane. He began folding up the chairs and she did the same.

Holding the table, he said, 'Do you get broody?'

Natalie made a face and shook her head. 'It hasn't happened yet, no. The idea of children, the possibility, is always there, of course, but I don't feel any pressure of time.'

'Where do you want to be when you are fifty? A professor? A professor and a wife? A professor and a wife and a mother?'

She shook her head vehemently. 'I haven't thought about it! Honestly. I find your questions faintly, faintly...'

The hubbub from the flamingos was, if anything, louder than ever. Although it wasn't late, shadows were beginning to encroach on the crater, its mountainous walls being so high.

'Faintly what?'

Natalie shrugged. 'You seem so ... you have your plane, your record player, your political committee in Nairobi, you are confident about the future here in Kenya, you seem to know such a lot of people wherever you go. Until now, you seemed – quite frankly – like a round peg in a round hole. Yet here you are.' She smiled. 'This will sound crazy, *fou* as the French say, but it's as if you are interviewing me for a job as your wife!'

Jack whistled as he clanged shut the rear airplane emergency door and fixed it with its lever. It was his turn to make a face. 'I put my lips together and whistle but you're not entirely wrong. No,' he added quickly, 'I'm not interviewing you for a vacancy, though such a vacancy does, unquestionably, exist.' He smiled. 'But there is something in what you say.'

311

He held the door open as she got back in the plane. Then he climbed in after her.

'What I mean is, and this interests me about myself, at some stage in your life, you do begin to think about time, about the fact that you are mortal. You begin to weigh up what you might achieve – in all sorts of directions. It never occurs to you in your twenties, that's too early, and maybe it's hit me sooner than it hits other people. If it has, I put it down to what's happening here in Kenya – independence, I mean. We are all going to be caught up in big events, great events, historic political changes, shaping a whole world. But, during that time, what happens to your private life?'

Jack leaned over and closed the window he had opened earlier. Everything needed to be battened down for take-off.

'I grew up with parents who had four children but were never really interested in us *as* children. We had toys when we were very young but the wildlife in the bush was much more interesting than those conventional things and we moved on as soon as we could walk and talk. I'm not sure I ever had a childhood in the normal sense of that term. Living the life we did, the life you are living now, we never really had a private life either. You must see that – it's why you like your late nights to yourself. Otherwise, you would spend all your days as part of a team, in a big family of sorts, where everyone knows what you are up to at all times.'

Jack started his check of the instruments.

'So yes, I do think about how my life might be

different. I don't necessarily want it to *be* different but, not having had a proper childhood, children interest me. It's more abstract than being broody.'

Natalie fixed her seat belt. 'When I spent the night with your mother, in her tent, she talked about her passion for the gorge, about your father's womanising and about how he had infused her with a love for palaeontology. She mentioned her children, but almost in passing. Were your parents not good parents?'

He checked the altimeter. 'How do children ever know how to answer that question? You only get one shot at it, don't you? Our parents expected us children to be adults as soon as possible. Is that being a good parent, or not?'

Natalie smiled. 'You don't seem to have turned out too badly.' When Jack said nothing, she added, 'Have you ever failed at something?'

He frowned. 'Like what?'

'Oh, I don't know. An exam? A relationship that you wanted to succeed? A job or a task?'

'Why do you ask?'

'Answer the question first, then I'll tell you.'

Jack seemed satisfied with the instruments and sat back in his seat. 'Just now, I mentioned a woman who died. She was called Roxanna and I said I nearly married her but that's a lot less than the whole truth. We had been going out with each other for several months and she, I know, was very much in love with me. I was just as much in love with her, at least to begin with, but then one big thing came between us. She didn't want children. Roxanna loved her career – she was an agent for actors and actresses and travelled a lot – and children would have slowed her down.' He fixed his seat belt. 'Well, I *did* want children. They were, they still are, the whole point of marriage for me. So I was preparing to tell Roxy that we should go our separate ways.' Jack took down his headphones from where they were hooked up on the dashboard. 'And it was at that point that she was diagnosed as suffering from leukaemia. She had been feeling tired for ages and once the diagnosis had been made she was given about a year to live.'

Jack rubbed his chin with his fingers again. 'We were both devastated, of course, and in those circumstances I couldn't leave her. It would have been too cruel. So I never said anything. I lived a lie – for fifteen months as it turned out, as I watched Roxy sink and die.' He put on his headphones. 'That felt like a failure, not being able to come clean.'

'I'm not sure that qualifies as real failure,' replied Natalie. 'It wasn't very brave, perhaps. On the other hand, it was kind. My point is that the psychologists say the most important years for determining character are the early ones, when we are infants. Others say our teens are important but I think that our twenties are the most important decade. Why? Because that's the first time that most of us fail in life. Your twenties are when life gets real. Families and school protect you from reality, to an extent. They are designed to do so, quite properly. But in your twenties you have your first job, you tend to get married, have children, you are finally an adult. And, for the most part, and for the first time, you have to confront failure. How you cope with your first real failure is all-important for how life will turn out.'

'And *your* failure?'

'You know about.'

'How are you coping?'

'I'll get by.'

'You're very beautiful. With longer hair you could be Veronica Lake. That must help. You'll always have men chasing you.'

She shook her head. 'Looks are a start, that's all, as I told you in Nairobi. There are all sorts of things that make up me that you don't know about. For instance, I was a difficult birth – in fact, I was a caesarean that went wrong. Because of my difficult birth, my mother couldn't have any more children.' She eyed Jack. 'My parents called me Natalie, they said, because my birth was precious, the only one God gave them. But of course, for me, even my name reminds me of what happened then, *why* my birth was so precious. Even my name is a reproach. That doesn't happen to many people.'

Jack nodded. 'Look,' he said, 'this is all very serious. This is the most serious afternoon I've ever spent in Ngorongoro, and I've loved it, but I want to take off while part of the crater is in sunshine. Otherwise, when you come out of the shadow into the warm air, you can get a few bumps. So can we continue this later?'

'Of course.'

'Good,' he said, pressing the button that fired the first engine. 'If you want, on the way back you can have your first flying lesson. It will have to be now because I'm going to Nairobi tomorrow.'

The second engine fired into life.

'Can I afford you, Dr. Deacon? What are your charges?'

Jack was listening to the tone of the engines. Then he looked across and smiled. 'I'm expensive – and I need a down-payment, right now. I'll take it in kind.' He leaned across and planted a kiss on her cheek.

Dear Russell,

Thank you for your letter. I am sorry I haven't written before but, to be honest, I am a little afraid of your strength of feeling so far as the gorge and the Deacons are concerned, and letters always risk being misinterpreted. I understand your point of view, of course I do, and in many ways I sympathise but, well, not in all ways. I'll come back to that.

First, professional matters. Several discoveries have been made since you left. Some of them are minor, but not all, and you should know that we have located a jawbone, three teeth and three nicely curved skull bones which, we believe, belong to the same individual as the knee-joint found by Daniel, Richard and you. That's what the anatomist Jonas Jefferson – you'll remember him – told us today, anyway.

I know that you always feared that just such a discovery might be made in the wake of your tibia and femur and that you may feel this subsequent find will overshadow yours. I am not at all sure that is true: the origin of bipedalism is much more important than fresh details about ancient man's brain size or diet, though the overall picture is clearly important. I

316

also think you should know, for the record and not out of any misplaced pride, that it was me who found the jaw, with the teeth and associated cranial bones.

We have also found a wall, which appears to be some kind of shelter, and have sent a paper on it to Nature.

Everyone here sends good wishes but we do all hope that you will think twice about making even more of a fuss than you have already stirred up. It is not dignified and doesn't help in the long run. If you have any feeling for me, please bear in mind what I say.

Natalie broke off and looked across the camp. She had showered not long before and was feeling relaxed. She could see Arnold Pryce sketching outside his tent, Daniel tinkering with the Land Rovers. Kees had a collection of stones on a trestle table outside his quarters. She loved the atmosphere of quiet busy-ness.

No sign of Christopher or Jack. The evening before, Christopher had stopped by her tent. She had thought his visits had ended.

She had been sitting quietly, smoking, and contemplating the very letter to Russell that she was now writing. She ought to have started it before, as she had promised Eleanor she would, but Russell's rawness was difficult to address in a letter; it risked being misunderstood.

'I hear you went to Ngorongoro,' Christopher had said, once she had invited him to sit down.

'Yes. Isn't it spectacular?'

He nodded. 'Much more so than the cave at Ndutu.'

Careful. 'No rock art in Ngorongoro.'

317

'Did you see any of those lions with their black manes?'

'Yes, we did. We had to scramble back into the plane when they turned up.'

'What else did you do?'

What did he mean by that?

'There wasn't time to do much else. We listened to the flamingos making their racket and – oh, yes – I had a flying lesson on the way back.'

'Jack's offered to teach you to fly?'

'Hardly. He just let me take the controls for a few minutes, see how the plane responded. But I loved it and, yes, I'd like to learn.'

'So he'll be taking you up again?'

Natalie hadn't replied immediately. Christopher wasn't just making conversation. His late-night visit wasn't a casual passing of the time.

On their visit to the cave at Ndutu, he had kissed her cheek. The day before, as they were leaving Ngorongoro, Jack had done much the same. She hadn't come to Kihara looking for romance but Dominic was a shadow hanging over her, a weight dragging her down, and she knew that she wouldn't get him out of her system without ... well, without someone else being around.

The cave at Ndutu had been a magical experience but, if she were honest with herself, it didn't begin to compare with the moment they had crested the ring of Ngorongoro in Jack's plane and she had seen what was below and beyond. Nothing had given her the sense of freedom, of exhilaration, of cleanliness: nothing had ever *thrilled* her like that moment.

And, she couldn't help but notice, Christopher had faded into the background since Jack had arrived, until tonight, save for that remark to Jack, the evening before they left for Nairobi for the deposition, when he had admonished his brother to bring back Natalie 'in one piece'.

Two kisses on the cheek by two brothers didn't amount to very much but the fact that they *were* brothers and that Christopher was here, asking the questions he was asking, suggested that something was going on inside him. Both Eleanor and Jack had spoken of Christopher's jealousy – was that what this late-night visit was all about?

Natalie said, 'You're learning to fly – you told me. Why shouldn't a woman?' That distanced the conversation from the three of them.

'It's a pity I haven't qualified yet. Otherwise, I could teach you. Lucky Jack.'

Christopher had got up and left then. Not in a huff exactly, she thought, but certainly rather brusquely.

She told herself she'd have to do something to make Christopher feel easier, with her and with himself. She didn't want to pit the brothers against one another, or get caught in the crossfire. She needed to be gentle but firm. With Christopher she could never–

She looked across to the refectory area and smiled. Some monkeys had got into the camp and Naiva was chasing them away. Natalie went back to her letter to Russell.

I can't face the way I used to face, when I sit and wind down at the end of the day. Since Richard's death, I don't want to relive what I saw that night. You've probably not heard but the local Maasai have said that if Ndekei is convicted and hanged, they will reoccupy the gorge and destroy it. Only in that way, they say, will the crime that Richard and you committed not be repeated. Of course, we are all devastated by this news, if it is actually carried through, but from it you will see that, first, it was right for Eleanor to send you away: you were definitely in danger. And second, you can perhaps imagine what it has done and is doing to my peace of mind. I must give evidence: it's the way I am made, the way I was brought up and I owe it to Richard and to you, Russell, but the dilemma is horrible, irreconcilable. In my first season of digging, amid all the exciting and important discoveries, I am going to be instrumental in destroying the very place that makes everything possible.

And I have to live with it every moment of every day. Every night, when I relax, or try to, it's all I can think of.

I repeat: if you have any feeling for me, Russell, think very hard and do not make more of a fuss than you have already made. You will be doing more harm than good.

I look forward to your next letter.

Natalie.

'Natalie, look down now. That's a sight you can't see anywhere else in the world.'

Natalie did as she was told, and looked down to her left. Set against the champagne colour of the grass was a long, luscious, red-brown streak, black in parts, shining and moving in the sun. Thousands and thousands of animals – wildebeest,

320

zebra, impala – all on the move, all nose-to-tail, all moving at a pace somewhere between a trot and a gallop, stretched out like a great stain on the landscape.

She judged that the aircraft they were in was flying at about a thousand feet, though as this was only her fourth time in Jack's Comanche she was hardly an expert. He had told her he liked to fly low, unlike Maxwell Sandys, who liked to fly high, above five thousand feet, where the air was thinner and faster but the view of the animals nowhere near as good.

It had been Jack's idea that she come. He was giving Christopher a flying lesson – his brother was at the controls right now – and Jack had combined it with an over-flying of the great animal migration that took place in the Serengeti and Maasai Mara, more or less throughout the year. Kees van Schelde was also with them.

'Where are they going?' asked Kees. '*Why* are they going?'

'Just keep her as she is,' said Jack to Christopher. 'Keep on a bearing of a hundred and ten degrees.' He turned in his seat so he could address Kees and Natalie together. 'They go in search of rain-ripened grass. That's what ungulates – hoofed mammals like wildebeest and zebra – feed on. The rains go in a rough circle – north at one point in the year, east at another, south later in the season, and so on – so the animals do too. Right now, they're heading east and south: back out of Kenya, down into Tanganyika.'

He turned back. 'Okay,' he said to Christopher. 'Climb to three thousand feet and then turn for home – that will be a bearing of one hundred and ninety-five degrees.'

Christopher pulled back on the control stick and the aircraft began to rise.

'Christopher!' said Jack in an irritated voice. 'What did I tell you? Say out loud what you are doing, so air traffic control at Kilimanjaro knows what to expect. There are other people in the sky, you know.'

'Bugger! I forgot again. Sorry,' said Christopher. 'Can't they see us on the radar?'

'Yes, but all pilots try to make it easy for them. Our lives may depend on them some day.'

Christopher held the speaker to his lips. 'Tango, Zulu, Delta, one, one, niner, Echo, rising to four thousand feet,' said Christopher.

'Copy,' said a disembodied voice.

'See?' said Jack. 'They *are* paying attention.'

Natalie looked down again and the wildebeest grew smaller as the aircraft rose. She was feeling good.

'Now turn for home,' said Jack to Christopher, 'and don't forget to announce your move in advance.'

'Tango, Zulu, Delta, one, one, niner, Echo. Turning for home on bearing one, niner, five,' said Christopher.

'Copy,' said the voice. 'Happy landings.'

'We are about thirty-five miles from the gorge,' said Jack. 'At this speed, that's about fourteen minutes. Lose altitude to two thousand feet and then stay at that height until you have the strip on visual.'

Natalie kept looking out of the window as they

came in to land. She could see Ngorongoro in the distance, the shimmering surface of Lake Natron, the escarpment of the Rift Valley itself. How she was coming to love this landscape.

'I have the strip on visual,' said Christopher.

'And there are the tents of the camp, to the left,' replied Jack, gesturing. 'Lose altitude to a thousand feet and fly over them. Then climb to two thousand feet, bank to the left and come in again.'

Natalie looked down as they buzzed the camp; she could make out Daniel and Arnold Pryce looking up. She waved.

The aircraft climbed again and Christopher banked the plane till the red-brown strip was ahead of them.

They lost height and speed, and the tone of the engines changed as the wing flaps went down to keep the nose of the aircraft in the correct 'attitude', as Natalie had heard it called.

'What's that!' cried Christopher suddenly. 'On the runway!'

'It's the cheetahs,' said Jack with a chuckle. 'Throttle forward, let your wheels bounce on the strip and go round again. The noise will frighten them away.'

Just then, however, two large cormorants flew across the strip and Christopher cried out. 'What!'

'Give me the controls,' said Jack, reaching across and putting his left hand on Christopher's right arm. 'I have command,' he added, as he pulled back on the control stick and pushed forward the throttle.

The sound of the aircraft's engines deepened as its wheels touched the strip and the plane started to rise again. The fuselage creaked and Natalie felt a sinking in her stomach as the aircraft banked up into the sky. She hadn't really had time to be frightened as Jack had taken over but the skin on her throat now broke out in a sweat. She looked across to Kees: he rolled his eyes and rubbed the palms of his hands on his trousers.

After rising a few hundred feet, Jack throttled back and banked the plane to the left again, steering a smooth circle until they were again approaching the strip.

'Come on, Christopher. Try again.'

'No, Jack, please!' Natalie wanted to cry out. But all she did was look at Kees. Once more he rolled his eyes.

'No, I can't–'

'Yes, you can. There are no cheetahs this time – look, the strip is clear. And all the birds will have gone, too.' He sat back and took his hands off the controls. 'Come *on*.'

The plane lurched and Natalie was immediately sweating all over again.

But Christopher took the stick and lowered the wing flaps; the tone of the engines changed for their final approach.

They lost height.

Natalie spotted the family of cheetahs, well away from the strip this time.

The plane's wheels bumped down – once, twice, three times ... and then the engine sound changed again as they slowed on the empty clay strip.

'Not the smoothest of approaches,' said Jack to

no one in particular. 'But we're safe enough.' He turned in his seat and smiled. 'No extra charge for two landings instead of one.'

'Park the car here, Daniel. Away from all the children.' Eleanor was sitting in the front of the Land Rover, with Natalie and Christopher in the back. Daniel pulled the vehicle over on to the edge of the track and switched off the engine. They all got down.

There was about an hour of daylight left. About two hundred yards in front of them was a large *boma*, or village. Perhaps as many as fifty mud huts, shaped like upside-down cups and built entirely, as Natalie now knew, of dried cattle dung. There had been a time when the very idea would have turned her stomach but not any more. It was amazing how herbivore dung, once it had dried out, became inoffensive. It didn't smell, it was soft, pliable and served admirably as a building material.

The huts were surrounded by the grey-white bulk of dead acacia thorns, fashioned in exactly the way the fence around their Kihara camp was built. Deep inside the *boma* was another ring of thorns: this inner fence protected the tribe's cattle and goats. That's where their wealth was concentrated and any predator – lion, leopard or other tribes – would have to break down two rows of defences to gain entry.

Daniel locked the Land Rover and the four of them began the walk to the village. So far as Natalie was aware it had no name, though a large rock nearby was called Tsuvata.

It had been a week since Jack and Natalie had visited Ngorongoro. Jack was in Nairobi, as he had said. That at least gave her time to think. He hadn't made a big thing about kissing her cheek in the crater. And there had been no more attempts at bodily contact. She was grateful for that. First Russell, then Christopher, now Jack. Yes, she was single; yes, she wasn't either stick-thin or balloon-fat; yes, they were isolated out here in Kihara; no, she didn't object to all the attention. To an extent, it reassured her in the wake of the business with Dominic. Still, the fact that two brothers had now done what they had done ... she would have to be more than careful how she let things proceed. And Eleanor was surely watching.

Today was the 'propitious' day when the Maasai had at last agreed to meet Eleanor and the others, and as they approached the *boma* a handful of men came forward to greet them, each dressed in a dark red cloak, carrying a metal spear and wearing a variety of black and white stone jewellery: bangles on their wrists; rings in their ears, several at a time in some cases; and layers of stone necklaces. None of the leaders smiled but some of the people behind them, especially the children, grinned.

Eleanor stopped and so did Daniel and the others. She said something in Swahili and one of the leaders turned to those in the rear and repeated what she had said in Maasai.

'I said I had some gifts for them,' said Eleanor, turning back to the others.

She now lifted her arms to present a large box

of matches and some firelighters. She knew this would go down well. Anything that made lighting fires easier in the bush was to be welcomed.

The translator finished speaking and one of the leaders stepped forward and accepted the bundle from Eleanor. He smiled slightly and then turned to the translator. The translator listened, and then spoke to Eleanor in Swahili.

'He has thanked us for the firelighters and matches.'

The elder nodded to Natalie.

'He wants to know if you are the witness – I told him yes.'

The elder was speaking again. When the translation was finished, Eleanor said, 'We are invited into his village. Be very careful. We may be offered food and drink. It is very rude to refuse and you must consume all you are given.'

She smiled at the chief elder and as he turned the others in the tribe stood back to open up a passage for Eleanor and him to proceed. Natalie, Christopher and Daniel followed, then the other elders came after them.

Inside the *boma* there were huts on either side of a wide passage which led to the second fence. Near this fence was a table with jugs and plates of food. As the party approached the table, two women came forward holding dishes and cups. On the dishes were what Natalie took to be dried meat. She took one slice. She was handed a cup and it was soon filled with a milky liquid.

The elders had all taken some meat and been given cups. The chief elder made a short speech which was quickly translated from Maasai to

Swahili. Eleanor turned and said, 'We are eating produce of the area: dried kudu and water with honey – the honey comes from local bees. He's making a point, I think, that this is what they do here: produce food. In other words the land is rich and we – the white people – are merely bystanders.'

Eleanor said something in Swahili, smiled, and then swallowed her kudu and drank some honeyed water.

Natalie tackled her meat. It was tough and strong-tasting. She sipped the water and immediately knew she would have a problem finishing it. The water was far too sweet for her. She'd just have to go on sipping and nibbling.

The chief elder – a tall man with a very flat nose and large hands, wearing more jewellery than most – waited for Eleanor to finish her meat and her drink, and then the cup was taken from her. Larger bowls were brought and they both washed their hands.

'This is important,' she said, turning to the others. 'As you can see, with so many predators around, *bomas* are built with defence as the first priority. They don't build villages near rivers as happens in Europe. Elephants might come through at any time and trample over everything. Which means that the water has to be brought a long way: it is very precious.'

Eleanor turned back to the chief elder. He had taken back his spear from the second elder who he had given it to, and now he sat on a chunk of wooden tree trunk that had been brought out. Another had been put in position for Eleanor, and she sat down.

The chief elder put his spear across his knees. Speaking through the interpreter, he began, 'I see you are familiar with our customs.'

It was a barbed beginning. If Eleanor was familiar with their customs, he was saying, how could she have allowed such a terrible thing to happen?

'Chief Marongo,' said Eleanor. 'Thank you for agreeing to see us.' She spoke without shouting but her voice was strong, forceful, pitched so that everyone could hear. 'Thank you for the kudu and sweet water. You are a welcoming man and a fine chief. I hope that you will have many more children and that your cattle will remain healthy.'

Natalie listened to the translator's murmur and marvelled at Eleanor's composure. Her African birth and her long years in the gorge meant she could utter these formalities without sounding in the least patronising – it was clear that she meant what she said.

But then she paused, while she took off her hat and spectacles.

'This is a dreadful situation,' Eleanor said. 'I cannot apologise enough for what has happened. But the two men who broke into your sacred burial ground didn't know any better. You must know that I have sent the second man away, as a mark of respect for your tribe and to preserve a life that I knew was at risk. Despite what has happened, I take your traditions very seriously.'

Eleanor sat upright. Natalie reflected that she had a dignified appearance and manner when it was needed. And it was needed now.

'You and I have known each other over many years,' continued Eleanor. 'Since before you were a chief. We have never had any quarrel before. We have exchanged gifts, you have seen our work in the gorge, we have never interfered with your farming. We have helped you and provided vehicles when members of your tribe needed to get to the hospital quickly.'

She didn't smile as she said, 'You are a wise man, Marongo, a fair man,' pausing just a little as she said this. 'And gracious. If you can find space in your heart, then you have the power to help me now.' She clasped her hands together. 'Please ask the elders to change their minds.'

The chief listened to the translation and then looked around him, at those standing behind him. He turned back to Eleanor and gripped his spear on his knees.

'Tell me, Dr. Deacon,' he said, 'was Dr. Sutton married?'

'No.'

The chief nodded, half to himself. He looked off to his left, and raised his arm, pointing, then beckoning.

Part of the throng of villagers which ringed Eleanor, Natalie, the chief and the others, shuffled to one side and a woman moved forward. She was small, with her hair in braids and she had a beautiful nut-brown skin, paler on her cheeks than elsewhere. She carried a baby and, behind her, two small children wrapped in tiny red cloaks followed, holding hands.

The woman walked up to the chief, who stood and put his hand on her head. He drew the two

330

children to him.

'This is Atape, Ndekei's wife.' He indicated the children. 'These are Tife and Sanga, and the new one, Nbole: the rest of his family.' He smiled as he spoke.

'They are lively children,' said the translator. 'Tife, especially, makes a lot of noise.'

But then the chief's features clouded.

'If Ndekei is hanged or sent to prison for many years, Tife, Sanga, Nbole and Atape will go without food and clothes. Their relatives will have to look after them, producing a widening circle of hardship.'

Chief Marongo's features cleared but he raised his voice. 'Is that fair or just? Ndekei did not break our laws – Maasai laws.' He gripped his spear and stamped it into the ground. 'On the contrary. After the desecration of our burial ground, the land of our ancestors, the elders met. It was noted where Ndekei worked and he was chosen for the task of retribution, as tribal law demands.' Another stamp of the spear. 'It was not a crime, it was an honour!'

The chief turned and spoke to someone behind him. Other heads turned, then an object was passed forward.

Natalie gasped noiselessly and held her hand to her throat.

'According to our custom,' said the chief, 'Ndekei had to bring us something that belonged to the victim, with blood on it, to prove he had done what the elders asked. He did so. Now it has been washed, cleansed of the blood of the victim, and it can be returned to you. We do not want it.'

One of the other elders stepped forward and handed Richard's watch to Eleanor. No one in the camp had noticed it was missing.

She took it without speaking, turned and handed it to Daniel.

As she turned back, the chief said, 'Come.' The elders had already made a gap for him to leave by and he waited while Eleanor and the others moved forward.

He led the way out of the *boma* through some trees, then around the side of a large red rock. Mosses hung in luscious swags from the rock but there was also a smell of burning, where some stubble had recently been cleared away.

Rounding the shoulder of the slope, with the large rock now behind them, they found themselves on the lip of a small valley, cut into by the dried bed of a seasonal stream. On the far side of the dried bed, the valley slope was sprinkled with trees – flat-topped acacias, figs, whistling thorns. Among the trees they could see goats grazing, watched over by two small boys.

The chief beckoned again for Eleanor and the others to come and stand near him. When they were gathered, he lifted his spear and pointed with it to the trees and goats. He spoke in short bursts, to allow the interpreter a chance to catch up.

'This is our burial ground. Notice how wooded it is, how fertile. The gods look after our ancestors. This is our land and has been for generations. Many of our warriors are buried here. We farm this land, we hunt here, we fall sick here and die here. The people we remember are buried here.'

He turned to Eleanor. 'Where will Dr. Sutton be buried?'

Natalie couldn't be sure but she thought she saw Eleanor blush. 'I don't know exactly. In America.'

'And where will you be buried, Dr, Deacon?'

'With my husband, in Nairobi.'

The chief didn't speak for a moment. Together they watched the goats moving between the trees on the slope opposite. The boys lay dozing on rocks, or against the trunks of trees, one of them always keeping a lookout for predators. The wind rose and fell in gusts. Chief Marongo was in no hurry. He let his words sink in.

'Nairobi. Where the government is. A white government that soon will go away. The black man will regain what is his.' The chief turned to Eleanor again. 'The government has its laws, laws introduced by foreigners, the white man. They may suit his way of life but we were never asked about those laws. They are not our laws.'

He pointed with his spear again to a cluster of trees at the upper end of the burial ground. 'Dr. Sutton and someone else stole the bones of one of our finest warriors, a great man. The man, Ollantashante, that your own son was named in honour of. The greatest honour we can bestow on someone from another people. According to our custom, such an act, despoiling a burial ground, is like stealing the bones of the gods themselves.'

'I know—' Eleanor went to speak but the chief

333

silenced her with a wave of his spear.

'The chief asks: Can you have the trial stopped?' the translator said.

'No. I'm sorry. The law must take its course.'

Hearing this, Marongo gave Eleanor a long appraising stare. At length, he spoke, 'And so too with our custom: it will take its course. You have your laws, we have ours. But Dr. Sutton's crime came before Ndekei's. It was unprovoked and therefore, according to our traditions, Dr. Sutton's crime was worse.'

'Please, Marongo,' urged Eleanor.

But the chief stamped his spear again. 'The elders have decided. Ndekei will plead not guilty to murder and will say he was acting according to tribal custom.'

He raised himself up and drew back his head. 'We are not a small tribe – look!' He pointed behind them with his spear.

Eleanor, Natalie and the others turned. Kees gasped.

Beyond the village, all along the skyline, was a line of Maasai warriors, each wrapped in a dark red cloak and carrying a shield and spear. There must have been hundreds of men, throwing a line of shadow from the setting sun. The silence, the sheer numbers and the shadows were very menacing. It was a show of force and a statement of intent.

Eleanor and the others turned back to look at Marongo.

He had taken hold of Tife's hand. 'Ndekei's family will be in court. Kenya is to have independence soon. We shall see how the newspapers respond to the trial.'

'I won't stay long. But I thought you might like to discuss what happened today – my mother has filled me in.' Jack spoke quietly as he lowered himself into Natalie's spare seat outside her tent. This was a new manoeuvre of his but she knew that he had only arrived back from Nairobi just before dusk and, after making the plane safe against the animals, had been late in to dinner. He had brought his own cigarettes and lit one.

Natalie was already smoking one of hers. The stars overhead were as close as ever, glittering against the immeasurable coal-black depth of the universe.

'What is there to discuss? It all seemed pretty straightforward to me. We are locked on a course for collision, all because of something I saw. You should have seen the number of warriors Marongo amassed. They stretched right across the skyline.' She fought to control herself.

Jack let a short silence elapse.

'What did you make of Marongo?'

Natalie drew on her cigarette and breathed out the smoke. She hadn't taken out the whisky tonight. She didn't know why.

'I liked him. Or, I didn't dislike him. You can see why he's a chief. He's strong and, with his own people, probably fair.'

Jack fingered the scar above his eyebrow. 'Before he was elected chief, he used to work here.'

'He did? As what?'

'Oh, nothing specific. He was very strong and

did all sorts of jobs, lifting and carrying. I once saw him and another Maasai, during the rains, lift a Land Rover out of a hole where it had got stuck.' He paused. 'He knows our ways better than we know theirs. And he's not just strong, he's ambitious.'

'Ambitious? I don't understand. Where does ambition come in?'

Jack drew on his cigarette again, and breathed out heavily. 'After independence, Marongo may run as a candidate in the new parliament. This case, this trial, will raise his profile, make him better known. He can't lose. If Ndekei is convicted and hanged, Marongo will become the representative of Maasai grievance; if Ndekei is acquitted, they will both be heroes.'

Natalie shook her head. 'How do you know all this? How *long* have you known all this?'

'You remember my mother was in Nairobi about a week ago, when we went to the crater? Among other things, she met Maxwell Sandys.'

Natalie crushed out the remains of her cigarette. 'Where was your mother tonight?'

Eleanor had not been present at dinner, but had had a tray sent to her tent, something Natalie had never known happen before. 'Is she not well?'

'She's well enough,' growled Jack. 'But I am afraid Marongo's implacability had a big effect on her. She thought–' He shifted in his chair. 'She thought that if she came to dinner, there would be an argument, a fight, that she might say things she would regret. She thinks all this business about "propitious" dates is nonsense. The meeting was held today because Marongo, cunning as he is, knew I would be away in Nairobi and he wouldn't have to come face-to-face with his boyhood friend. The elders were never going to give way.' He sighed, reached forward and put his hand on hers. 'She's right.'

'Hmmn.' Natalie snorted. 'I'm not sure I buy that, Jack. I don't know your mother as well as you do, naturally, but I do know that she's not one to avoid confrontation. She's her own woman, strong-willed, she knows her own mind and this is her home ground. Sulking in her tent is very definitely not your mother's style.' She took a deep breath, considered reaching for the whisky, thought better of it. 'So what's going on?'

Jack took his hand off hers and leaned back. He chewed at his lower lip, taking a fresh cigarette from his pack and lighting it. He breathed out the smoke.

'We had a fight.'

Natalie played with her mother's watch on her wrist. Baboons screamed across the gorge.

'Go on.'

The smell of the campfire came at them in wafts.

'She was sitting in her tent – in that outer room she has, the one with the radio and the first-aid kit. She had just been talking to Maxwell Sandys on the radio-telephone and he had told her about Chief Marongo's political ambitions. She was very low.' Jack brushed his hair off his face. 'Until then, I think, she had hoped that a solution might be found. Yes, Marongo was fairly intractable when you were all in the *boma* but that might have been a negotiating position. After all, I'm

337

sure we could do something to help Ndekei's family – financially, I mean, and Marongo knows that.'

He drew on his cigarette again.

'But once she heard about the chief's political aims, she realised that nothing she could do would make a bit of difference. Either the trial has to be stopped or the gorge will be reclaimed – either outcome suits Marongo's wider aims.'

The drone of a jet reached them from way up high. 'So what did you fight about?'

Jack leaned forward, resting his elbows on his knees. 'I told her she was being defeatist, that it wasn't necessarily a question of Ndekei or us, that we still have plenty of room for manoeuvre.' He fingered his cigarette pack. 'I said: Look–' and he put the forefinger of one hand against the thumb of the other, 'one, we have a knee-joint.' He moved his forefinger to the forefinger of his other hand. 'Two, a jaw with teeth; three, some skull bones; four, a wall; five, some obsidian.'

He risked a smile. 'That's a hell of a lot for a two-million-year-old skeleton.'

'And? So?' Natalie felt like another cigarette but didn't want to smoke more than one a night.

'I suggested that we put our thinking caps on, work out what this creature was like – how tall, what sort of brain size, what his hands were capable of, whether he or she could speak, did he or she have an opposable thumb, what he or she ate – and then call a major press conference, to announce what we have discovered.'

Jack crushed the remains of his second cigarette into the ashtray on the table.

'There's no doubt in my mind that, put together, what we have is of world significance – hugely important. And if we announced what we have, and at the same time made public the threat to the gorge, it would put immense pressure on the authorities to do something, to rein in Marongo and the elders. Our discoveries will put Kenya on the map, culturally but also financially and therefore politically: it adds to the country's importance, will attract tourists and scientists. The economic impact could be significant.'

Natalie nodded. 'I see all that but I don't see what your mother and you had to fight about.'

He sat back again. 'First, my mother *hates* the idea of a press conference because, being of the old school, she believes we must publish in the scientific literature first – in *Nature* or *Science* or *Antiquity*, preferably all three. Second, and even more important, she hates linking the gorge – science – with politics; she hates raising the spectre of the trial in the same breath, so to speak, as the discoveries in the gorge. She thinks it's demeaning, that it tarnishes what we do here.'

He let a pause go by.

So did Natalie. 'I can see all that would make Eleanor uneasy but is that really what you fought about?'

More screaming from the baboons.

Jack nodded. 'It got pretty heated, yes. We were both steamed up, shouting. But it didn't boil over until I said – in the middle of her resistance – that it was a pity our father wasn't still around, that Jock would have instinctively understood what

339

was needed now–'

'Oh, Jack!'

He raised his hand. 'It's true enough. Dad would have *revelled* in this situation. He knew Kenyatta in the old days, argued with him, shouted at him, and Kenyatta shouted back, but there was a respect there, a mutual respect. Dad would have known that the solution to this crisis doesn't lie in secret deals or negotiations with Marongo and the Maasai. It's really about what kind of country Kenya wants to be – a tribal backwater or a modern scientific centre.'

Jack was hunched forward over the table again. He lowered his voice. 'You know, I think the real reason she didn't come to dinner is that she wanted to calm down, to think about what I had said, before she heard what the rest of you had to say. She's jealous of her authority, as you know, but she also knows she has to give way soon – to me and/or Christopher. She just didn't count on me having this particular idea, now. She's not happy with it, and she knows that a lot of publicity, much of it hostile, goes with the territory, but she also knows – deep down – that it could be a way out, a way forward.'

Another long silence, save for the baboons, among whom something disagreeable was clearly taking place.

'What do you think?' He leaned forward.

Natalie rubbed her eyes. The vapours given off by the hurricane lamp were stinging them.

'I can understand your mother's objections. The scientific journals don't like it if you go public first. But yes, I agree, it may be a solution.'

340

In fact, her heart had been lifted by what Jack had said, in a way that it hadn't been lifted in weeks. 'What gave you the idea?'

'Well, in a way, you did.' Jack put his hand on hers again.

'What do you mean? How?'

'When we were in the crater, you said you had talked with my mother about Father's womanising. You also talked about failure, being in your twenties and failing and coming back from failure.' He rubbed the scar over his eye. 'Well, you couldn't know it, but Father would never accept failure. The battles he fought, in the early years of the dig, were amazing and half the time he fought those battles in public, in the media, manipulating them where he could, cajoling where he could, and – I am sure, though I don't know for certain – exaggerating here, fibbing a bit there, being creatively ambiguous somewhere else. All to get his own way, to recover from setbacks.'

Jack smiled ruefully.

'Thinking about my father, and how different he was from my mother, what a showman he was, I suddenly saw that he would have responded to our predicament over the trial in a very different way – and in no time the solution came to me. That's another thing my mother finds hard to swallow: that I've inherited something of my father and that maybe, just maybe, *his* genes could rescue us.'

Natalie was still longing for another cigarette but, for the moment, held off. 'Say you do hold a press conference along the lines you suggest.'

He nodded.

'Wouldn't it provoke the Maasai? Maybe they would move on the gorge *before* the trial. All those warriors are just waiting.'

Jack shook his head. 'That would show them to be savages. Marongo wouldn't want that. His political power will come, if it does come, from showing that their customs are as evolved and as dignified as ours. Don't worry about that.'

He smiled. 'Worry about this instead.' He lifted Natalie's hands and bent his head to kiss them.

For a moment, Natalie allowed her hands to be kissed. But she said nothing and then she slowly disengaged herself. 'I feel a whole lot better than I did half an hour ago. I realise there's a long way to go and that your mother may take some convincing, but your idea has lifted a load from my mind.'

She was impressed, too. Impressed that he had used his interest in – and knowledge of – politics to come up with a solution. What might be a solution.

Jack looked at her, a half-smile along his mouth. Slowly, he reached up and touched the ball of his thumb to her lips, and then to his own lips.

'I said I wouldn't stay long but I have. Forgive me.' He got to his feet and picked up his pack of cigarettes. 'But,' he whispered, 'I'll be back.'

'Found any more obsidian, Kees?' It was the end of the next morning's digging and Natalie was stowing her kit into the Land Rover as Kees approached. They had been working near each other and would drive back together to the camp.

'No. Why are you so interested?'

'You know Mgina? That pretty girl who cleans our tents, who brings the hot shower water?'

Kees nodded.

'She's getting married soon. I wondered if obsidian would make an ideal wedding gift: it's local and she could maybe have it turned into jewellery.'

'Nice idea,' said Kees, 'but I'm afraid I've not come across any more.' He threw some of his things on to the back seat of the Land Rover.

'You know,' she said, opening the driver's door, 'some anthropologists think that obsidian made the first mirrors and they speculate that that's why obsidian was so valued in ancient times – it was felt to have mystical powers, throwing back images of people as if from another world.'

Kees frowned. 'Wouldn't ancient man have seen his reflection in water – in rivers and lakes?'

She nodded. 'Rivers and lakes were worshipped, too, for all sorts of reasons, of course, because life depended on them, but I can quite see that reflections could have been very mysterious to early mankind.'

'When is this wedding?'

'I don't know, in a few weeks I expect.' They both climbed into the Land Rover, with Natalie in the driving seat. Before she could switch on, Kees said, 'I'll keep looking and let you know if I find anything. By the way, I very much admire the stand you are taking over Mutevu.'

Natalie looked at him. 'I didn't think you were on my side.'

He shook his head. 'I'm not. I just mean to say that I admire and sympathise with your inner strength, your steel. I wish I had it.'

Natalie put the key in the ignition. 'I don't understand, Kees. If you agree with everyone else, with the majority, why do you need inner strength? Why is steel so important all of a sudden?'

Kees wiped the beads of sweat from his face with his small towel. 'There's nothing sudden about it. I'm in a much more – what's the word? – a much more *profound* minority than you and I've been *in* that minority for years without daring to tell anyone. That's why I admire you.' He stuffed his towel in the back pocket of his trousers. 'I'm homosexual.'

Natalie said nothing at first. But for a moment she forgot the heat. She reached out and put her hand on Kees's arm. She didn't say anything. She didn't say anything because she couldn't think of anything to say. She knew, at least in theory, that such a thing as homosexuality occurred but she was not aware of having met anyone before who was homosexual, or 'queer' as the unpleasant slang in Cambridge had it, though she was pretty sure some of the fellows at Jesus College were that way inclined. But until now the whole matter had been abstract, distant for her, theoretical. She hadn't really thought about homosexuality except in the most general, disinterested way.

'Why are you telling me this, Kees? And why now?'

'I ... I thought it might give you some comfort to know that I understand what you have been going through, that's all. In some places of the world, people like me are illegal, we are jailed, the churches are against us, no one wants to know us.'

344

He wiped his lips with his hand. 'You feel ... you feel at times that you are all alone here in Kihara – I know, I've seen the way your face tightens, the way you look inside, the way the shine goes out of your eyes and they deaden. Like the other day, after you argued that Western "modern" practices are as old as Maasai traditions, if not older. I should have said something before, I suppose, to comfort you. But I couldn't... I couldn't because it meant ... it meant telling you what I'm telling you now and, with your background, with your father being what he is, doing what he does in the church, I couldn't be certain how you would react.'

'But now you've changed your mind?'

Kees shrugged. 'I've been meaning to say something for days now, as the pressure on you has started to mount. But, as I say, I couldn't bring myself to do it. Now, here we are, just the two of us, with no one else around.' He wound down the window. 'When you are homosexual, you can't help but be sensitive. Remember when I snapped at Jonas, when he was talking about Amsterdam's red-light district? Of course, he assumed I was heterosexual – and part of me hated that assumption. But I was too frightened to come clean: that's what made me snap.' He rubbed his jaw. 'I'm pretty sure that's why Richard Sutton had such a temper–'

'You think Richard was homosexual?'

'I do, yes. I caught him looking at me in a certain way once or twice. I think he had his suspicions about me.' Kees smiled wryly. 'Had we discovered each other, so to speak, then life here wouldn't have been so ... well, it would have been different. But then he was killed and that was that.'

Natalie turned the key in the ignition and the Land Rover's engine sparked into life. She let out the clutch and the vehicle eased forwards.

'I'd be grateful if you didn't tell anyone else what I've just told you, Natalie. Some of my friends back in Holland are beginning to go public – "coming out" they call it – but I'm not ready, not yet.'

She nodded. 'Don't worry, I wouldn't dream of telling anyone else.' She changed up and accelerated as they reached the rough track that led back to the camp. 'But Kees, may I ask you a question?'

'Sure, fire away.'

'I know next to nothing about homosexuality but could a man ... can a man be both homosexual and married?'

He smiled. 'Oh, yes. It's much more common than you might think.' He drank some water from a bottle and passed it across to Natalie. 'I share a flat in Amsterdam with an older man, the cello player I told you about. Hendrik is forty-nine and until five years ago he was married with two children. But, he says now, he always knew, deep inside him, that he was ... well, the way he was, is. And because of the way he was, sex with his wife tailed off, she had an affair – and what Hendrik felt most at that point was, he says, relief. Relief that he could, as he put it, escape. Of course, the children have suffered but for the first time in his life, he is content. He's a wine merchant and didn't want me to come on this dig, but I couldn't turn it down.'

Kees took back the water bottle from Natalie. 'So you see, I – we, Hendrik and me – know all about being in minorities, how tough it is, how you can hardly think about anything else. But at least with you it will all be over after the trial. With me it's going to last a lifetime.'

Natalie nodded as she slowed the Land Rover to negotiate a tiny dried stream-bed. But she didn't really hear what Kees was saying. She was thinking about when she had returned the wellington boot to Mutevu Ndekei and found Richard Sutton standing close by, in the storeroom next to the kitchen.

'Jack! Jack? Are you there?' Natalie scarcely raised her voice. There was more than an hour to dinner, the sun was rapidly setting and the colour was beginning to go out of the day.

Jack appeared. He was holding a book. He smiled. 'A visit from Lauren Bacall. This is a first. Things are looking up.'

'Yes,' she said. 'Fair's fair. You've been to my tent lots of times. I've come to see how you live. Is your tent as tidy as your plane?'

'*Nowhere* is as tidy as my plane,' he growled, grinning. 'So no, you can't come in. I'd be embarrassed and ashamed.'

Natalie grinned. 'That gives me an advantage immediately. As you say, things are looking up.'

She sat on one of his chairs and he sat on the other. 'What's the book?'

Jack showed her. '*Lolita*. For an hour before dinner, I like to break away from the gorge–'

'And read pornography?'

'This is great literature, Dr. Nelson. Sexy, yes, but beautifully written. Have you read it?'

She nodded.

'You think it's pornographic?'

'I think it's pornographic *and* great literature.'

'Can a book be both at the same time?'

'Another time, Jack. What I really came to ask is if there is any news yet on your press conference idea? Has your mother bitten the bullet?'

'No. Complete radio silence so far. Sorry.'

'Can't you push it?'

Jack shook his head. 'It would be counter-productive. We just wait.'

At that moment, however, there was a commotion.

'Jack! *Jack!*'

They both turned. Daniel was running towards them.

'Daniel, what is it?'

'Wildebeest drowning, the Mara river at Olpunyata.' He took a deep breath. 'Thousands of them.'

'Oh no!' cried Jack, jumping to his feet. 'Not again!'

Daniel turned on his heel, without saying any more, and ran off in the direction of the Land Rovers.

Jack threw his book into his tent.

'Jack? What's going on?' Natalie had stood up too.

'Come with me. I'll explain as we go. We must hurry. Leave everything, my mother will make sure all our tents are closed up. We may be some time. *Come on!*'

Natalie, perplexed, followed as Jack pursued Daniel towards the Land Rovers. As they approached, she could see him throwing ropes into the back of the vehicles, loading large game lights, a primus stove and several cardboard boxes.

Daniel and Aldwai got into one vehicle and led the way out of the camp. Jack and Natalie got into the second, with Christopher and one of the other guards in a third. They drove on to the rough, dirt road outside the camp and headed north, which took them down into the gorge and then up the other side. It was coming on to dusk and when Natalie went to speak Jack held up his hand.

'Not just yet. This track is tricky at night, or dusk. Wait till we get through the gorge. It's flatter on the plain.'

All three Land Rovers had their headlights on now though Jack didn't drive too close to Daniel, not wanting to blind him.

They rocked over stones and gullies, slowing every so often so as not to put too much strain on the axles. Jack engaged the low four-wheel drive to ascend the far steep side of the gorge. When they got to the lip and looked on to the plain, Daniel's Land Rover was already a hundred yards in front.

'Now,' said Jack, as the terrain became flatter and smoother and softer, 'you remember that long line of wildebeest that we saw from the plane the other day, when I was giving Christopher a lesson?' He didn't wait for an answer. 'One of the

349

great mysteries of the wildebeest migration is that, although it has been going on for – oh – tens of thousands of years, if not more, every so often the animals choose to cross rivers that are, at the point where they make the crossing, literally impassable. Deep, swift-running, steep-sided. No one knows why, no one knows why they haven't evolved the skill to choose safe crossing places, but every so often a catastrophe occurs. Sometimes ten years pass without anything happening but when it does, when it does, thousands – *thousands* – die. That's what's happened now. We try to save as many as we can.'

Natalie let this sink in. Around them the landscape was indistinct, the darkness descending.

'How far is it?'

'Olpunyata? About an hour and a half.'

Natalie turned in her seat. Christopher's Land Rover was about a hundred yards behind.

'Aren't wildebeest rather big? Big and fierce: dangerous, I mean. What can we do?'

Jack squeezed her knee. 'Yes, wildebeest are huge, savage creatures, with long, curling horns. We can do a number of things, none of them very effective but better than nothing.'

He swerved to avoid a termite mound that suddenly loomed into view.

'People will be converging on Olpunyata from all over the area, just as we are, in their four-wheel drives. Some of us will drive between the animals, try to divert wildebeest who haven't reached the river to cross someplace else, somewhere safer. Then, together, we will shine our headlights on that stretch of the river where they are floundering. That will help at least some of the wildebeest find their way out of the ravine and it will keep predators – crocodiles, lions, hyenas – away. Obviously, in such a catastrophe, such a panic, with wildebeest thrashing about in the water, drowning and being knocked about by the others, they are sitting targets for predators.'

Jack changed gear and drove a little faster, closing the distance between them and Daniel.

'The final thing is to lasso the young. Normally, wildebeest don't calve until December or January but as it's now mid-November some of them will already have produced their young early. They are not so heavy, or anywhere near as fierce, and their horns aren't formed so a couple of men can usually haul them to safety. Sometimes they get separated from their mothers but we can't help that and it's better than dying.'

Natalie looked about her. It was too early for the moon and she could make out almost nothing at all, except the flatness of the plain.

'If it takes two men to pull out even a baby wildebeest why am I here? Won't I just be in the way?'

He grunted as a family of birds, caught in the Land Rover's headlights, hurried out of harm's way. 'Three reasons. We're going to be here all night and well into the morning. Daniel's loaded a primus stove and some tins of soup. We'll all need a break from time to time. Also,' he changed down, to negotiate a deep rut in the track, 'it's quite a sight, all these animals thrashing about in the water. I thought you'd like to see it.'

Natalie nodded. 'And the third reason?'

He changed up again, and accelerated. 'Don't let this go to your head, Dr. Nelson, but I like having you around.'

'Is there any of that soup left?'

'There's plenty – and it's piping hot. Let me get you a mug.' Natalie reached into the back of the Land Rover and took an enamel mug from a cardboard box. She took it to the primus stove and poured the tomato soup into the mug.

'Here you are,' she said softly, handing the mug across. Daniel looked exhausted, she thought.

It was an hour off dawn, almost four-thirty, and they were all dirt-tired. What a night it had been.

Some two dozen four-wheel drive vehicles were drawn up on either side of the Mara River at Olpunyata. All had their headlights full on and some had game lights fixed to their roofs as well, beaming across the river.

When Natalie had first seen the heaving mass of bodies – the wet, black-brown torsos, writhing and flailing, sinking and re-emerging in the water, screaming, squealing, roaring into the night, the white flashes of their distended eye-balls, their horns piercing the flanks of their neighbours, their glistening hooves sinking down the steep riverbank, plunging head-first after the creature that had gone before – she thought she had never seen anything so awesome, so terrible, so final, so *catastrophic*. It was like a scene from one of those huge Victorian paintings about the damned in hell.

Between them, Daniel and Jack and Christopher, with Aldwai's help, had managed to lasso perhaps a dozen young wildebeest and haul them to safety. It was plain, to Natalie at least, that the poor creatures didn't want to be helped and though she couldn't be sure, because outside the range of the headlights it was deadly dark, she suspected that more than one young wildebeest, once released from its rope, had plunged back into the river all over again.

Natalie had found a flat stone between two vehicles where she could light the primus and warm the soup. Daniel had packed a dozen mugs so she had been able to help men from other locations who had answered the call that had gone out on the radio-telephone.

She was standing now, a mug of soup in her own hand, looking down over the lip of the riverbank. She supposed their presence was having some effect but the shapeless, writhing mass of contorted bodies below her seemed as dense and as demented as when they had arrived. The shrieks and squeals and yowling had not ceased. The stench was as bad as ever.

Jack and another man were jointly holding the same rope which was looped around the neck of – as Natalie could now see – a wildebeest that, though not a fully grown adult, was on the large size for a newborn infant. Even by the light of the Land Rover headlights it was difficult to make out the age of the creatures in the mayhem of the river.

Jack and the other man were winning, sort of. Both were lathered in mud and they edged back on to the flat ground at the top of the riverbank. But the animal didn't want to be helped, and writhed and thrashed, pulling them back towards the river. And this one had horns.

The two men heaved, and heaved again, and were back on level ground.

Suddenly Jack took the end of the rope which he had wrapped around his lower back and threaded it into a metal hook on the front of the Land Rover. He tied it in a double knot.

'Good idea,' shouted the other man.

'Hold it there, Ted,' gasped Jack, almost out of breath. He jumped in the Land Rover, switched on the engine and threw the four-wheel traction into reverse. Slowly, he moved backwards as the animal was dragged up the river bank.

Ted whoever-he-was peered over the lip of the riverbank and motioned for Jack to continue. Jack reversed the Land Rover away from the lip of the bank, his wheels spinning in the mud, and Natalie watched, transfixed, as the wildebeest was hauled steadily and reluctantly into view. It thrashed for a moment, squealed, reared up, and then slumped into a sullen stillness. Then it writhed again and called out. Then it lay still again. It moved its head from side to side, looking for someone to blame.

As it reached level ground, however, Ted backed away. Jack killed the Land Rover's engine and got down. 'Watch out!' he yelled as he disengaged the rope from the metal hook.

With the smaller animals, as Natalie now knew, several men would lie on the newborn wildebeest while someone else unwrapped the lasso from around its neck, so it could be used again. But this creature was too big for that. What was going to happen this time?

Sensing level ground, the wildebeest got to its feet and looked around. Steam escaped from its nostrils, rose in clouds from its wet haunches; mud clogged its legs, dripped from its horns. The creature's eyes stared wildly, it was angry and bewildered at the same time. The animal shook its head, swirled its tail and kicked out with its hind legs. Then, lowering its head, it rumbled forward. It was in a panic, understandably enough, entangled in rope, and it charged straight ahead.

Towards Natalie.

'Watch out!' cried Jack again. 'Get out of the light!'

The wildebeest picked up speed surprisingly quickly and Natalie was disconcerted to see how wide apart the tips of its horns were. She stepped back.

Still the animal seemed to be making for her. Natalie was still in the shaft of light from the Land Rover's headlamps. She stepped back again.

On to nothing. There was nothing behind her. Without knowing it, because outside the light beams it was deadly dark, she was on the very lip of the riverbank and had stepped over the edge. She cried out as she fell, dropping her mug with the soup in it, and slithering down the mud of the near-vertical bank, smelling its wet smell. She dug her fingers into the earth, feeling them slither through the mud, encountering small stones but nothing she could hold on to. Her body kept going.

Suddenly her hand encountered something

substantial but she immediately cried out. It was a whistling thorn bush and the spikes punctured her flesh and drew blood. Her face scraped the riverbank, her hair sluiced through the mud, mud caked her eyes, she tasted it on her lips. It clogged her nostrils. Again she dug her fingers into the mud. Again, all she encountered were stones and thorns, too sharp and too quickly gone to hold on to. Still, her body kept going.

She hit a rock and cried out, her clothes snagged on thorn bushes but didn't break her fall. Thorns scored the flesh of her arms as she went by and she called out again in pain.

Her skin was wet, wet with mud, wet with sweat, wet with blood. Like the wildebeest she'd been so close to, the sweat was steaming off her.

How far had she fallen? How far was she going to fall? Was she going to end in the river, a river of sand, mud, blood, all manner of excretable substances and fluids and the natural habitat, as Jack had pointed out, of crocodiles.

Despite the taste of mud on her lips, the hot streaks of pain where the thorns had scored her skin, the grit in her eyes and that clogged her nostrils, she reached out, hoping to hit a branch, a firm rock, something – anything – that would stem her fall.

Nothing. Just mud and thorns, sharp rock that buffeted her shoulder, pummelled her hips, bounced off her skull. Thorns ripped into her neck, sliced into her wrists, drew blood from her cheeks, tore at her shirt. How much further was the water?

Suddenly she hit something and immediately

stopped falling. What she had hit was firm, solid, but not stone-solid – and it was warm. She had, she instantly realised, landed on the newly-dead drowned carcass of a large adult wildebeest, half-in and half-out of the river. All around were thrashing, writhing, vast contorted bodies of animals still alive, still panicking, still squealing and moaning, still kicking, still biting – their twisted, bayonet-sharp horns slicing through the night air, gouging the eyes, necks and bellies of other animals.

The smell of wildebeest was overpowering, the stench of their hot, panic-stricken breath even worse. The dead animal that had broken her fall was being kicked, knocked, pummelled in the mayhem.

How long would Natalie remain safe? What could she do? No one could see her. The lights were shining elsewhere.

She had hit the wildebeest's rump. It was, she realised, lathered in mud and fresh, wet, warm dung. In its panic it had defecated. But she wasn't yet in the river and she had something to hold on to: the animal's tail.

Blood was caking her cheeks, Natalie felt it running across her arms where her wrists had been torn, her hip hurt and her head hurt where she had bounced off some rocks on her way down.

The way she had fallen, she was looking at the river. The light from the four-wheel drive vehicles was mainly up-river of her but she could make out the dense shadowy form of one wildebeest after another, flailing and kicking and twisting in the water. Then she saw – or thought that she saw – a smoother, more sinuous, far more controlled form as it whipped out of the river and, in no time, smoothly slapped back into it. No more than a second passed before she realised she had seen a crocodile swoop on a young wildebeest – one they had obviously not rescued – crush it in its jaws and drag it back down, under water.

What if a crocodile came for the dead animal under her?

Instinctively, she tried to crawl up the river-bank. After two steps, she slithered back down again till she came to rest on the warm, dead wildebeest.

She had to get away. That much was obvious.

Holding the wildebeest tail with one hand, she shook herself free of one half of her jacket. Transferring the tail to her other hand, she shook herself free of the other half. Another wildebeest blundered against the dead one she was holding on to, and she dropped her jacket. It disappeared into the night.

Crying out, she searched frantically with her free hand. Her fingers found the woollen sleeve and she snatched it to her. It was lathered in dung.

Holding the wildebeest tail and her jacket in one hand, she took one step up the river bank and reached upwards. Her hand struck a thorn bush and she whelped in pain. But now she reached down, snatched at her jacket and threw it over the thorn bush. Then she scrabbled for a branch to hold on to, her flesh protected from the needle-sharp thorns by her jacket.

Natalie found a branch; her fingers closed over it. Her jacket did its job and her flesh was spared the thorns. She pulled herself clear of the wildebeest and lay on the bush, *in* the bush, her hand gripping the branch. She pulled her knees up to her chest. Her clothes were plastered in mud, blood, dung and sweat.

She saw all this more clearly, she now realised, because the light had suddenly changed. A game light must at last have found her and was playing on her shape.

She could now see clearly the animal that had broken her fall. It was dark, almost black, a huge bull wildebeest whose carcass was mostly in the water, though its massive horns poked up out of the river into the night air. At least two of its legs were broken and its belly was bleeding where another animal's horns had ripped deep inside, penetrating its heart and killing it. Maybe its back was broken too.

Natalie wanted to look up, to see if anyone was coming for her but her main worry was crocodiles. While she was hanging on to her thorn bush and the massive bull wildebeest was between her and the water, he would surely be the crocodile's easiest prey. But if he were to be taken...

Steam and mud slithered past her. Someone was coming.

As she thought this, the horns of the dead wildebeest rocked from side to side as the animal's head was pulled into the river, until just its hind quarters were left above water. There was only one explanation for that.

Natalie tried hard to crawl further into her

thorn bush but she was no more than six feet from the water's edge. The riverbank was steep but she simply had no idea whether that would deter a crocodile.

A moment later mud cascaded on her head, lodged itself in her eyes, wedged itself in the corners of her mouth. She spat it out. She could feel her hair caked with yet more mud and grit, some of the mud already drying.

She was engulfed in shadow. Then she cried out, a despairing gasp. Something – or someone – hit her hard and knocked her out of the thorn bush, down towards the river. She shouted but her shout was stifled as a hand grabbed her by the back of her collar and the front of her shirt was pulled up against her throat, blocking her windpipe, choking her, so that she coughed and coughed again.

But at least her fall towards the river was broken.

Natalie felt an arm worm its way around her abdomen. It pulled at her shirt so that the skin on her stomach was exposed and she felt thorns scratching her flesh. She was gasping, almost crying, but she felt another arm going round her, and wedge itself under her armpit. She was pulled upwards, then, the arms went all the way round her chest and closed over her breasts. She was held in a tight embrace.

Still the wildebeest stampeded in the threshing water, still the squeals and whinnies bounced off the steep walls of the riverbank, still the stench of dung and blood polluted the air.

The heels of her boots were in the water.

The hands of whoever had come for her tightened over her breasts.

'Okay! I've got her. Pull!' shouted a voice, Jack's. 'Quick, *pull!*'

Off to Natalie's left, animals were still blundering into the river, still sending showers of muddy water over everything. There was the sound of a gunshot.

'One less to worry about,' murmured Jack. Then he shouted again, 'Pull!'

Suddenly, she felt her body jerk upwards. The flesh on her back where her shirt had been pulled free of her trousers scraped against the thorns of the bush she had lain in and she could feel that yet more blood had been drawn. She tried not to call out, but failed. Sweat and tears mingled in her eyes, her nose was running – but her boots were no longer in the river.

'Again!' shouted Jack. 'Pull!'

Another jerk, another rise of a couple of feet.

The smell of Jack was hardly better than her own. He'd been straining all night, in the mud, wrestling with one newborn wildebeest after another. He had as much dung on him as she did.

Another jerk, another thorn bush, then a sharp rock, hard and jagged which scraped against her already-raw shoulder. Natalie cried out again.

Her hair was plastered to her face, it was in her mouth, mud had slipped down inside her trousers where her shirt had been pulled free.

The glare of the game light was very bright now. She could hear other voices.

'Careful!'

'Hold that rope!'

'Watch it doesn't slip!'

She could see the scratches and lines of blood on the backs of Jack's hands that were held over her breasts in the tightest of squeezes. She could now make out the blood and mud and dung on her own trousers and boots.

She felt a hand grab the collar of her shirt. Other fingers were inside her belt and, suddenly, with a heave, she was lifted through the air and then soft grass was under her. Jack was next to her, his arms still wrapped tightly about her.

They both lay there for a moment, exhausted, breathing heavily. In the weird contrasts of the Land Rovers' headlights, she was aware of shapes standing over her.

'Are you all right?'

'Any bones broken?'

'You were lucky you hit that dead animal. We had to shoot that croc. He was taking an interest in you.'

She was too winded to offer any reply. Tears and sweat mingled in her eyes.

Jack too was breathing heavily but he loosened his grip and propped himself up on one elbow. He noticed the blood on her wrist and leaned over, pulling a short branch of thorn from where it was lodged between her shirt sleeve and the flesh of her arm.

'Nearly lost you there,' he said softly.

'That would have solved a lot of problems, eh?' she managed to say.

Jack gave a hard laugh. 'It would have suited my mother – I suppose you're right.' He wiped the blood from her hand with a handkerchief. 'But it wouldn't have suited me.' He kissed her on the cheek. 'Oh, no.'

He gently turned her head towards him with his hand.

'That button on your shirt, the one you didn't do up on the flight back from Nairobi,' he kissed her cheek a second time, 'it's come undone again.'

Threats

Natalie crouched over a patch of sand-soil, feeling the high sun on her back. Her eyes were aching, her spine complaining, her knees sore. Sweat coursed down her face, seemingly intent on searching out her eyes and stinging them. For the moment, palaeontology had lost its allure.

For about a week now, Daniel and she had been searching the wall of the gorge for any more remains of the skull she had spotted. Experience told Eleanor that such fragments could be no more than the size of a fingernail, and that the only way to distinguish them from the surrounding rock was by small gradations in colour and texture. It was like looking for a needle in a haystack that was on fire. And nothing more had been found.

This morning was no better and Natalie decided to call it a day. The others had already gone back to camp and although her discoveries had whetted her appetite for more, the heat was still a problem for her and today the promise of the early afternoon shower was especially tempting. She waved to Daniel and gestured that she would meet him at the Land Rover.

The minute they arrived back in camp, Natalie could see that Eleanor had company. She was sitting outside her tent with a tall, grey-haired man wearing horn-rimmed spectacles. Natalie didn't interrupt them but made straight for her own tent where Mgina soon brought her the

367

buckets of hot water she could shower with.

As Natalie soaped her hands and ran the warm water over her neck – which was comfortingly cooling as it evaporated – she reflected that nothing more had been said about Jack's idea for a press conference to publicise their findings and to force the authorities to confront the dilemma being faced in the gorge. Natalie had asked Jack twice since the conversation outside his tent before the wildebeest stampede if there had been any developments. He had replied that his mother was still making up her mind and that it would be unwise to press her. Natalie could believe that but it didn't help her own predicament, her own peace of mind, and time was passing.

On the night when he'd first told Natalie about his idea for a press conference, when he had kissed her hands, Jack had said he would be back and he had been as good as his word. He didn't visit her every night, but every three or four nights: nights when they finished dinner early, when the conversation didn't linger and for one reason or another no music was played. And he stayed for one cigarette only. That allowed her her privacy and at the same time they learned more about each other – his early life in the gorge, her time at Cambridge, his siblings, her father, Jock Deacon's showmanship, her Ph.D., his Ph.D. Each night as he left, he kissed her hand. But nothing more; he didn't crowd her.

Christopher had stopped coming and had stopped asking her on game drives. She was friendly whenever they sat together at the table, or dug near each other in the gorge, but he was more reserved now than he had been earlier on. There were moments of unease but, overall, Natalie was happy enough.

She cleaned her teeth and brushed her hair. Their discoveries in the gorge, and Jack's attentions, meant that she was thinking about her father less, and Dominic too. There were always the nights to get through, of course, but, somehow, she managed that.

Natalie walked over to the refectory tent. The others were all there, including the tall stranger, who sat on Eleanor's right. A place had been left for Natalie on his right.

He stood up as she entered the tent.

'Natalie,' said Eleanor, 'Natalie Nelson, this is Henry Radcliffe.'

They shook hands and sat down.

Deep runnels ran down the flesh on his face. The stubble on his chin was prominent as was the Adam's apple at his throat. His hands were large. He wore a checked shirt and corduroy trousers, which must have been very hot. He reminded Natalie of her father.

'Henry,' said Eleanor, 'is African field officer for the Bell-Ryder Foundation, the foundation that supports this dig.'

Natalie put on her best smile. 'Have you come to see how your money is being spent, Mr Radcliffe? Or to be updated on the discoveries? It has been an exciting season.'

Naiva came in with the lunch: stuffed vegetables. Natalie helped Radcliffe to water, then filled her own glass.

'I am interested in your results, of course,' he

369

said, reaching for his glass. 'But that's not the main reason I'm here. I'm here because of this.'

He reached down beside him and took a folded newspaper from where it was wedged between his thigh and the edge of the chair. He placed it on the table in front of Natalie.

All eyes were on her. Eleanor, Jack, Kees, Christopher, Arnold Pryce, Jonas Jefferson and Daniel all leaned forwards. Natalie felt a wave of sweat break out at her throat.

The newspaper, she could see, was the *Los Angeles Times*. It was dated only a few days before – someone must have sent it to Africa in a great hurry. It was open to the Op-Ed page where she could see that the main article was headed: 'MY STOLEN DISCOVERY' and underneath that it said, *'Californian Scholar Reveals How a Feud in Africa Forced Him To Abandon the Find of a Lifetime.'*

Natalie forced herself to read Russell's article at a pace that was comfortable for her, so she could take everything in, while lunch was served around her and people began eating.

Russell had certainly gone to town, that much was clear. The *Times* had given him most of a page, and he had not spared any of the grisly details. In fairness, he hadn't spared himself either, blaming himself and Richard Sutton for a silly and tasteless 'prank', as he put it, in raiding a 'local burial ground'. But the blame he attached to himself was nothing to the blame he attached to Eleanor for expelling him from the dig. He described the finding of the knee-joint in full glory, then spent several paragraphs expatiating on what he thought was the significance of the find and then set out what else he could have expected to unearth, had he been allowed to stay. And, as Natalie could see all too clearly, in this regard Russell had been uncannily prescient. He hadn't foreseen the finding of a primitive shelter but he had anticipated the discovery of a skull and jawbones, with teeth – and he would be receiving Natalie's letter any day now, if he hadn't already done so. He ended by saying that the Deacons had had things their own way for too long: he repeated his mantra that there was no room for a 'royal family' in archaeology, that they were putting the interests of the dig before the interests of justice, that more light needed to be let into the 'closed world of African palaeontology', as he put it, and that, as an associate professor at a distinguished university, he would be approaching the Bell-Ryder Foundation to request that they review their procedures in future.

Natalie finished the article and, without raising her eyes, folded the paper and pushed it to one side. She pulled her lunch towards her.

'What do you think?' said Christopher. He was sitting next to his mother, directly across from Radcliffe.

'He's delivered what he promised,' said Natalie, chewing, still not looking up. 'No more, no less.'

'He's accused me of unprofessional conduct, of damaging his career, of being an authoritarian. Highly damaging – I could sue.'

Now Natalie did look up, to see Eleanor staring at her grimly.

'You won't though, Mother, will you?' said Jack.

'That's just what Russell would want – a real scrap in court, in front of the press. He couldn't lose.'

Eleanor ignored him. She picked at her food without any real enthusiasm. Addressing no one in particular, she said, 'Does anyone think I should reply? Or would that be prolonging the fight?'

Radcliffe put down his knife and fork with a clatter and all eyes turned to him. 'I think yet another article would be a mistake, Eleanor, though of course you must make up your own mind.' He drank some water. 'But I'm bound to say that I didn't just come here to update myself on your results – though that's why I usually come.'

Everyone had gone very quiet. Eleanor gently laid down her fork and leaned back in her seat.

'I have a message from head office in New York. They've been got at by Richard Sutton's father, Richard Sutton Senior. He is apparently a big donor and he's been throwing his weight around, threatening to–'

'I don't believe this,' hissed Eleanor. 'The foundation ought to be bigger than that.'

'It is!' Radcliffe reacted sharply. 'It is. He was given very short shrift, I can tell you. As you know, we have an academic committee and a finance committee and a public affairs committee, and their activities are kept entirely separate. Only the secretary general of the foundation sits on all three.' He gripped his water glass. 'But I can't hide from you the fact that the foundation hates this sort of controversy, and the sort of lurid sensational publicity it engenders. It's not what palaeontology is about and it frightens away potential donors.'

'Then tell your secretary general about the discoveries we have been making, the ones we have made since Russell was forced to leave – the discoveries mostly made by Natalie here.' Eleanor reached forward and laid her hand on Radcliffe's arm. 'Henry, we're having one of the best seasons we've ever had. Perhaps *the* best.'

Radcliffe nodded. 'I'll do my utmost, certainly. You know I will.' He glanced briefly at Natalie and smiled, then turned back to Eleanor. 'But you must let me deliver my message. If there is any more bad publicity, any more controversy which has nothing to do with science, then I am instructed to tell you that you can forget funding for next year.' He finished his water. 'I'm sorry.'

There was silence around the table. But only for a moment, before Christopher said, 'But you know there's going to be a trial, right? That's inevitable. Does that count as bad publicity?'

Radcliffe took a pair of spectacles from his pocket and began polishing them with his napkin. '*Is* the trial inevitable? Trials sometimes get called off, for any number of reasons. What's the latest?'

'Worse even than you know.' Eleanor sat back again and took off her eye glasses, laying them on the table in front of her. 'Not only does the trial go ahead, with all speed, but the local Maasai have told us that if Ndekei is convicted and sent to jail or hanged, as he certainly will be if the verdict goes against him, they will reclaim the gorge and destroy the areas where we have been digging. The idea behind that is to prevent a recurrence of the original crime, the raid on the burial ground. So if Ndekei is convicted we shan't need your funds, Henry. There'll be nowhere to dig.'

This time a much longer silence fell over the table, during which Naiva took away the plates. On several the food had scarcely been touched.

At length, Radcliffe spoke. 'Will Ndekei plead guilty, or not guilty?'

All eyes turned to Natalie but Jack answered. 'He will admit to killing Richard, but he will say he acted under local Maasai law, as retaliation for the attack on their burial ground. He will say he was chosen by the elders for the task–'

'Which is true enough.' Eleanor was unable to contain herself any more. 'We paid them a visit, met the woman who will be widowed if Ndekei hangs, and his children. Ndekei was acting according to Maasai custom.'

'This gets more difficult,' said Radcliffe after yet another silence. 'We have a new policy document coming out later this year, and respect for local customs is high on our list of priorities. We shall be requiring all recipients of Bell-Ryder funds to sign an undertaking that they will abide by local customs.'

Another long gloomy silence around the table.

Then, very quietly, Eleanor said, 'Jack has had an idea to get us out of this mess.'

All eyes turned to her.

'I'm in two minds about it myself, because it's unscientific but ... well, Jack, you tell Henry.'

374

Jack drank some water. 'My mother is right. We've had, we *are* having, a very successful season, and it's not over yet.' He outlined his plan for a press conference, to publicise what they had unearthed and how it would counter the threat by the Maasai to reoccupy the gorge.

Radcliffe listened intently. When Jack had finished, he said, 'When is Ndekei's trial scheduled for?'

'Early to mid-February,' Eleanor replied.

'So your press conference would have to be before that.'

'Yes, of course,' Jack said.

'Today is the twenty-first of November. You wouldn't have time to publish your results and your inferences, your interpretations, before the conference?'

'No!' snapped Eleanor. 'That's what I meant when I said it was unscientific. We would be acting like *journalists!*'

'But it might break the logjam,' said Jack, equably but forcefully.

'How, exactly?' queried Radcliffe.

'We would be facing the authorities – black Kenyans and white Kenyans – with what kind of country they have, or want to have. Do they cling to their old customs or look forward? The Second World War is long over, colonialism is coming to an end, the empire is being dismantled, air travel is growing, more and more people will have holidays abroad – why not in Africa? Why not Kenya? Why not the gorge? The gorge is where mankind began, *all* of mankind. The gorge shows we are all one people. In some ways it's the most precious location in the entire world – who would want to destroy it? The Maasai would have the whole world against them.'

Radcliffe nodded. 'But what could the authorities do? Have troops occupy the gorge? I hardly think–'

'No! No! Nothing like that.' Jack was almost shouting. 'But Chief Marongo has political ambitions. With a man like that there's always the chance of a deal.'

Radcliffe wiped his lips with his napkin. 'Eleanor, what do you think?'

'I don't know what I think, that's why I haven't brought it up before. Jack first mentioned his idea a little while ago and I tried to put it out of my mind. It's not science, the editors of *Nature* and *Science* and *Antiquity* would hate it and might not publish our findings any more. It's ... it's *showbusiness!* We'd be a laughing stock.' Her fingers grappled with her spectacles.

Radcliffe rubbed his eyes. 'I'm not sure the foundation would be in favour. I don't think we'd object to a press conference in itself, not if you timed it to coincide with publication. In fact, we'd approve. But if you went ahead *before* publishing and were then criticised, or shown to have got something wrong, and if the professional journals turned against you because you'd gone the showbusiness route, as you call it, I don't think that would go down well.'

Jack slapped the table. 'It's *exactly* what my father would have done, in the circumstances.'

Radcliffe looked bemused. He wasn't often spoken to like this, not in remote parts of the world where the foundation's funding was the sole means of support. He looked across to Eleanor but Jack didn't give him chance to speak.

'This is a crisis, Henry. The usual rules don't apply. We have a knee-joint, a jaw, with teeth and some skull bones, all from the first form of humanity that walked upright. These fossils exist whether they are published in *Nature* or not. Together, they rewrite early history. Think what else we might find here.'

He slapped the table again.

'We also have a wall, mankind's first construction. That's a whole sensation in itself. Hardly the beginnings of high culture, but the beginnings of *something* and maybe something more important. If my father were alive, he'd grasp the dilemma instinctively. He never minded the showbusiness side, as my mother dismisses it. A little showbusiness – make that a *lot* of showbusiness – has often been necessary in the past to raise funds and attract attention to what we are doing here.'

He took a deep breath. 'In my view it's necessary now. If the future of the gorge is more important than Richard Sutton, then it's more important than the niceties of where we publish our articles.'

'Yes, but–'

'I haven't finished!' hissed Jack.

He pointed at Natalie.

'Two of the discoveries were made by Natalie here. It's her first season in the gorge but obviously she has the eye. And she, of course, is the one who saw Mutevu Ndekei sneaking through the night on his way to...' and he tailed off. 'We owe it to her to ... she's been put in an impossible position and if we take the fight to the authorities, broaden the context, it lifts some of the pressure off her.'

Another long silence followed. The only sound came from Naiva moving around, lifting plates, placing the fruit bowl on the table, refilling water glasses from the jug.

At length, Eleanor said quietly to the table in general, 'Shall we take a breather, cool down, reconsider?'

Radcliffe shook his head. 'I don't need to. I can tell you what the foundation's position will be right now. I understand Jack's argument, and I can even see that what he proposes might make sense tactically in the circumstances. I also agree that Jock would have been up for a fight, ready to make a spectacle of the whole business.'

He drank some water. No one else spoke; he had the floor.

'But Jock's been dead for however long it is – five, six years – and the world has moved on. Kenya is about to get independence and the new government, whoever it is, will no doubt want to make its mark. So who can possibly predict how they will respond to what you throw at them? I don't know and you don't know either.' He took a deep breath. 'So I have to tell you that any departure on your part from regular scientific procedures will incur the censure of the foundation and the immediate cessation of all funds. In other words, and to make everything absolutely plain, if you go ahead with this press conference *before* you publish formally, in one of the foundation's approved journals, the next tranche of your money, due on the first of February, will be forfeited.'

Henry drank more water. He gulped at it as if it were something stronger. 'Would you like to take a breather now, and reconsider *that*?'

Somewhere, a long way overhead, an airplane droned across the black sky. Natalie looked for its identification lights but could see only fathomless numbers of stars.

What a roller coaster this evening had been. No one had wanted a return to the fight at lunchtime so the conversation had been confined to science – to the discoveries they had made and what the implications were. And Eleanor had taken the lead in suggesting they have coffee next to the fire, listening to Jack's records. So far, so good.

But then Jack and Christopher had started arguing over where else, in the Rift Valley, was the best place to dig if Kihara was taken away from them. Radcliffe's advice had been sought – his foundation supported other excavations and he visited those sites – but that raised the question of funding and in no time the arguments of lunchtime were reheated.

Natalie had left in the middle.

She had never thought much about funding and mention of the February deadline at lunch had alarmed her. So much was happening so quickly. At least Radcliffe had been crystal-clear in what he had said, however unpalatable his message was. How different from what Kees had told her. He didn't know its significance but it had ... well, it hadn't so much alarmed her as perplexed her and that was just as bad. Had Richard been homosexual? Had he been in the storeroom with Ndekei for some bicarbonate of soda or for some other reason? What was she thinking? That there was some sort of relationship – a sexual relationship – between Richard and Mutevu? And, if there was, did it have something to do with Richard's murder? And if it did, how did that change her understanding of the upcoming trial? Had Mutevu killed Richard for personal reasons and was he now hiding behind Maasai traditions? If so, then she had all the more reason to give evidence.

But how could she ever be certain that Richard was homosexual? Who could she ask? Kees had sworn her to secrecy over his own situation.

'I'll swap you another free flying lesson for a shot of whisky. I badly need a drink after the day we've had.' Jack slumped into the spare seat.

She had the small cap in front of her.

'Take it all,' she said, moving it across the table. 'You earned it.'

He sipped some whisky and looked up at the stars.

Natalie watched the muscles in his throat as he swallowed. Tonight he looked more like Montgomery Clift than ever. 'Will your mother come round, do you think?'

He shrugged. 'I really have no idea. In any case, it's not so much *if* she comes round, as *when*.'

'Oh? Why?'

He broke off a piece of chocolate and handed it to her. 'We can't just hold a press conference any

380

old time, in any old place. It takes time to arrange and it will have to be in London or New York.'

'What!'

'Sure, the big British and American newspapers aren't going to send reporters all the way to Nairobi for a press conference. We have to go to them. All that takes time and money to arrange *and* we have to prepare what we are going to say.'

Natalie listened in silence. It hadn't occurred to her that the press conference would have to be in London or New York but she could see it made sense both practically and politically, and the thought filled her with gloom. It would take time to organise and be costly. Then another gloomy thought occurred to her. 'If you hold the press conference in London or New York won't you only succeed in putting up the backs of all the Kenyan politicians who are in a position to help you? Won't they see it as – what's it called – cultural colonialism?'

He grunted. 'Maybe they will, but if we can get our achievements, and our dilemma, into the London and American papers they can exert much more pressure than the local rags here. We're in a fight and we need to use the biggest weapons available to us.'

Jack reached across the table and pushed the whisky towards her. 'Look,' he said softly, 'I think we should take matters into our own hands.'

'What do you mean?'

'It will save time. You write up your findings on the jaw and teeth, and what you think they mean. Arnold Pryce can help you on diet. I'll do the skull, since I'm more experienced in that department than you. Russell's already done the knee-joint. Kees can do his hand-axe analysis. We'll get a set of papers all ready to send to *Nature*, technical stuff, but we'll also collaborate on an interpretive paper. That will become the basis of any press release. That way, if and when my mother does come round, we can be ready to move immediately. What do you say?'

'Won't she see it as us going behind her back?'

'No, it's not as if we are planning to publish anything without telling her. This is just preparation. If she finds out, it may help her make up her mind in our favour.'

'*Our?*'

Jack grinned.

'Don't get me wrong, I still have that dreadful view: that the gorge is more important than Richard Sutton. I know that offends you. But in my judgement Marongo's political ambitions are his weak point and the best chance we all have is to exploit that. Which makes you and me temporary allies.'

'Temporary?'

'For the duration of the fight, certainly.' He got to his feet and stood over her. 'After that...'

He bent down and kissed the hair on her head.

Dear Natalie,

I still haven't heard from you. What am I to conclude from that? That you are too busy to write? That you have already forgotten the intimacies we shared? That you have so gone over to the other side that you now cannot be bothered to keep me in touch with what is rightfully mine?

Let me ask you this, Natalie: do you really want to make an enemy of me? Palaeontology is a small world, a small world in which I am not without friends, without allies, in which I am not a bit-player, even if I say so myself.

Remember that the future of the discipline is here, in America; this is where the funds are and therefore this is where the action will be. Do you really not understand that? Is it too much for me to ask you to write?

Remember that Richard Sutton Senior used to fund the digs that his son was a participant in. So beware: he knows the score and he knows how to make things happen. If he decides to continue his interest, as a memorial to his son, you might be part of that, but not if you continue to act as you are acting – or rather, not acting.

Please write soon, or I shall conclude the worst.

Fondly, for the moment,

Russell

Natalie put the letter on her table. Radcliffe had brought some post and Eleanor had given it to her at dinner.

Oh dear. Russell, hunkered down in California, miles from the action, as he no doubt thought of it, was growing increasingly bitter. Her letter must have crossed with his – it clearly hadn't reached him yet. And when it did, would it help?

She stared into the darkness, listening to the theatre of the night. Had she mishandled Russell? Was that question fair to herself? His 'stampede' mode had got the better of him. Did he know any better? Could he behave any

383

differently? She doubted it. That was the mode that had brought this whole mess into being in the first place.

But, another thought struck her: if Kees was right about Richard, and Richard *hadn't* been killed because of the break-in at the burial ground, Russell had been wronged. What a mess.

She allowed her thoughts into areas she wasn't sure she wanted them to go. Lately, some of Natalie's thoughts had developed an energy – and a direction – all their own. She knew why, even as she was reluctant to acknowledge it.

Months ago, years in fact, Dominic had awakened her sexual side. She had been lucky. He was an experienced man, even an expert if that word applied in such a context. When the affair had ended, she had resumed the existence she had had before Dominic: celibacy. She hadn't expected anything different.

But then, amazingly, and secretly, and totally surprisingly, amid the danger and panic and smells and shadows of the wildebeest catastrophe, Jack Deacon had rescued her and, in the process, wrapped his hands around her breasts.

And she could admit it now, at this distance, she had *enjoyed* the sensation. More accurately, she had enjoyed the thrill. More accurately still, she enjoyed the memory of the thrill, for if she were truly honest the memory was more potent than the original sensation, which had been alloyed with fear. Was that normal? Was *she* normal? Dare she admit any of this to herself? Dare she admit that, after however many months it had been since Dominic's abrupt and humiliating departure, her body – if not yet her mind – was giving notice that what had once been awakened could never again be entirely dead, totally inert? That there was something inside her that brought to mind a word, a feeling that she was half-ashamed of, half-embarrassed by, that didn't fit the sort of personality she thought she was, that she wanted to be. That feeling, that word, was *craving*.

Natalie was embarrassed by these thoughts, yes, but she was now beginning to realise that they were too recurrent to dismiss. When Jack had put his hands on her breasts, he may or may not have had thoughts other than of her immediate safety in mind but whatever his intention, or lack of it, something had been triggered – rekindled, reignited, rescued – in Natalie. It made her uneasy to feel this way, but that she felt as she did there was no denying.

Did that mean her body had got over Dominic before her mind had? Was that how these things worked?

An image of the black-maned lions of Ngorongoro came into her head, and their rapid copulating. So far as she knew, animals didn't have the kind of problem she was preoccupied with; they were too busy surviving.

Her thoughts went back to Kees. He was busy surviving. How terrible to be locked away in a world that couldn't be acknowledged. Not for the first time she told herself that her isolation would end with the trial, but would he ever be liberated?

In the distance an elephant trumpeted. She loved that sound, it was so joyous, and she waited to see if any other elephants answered. But none did.

Natalie sat brushing her hair. Although she was normally obsessive about her hair-brushing, this morning it had a different aim. It was what the ethologists would call 'displacement activity' or 'avoidance behaviour'. She knew, from things she had overheard the previous day, that Radcliffe was leaving after breakfast and the blunt truth was she didn't want to see him again before he left. She knew it was weak of her, that the arguments wouldn't leave with him, but even with Jack's brainwave about the press conference she felt badly outnumbered as it was, without Radcliffe adding to the arithmetic. Alongside the others on the dig, she could lose herself in work – and they let her. Radcliffe, on the other hand, was a standing reproach, an implied threat, and a symbol of the consequences of her giving evidence. She brushed away.

A cup of coffee wouldn't have gone amiss but there was no sign of Mgina.

Suddenly, Natalie heard a plane. She went out and looked up. The sun was as fierce as ever and the plane was coming out of the sun, which beat down on her face, hurting her eyes. Who was it now? Radcliffe's plane had over-nighted with him, so their little airstrip was going to be choked.

The plane came closer, lost height, and then buzzed the camp. It was a white and blue twin-engined six-seater and it climbed away in preparation for the circuit it must make before approaching the strip. Was it someone to do with the trial? God, she hoped not. She returned to her hair-brushing.

For half an hour, she fiddled with her clothes and her tent, rearranging this, refolding that, airing something else. She tried to convince herself it needed doing but she knew she was just killing time. It was still not seven o'clock when she heard one of the Land Rovers start up. Natalie looked over to the trees, where the vehicles were kept in shade. One of the odd-job men was driving out of the camp with an empty vehicle. So this was not Radcliffe leaving but someone else being picked up from the airstrip.

Normally, at this time, she would have already breakfasted and be making her way down to the gorge. But this morning there was no sign of anyone going that way and she knew there wouldn't be until Radcliffe had departed. Natalie couldn't imagine what had been said the evening before, after she had left and Jack had followed her. Had the others talked on into the night, trying to work out what to do? Were they still discussing it now, at breakfast?

There was no more she could do in her tent. Everything capable of being tidied had been. There was not a wrinkle on the covers of her bed, not a speck of dust anywhere, nothing was out of place. But there was still no sign of anyone gathering at the Land Rovers, ready for work or Radcliffe's departure. She sat at the entrance to the tent, where the flaps were pulled back.

The argument between Christopher and Jack the previous evening had upset her, and it had embarrassed everyone else. They had been discussing a potentially straightforward theoretical issue – where else in Kenya or Tanganyika they could dig if the gorge was reclaimed by the Maasai and closed to excavation. Jack had favoured a site in the north, near Lake Rudolf, on the grounds that a lakeshore was a likely place for human settlement. Christopher had favoured a smaller gorge in a different tribal area, to the west.

The discussion had been fairly equable until Eleanor had remarked that she inclined to Jack's view, when Christopher had exploded.

'You always take Jack's side,' he had shouted. 'You always did, even when we were children.'

'I did not!' hissed Eleanor, her face colouring. 'And if I do now, it's for a reason. Lake Rudolf is miles from the Maasai.'

'I thought Jack was supposed to *be* a Maasai,' Christopher said. 'Fat lot of use he's been so far.'

'Christopher!' cried Eleanor again.

'No,' Jack had intervened but gently. 'He's right.'

Eleanor wouldn't be quietened. 'What ideas have *you* had, Christopher, what have *you* done to help?'

Jack put his hand on his mother's arm. 'Steady.'

'See!' cried Christopher, getting up and pointing at Jack's hand on his mother. 'What a lovely couple you make.' And he had stormed off into the night.

In the embarrassed silence that had followed, Natalie had found herself wondering if, unconsciously and despite what she had said, Eleanor did favour Jack, if not above her daughters, then

388

above Christopher. As an only child, Natalie had never experienced jealousy – not the familial kind, anyway – and, much as she liked Jack, she felt for Christopher. If Jack was his mother's favourite and now she, Natalie, had developed a similar preference, then on top of what had happened with the Gisella woman, Christopher must be suffering.

She felt for him, but there was nothing she could do.

Natalie looked up. The Land Rover was back, clattering into the camp and pulling to a stop in the shade of the thin trees where the other vehicles were parked.

Natalie polished her sunglasses as she watched a white man and woman get down from the Land Rover and follow the black driver as he led them to the refectory tent. The man was tall, thin, wearing a sand-coloured lightweight suit but with no tie. The woman, smaller, stocky and broad around the hips, wore jeans and a white shirt. She also had on a pair of large sunglasses. Even from where Natalie was seated she could make out the woman's lipstick.

Mr and Mrs Richard Sutton Senior.

She sighed. No more work today.

On the other hand, and looked at in a different light, reinforcements had arrived.

She heard a burst of conversation from the refectory tent. Introductions were being made. It was time she put in an appearance.

Natalie went to the mirror that hung from a post in her tent. She made sure again that her hair was tidy, that her shirt was neatly tucked into her trousers, and the buttons were properly buttoned, that her nails were clean, and she treated her mouth to just a touch of lipstick. Then she set off.

The scene resembled a cocktail party. A dozen people were all standing in the small area outside the refectory tent, next to the dining table, shaking hands and making introductions. As Natalie approached, Eleanor stepped forward, and said, 'My dear, *there* you are. We wondered what had happened to you. Come and meet Mr and Mrs Sutton, who've just flown in.' She waved Natalie forwards with a vague gesture.

Radcliffe was in the background, bending and listening to something Mrs Sutton was saying. Everyone was being very polite, painfully polite, Natalie decided. The fireworks would come later.

'This is Richard Sutton Senior... Dr. Natalie Nelson.'

Natalie held out her hand and Sutton seized it with both of his. 'Russell told us all about you. I'm pleased to meet you. We are relying on you, for justice.'

Nothing like being plunged in at the deep end.

Sutton had turned and was calling to his wife. 'Nancy. *Nancy!* Come and say hello to Dr. Natalie Nelson, the woman who's going to be a witness. The woman Russell North told us about.' He turned back to Natalie. He still hadn't let go of her hand. 'Nice guy, Russell North. I understand you and he were great buddies.'

Natalie nodded weakly. 'Buddy' was not exactly how she would have described Russell.

Nancy Sutton eased her way forward and held

390

out her hand for Natalie to shake. Only now did Richard Sutton relinquish control.

'My!' Mrs Sutton said. 'You are every *bit* as pretty as Russell said you were.' She took Natalie's hand. 'I am only sorry we have to meet in such dreadful circumstances.'

Natalie nodded again. 'I'm really sorry, too, for both of you. It was brave of you to come.'

Nancy Sutton shook her head. 'No,' she said in a half-whisper. 'When something like this happens, you want to see everything for yourself.'

'And so you shall,' interjected Eleanor, who had been listening to this exchange. 'I will show you everything myself, but I must just say goodbye to Dr. Radcliffe here, who is flying to Nairobi this morning. He and I just need a few words together, then I can give you my full attention.' She beckoned to Naiva, standing by the dining table. Turning back to the Suttons, she said, 'Would you like some coffee? You must have got up very early this morning to be here by now. You must be dying for something.'

'Coffee would hit the spot,' said Richard Sutton.

'I'll be ten minutes, no more, I promise,' said Eleanor. And she led Radcliffe away. As he went, he nodded to Natalie and mouthed, 'Goodbye.'

Natalie, having gone without breakfast, suddenly realised how badly she needed a coffee herself, and she ran after Naiva, to tell her to bring an extra cup.

When she returned, Nancy Sutton stood up. 'Is there such a thing as a ladies' room, my dear? The plane *was* tiny.' She smiled.

Natalie smiled back. 'You can use the one in my tent. Come on.'

Natalie reached her tent first and showed Nancy Sutton through to the back, where the shower and latrine were located. 'I think there's everything you'll need but shout if anything's missing. I'll be out front.'

'Thank you, dear. I'm sure I'll be just fine.'

Minutes later she reappeared. Her lipstick had been freshened, her hair brushed, and a bright blue bandana had been tied around her neck. It brought out the blue in her eyes and provided a lift to her appearance, drawing the eye away from her figure. Natalie admired that.

As they approached the refectory tent, they could see that Eleanor had returned. She was talking to Richard Sutton and helping herself to coffee. She lifted the cup and addressed Natalie.

'Radcliffe got off okay. I gave him copies of your paper. I haven't had chance to tell you yet, but I heard this morning on the radio-telephone from *Nature* – it's been accepted.'

'But that's wonderful,' said Natalie, her features creasing into a smile. 'Great news.'

Eleanor nodded sardonically, as if to say 'Yes, but...'

'What paper is this?' Richard Sutton put his coffee cup back on the table.

'Natalie discovered what we think is a wall, a shelter. Maybe man's first construction. We think it may have been built by the individual whose knee-joint Richard and Russell and Daniel found. I'm sure Russell told you–'

'Yes,' said Richard Sutton quickly. 'Yes, he did.'

Eleanor nodded. 'Look, if you're rested and refreshed,' and she looked at Nancy Sutton, 'why don't I show you the gorge, the general layout and where our various finds have occurred?'

'And will Natalie come with us?' Sutton had taken off his jacket. His shirt revealed a slight build.

'I think not.' Eleanor almost snapped the words, and then seemed to regret her tone. 'You can see Natalie when we return. And if we are to talk about your son, it should be confidential.'

Sutton shrugged. 'So long as we can talk with Dr. Nelson afterwards, it's fine by me.'

Eleanor led the way across to the Land Rovers. Natalie guessed why she wanted the Suttons to herself: they could make trouble and Eleanor needed to get across her point of view first and uncontaminated by anything Natalie might say.

She watched them get into the vehicle and drive out of the camp. She sat at the refectory table and helped herself to what was left of the coffee. Natalie reflected, as she had reflected before, that in some ways science, though she loved it, sometimes misled her. So enamoured was she of the scientific process, of publication in professional journals, where the best arguments eventually won out, that she tended to look upon her private life in the same way. In this whole murder business, she had assumed that she had the best argument and that the judicial process – as much a rational world as science – would take its course. Her evidence was, in a sense, impersonal. She had seen what she had seen, made an observation much like a scientist carrying out

393

an experiment. It was for the court to decide the value of her observation.

But that, of course, was not how others saw it. It was not how Eleanor or Jack or Daniel saw it. It wasn't how the local Maasai saw it, it wasn't how Russell saw it and, almost certainly, it wasn't how the Suttons saw it. Eleanor was getting her argument in first, so it would have maximum force. It was hardly scientific but it was very human.

Natalie walked back to her tent. There had been no sign of Jack and no sign of Daniel. Maybe they had gone into Karatu, for supplies. With no prospect of work today, she tried to read while she waited for the Suttons to return from the gorge but she found she couldn't concentrate. She lay on her bed and, to her surprise, almost immediately felt drowsy.

That was very unlike her, she told herself. This whole business must be taking its toll.

Kees couldn't have known when he had told Natalie about Richard being homosexual what effect it would have on her. But the extra level of complexity, the confusion and mystery it sowed in Natalie's mind about the real reason for Richard's death only served to tire her even more. It was a conundrum she might never resolve.

She lay back on the bed. There was still no sign of Mgina.

Natalie jerked awake when she heard a Land Rover. Lord, how long had she been asleep? Her watch said 10.45 – more than two hours had passed.

She rolled off the bed and looked out of her tent. She was conscious that her shirt had come out of her trousers and, absently, she tucked it back in. Her flesh still showed scratches and bruises where she had been cut and knocked during the wildebeest stampede.

Jack and Daniel were getting down from one of the Land Rovers. Jack looked over and waved. She waved back. They had been shopping, for each was carrying bags: bulging leather carriers like those used by cricketers back home. Before they had gone very far, though, another Land Rover entered the camp, generating another cloud of dust. Eleanor and the Suttons were back.

Natalie tidied her bed for the second time that morning and sat on the canvas chair outside her tent as the Suttons got down from their vehicle. Eleanor was talking to Jack, then turned back to the Suttons before gesturing towards Natalie. She pointed to her watch – perhaps telling them what time lunch would be – then she trudged after Jack and Daniel.

The Suttons looked across to Natalie and started to walk towards her.

She went back into the tent and retrieved the second canvas chair. She pulled back the flap of the tent further. Someone could sit on the bottom end of the bed.

'How was the gorge? What you expected?' She waved Nancy Sutton to her own chair and waited while her husband chose which seat he wanted. He opted for the bottom end of the bed.

'Well, a gorge is a gorge,' he said, sitting down. 'The heat doesn't hit you until you are right there, and the vegetation's pretty exotic but, well, I'd seen photographs, so yes, it was pretty much as I expected.'

'And Eleanor showed you where Richard and Russell made their discovery ... the knee-joint?'

'Of course.'

Richard Sutton fell silent. There wasn't much resemblance between father and son, Natalie thought. Richard Sutton Senior had none of the cockiness of Richard Sutton Junior. His movements were neat and tidy, his voice was quiet, his shirt and shoes were understated but expensive. Nancy Sutton was wiping her face with a handkerchief. Then she wiped her hands. She didn't speak either.

The silence lengthened.

'So,' Richard Sutton finally said, 'you were sitting here, more or less, when you saw this cook – Ndekei? – sneaking through the night?'

'I didn't think he was sneaking. I mean, I didn't know what was about to happen. I thought ... I thought he was visiting a woman, so I didn't really pay much attention. It was only the next morning, when I was walking across the camp and saw a monkey run out of Richard's tent carrying a camera that I realised something must be wrong.'

Another silence. 'But, yes, I was sitting in that canvas chair, right there.' She pointed to Nancy Sutton. 'Having a late-night smoke.'

Richard Sutton nodded. 'Can you ... would you mind telling us what you found?'

Natalie breathed in audibly. She looked at Nancy Sutton. 'Are you *sure* you want to know?'

She shook her head. 'It was horrible.'

Richard Sutton Senior didn't say anything straight away. Then, 'I understand it must have been an ordeal for you, Dr. Nelson, and that you may not wish to... But I served in the United States Army as a young man, so I've seen a few dead bodies in my time. Nancy here was a nurse. We've flown eight thousand miles to see where our boy was killed. We saw his body before it was buried so we know he had his throat cut, though the wound was all closed up by then.'

He waited. He didn't push but for Natalie, she knew, there was no escape.

'Very well.'

And she relived that dreadful morning: the cloud of flies, the insistent sounds of their buzzing, the small black insects crawling in and out of Richard's eyes and nostrils, his mouth, the escaping monkeys, the smell of blood and urine, the total stillness of the body.

When she had finished, Nancy Sutton was quietly weeping. Richard Sutton just sat, very quietly, listening. His eyes never left Natalie, hardly blinked, gave nothing away.

Eventually, he said, 'There are no other witnesses?'

Natalie shook her head.

'And that means the prosecution's case rests entirely on you?'

'Yes and no.' Natalie shifted in her chair. 'I am the only witness – yes. But a piece of the cook's apron was found on a spike of thorns that forms the wall of the camp, near Richard's tent. And an imprint of his rubber boot was also found in the dust outside the tent. Ndekei took Richard's watch, to prove he had done what was asked, and the Maasai gave it back to us.' She didn't say there had been blood on the watch at one stage. 'That's all circumstantial evidence, of course, but put together with what I saw it's very damaging.'

She passed her fingers through her hair.

'But, in any case, as I'm sure Eleanor told you, Ndekei is going to admit the killing, but still plead "Not Guilty". He'll say he was acting according to local Maasai law, that Richard and Russell had desecrated their local burial ground and that he had been ordered by the elders to kill Richard as revenge for what he and Russell had done.'

'Jesus! Will that wash?' Richard Sutton neatly peeled off his jacket and carefully laid it on the bed beside him. He was clearly a very tidy man.

'What did Eleanor tell you while you were in the gorge? You must have discussed it.'

'Oh, we discussed it. Nancy 'n' me have come eight thousand miles to discuss it. Dr. Deacon gave us some flim-flam about how good our boy was – well, we knew that. Then some soft-soap about how important the discovery was. We knew that too. Russell had filled us in plenty in New York.'

He carefully rolled up his shirtsleeves. 'Then she made her point. Clearly and forcefully, you might say. She said that the raid on the burial ground was the worst thing that has ever happened to her in nearly forty years of digging. She said that Richard and Russell were foolish – foolish verging on the criminally insane. That she had sent Russell away to save his life and that she blamed herself for not sending Richard away sooner, so he would not have been killed. She said that the trial threatens to turn ugly, that politics may be involved, and that the whole dig is still threatened. But she said that you are unwavering in your testimony and that you fully intend to give evidence. That's what Nancy and I want to hear, but we want to hear it from you.'

Richard Senior leaned forward. The fingers of one hand played with the gold watchstrap on his other wrist, but his eyes were on Natalie.

She returned his stare. His neat and tidy manner, his precise movements, his quiet voice were forceful, unnerving. Here was a man who didn't need to raise his voice to be obeyed, who loathed waste or extravagance or show in any form, who was used to getting his own way. She didn't want him to see or sense the doubts within her. Eleanor couldn't, mustn't know how she had wavered – was *still* wavering; once she showed weakness, the pressure on her would surely increase. But the very fact that Richard Sutton Senior was here at all emphasised that she was right to hold the view that she did. She couldn't abandon his dead son now.

'Of course I'm giving evidence. I saw what I saw. I've signed an official statement for the court and I can't go back on that without putting myself at risk of perjury or contempt of court. Not that I intend to,' she added quickly.

Sutton leaned back on the bed, not speaking. He looked at Natalie, then into the middle distance, then back again at Natalie.

'Dr. Deacon made it very clear that you are in a minority of one in the camp, that everyone else thinks the local law *should* take precedence, that it is more important to keep the dig going than to avenge Richard's death. She even said that that is what Richard himself would have wanted. She wanted us to talk to you and get you to change your mind, and withdraw your evidence.'

'And you agreed?'

'I didn't say that.' His eyes bored into hers. 'I wanted to hear what you have to say first.'

'And now that you have?'

He spoke even more quietly. 'I'm Richard's father, Dr. Nelson. My son – a talented, beautiful, intelligent man – was cruelly hacked to death by a savage, a barbarian, an inferior form of life acting in accordance with some primitive, stone-age custom.' He nodded. 'Yes, I'm all for respecting ancient traditions, provided they don't get too much in the way of progress, but to be sliced to death all because...' Sutton checked himself. His words were becoming more emotive than he was used to. 'All because a burial ground was ransacked. The very idea fills me with ... loathing isn't a strong enough word.' He shifted his frame on the bed. 'I *dislike* strong feelings, Dr. Nelson. I *distrust* them.' He tapped his temple. 'They interfere with what goes on up here and in my business life I have learned to control them.' He shook his head, though he did even that tidily, without waste or show. 'But at the moment I'm so ... so bitter, so dripping in fury, so coiled up inside, so full of *fire*, that I'm almost ready to kill, myself.'

He refolded his handkerchief, neatly, and slid it

back inside his pocket. 'So, as you can imagine, I am relieved, to put it no stronger, that you are acting according to a conscience that I recognise. Russell North said some good things about you in New York and I'm glad that you have lived up to the advance publicity.'

Sutton allowed himself a smile. 'But I want to tell you something else, Dr. Nelson, Natalie, something I want you to keep in mind after Nancy and I leave later today.' He brushed dust off his shoes with his fingers. 'The trial is still weeks away and you will be cooped up here, surrounded by people who disagree with you, people who – in some cases – are your seniors in professional terms.'

He reached across to the small table just inside Natalie's tent, and picked up the water jug. 'May I?'

Natalie nodded, and Sutton poured half a glass. He offered the remainder to the two women but both of them shook their head. He finished the water in several small swallows. He took out his handkerchief again and wiped his mouth.

'As the trial approaches, the pressure on you to change your story, to withdraw your evidence, is likely to mount. You may get to the point where you feel that such pressure is irresistible.' He shook his head and bit his lip at the same time. 'If you even consider changing you mind, Dr. Nelson, remember this – I will not sit idly by and let my son's death go unavenged.'

He was now looking intently at Natalie.

'If Ndekei is convicted, then it is not very important to me whether he is hanged or sent down for a very long time. But if he never faces trial, because you change your testimony, because pressure has been put on you, then you may rest assured that Richard Sutton Senior will not stand aside until he has seen justice done.'

There were beads of sweat at his temples and Sutton again dabbed at them with his handkerchief. 'This is not an empty threat, Dr. Nelson, by a distraught father in the first flush of grief.' He poured himself more water. 'Nancy, why don't you go back to the main tent where it's cooler? Let me finish up here with Dr. Nelson alone?'

It wasn't a request and Nancy Sutton got to her feet, smiled a tight smile at Natalie and headed back to the refectory area.

Richard Sutton watched her go, all the while wiping his forehead with his handkerchief. 'In New York, Dr. Nelson, I'm a lawyer, a corporate lawyer. I work for a big property developer and it is in the nature of the property business that, legally speaking, corners get cut, toes get trodden on, strings get pulled. My job, one of my jobs at any rate, is to sort out the messes.' He nodded briefly again. 'Yes, I think I can say I've sorted out one or two messes in my time. New York is ... well, I'm sure you know all that. I know a lot of people. The property business has a rough end, where it joins up with the construction business, and there are all sorts of things I can do.'

He reached forward and touched her knee. 'I'm not picking on you, Natalie, or not only you.' He gestured around him. 'Now that I've been here, I know what Dr. Deacon's outfit amounts to – the camp, the gorge, the neighbours – I know what I'm dealing with.'

He let a long pause go by before adding, 'And I'm a man of the world, Dr. Nelson, the real world, the twentieth-century world, not the million-year-old world that you and Dr Deacon inhabit, and my beloved boy inhabited, and all these bones inhabit.'

Another silence. The broadside was over.

Natalie's anger had risen as he had spoken. But she had fought it and was now wondering instead how Richard Sutton Senior would respond to being told his son was homosexual. Did his wife know? Would it make any difference? She said nothing as he reached for his jacket and stood up.

'You probably weren't expecting any of that. I understand your father runs a church choir, so I may have sounded heavy-handed. But I don't want you to underestimate me. If you give evidence, as you have just promised, then that's all I ask, and everything will be over. If you don't...' He put his hand on Natalie's shoulder. 'I hope it won't come to that.'

Sutton stepped away, then turned back. 'I'm going to look at Richard's tent. See you at lunch.'

Jack placed his canvas chair next to Natalie's table and sat down in it. He laid some chocolate next to the flask of whisky and leaned back.

Natalie drew on her cigarette. Around them the night was very dark – no moon yet. There were the sounds of baboons and elephants in the distance. She didn't speak. A hurricane lamp burned just inside the tent, throwing a weak yellow light

403

over the thin earth and straggly grass that had
been trampled in the constant coming and going
in and out of her tent. The smell of paraffin hung
in the air.

Jack scratched his head. 'Exhausting day. I
gather they gave you a going over before they
turned on the rest of us.'

The briefest of smiles played over Natalie's
features. Lunch had indeed been a high-octane
affair. Richard Sutton Senior had let lunch be
served before repeating his threats to the entire
assembled company. He had still kept his voice
low, his movements precise, but his eyes had
raked back and forth over everyone at the table,
like a searchlight in a concentration camp, looking for resistance, weakness. He let no one escape.

He was like an animal in the wild, Natalie
thought, defending its young, or its territory. In
theory Natalie should have been relieved that she
was, for the time being anyway, no longer in a
minority of one, that Sutton was taking her side.
But his manner of doing it, the menacing con-
tradiction behind his precise movements and
vague threats, the raw force in his quiet tone,
merely embarrassed her and caused her to doubt
the strength of her own position.

Matters had deteriorated even more when
Sutton had said that, during the afternoon, he
wished to be shown the Maasai burial ground.
Eleanor had refused point blank and forbidden
anyone else to go there.

Whereupon Sutton had turned to Natalie. 'You
can show me.'

Natalie had coloured. 'I will not.'

'What do you mean? I wish to see the burial ground. So does Nancy.'

'No!' said Natalie vehemently. 'It will make the situation worse.'

'Not for my son it won't. I wish to know if this is a proper burial ground – or some primitive jungle junk yard?'

'Stop!' cried Natalie. 'Stop. I've told you about my testimony, I've told you I won't change, that I will tell the court what I saw. Yes, I believe that your son didn't deserve to die.' Natalie's throat was clammy with sweat. 'What happened to him was barbaric and unjust. How many times do I have to say that?' She pushed her plate away from her. 'But I will not take you to the burial ground. Things are complicated enough as it is, and it doesn't matter what sort of burial ground it is – it's sacred, and I accept that we have to respect that. It's not a tourist attraction.'

'Listen–'

'No!' Natalie jutted forward her chin. She wasn't often stubborn but she was good enough at it when she needed to be. 'No.' She breathed out audibly. 'No.'

Sutton sat upright, motionless, and without speaking. His eyes again swept from one person to the other. They came back to rest on Natalie. He nodded. 'Have it your way.'

Then he looked at Eleanor, and in the same quiet tone, added, 'I want justice for my son, Dr. Deacon. Call it vengeance if you prefer. It's all the same to me. But don't underestimate me. I can damage you and,' he pointed at Natalie, 'if

405

she doesn't give evidence, you'll find out what I mean.'

'Are you threatening me, Mr Sutton?' Eleanor too was sitting very upright.

Sutton shrugged and got to his feet and they had left.

He had made a point of shaking hands with Natalie but he'd said nothing else. Presently, they had all heard the sound of the Suttons' plane taking off and disappearing into the afternoon sky.

Now Natalie stirred in her chair and turned towards Jack. 'Yes, I'd been subjected to the Sutton Senior species of charm when they visited me this morning. Even though I had told them I was giving evidence, Sutton still felt the need to–' She formed her fingers into a pistol shape and pointed them at her head.

'You *are* still determined to give evidence then?'

'Jack, please!' She stubbed out the end of her cigarette and reached for another. 'I have to. I must. Please don't try to–'

'I won't, I won't,' he said quickly. He rubbed his eyelids. 'It's just that we've all had a wearing day – a difficult few days, in fact. I just wondered if you'd wavered, that's all.'

Natalie couldn't let even Jack see that she had doubts. The moment she did that, she knew, she was lost.

She shook her head firmly. 'No. It's funny, I see the arguments of the other side very clearly and, intellectually speaking, they worry me. But in here,' and she pointed to her heart, 'I have never wavered. Years of upbringing, I suppose, and yes,

406

maybe, having a father who's religious. I saw what I saw and it's my duty to tell it in court. I know what the consequences are likely to be and I'm far more worried about the threats from the Maasai than from Sutton. But I have to give evidence. It's the tradition I was brought up in.' She pulled on her cigarette. 'I can't change.'

She breathed the cigarette smoke out through her nostrils. Was that true? she asked herself. Was that true?

'There, look at that.' Jack pulled on the handbrake of the Land Rover and switched off the engine.

'What exactly is it that I am looking at?' replied Natalie.

They were on their way to Karatu to shop for supplies, visit the pharmacy and to collect the post – some deliveries were made by air, when it was convenient to do so, otherwise regular post came by road to a *Poste Restante* in Karatu.

Jack had pulled up near a thicket of acacia trees and thorn bushes.

'You haven't been working on your bush eyes lately,' he said softly. 'Follow the top line of those flat-topped acacias, from left to right. About a third of the way along, there are the heads of two giraffes.'

She followed his directions. 'Oh yes,' she breathed after a moment. 'Cute.'

'Don't you think,' murmured Jack, sipping water from a bottle, 'don't you think that, from a distance, the way giraffes stand, the way they are built, it always looks as though they are kissing, or about to kiss, or whispering in each other's ear?'

Natalie smiled. 'I hadn't thought about it, but now that you mention it, I suppose so.'

'And they're usually in twos, not herds. That strengthens the impression. And look.' He pointed. 'Lower your eyes, underneath the adults, see ... a young, infant giraffe.'

Sure enough, Natalie could just make out a baby giraffe caught up between the legs of the adults.

'I've always thought it would make a good book,' said Jack. 'How the so-called wild animals of Africa look after their young. They can be quite ferocious about it, though it's mainly the mothers of course. Fathers don't seem to have that instinct so much, though in humans we do.'

'You think so?'

'Oh yes, don't you? Even if a father's instincts are not as strong as a mother's, human males take a much greater interest in their offspring than, say, male lions or baboons do in their young. How and why and when did that feeling evolve, I wonder?'

She weighed what he said. 'You *are* feeling broody.'

He laughed, put the Land Rover in gear and waved farewell to the giraffes.

They drove across the plain for a while, before joining the tarmac road from Elangata. They saw more people now, walking along the road and working the land. There was more traffic too. Most of it, just as Jack did, drove along the smooth central crown of the road almost until a

408

collision seemed certain, then pulled off to the rougher edges.

And then, laid out before them, about half a mile away, were two rows of buildings, set back from the road. Dust was being churned by the amount of traffic and a spindly radio mast shot up above everything else.

'Welcome to Karatu,' said Jack, as he pulled the Land Rover off the highway and into a filling station. 'Can you fill her up with diesel while I go across the street to the post office?'

'Sure.'

They both got down, Jack taking with him the leather pouch he'd been keeping behind the driver's seat. He handed her some money. 'That should cover it.'

'Where do I find you when I've filled up?'

'Well, don't forget you need to fill up all the spare cans in the rear, as well. That will take a while. But if I'm not back, the post office is that green-painted building over there.' He pointed. 'The one with all the security grilles.' He made off.

A group of small children had gathered to watch Natalie, and a wizened old man, with no teeth and grey hair, appeared to be the attendant. At her request he started filling the Land Rover's tank while Natalie laid out all the spare cans in a line, so they could be filled afterwards. As the attendant held the nozzle of the hose wedged in the Land Rover's pipe, Natalie looked about her.

All of the buildings were the shape of shoeboxes – there was no architecture, as such, in Karatu. There were several shops, selling food or hardware, a hairdresser's, a shop where you could have letters written, a shop with a display of boots outside and a pawnbroker's. No book-shops. The only books she had brought with her to Africa were work-related. But she found she warmed to Jack's idea of spending an hour or so a day off their main concern. It made sense. Like his interest in politics, it enlarged him.

The attendant transferred the nozzle to the first of the spare cans.

A bus chugged into town, billowing black diesel exhaust from somewhere deep underneath. It stopped and countless people were disgorged, several of whom climbed up a ladder at the rear of the bus to reclaim their belongings on the roof. In no time the bus was on the move again.

The cans were filled. The attendant helped Natalie lift them into the back of the vehicle and she handed over the money. There was a little change and she waited while it was brought.

She drove over to the post office and parked in front of the building. Another bus, just as laden and swathed in black exhaust as the first, was pulling up. Natalie locked the doors of the Land Rover but as she did so, Jack appeared through the door of the post office. He held up a bundle of letters.

'Look,' he said, holding out a long airmail envelope. 'It's from Russell.'

The Californian postmark was not the only giveaway. Russell had scrawled his name and address on the envelope, as Americans tended to do. She felt the paper between her fingers. A couple of pages at least. Or else he had enclosed something in addition to whatever he had written.

She folded the envelope and put it in her pocket.

'We're all set with the diesel,' she said. 'By the way, why so many spare cans? I thought Land Rovers came with especially large tanks of their own.'

'They do,' said Jack, throwing a bundle of letters on to the back seat. 'But some of the cans are for use with the plane. I have to fortify it with tetra-ethyl lead but if I refuel myself at least I know the right type of juice is being used.' He opened the door to the driving seat. 'You do hear stories of people getting mixed up at big airports and confusing jet fuel with Avgas. It happened not long ago, near Mutonguni. Two KANU politicians and their pilot were killed. They still don't know if it was an accident or deliberate.'

He got behind the wheel. 'Now, I have one more errand before we head back. I need to stop by at the clinic, pick up some spectacles for Daniel. They're being repaired. Then we can hit the road home.'

The clinic was on the far side of town, down its own bumpy track, and it took them about fifteen minutes to complete the drive. The building, when they came to it, was a white-painted hut with a thatched roof. 'I shouldn't be long,' said Jack, switching off. 'You don't need to come in.'

He was obviously sensitive to the fact that she was anxious to read her letter from Russell, all alone. He entered the clinic without looking back. Natalie took the envelope from her pocket

411

and slid her finger under the flap.

The letter occupied one sheet of paper only, though it was written on two sides. But there were two other type-written sheets enclosed with it. A cursory glance told her it was a copy of the raw text for his article in the *Los Angeles Times* and which she had already seen. She put those sheets to one side.

Dear Natalie,

I'm at a loss how to start. I had planned to discuss just the enclosed article, which you may have already seen, or at any rate heard about. But, having received your letter, all that has changed.

I knew, I <u>knew</u>, when I left Kihara, that I shouldn't go, that I should have put up more of a fight. I <u>predicted</u> that other discoveries would be made but you prevailed on me to leave. And now you, and her ladyship, have made the discoveries – a jaw, a skull, a construction even – that should have been <u>mine</u>. A whole new species, the ancient ancestor that first walked upright and created culture, that <u>I</u> should have found and named.

Forgive me, Natalie, but right now I'm feeling very bitter and yes, for the first time, some of it is spilling over on to you. We could have found this creature <u>together</u>, think how that would have cemented a relationship between us. As it is, my find – Daniel's and Richard's and my knee-joint – will be over-shadowed by the rest of your discoveries. I'll be an also-ran alongside yet another Deacon-led triumph.

On top of everything, your letter was – or rather it wasn't – the friendliest letter I have ever received. Have I not earned more warmth from you?

I will give you the benefit of the doubt until I receive your next letter, to give you the chance to explain yourself, and I hope I like what I read. But until then all the promises I made to help in your career are on hold – is that clear? You seem to have changed and I need to know that you have not. Give me your views as soon as you can, please.

If you haven't had a visit yet from the Suttons you soon will. If they have been and gone you'll know by now what a force of nature Richard Snr. is. To tell the truth, I didn't altogether take to him. A little too controlled (and controlling) for my taste, but there's no doubting his energy or his will. He's not someone I would like to cross and I hope you are not planning to do so. I'd like you to reassure me on that point too, when you write.

Please make that soon. My LA Times article has aroused quite a bit of interest within the profession – most of it, I have to say, sympathetic to me and, partly on the strength of it, I have been offered a place on a big dig next year at Lake Rudolf, in the northern stretch of Kenya. You could probably join me if you wanted but that rather depends on … you know what it depends on.

I had wanted our letters to be more, well, softer, more intimate, cosier, not only professional, but it's hard at the moment with all that is happening. Your next letter is crucial, but I'm sure you sense that. I'll be on edge till it comes. Don't make me wait too long.

My personal feelings haven't changed; I still recall out nights under the stars, and our illicit drinking. I am back in California now, in my study overlooking the bay, and feel more than ever that you would fit in here perfectly among the pine trees and its pastel colours. I hope it's not over between us, but that's up to you.

Russell

Natalie looked up, to see Jack leaving the clinic and coming towards the Land Rover. She folded the letter back into its envelope. Jack threw the spectacle case on to the driver's seat and climbed in after it.

'All set,' he said. 'How's Russell?' He started the engine and put the vehicle in gear.

'Still wounded,' replied Natalie in a whisper. '*Blessé*. Still wounded.' She stuffed the letter into her pocket and added, half to herself, 'And still dangerous.'

Three mornings later, Natalie came back from the gorge and, as she entered the camp, it was immediately clear that there were new visitors. Two men – one grey-haired, one dark – were seated with Eleanor outside her tent. But Natalie was tired. She hadn't exactly done much today, save sift soil-sand through a sieve, watching the Maasai who were now increasingly patrolling the gorge. But the bucking of the vehicle on the drive back from where they had been digging and the constant grime from kneeling among the dust and dung had taken their toll. She needed a shower and she needed a rest. She also needed to re-read Russell's letter, one more time, to see if there were any subtle messages she had missed. She'd no doubt meet the strangers at lunch and that was soon enough.

Mgina brought the hot water.

414

'Is all going well with the wedding?' Natalie asked.

'Yes, Miss Natalie. My sisters are making my wedding jewellery.'

'What is the jewellery made off?'

'Black stone, white stone, ostrich beads. Jewellery must come from the land, so you will remain here always.'

Not for the first time, Natalie remarked on the simple – but sensitive and sensible – iconography of Maasai customs. *Most* Maasai customs.

She changed, brushed her hair, put on her shoes, lighter than her boots, and tried a little lipstick. She always felt better after that.

As she approached the refectory tent, the men turned toward her.

With a start she realised that it was the deputy attorney general she had met in Nairobi – what was his name? The other man she didn't know.

They stood up as she approached. The deputy attorney general was virtually unrecognisable out of his lawyer's uniform of gown and wig. He wore an open-necked shirt and green-cum-khaki trousers. He was sweating. The other man, the dark-haired one, was more elegant, in a pale linen suit.

'Natalie,' said Eleanor, rising from her chair. 'I am sure you remember Maxwell Sandys. And this is Peter Jeavons, he's British minister of state for science. He's here to see what we do.'

Natalie shook hands with them and then sat in her place. Sandys' name had come to her just before Eleanor had mentioned it. 'You are a long way from court,' she said as she sat down. 'Is this work or pleasure?'

Sandys opened a cardboard folder he was holding and took from it a newspaper. He handed it to Natalie. 'We're here because of this. It's an editorial in the *East African Gazette* that appeared three mornings ago. Will you read it please?'

The knot of foreboding that had been finding a regular home in Natalie's stomach reformed itself in no time. She took the newspaper and read the article carefully, in her own time. It described a case where John Tudor had been the judge, and where a white security guard had beaten a black burglar fourteen times with an iron bar, so badly he was still in hospital and couldn't attend his trial. Tudor had dismissed the charges against the security guard and freed him.

When she had finished reading the long editorial that attacked the judge's behaviour, she handed the paper back to Sandys.

Jack was right about John Tudor being a racist. 'Fourteen blows is fourteen too many,' Natalie remarked.

Sandys nodded. 'We're agreed there, Dr. Nelson. But this isn't the first time Tudor has shown undue leniency towards white security guards when they have attacked and injured black robbers or burglars. He's giving people – white people – licence to ill-treat blacks if they catch them committing crimes. No one wants to condone robbery, of course, but Tudor is showing no sense of proportion and, as I am sure you can see, this only exacerbates a situation that is already very sensitive. Tudor, as I think you have been told, is to be the judge in the case where you will give evidence. It is fair to say that any case coming before Judge Tudor from now on, and which pits a black person against a white person, is going to be big news, the focus of potentially sensational newspaper coverage and will almost certainly stoke the political fires.'

He reached forward and lifted a water jug, filling their glasses one by one as he went on speaking. 'Your case, of course – if I can phrase it in that way – is even more sensational, at least potentially, because of the defence Ndekei is running: that he was acting according to tribal law. That hasn't reached the papers yet, but it will, it will.'

Natalie drank some water. It always smelled a little of the purification pills that were needed to keep it sanitary.

'However,' Sandys went on, 'I am afraid we have been dealt another blow that I suspect you know nothing about.'

Natalie bit her lip. What was coming?

'We now have a date for the trial – February the twelfth.'

'Why is that significant?'

He drank some water himself and looked at Eleanor. 'That is exactly one day before the opening of the independence conference in London. It couldn't come at a worse time; black–white relations will be under intense scrutiny and if Tudor steps out of line, or makes one of his racist gaffes, who knows what will happen? The whole thing is a tinderbox.'

'Can't you change the date, or change Tudor?'

Sandys shook his head. 'Cases are set by

417

rotation, Tudor has already been assigned to the case and he refuses to back down – I actually think he's looking forward to it.' He shook his head. 'As for the date, he won't hear of that being changed either. In any case, the Lord Chancellor's department, which administers the judges and the courts, has already begun its transition to independence – the deputy in that department is himself black and is not about to do us any favours. I think he is looking forward to this case, too.'

Sandys shifted in his seat. 'We also know that the American ambassador in Nairobi is taking a keen interest in the trial. Richard Sutton Senior went to see him while he was in town and reminded him he was a big donor to the president's campaign. That's another reason this case is a tinder box. There's nothing to be done. The case goes ahead.'

Natalie said nothing. Why was Sandys here? She suspected she was about to find out.

'Tudor has seen the case papers – they are passed to the judge as a matter of routine, once a date is set. So he knows the nature of the evidence against Ndekei; he knows that your evidence is the main plank in our case.'

He paused, sipped some more water.

'We all know, Natalie, that the only way this case will not go forward is if you withdraw your testimony – now, before you jump down my throat, let me finish.' He raised his hand as if to stop her physically attacking him, though she had no intention of doing so. 'I know how committed you are to giving evidence; how you feel loyalty to

Richard Sutton, and to Professor North; I know you feel that you must tell the court what you saw. And I know from Eleanor here that you are from a religious family and that too affects your attitude. But I want to mention one argument that will, I hope, persuade you to change your mind.'

Sandys leaned forward in his chair.

'This latest outrage by Tudor, and the fact that Ndekei will be sentenced to hang, perhaps on the very day that the independence talks begin in London, mean that we could see riots in Nairobi, riots in which people – maybe *dozens* of people – could be killed. Is that what you want?'

He shook his head. 'I appeal to you as a scientist, a pragmatist. I ask you to consider that circumstances have changed. I know that Eleanor has used the argument that the work of the gorge is of more importance than the life of one man. I happen to agree with her but I know you don't and that's not the argument I am using now. I simply point out that the situation has changed. This trial could be a major political event, it could inflame passions, it could set off riots, it could cause far more deaths than have occurred already.'

He wiped the palms of his hands with the handkerchief.

'All I'm saying is that, in the new circumstances, it would be natural for you to decide that you can't be sure, any more, of what you saw that night. You have already said that you didn't see Ndekei's face but recognised him only from his shuffle. Anyone can make a mistake, read too much into what they saw in the night. If the figure wasn't shuffling, it could have been anybody.'

Pause.

'But I *did* see him shuffling and in any case he has admitted the killing.'

'Yes, I know, we all know. But we all know too that he is not required to mount his defence until after the prosecution have presented their case. If there is no case to answer, he will not have to explain himself. The racial element, the tribal element, the tinderbox issue of skin colour, will go away. By letting Ndekei go free – one individual – you may be saving many lives that will be lost if the case sparks rioting.'

A long pause.

Outside the shade of the tent, the sun beat down. The smell of diesel was strong today, so many vehicles had been used. Natalie was sweating all over. Her shirt clung to her flesh: the damp, dark patches showing through. The cooling effect of the shower had quite worn off. She wiped her brow with her sleeve.

She had rehearsed so many of Sandys' arguments in her head over the days and weeks.

Natalie shook her head. 'I'm sorry, but nothing of what you have said convinces me. I do recognise your arguments, of course I do. What Judge Tudor did was hateful, *hateful*. But I just don't think a murder, the loss of a life, can be swept under the carpet – which is what you are suggesting, however many fine words you use to disguise it.'

She unbuttoned one sleeve of her shirt and rolled it up her arm. 'I could, if I wished, paint a very different picture. I could say that the people of Kenya will be so obsessed by the independence conference in London that they will pay no attention to this trial–'

'You know that's not true!' Sandys shouted.

'No!' cried Eleanor at the same time.

'But I have another argument that I'd like you to consider. One that you people outside the camp don't know about.'

That got Sandys' attention. He looked at her without speaking.

She couldn't tell him what Kees had said about Richard Sutton's sexuality. He, Kees, was sitting right across the table, unaware of the significance of what he had said. And it might not be true anyway. But she could tell Sandys about the threats made by Richard Sutton Senior while he was in her tent during his visit. Natalie spoke about his promise to make her life a misery, to ruin her career, if she didn't give evidence. She did her best to remember the exact words Sutton had used when he had threatened her.

When she had finished, they all sat in silence for a while, their breathing the only sound.

'Isn't that all a bit, well, extreme?' Sandys said at length. 'I mean, are you sure you are not reading too much into his words?'

'Oh no!'

To Natalie's surprise, Eleanor answered for her. 'Here I'm on Natalie's side, Max. Richard Sutton Senior is a very unpleasant man. When I showed him round the gorge – this was early in his visit, and Natalie was not present – he made threats to me too. He said that if Natalie didn't give evidence I would regret it, that his people in the construction business had the power to make our lives "very difficult"; those were the words he used.'

'Melodramatic, I agree,' said Sandys. 'But anything more than that?'

'Why don't you find out for us, Max?'

All eyes turned to Eleanor.

'What do you mean?'

'You're the deputy attorney general. The British government must have a legal counsel, or a police liaison officer at its consulate in New York. Set them on the case. If Richard Sutton is as black as he makes out, it shouldn't be too difficult to smoke out what pies he's had fingers in. All it takes is a phone call from you, to set things in motion.'

Max looked at Jeavons. Before he could say anything, Eleanor went on, 'He won't be expecting us to check him out. He probably thinks we are unworldly academics who don't know the difference between a felony and a misdemeanour.'

'*Do* you know the difference between a felony and a misdemeanour?' said Sandys with a smile.

'I think so,' said Eleanor, smiling back. 'What Ndekei did was a felony. So will you do it, Max? For me, for us?'

'Ah!' thought Natalie, an interesting exchange. Eleanor clearly had some sway with Sandys, still, so maybe the rumours about an affair were true, after all. Watching them, it was as if they tried to keep their familiarity with each other out of sight, but it kept breaking through. They had a past together, Natalie was more certain of it now.

'I'll see what I can do, Eleanor, but how will it change things, how will it help?'

'Oh, it will help all right, I can assure you. Just find out what you can and let me know, let *us* know, as soon as possible. Now, let's have lunch.'

Over lunch, all talked revolved around Jeavons, as they filled him in on the work being done in the gorge. He was not a scientist by training – he was a politician, a lawyer – but he seemed interested enough, asking intelligent questions and listening carefully to the answers. It turned out that he was the member of parliament for Rossington, a constituency adjoining Gainsborough, so he and Natalie had that in common. She asked him what the main local issues were, politically speaking. He replied that they were housing – there was a great need for more council houses, even this long after the war – and that race was becoming an issue, a problem. West Indians were moving into an area that had been whites-only until recently.

'There's a lot of local feeling,' Jeavons said. 'I suspect that race is going to be a big issue in British politics in the next few years. It's not just Africa and the United States where skin colour matters.'

Natalie had been shocked to hear what Jeavons said. As a Q.C., he told her he was fascinated by her own dilemma but, like a good politician (so she thought), was careful not to take sides.

Because he was leaving early the next morning – he and Sandys had flown down from Nairobi, piloted by Sandys – the minister was driven out to the gorge by Eleanor in the heat of the afternoon. Natalie was glad she wasn't going with them.

She spent the afternoon hours writing her paper that would form part of a press conference, if there was one, as she had promised Jack. While she was sitting in the shade of her tent, she was approached by Mgina, who had a young man with her. He was a shade taller than she was, but every bit as shy in the way he held himself.

'Please, Miss, this is Endole, the man I am to marry.'

Natalie got to her feet and shook hands with the young man. 'Congratulations,' she said. 'I am very happy for you. When is the wedding?'

'In one week, Miss.' Endole had a very deep voice but still soft and gentle, like Mgina's.

'And after you're married, Mgina, you will live with Endole's family?'

Mgina nodded.

'As the third wife?' It pained Natalie to say it, but she wanted to see their reaction when they were together.

Mgina nodded and smiled. Endole said nothing; his expression never varied. They were both perfectly content.

'Hold on,' said Natalie. She dipped into her tent and brought out her camera. She took several pictures of Mgina and Endole. They smiled and laughed in embarrassment.

'Now we must tell Mr Jack,' whispered Mgina when Natalie had finished. She turned away, then turned back. 'I must learn to call him Doctor Jack now, yes? But he's not a medical doctor, is he?'

'No, he's not. I don't expect he minds what you call him. He has a Maasai name, you know–'

Too late, she realised her mistake. Jack's Maasai name evoked the drama of the burial ground.

Mgina and Endole looked at each other, then sheepishly walked away towards Jack's tent. They didn't want to resurrect memories of the murder any more than Natalie did.

The chatter around the dining table was unusually loud tonight and the reason wasn't hard to find. In honour of the minister (or was it out of affection for Sandys?), Eleanor had suspended her 'no alcohol' rule and allowed a little wine and beer (for Arnold Pryce) to be brought from the locked storeroom, the only brick-built construction at Kihara Gorge.

Natalie was discussing with Pryce and Jack what they were going to give Mgina and Endole for a wedding present. Jack was thinking of giving the couple a flight to Nairobi, if they wanted, but Natalie preferred something more personal, something that would last: a framed photograph perhaps.

All of a sudden, voices were raised at the other end of the table, where Eleanor was sitting between the minister and Sandys.

'And I repeat,' insisted Jeavons, 'that the prime minister would like you to change your mind. It will be good publicity ahead of the independence conference. Do say you will.'

'No,' said Eleanor firmly, shaking her head, her chin jutting forward in the way that Natalie was now used to.

'Yes, come on, Eleanor, if I can accept, why can't you?' Sandys laid his hand on Eleanor's arm.

Slowly, she withdrew it. 'I think the whole idea stinks. No.'

'What idea stinks?' said Jack affably.

Eleanor, the minister and Sandys looked sheepish.

'We can't really talk about it,' said Jeavons in a low voice. 'Not yet, anyway.'

'Come on, Mother, out with it. What's got Max here all hot and bothered? What has he accepted that you haven't – oh, I know, I get it. *Of course.* It's that time of year. Am I right?' He grinned. 'Am I right?'

Eleanor nodded.

'Is someone going to tell the rest of us what the mystery is?' said Natalie, transferring her gaze from the minister to Sandys to Eleanor. When neither of them replied, she turned in her seat. 'Come on then, Jack, what's the answer to the riddle?'

Jack nodded, drinking a slug of wine. 'What Max has that our mother doesn't is a knighthood.' He wiped his lips with his hand. 'My guess is that she has been offered a Damehood in the New Year's Honours list and she, bless her, has turned it down.'

All eyes were on Eleanor.

'Eleanor,' said Natalie, 'is it true?'

'Well, I've had a letter from the palace, yes. They never say you're getting anything definitely, just that her majesty "has it in mind" to consider you for an honour and, if granted, would you accept?' She fixed her gaze on Natalie and shook her head. 'I said no. I think all the wrong people are rewarded in Britain, all the attention-seekers and snobs rather than real achievers. Your work should speak for itself. Added to which, in this case, there's a political element. I was chosen because of the upcoming independence conference and that's not right.'

'But Eleanor,' said Jeavons, 'you're very deserving – I'm surprised you haven't been asked before.'

'But I *have!* Three years ago. I said no then, too. That's how Jack could read between the lines.' She leaned forward. 'And I tell you, minister, there are lots of deserving people, unknown people who give their lives to good causes, who never get honoured. Who gets honoured? I'll tell you who gets honoured – well-paid, overweight businessmen who aren't satisfied with being well paid, but who want a gong to hide the fact that they are, most of them, very ordinary human beings. It's a rotten system, Mr Jeavons, and I want nothing to do with it.'

She wiped her lipstick off her glass with her napkin.

'Normally, if you are offered something and turn it down, you must wait at least five years for another offer. The fact that they've waited only three years in my case shows this is politically motivated. So I want it even less. You can tell the prime minister from me that–'

'Eleanor!' Sandys again put his hand on her arm. This time she did not remove it. 'Calm down. Think for a minute. We all know, around this table, the threat you face. If you were to be honoured, it

427

would be much more difficult for the authorities – whoever they are – to close you down.'

That thought had occurred to Natalie at precisely the same moment.

Now Eleanor took back her arm. 'Maybe so, maybe so. But I don't like it – it's wrong. The work should speak for itself.'

'I wish everyone felt like you, but I fear they do not.' The minister spoke quietly. 'You'd be surprised how a title attracts attention, even these days. Why not sleep on it–'

'No!' She softened her tone. 'No. My mind's made up.' She looked up and scraped back her chair. 'Jack, how about some music to go with the wine? Let's spoil the minister with all our luxuries at once.'

'Sure,' said Jack. 'What's your taste, minister: Beethoven, Brahms, Basie?'

'Oh, Basie, please.'

'*Shoe Shine Boy* suit you?'

'I never thought I'd hear *Shoe Shine Boy* in the Bush – amazing.' Jeavons beamed.

'The Count Basie Big Band coming up!' said Jack as he got to his feet.

Suddenly he stopped, winked at Natalie and then looked at his mother. 'Having a title worked for Basie – it worked big time.'

He left the tent grinning as his mother threw her napkin at him.

Natalie didn't mind jazz, but she didn't find it moved her anywhere near as much as classical music. She didn't like the endless repetition and the heavy syncopation which she found intrusive.

428

Classical music let you think.

Still, as she sat near the fire, listening to *Shoe Shine Boy*, she could see that the minister was extremely relaxed and nodding his head – his very fine head – in time to the beat. He had a sharp, legally-trained mind and seemed to see the point of jazz, so maybe she was missing something. But she had in particular been fascinated by what he had to say about politics in Britain, especially race. *Could* it become as important an issue as in Africa or the United States? Surely not. But Jeavons seemed to know his own mind, and he was a minister after all.

As soon as was decent, she got up from her seat, said goodnight to everyone and retreated to her tent. She had Russell's letter to answer, and she wanted a smoke. Given that tonight they'd had wine at dinner, she didn't bother with whisky.

Jack played *Shoe Shine Boy* three or four times then the camp fell silent. One by one, the people around the fire got up and returned to their tents. The minister was one of them – he and Sandys were using the two guest tents at the far end of the row, well away from Natalie's own quarters. Soon only Jack, Eleanor and Sandys were left but as Natalie watched, she saw Jack get up, kick some sand on to the fire to kill it and then he retired to bed.

Sandys and Eleanor both stood, kissed on the cheek, and then Eleanor went back to her tent and Sandys strolled to the guest tent he had been allocated.

Natalie finished her cigarette, put out her own

lamp, moved the chair and table inside the tent, and then sat looking out.

The camp had closed down for the night and all was quiet, save for the noises of the Serengeti – shrieks, high in the trees, a rush of hooves as a herd of something tried to escape a predator, the flap of wings from a large unseen bird, slow and rhythmical.

She sat on. She had set herself to wait for half an hour, to see whether something might happen, something that she thought *would* happen, and she had a bet with herself that, if her instincts were right, she would treat herself to another cigarette.

Ten minutes passed, fifteen. Just on twenty she saw a figure walk quickly from the area of the guest tents towards Eleanor's tent. Sandys. He didn't look round and he certainly didn't shuffle, as Ndekei had done. When he reached Eleanor's tent he went straight in and disappeared.

Natalie reached for her packet of cigarettes.

'Over to your left,' said Daniel, pointing, 'That's what we call a sausage tree.' He slowed the Land Rover.

Natalie was sitting next to him, with Kees in the back. It was a week later.

She looked to where Daniel was pointing.

'Isn't that a leopard?' said Kees.

'Your eyes are good,' breathed Natalie. 'I can't see it.'

'Well done, Mr Kees,' said Daniel. He pointed again, for Natalie's benefit. 'About ten feet off the ground. Leopards like sausage trees.'

With difficulty, Natalie located the leopard. 'I'll never get the hang of seeing things in the bush.'

'Hmmn,' growled Kees. 'I'm long-sighted. I need specs for my work and for writing. Look,' he added, 'I see Maasai ahead, over to the left. Do you think they want a lift somewhere?'

'What are they carrying?' said Daniel, lowering his voice.

'Something glinting in the sun,' replied Kees.

Daniel turned off the track and drove through some scrub thorn bushes.

'They are a long way off the road, aren't they?' said Kees softly.

'Why does that matter?' Natalie was itching to get back to camp.

'Well,' said Kees. 'If you are on foot you can go anywhere, of course. But if you stick to the tracks and roads and we come along, or someone like us, in a vehicle, you can get a lift. It's odd that these two are in open country.'

They all watched in silence as they approached the Maasai, who stood still as the Land Rover came near.

Daniel pulled up close.

The two Maasai were tall, grown men rather than boys, and they had their red cloaks pulled around them. He turned off the engine, leaned out and spoke to them in Swahili. They shook their heads so he switched to Maasai.

They replied, but briefly.

'They say they are looking for lost cattle but I don't believe them.'

'Why ever not?' Natalie looked at Daniel. 'Why would they lie?'

'Look around. The soil is undisturbed. Nothing has been this way.' He nodded his head to the left, to the south. 'They are coming from Olinkawa.'

'Why is that significant?'

'It's inside Tanganyika.'

'So?'

Daniel turned in his seat. 'Do you have any cigarettes?'

'Not on me, no.' Natalie shook her head.

'I do,' said Kees. 'But I thought we weren't allowed to give Maasai cigarettes?'

It was true enough. Cigarettes were very popular among the Maasai but they were a fire risk.

'Give me your pack,' said Daniel, still speaking softly.

Mystified, Kees took the cigarettes from his shirt pocket. Daniel undid the pack, leaned out of the Land Rover window again and held out the pack to the two Maasai. Their faces broke into grins and they both stepped forward.

As they did so, the cloak worn by the taller of the two men fell open – and Natalie gasped.

Under the cloak, something shiny was revealed, something metallic.

A gun.

The Maasai, embarrassed by what had happened, angry at being tricked by Daniel, took a step back, shouted at him, pulled their cloaks more tightly around them and, spurning the offer of cigarettes, started walking away from the vehicle.

Natalie, Daniel and Kees watched them go.

'What was that all about?' she said at length.

'It's a Russian gun,' breathed Daniel. 'A Kalashnikov. They got it in Tanganyika. I've been hearing rumours for days now, weeks. Some Tanganyikans were trained in Russia and the Russians were invited back to train more Tanganyikans. To train the army, I mean, special forces. And they bring Russian guns. These men will have got that Kalashnikov in Olinkawa – that's about twenty-five miles from here. They will have left in the dark and crossed the border in the dark. That's why they are off the tracks.'

'How will they have paid?' said Kees. 'Those guns don't look cheap.'

'Cattle maybe. Precious stones. The Russians are trying to sow trouble, so the guns may not be as expensive as they look.'

'And what's it *for?*' Natalie suddenly had a craving for a cigarette herself.

'Let's ask them,' said Daniel. He started the engine and caught up quickly with the two Maasai.

There was another exchange though this time they didn't stop walking and Daniel was forced to keep the Land Rover trundling along. Eventually, he braked and let them go on.

He looked across to Natalie. 'They say that, in the first instance, the gun is to guard the burial ground. So there is no repeat of the break-in.' He put the Land Rover in gear. 'And then, when the time comes, it will be used to defend the gorge.'

The strains of Sibelius' *Karelia Suite* filled the night air, the strings offering a cooling image of a near-frozen fjord – clean, compact, crisp. Natalie stared into the scarlet and crimson embers of the

433

campfire. She was thinking about Christopher and Jack. This evening at dinner they hadn't fought exactly but there had been niggles throughout. Eleanor had been away for a few days in Nairobi, visiting the bank, picking up money with which to pay the ancillary staff and doing other chores. In fact, she had only just returned as they were finishing dinner, having driven there and back. It turned out she hated flying and, when she could, took the Land Rover, even if it meant driving through many hours of darkness on dirt roads.

At one point during the evening, the conversation had turned – as it inevitably did turn, most nights – to the trial, and what might happen to the gorge. Everyone was even more gloomy, now that the Maasai had increased the pressure by acquiring a gun. Jack had tried to lighten the mood by explaining that the practice of burying the dead was not only a Christian idea, but had been taken over from the Datoga tribes-people, who had been conquered by the Maasai in the early nineteenth century.

'The Datoga buried their famous warriors and it seems fig trees – which can grow to massive proportions – like the soil where humans are buried. That's why you have the tradition, in this part of the world, of worshipping fig trees. They are sacred because they are infused with the spirit, the blood, of powerful ancestors. Because the fig trees that grow over the graves of past chiefs are especially vast, that proves how powerful their spirit is.'

'Nonsense!' Christopher had cried. 'Romantic rubbish.'

Jack had fallen silent.

'Look around,' said Christopher. 'There are fig trees all over the Serengeti – small, large, massive. Their size has nothing to do with who's buried where, but how close they are to rivers, how deep the soil is, how exposed to the wind they are. Like all plant life.'

'I was just explaining Datoga and Maasai beliefs–'

'Why do only men worship the fig trees, then? The women worship those shifting sand dunes. That has nothing to do with the Datoga.'

'Those dunes aren't very big. Maybe they didn't exist in the nineteenth century.'

'You have an answer for everything, Jack.'

Christopher had left the table then and stalked back to his tent.

Jack had gone and sat by the fire and, after a few minutes of desultory conversation, everyone else dispersed, embarrassed by the brothers' behaviour. Some went to their tents, Natalie to join Jack, just sitting, letting the shadows from the fire play over his face.

What was Jack thinking? she asked herself. Was Christopher smarting from his piloting error in front of her and Kees?

Suddenly a figure slumped into the chair across the fire from hers.

Eleanor.

Jack looked up at his mother and smiled.

'You must be exhausted,' said Natalie. She looked at her watch. 'It's gone ten.'

'Those last thirty miles *are* bumpy,' Eleanor said. 'We saw a lot of zebra and rhino, and had to wait for them to move on. But I'll live.'

She looked up as Naiva brought her a coffee and a small plate with a sandwich on it.

She sat, leaning into the fire, drinking her coffee and biting into the sandwich.

Jack hunched forward. 'You heard about the Kalashnikov?'

Eleanor nodded. 'Nasty. Highly illegal, of course, they won't have a permit, but then they make a point of not recognising Western – white – law. I'll tell the local rangers but I doubt they'll move in for just one gun. If they get more, however...' She shook her head.

'Did you get done what you needed to get done?' Jack kicked the fire.

Without speaking, still eating, Eleanor nodded. When she had finished swallowing, she said, 'More than that. I saw Max. He had news from New York.' She bit into her sandwich again, chewed again, swallowed again.

The others waited.

Eleanor looked from Natalie to Jack and back to Natalie. 'It would appear that Mr Richard Sutton Senior is, as they say in America, a real piece of work.'

More biting, chewing and swallowing. Eleanor was very hungry.

'So far as I can make out, he or his company have been the subject of more than one investigation by the New York Police Department but they have never been able to get enough evidence to make the charges stick.'

'Those charges being?'

Eleanor was again nodding and chewing at the

436

same time. 'Tenants, tenants in apartment blocks, are quite protected under American law. A landlord can't just evict them, if he wants to upgrade a building, say, and sell it on. Sutton's employer, however – the man who actually owns the real estate company – has a reputation for bringing pressure to bear on tenants: beatings, excrement through the letter box, their cars vandalised, that sort of thing. Of course, the tenants who receive this treatment are much too frightened to tell the police. They up sticks and move on, which is what Sutton's employer wants. And Sutton himself is the one who handles all the court cases and applications.'

She finished her sandwich. 'But that's not all, or the worst of it. Apparently at one point – this was a couple of years ago – he was involved in a bidding war over a piece of land being sold for redevelopment. There were just two people competing for the land, Sutton's employer and someone else. During the course of the bidding, the other man's daughter was kidnapped – she was seven. Naturally, this other man, Sutton's employer's rival, lost interest in the bidding and dropped out while he searched for his daughter. The girl was returned, safe and sound, and no money changed hands. But, of course, that's what makes it so suspicious. The handover of the money is always the most dangerous point for a kidnapper. In this case, the girl was just left outside a church. The only beneficiary of the whole business was the company Sutton is the corporate lawyer for, but again nothing could be proved.'

'The girl wasn't harmed, you say?'

'Well, she wasn't harmed physically. I can't say what psychological damage she suffered and Max, or Max's contact, didn't know either.'

'That's not what I meant,' replied Jack. 'Do we think Sutton, or Sutton's contacts, are capable of violence, real violence?'

Eleanor finished her coffee. 'Beatings, intimidation, kidnap: if it's true, it's bad enough. And think. Those actions were to secure buildings, they were done for money, for financial gain. In this case, in Natalie's case, it's Sutton's own son, his *only* son who is the centre of the whole weather pattern. How much more determined will that make Sutton now, how much more ready to commit violence?'

She nursed her empty cup with one hand, warmed the other over the fire. 'It was a long drive back from Nairobi and, yes, wearing. The roads are hard. But it gave me a chance to think and I've come to a decision, two decisions actually.'

Her son looked at her.

'Max also happened to let slip that the British government is flying out a cohort of British journalists for a background trip on Kenya ahead of the independence conference in London in February. They're coming during a quiet time for news, between Christmas and the New Year. That seems too good an opportunity to pass up.' She paused. 'We can't dissuade Natalie from giving evidence, Jack – that would put her safety at risk. I see that now. Your solution, your idea, is the only road open. Let's call a press conference. But here in Kenya, in Nairobi.'

Natalie's heart lifted.

Jack, obviously pleased that his mother had come round to his view, nodded and sat back. 'You said two decisions.'

It was Eleanor's turn to nod. 'Yes, I've added in a little thought of my own.' She stood up. 'When we announce our discoveries, we shall say we think we have found an early form of mankind, a new species which not only stood upright but built man's first structure. And we shall name him *Homo kiharensis;* we shall name him after the gorge. Let's see the Maasai – Marongo and his elders – deal with that!'

Eleanor sat bolt upright in the refectory tent and tapped the table with her pen. 'Let's make a start, shall we?'

She looked around her. 'Now that the decision has been taken to hold a press conference – and I can't pretend that I'm any happier about it than some of you are – we need to make sure that we conduct ourselves as efficiently and effectively as possible. I have given some thought to logistics and how we might divide up the responsibilities between us.'

She had a sheet of paper in front of her and consulted it now.

'I will myself handle the invitations. I don't think I'm being immodest if I say that my name, the Deacon name, is best known in relation to ancient man in Kenya, so we must use that. I can liaise with the High Commission in Nairobi, find out which newspapers are coming, add in some

East African papers, the wire services like Reuters, and some American papers, who have correspondents here or elsewhere in East Africa, and I can also find out when the British delegation has its freest day.'

Eleanor looked up. 'Christopher, I'd like you to find a place where we can hold the conference. Not a hotel, of course, all the main ones are whites-only. I suppose a lecture room in a college somewhere would be a suitable alternative. And I'd like you to be in charge of the exhibits themselves – the jaw, the teeth, the skull and the vertebrae. Good boxes, polished wood, coloured cotton wool or satin, something that shows them off clearly and makes them seem special. Yes?'

Christopher nodded.

'You will do the pictures as well, of course, Christopher – very important. The knee-joint, the jaw and teeth, the boulders. These must be as clear as possible. If we are successful they will be used in newspapers right across the world, so I want lots and lots of copies. Okay?'

Christopher nodded and smiled.

'And I want a few slides. That means we can darken the room where the conference is held, to make more of a dramatic impact. Can you do that?'

'Yes, of course. No problem at all.'

'But that's not enough!'

All eyes turned to Jack.

'I'm sorry, Mother, but this is journalism, not palaeontology. We need general shots of the gorge, of the places where these objects were found – and above all of the people who found them, *us:*

440

Daniel here, Natalie, you, the rest of the team.'

'Surely they will have their own—'

'You know I'm right. Not every paper will send a photographer on a background trip. If we want the coverage we do want, now that we have decided we need it, we must make it as easy for them as we can.'

Eleanor looked at him for what seemed an age. Then, 'Very well. See to it, Christopher, please.'

Christopher made some notes on an old piece of paper he had in his pocket.

'Jack, I'd like you – with Natalie, Jonas and Arnold – to draft the actual document, the press release itself. Obviously, I want to see it and finalise it, but I'd like you four to do the preparatory work. We'll keep Kees in reserve, in case something goes wrong. We'll decide which of the team, which of us, actually faces the press nearer the time. We don't need to take a decision on that right now.'

She looked around the table. 'Any questions?'

No one spoke.

'Good. It's now the eighth of December. The Christmas break isn't far away, when many of the ancillary staff have a week off anyway – people like Aldwai, and the other guards – so the timing is fortunate. I'll let you have a date for the conference as soon as it is settled, but I think we want the press release and the photographs ready by – what? – let's say, the twenty-eighth of December. I'll make sure the conference isn't before the thirtieth. Is everyone clear on that?'

No one said anything, but they all nodded.

Eleanor scraped back her chair and stood up.

441

The meeting was over.

As everyone dispersed, Jack took Natalie's arm and led her across to Arnold and Jonas. 'Look,' he whispered, 'Natalie and I are ahead of the curve here. We anticipated this and have been working on a press release. It's too hot now but let's gather at my tent before dinner tonight and we can start going through the drafts we have prepared. What do you say?'

'What time?' said Jonas.

'Six, six-thirty; that will give us an hour and a bit before dinner.'

Arnold grinned. 'I'll bring the sherry.'

Lost

'Kees, what on earth are you doing?' Natalie stood over the Dutchman, near the wall of the gorge. It was another baking day.

Kees was kneeling before two piles of stones. He wiped his brow with his sleeve. 'So far, I've been looking at the shape of the hand-axes we found here, trying to fit them into some sort of sequence. This pile on the right', and he gestured, 'are from below the two million years level. The others, on the left, are from above that level. See, they are – on the whole – smaller, with sharper edges, and narrower points. It looks as though we have a change in technology, associated with your wind shelter, if that is what it is, and with the skeletal remains we have found.' He looked up. 'Something else for the press conference, maybe.'

Natalie examined the piles of stones. She could see that what Kees said was right. 'But this is wonderful. I can see the change clearly. Have you told Eleanor?'

'I've hinted at it, yes.'

'You must tell her immediately. If you are right, it's major news. Why haven't you brought these stones back to camp?'

He sat back on his haunches and wiped his face with the towel he kept in the back pocket of his trousers.

'Because I wanted to be certain about my second idea.'

Natalie crouched down alongside him. 'Go on. I'm all ears.'

He pointed to the stones. 'Look at the hand-axes. Whether they are the earlier, bigger, blunter shapes, or the later, narrower, more pointed ones, they are greeny-grey in colour and very hard. Geologically speaking they are chert.' He waved his arm in a horizontal sweep. 'Look at the gorge. Here it's relatively soft, reddish rock, quartzite, because it has iron oxide in it. So where did ancient man find the stone for his tools?'

Kees replaced his towel in his back pocket. '*Homo kiharensis*, as we are calling him, obviously found out by trial-and-error that chert is harder than quartzite, but where did he find chert in the first place?' He coughed. 'What I'm saying is that, somewhere near here – I assume it's near here – will be a mine, man's first mine, a place where he dug for chert, dislodged lozenges of hard stone to make chert hand-axes. It may be an old stream bed.' He looked up and smiled. 'That's my next project, to look for the mine. That should get me my Ph.D.'

'Brilliant, Kees,' breathed Natalie. 'But how do you start looking?'

'As I say, chert is harder than sandstone. It produces smoother terrain, is covered by fewer trees, more likely just savannah grass or is washed out by streams when they break cover. I'll get all these axes back to camp today and start looking for the mine tomorrow.'

'Let me help you now.'

'Great, thank you. Just make sure to keep the piles separate. I've painted a little number on

446

each one, in white paint. And I have a map here in my pocket, recording where each one was found.'

'Sounds like another Ph.D. to me.' Natalie smiled at Kees as she picked up some of the stones and started the trudge back to the Land Rover.

How good it was to be back in the gorge, what she thought of as her natural habitat now, despite all its attendant discomforts – the heat, the airlessness, the smells. Today's variety was baboon dung again: she was becoming a connoisseur. She reached the Land Rover, with Kees not far behind. They put one set of axes on one towel, the others on a second, a different colour, so there could be no mix-up. Then they went back for the rest. Aldwai, leaning on his gun, watched all this from a distance.

'How far away might this mine be?' Natalie asked Kees as they retraced their steps.

'How long is a piece of string?' He smiled. 'All we know so far is that early man acquired obsidian from as much as one hundred and fifty kilometres away. I don't expect the mine in this area to be anywhere near as far away as that. Obsidian is light and the objects it makes, as you have seen, are small and for ceremonial use. Chert is much heavier and those early hand-axes, as you can see, are quite big, for everyday use. I don't think early man would have ventured more than – what? – five to fifteen kilometres away, though you never know. Anyway, tomorrow I start looking. If I find something, it will be an extra announcement at the press conference.'

They reached the remains of the axes they had left behind, and both stooped to collect what was left.

As they did so, Natalie said softly, 'You remember you said to me – that time we were discussing obsidian mirrors, when you first told me you were homosexual – that Richard Sutton was also that way inclined.'

Kees nodded, but immediately looked around, to double-check no one else was within earshot.

'Do you still stand by that?'

'Yes, I think so. Why do you ask?'

She picked up a number of stones. 'Well, you couldn't have known this but, once, before Richard died, I went into the storeroom to return Ndekei's wellington boot – which had got lost and I had found – and Richard was there and he and Ndekei were standing very close. Richard *said* he had indigestion and was there for some bicarbonate of soda, but, well, I wonder if he was, really...' She tailed off.

Kees whistled. 'What are you saying? That you think Richard and Ndekei...? Is that why you asked if married men could also be homosexual?'

She nodded.

'But that means if you are right, the real reason Ndekei acted as he did was not what he told the police.'

Natalie nodded again. 'Maybe the two reasons coincided. But you see why your hunch about Richard is so important. It's important to me, because if Ndekei killed Richard for – oh, let's say for something having to do with sexual jealousy – then that changes the whole picture, and it means the Maasai threat to destroy the gorge is founded, at least partly, on a lie.'

Kees nodded. 'I can see that, yes. But I can't give you a firmer answer, Natalie. I did notice that Richard looked at me in a way that I am familiar with. If he had looked at me in that way in Amsterdam, I would have had no hesitation in approaching him. But in Amsterdam rejection, if it happens, is fairly anonymous. Not here, which is why we never ... why nothing ever happened. I can't be much more help, I'm afraid.' Kees tailed off.

She nodded. 'I did wonder, at one point, whether to talk to Maxwell Sandys when he came in from Nairobi the other day, to test how what you know changes things–'

'You didn't say anything did you? You *promised!*'

'No, I didn't! Don't worry, I didn't. But, but I do think things will only change, Kees, if you *make* them change, stand up for yourself, get organised politically.'

Kees was shaking his head and biting his lip. 'I can't think politically, not for now.' He hesitated. 'I remember that last time we spoke I told you I was in a minority, like you. Well, my minority just got smaller, by one.'

'What do you mean?'

'Remember I told you about Hendrik, the man I share a house with in Amsterdam?'

'Yes. Yes, I do.'

'And you may remember I told you he is a wine merchant. I had a letter from him in the last batch of post. He's been to California, to buy some wine from their phylloxera-resistant vines

449

because the European vines have this disease, and it's affecting wine production, and therefore prices.' He paused, his features clouding. 'While there ... while there he met someone else.' Kees breathed in and swallowed hard. 'He means a lot to me, but his letter said he has met someone else and that he is emigrating to America, to San Francisco, with this other person. That it is all over between us. So now I feel...' He caught his breath and resumed picking up the hand-axes.

Natalie didn't know how to respond. She had no experience with this kind of situation.

'I don't know what to say, Kees,' she whispered, as they both began the trudge back to the Land Rover. She was about to say that she, too, had recently split up with someone when she realised she hadn't thought about Dominic for days. She said nothing.

'Ah, here's Naiva.' Eleanor reached out and gripped the other woman's arm. 'Before we start dinner, can you tell us, Jack, are you going to do this Christmas what you did last time – for the children of the staff, I mean?'

Jack, swallowing some water, nodded his head. 'Circuits and bumps, you mean? Yes, I don't see why not. They seemed to enjoy it, all those who weren't scared stiff of flying.'

'What's all this?' said Arnold.

'It's Jack's idea: a collective Christmas gift to all the children of the ancillary staff.' Eleanor held out her glass, so Jack could fill it with water. 'If they want to, and if their parents give them permission, he takes them for a ride in his plane. Not for long: they fly over their own villages, so they can see them from the air, they look at some animals from up there, and he lands and takes off again immediately, so they have some impression of speed. One or two of the very young ones were scared of the noise and the idea of leaving the ground, but most of them loved it.'

She turned back to Naiva. 'There you are, my dear, you can tell everyone that Mr Jack will fly anyone who wants to – let's say on the afternoon of the day before Christmas Eve, December twenty-third. Is that okay, Jack?'

Jack nodded.

Naiva beamed.

'Now you can serve dinner,' said Eleanor, sitting back.

She waited for a moment, as Naiva moved around the table.

'Where's Kees?' Eleanor said. 'He wasn't here at lunch. He must be back by now.'

'I'll go look for him,' said Jack, getting to his feet.

Naiva placed a large bowl of pasta, smothered in a tomato sauce, in the middle of the table, from where they could help themselves.

She was just bringing a jug with more sauce when Jack arrived back, running. 'There's no sign of him. His bed is all smooth, his tent flaps were tied, everything inside is neat and tidy.'

'He's never gone off before,' said Eleanor. 'I don't like this. What can he be doing?'

Natalie put down her water glass and relayed the substance of her conversation with Kees a few days before, about looking for a chert mine.

451

'Oh dear,' breathed Eleanor and looked from Jack to Christopher to Daniel. 'If he got too much sun, became sick, delirious, he might have lost his bearings, stumbled across all manner of predators.' She got to her feet. 'We must go and look for him. Jack, you take one Land Rover and head south, Daniel you take another and drive east, I'll drive the third and go north. If he'd gone west he'd have been in the camp. Arnold, you come with me, Natalie go with Jack, Christopher with Daniel. Jonas, you stay here in case your medical skills are required. If anyone finds him, we'll radio in and you can drive the other Land Rover to wherever he is.' She turned to Naiva. 'Sorry, my dear, keep some food warm if you can. I don't know how long we shall be.'

She led the way to the Land Rovers.

'Don't forget the game lights,' shouted Jack to no one in particular.

He took the second Land Rover and made sure a game light was in the back. He drove down into the gorge and up the other side, turned right along the northern edge, driving as fast as he dared. After about twenty minutes he turned right again and sank down back into the gorge and up the other side, on the southern bank.

'Kees said that chert is a hard rock and that it probably supported only grassy vegetation rather than lush trees, but is sometimes found in river beds.'

'So we keep to the open spaces rather than the thickets and forests: that's worth knowing. And we look out for dried river beds.' Jack pointed to a socket near the transmission. 'If you plug the

452

game light in there, you can use it to shine to the left and right of the vehicle. It's far more flexible than the headlights.'

Natalie did what he said.

The game light, she found, was not only more flexible than the headlights, but far more powerful.

'Keep an eye out for animals,' said Jack. 'You'll notice their eyes first: their eyes reflect the light, like cat's eyes on a road. If Kees has been attacked by a predator, then those eyes may be the first sign we have that we've found him, or his remains.'

'Bit ghoulish, aren't you?'

'It's night-time in the bush, Natalie. You know full well that most of the animals we see during daytime are resting in the heat, and they come alive at night. Kees is in even more danger in the dark than he is during the day. During the day, his chief enemy is the sun. If he was searching less-covered areas, less-covered with trees, I mean, he was at risk of sunstroke. If that's what happened, I don't think he will survive the night. I'm sorry, but that's the reality.'

They drove on in silence, Natalie playing the game light in all directions. They saw impala, a lynx, countless baboons, wildebeest, foxes. At one point they saw four lionesses and Jack brought the Land Rover to a halt. 'I'm going to approach them slowly. Wind up your window. Look for blood, signs of human remains.'

Natalie looked at him. 'You really think–?'

'Yes, it's possible. Of course, it's possible. That's why we are out here, now, looking for him.'

But they could see no signs of blood near the lions, nor any other suspicious remains, and they pressed on.

At midnight they heard Eleanor's voice over the walkie-talkie.

'Anyone seen any predators?'

'No,' said Daniel's voice.

'Lion,' said Jack. 'Four lionesses, by Kilkoris Stones, but no blood, nothing.'

'I'm with some elephants now,' said Eleanor. 'Near Sekanani, but they're not moving.' She was silent for a moment. 'Let's give it another hour.'

After another hour, however, there was no better news when Eleanor came back on the walkie-talkie. 'We need a change of plan. Daniel, you have the best eyes, so you and Christopher can continue looking. Jack, assuming Daniel doesn't find him during the hours of darkness, you need to take off at dawn, so you and Natalie should get some sleep. I'll turn in too, so I can raise the alarm at dawn and get some of our neighbours to lend us the use of their planes. We must pull out all the stops in the morning. Is everyone clear?'

'Understood,' said Jack.

'We'll keep at it,' said Christopher.

'If you find him, radio in, whatever the time. Clear?'

'Copy.'

Jack turned the Land Rover and headed for home. 'Keep looking,' he said to Natalie. 'You never know.'

As they drove, he said, 'If we have to go looking for Kees tomorrow – by plane, I mean – if

454

Christopher and Daniel don't find him tonight, are you okay about that?'

'What do you mean? Why shouldn't I be?'

'The hairy landing the other day. It didn't put you off?'

She thought. 'I can't say it's up there with Brahms's *Deutsche Requiem* as one of life's must-have experiences, but, well, I don't have much flying experience but you seem, you seem... I'm not put off.'

Jack nodded and changed gear, to negotiate ruts in the track. 'And when I dared to kiss you the other night, during our other nocturnal adventure, did that put you off?'

Natalie didn't say anything.

'If you don't answer, I'm going to stop the Land Rover and let you walk the rest of the way home.'

'That puts me off.'

She grinned and let another silence elapse, and so did he. 'How long can someone survive in the bush?'

He swung the wheel over, to avoid a rock. 'Well, obviously it depends on whether he meets any predators, whether he has the sense to keep in the shade, whether he knows which plants are edible or not so he can take on water.' Jack took some chocolate from the breast pocket of his shirt and handed it to Natalie. 'Four days, I'd say.'

Natalie stripped the silver foil from the chocolate, broke off two squares and handed them back across to Jack.

He held her hand in his, moved her fingers to

his mouth, took the chocolate and brushed his lips across the back of her hand. Then he let go.

It took them almost another hour to reach the camp, so that it was two o'clock before Jack reversed the Land Rover under the acacia trees where it was normally parked. Someone had kept the campfire going, the hurricane lamps were still burning in the refectory tent and they could see three or four thermos flasks on the table, alongside a tea towel draped over something. Naiva was in bed but she had left them coffee and chicken sandwiches. They had gone without dinner.

There was no sign of Jonas either. He must have gone to bed.

'Do you have an alarm?' said Jack, as they stood, munching sandwiches and washing them down with hot coffee.

'Of course.'

He nodded. 'Let's meet at the Land Rovers at five. It gets light around five-thirty but Naiva will be up, with breakfast, and we need to get the plane ready. We take off at six, once we can see clearly.'

When Natalie reached her tent, she realised she was exhausted and she felt as though she was covered in dust. Part of her would have loved a shower but there was no Mgina at this hour and certainly no water. The other half of her was longing to collapse on the bed but she forced herself to clean her teeth and, after she had got undressed, she brushed her hair for a few minutes.

She set the alarm; five o'clock was now just two

and a half hours away.

Natalie lay back and thought of Kees. How terrified he must be, right now, if he was still alive. She had listened to the theatre of the night so often from the safety of her tent in the camp, but to be out there, amid the screams and skirmishes, the sudden rush of hooves, the roar of lions, the menacing silences: if the sun hadn't driven Kees mad, night-time surely would.

She turned on her side. She realised she was still hungry. The sandwiches had simply stimulated her appetite. The camp kitchen was closed but there were the remains of Jack's bar of chocolate which she had left in the Land Rover. Should she get them?

Jack. Once again he had gently touched her but made no attempt to press himself further. He was letting her get used to him, showing her how he felt but leaving her breathing space.

She liked that. He was willing to wait. Like Dominic had been.

Jack slumped into a chair next to Natalie and they both stared at the flames of the campfire.

'What can you see in the embers, Dr. Nelson?'

It was three nights later. Despite day-long searches, by plane and Land Rover, Kees had not been found. This evening, at dusk, the search had been called off.

She shook her head. 'I'm not looking and I'm not thinking. My mind is numb. Say we never find Kees' body, how are we going to deal with that? I mean, there'll be no end, always a doubt – not just as to whether he is actually dead but as to how, exactly, he died, if he did die. It's all so ... so *cold*. If my father were here, he would pray for Kees. I can't do that but not being able to do anything ... it's worse.'

'How well did you know Kees?'

Natalie shook her head again. 'Not well, not well at all. He talked to me about his beloved hand-axes and the stone they were made of, that's about it. You?'

'Some. He was interested in flying, mainly because it helped him see rock-formations from above. He was one of the most interesting passengers I ever gave a lift to, explaining what we were over-flying all the time.' Jack shifted in his seat. He let a few moments go by. 'I can see you are upset, Natalie. Why don't you let me take you to Lamu for Christmas – just a couple of days. It will take our minds off things. It's only about three hours by plane.'

Natalie didn't seem to hear him. Then, 'What's at Lamu?'

'It's on the coast, an old Swahili village that used to be a centre of the slave trade. Totally different from here. There's also a very nice reef: we could go snorkelling, work on our tans.'

She looked across and gave him a sad smile. 'I don't know, Jack. I don't think... I'm not ready to have a good time while we don't know what's happened to Kees. It doesn't seem right.'

Eleanor stopped buttering her toast and tapped her enamel breakfast mug with her knife. 'Now, it's going to be a difficult day today and there's no point in hiding it. We have got to try and get

458

back to a normal routine, doing what we came here to do. We'll go through where we are on the press conference before dinner tonight, but as for the gorge we need to keep sieving and digging; we have a few days yet and we may still come across more bones of our man, or woman, which may enlarge on what we already know.'

She drank some tea. 'But – and I know this is bolting the stable door after the horse has escaped – *but* from now on we only dig in pairs; outside the camp, we only do *everything* in pairs. I don't want anyone else straying like Kees did. I shouldn't need to say this but do I make myself absolutely clear?'

'Don't worry, Mother,' breathed Christopher. 'There's no need to rub it in.'

Eleanor nodded. 'Good, good. So, how shall we pair off?'

Suddenly a Land Rover drove into the camp at high speed and sounded its horn. The horn sounded again and again. A black driver got down. 'We've found him! We've found him! Doctor Jonas, come quickly, he's very weak! By the Nimanu Road.'

Jonas was running to his tent to fetch his bag.

Jack was on his feet, pulling Christopher with him. He stopped for a moment and shouted, 'Remove the back seats from the plane and put in a mattress. I may have to fly him to a hospital. Hurry!'

Christopher had started the Land Rover's engine and Jack jumped in alongside him. Jonas got in the back and the two vehicles accelerated away through the camp gate.

They returned in just over an hour. 'He was six miles away,' said Christopher, getting down. 'He's conscious but delirious – and he's lost a lot of weight, *a lot*. Dehydration.'

Natalie looked in the back of the Land Rover. She shuddered in shock. She couldn't help it. She had seen Kees barely five days before but he was now just skin and bone; he must have lost fifty pounds, more. His facial skin was stretched tight over his jaw bone, the stubble of his beard dark against the rust red of his cheeks. His eyes, deep in their sockets, like tiny craters, raked this way and that, unfocused, fearful and bewildered at the same time.

But Kees was alive.

'Where are we going to put him?' said Arnold.

'We're not,' said Christopher. 'We're going straight to Jack's plane. We only came back here so Jack could pick up his keys and Jonas could get some medicines from the refrigerator. Did you take out the seats as we asked?'

'Yes,' said Natalie. 'The plane is ready. I also filled it with Avgas.'

Jack, who had arrived back from his own tent, heard this. He stretched his arm around her and squeezed. 'Thank god for Dr. Nelson. You've saved us fifteen precious minutes. If Kees makes it, you may have saved his life.' He turned to Jonas. 'Ready?'

Jonas nodded.

As they got into the Land Rover, Jack shouted to his mother, 'I'll radio in from Nairobi.'

Christopher and Natalie followed them in another Land Rover as they sped out to the strip.

Christopher helped Jonas lift Kees into the back of the plane to save time as Jack did his pre-flight checks. Then they watched as first one engine, then the other, cranked into life. Jack taxied to the far end of the strip and took off, waving briefly as he banked eastward.

The waves of human voices built on each other, like rollers thudding on to a beach, each one more powerful than what went before. The third movement of Brahms's *Deutsche Requiem*. How different male voices were from female ones, Natalie thought. Not just a different sound but different moods. Female choirs soared, male voices consoled.

Dinner this evening had been close to a riot. In view of the fact that Kees had been found alive and after Jack had radioed in to say they had reached the hospital in Nairobi safely, Eleanor had allowed a bottle of champagne to be brought from the fridge. As usual, there hadn't been enough for more than one glass per person but even so tongues had been loosened in heads that were relieved that the cloud hanging over them had been lifted.

There had been much laughter at dinner, as if not being allowed expression for days it was now pouring out of everyone. And, with Jack away, they were playing as many of his records as they could, one after the other, jazz alternating with classical in random order.

Natalie sat next to Christopher. 'Tell me, where exactly was Kees found? *How* was he found?'

Christopher edged his chair closer to hers. 'He

was between two large boulders, in the shade. But he was near a track and he had pulled a log across it, forcing anyone who came by to stop, to move it out of the way. As far as we could make out, he had wandered in the sun for the first day, because the kind of rock formation he was looking for didn't support much vegetation. He didn't realise he had been in the sun for so long until it was too late, when he felt sick and had to rest. He fell asleep and woke in the middle of the night. His sunstroke was bad the next day and as the sun moved round, during the afternoon, his shade disappeared. He tried to move, fell, hit his head and passed out in full sunlight. Again, when he woke it was dark.

'It was amazing no predators found him but since he wasn't near any trees, that helped. By the third day, he was severely dehydrated and, though he heard the planes looking for him, he was too weak to stand or wave. The only thing he could do, had done, was the log he used to block the track he was near. But that track is hardly used at all these days and Iku Liguru only drove that way this morning because he had fought with his daughter and wanted to make it up to her by picking some rare wild flowers which grow in that area.'

Christopher stopped speaking as the music fell silent. Then, 'I'm sorry if I frightened you – the other day, I mean, in the plane. I suppose I panicked.'

Arnold Pryce, in charge of the gramophone tonight, put on some jazz – loud, fast and, to Natalie's ears, crude.

462

'I'm not sure I have the temperament to be a pilot.'

'Don't be so hard on yourself. It was a momentary slip.'

'If Jack hadn't been there–'

'But he was!'

'Were you very frightened?'

She paused. 'It all happened so quickly, there wasn't time. Jack reacted before I did.'

Christopher nodded. 'He was quick to see what was happening. Those bloody birds.' He let some time go by. The jazz got faster still.

A water buffalo moaned in the gorge.

'I need more lessons.' He breathed out. 'But not from Jack. Jack makes me nervous. I suppose it's him being my brother.'

Natalie said nothing. Where was this going?

The jazz ended in what sounded to Natalie like an apocalypse of drums.

'Look,' said Christopher, leaning forward, 'it's Christmas in just over a week. The ancillary staff get a few days off, and the guards, and with this new ruling of my mother's that we must only be in the gorge in pairs – we are all going to stand down for seventy-two hours. I wondered, I wondered if you wanted to drive over to Kubwa. It's on the slopes of the mountain before you get to Ngorongoro and there are some hot springs. The water is very restorative and, well, since we have had such a wearing few days, I thought it might help us unwind, get the cobwebs out of our hair, prepare us for the ordeals to come: the press conference and the trial.'

Ah, Natalie was relieved to hear Chopin's

Poland Waltz. For her, the piano beat the drums any day. But how did she respond to Christopher, who had just handed her a nice little dilemma?

'Jack has already asked me to spend Christmas with him, at a Swahili village called Limu, Lomu? On the coast, anyway.'

'Lamu. It's not far from the Somalia border. Did you say yes?'

She shook her head. 'I haven't given him an answer yet, no.'

'Then you are going to have to choose between brothers.'

'Oh no,' replied Natalie, shaking her head again. 'Oh no. You've both put me in an impossible position and there's only one way out.' She stood up. This had gone far enough. 'I'm going to say "no" to both of you. Goodnight.'

When Natalie reached the breakfast table the next morning, Eleanor and Christopher were discussing the press conference.

'Most of the British delegation will be staying at the Rhodes,' Christopher was saying. 'That's not far from the Coryndon Natural History Museum, where the director has said we can use their premises. It's central and the room will be filled with natural history specimens – that will produce the right atmosphere, don't you think?'

'Yes, it will. Excellent. Well done, Christopher.' Eleanor looked up and smiled as Natalie sat down. She let Natalie sip some coffee and slice into her fruit before asking, 'And the documentation, Natalie, how is that coming along?'

'Well, no one has worked on it for a few days,

for obvious Kees-related reasons. But we're almost there, I think. Once Jack gets back from Nairobi we can polish what we have, and you can see it soon after. Forty-eight hours at the most, I should think.'

Eleanor nodded. 'Good. Things are falling into place. I still can't say I'm happy with the route we are taking but since we are going that way, we must give it our best shot, as the Americans say.' She looked across to Natalie. 'There's been no further word from the odious Richard Sutton Senior, or from Russell, I suppose?'

'One short note from Russell. He's still not happy.'

'And did you try to soften him up?'

'Yes, of course. I haven't heard back. My letter crossed with his.'

She swallowed some fruit.

'I don't think Russell *will* soften, Eleanor.'

Eleanor nodded, removing her spectacles at the same time. Just then Naiva brought in a large plate.

'Ah, eggs!' cried Eleanor. 'Christopher', and she looked across, 'I'm famished. Be an angel, go and radio Jack. Find out how Kees is this morning.'

Christopher got to his feet and, taking his coffee mug with him, crossed to his mother's tent, where the radio-telephone was.

Eleanor waited, as usual, while everyone else was served, before spooning two eggs on to her own plate.

'Arnold, how close are you to finishing your part in the press conference?'

465

'It's just a matter of tinkering, don't worry. This creature – I take it we are still calling him, or her *Homo kiharensis,* yes?'

Eleanor nodded.

'Well, we now know more or less what his or her diet was and–'

'Before you go into that, may I say something?'

Everyone looked at Natalie.

'Sorry, Arnold,' she said. 'But I'm sure your news about diet will be accepted by the rest of us. I wanted to raise a point where I don't expect universal agreement.'

'Go ahead,' said Arnold. 'These eggs are too good to let them get cold, anyway.' He attacked his food.

'I can understand why you want to call these remains *Homo kiharensis.*' Natalie swallowed some coffee, and looked over her mug at Eleanor. 'I see how that fits into what we are trying to achieve. But I wonder if we are not ... if we are not missing a trick here.'

Eleanor wiped the remains of egg yolk from her plate with some bread. 'I don't follow.'

'Consider an alternative name,' replied Natalie gently. 'Consider *Homo suttoniensis.*'

Eleanor gave a stunted gasp. 'What! I don't believe...' She tailed off.

No one else spoke.

'As a mark of respect, as an acknowledgement that he, and Russell and Daniel here, found the first bones.'

Eleanor was shaking her head. She was just about to speak when Christopher stood over her. She looked up. 'Yes?'

Natalie noticed a stain on Christopher's shirt. He had spilled his coffee over himself.

'I spoke to Jack,' he said quietly, very quietly. 'Kees died in the night.'

'What! No. *No!*' Eleanor wrapped her fingers around her mouth, but said nothing more.

Behind her spectacles, her eyes glinted. Natalie, shocked herself, couldn't make out whether or not there were tears in Eleanor's eyes.

'Jack and Jonas will stay in Nairobi today, alert the family and make the arrangements to fly the body back to Holland. They've already started. He died in hospital so there are no legal problems.' Christopher looked around the table and put his hand on his mother's shoulder. 'Apparently, his internal organs had suffered and withered too much for him to survive. He died at 4.15.'

Eleanor scraped back her chair and hurried to her tent. She disappeared inside.

Christopher sat back down at the breakfast table. 'I know I shouldn't say this, but I'm starving.'

'Eleanor? Eleanor? It's Natalie. Are you there? May I come in?' Natalie stood by the radio-telephone at the entrance to Eleanor's tent. In more matter-of-fact tones, she repeated, 'Eleanor.'

Following Christopher's devastating news, the high spirits in the camp that had carried over from the night before had vanished entirely. No one now felt like exposing himself or herself to the airless heat of the gorge and people found chores to do in camp. Grief shared is grief lessened.

Eleanor hadn't been seen all morning. There had been no more activity on the radio-telephone. Jack and Jonas were obviously shouldering the burden of telling the next-of-kin and making the other arrangements – finding a coffin, making the airline booking, liaising with the Dutch embassy over customs/immigration clearance and whatever else was needed.

The flap to Eleanor's tent moved and she appeared.

Yes, she was diminished, Natalie thought. Her hair was less than its immaculate self, her skin had lost its sheen, her fingers were shaking. She was still in shock. For the first time, Natalie thought, Eleanor looked old.

'Yes?' she said, in a flat, cold voice. 'I can't face talking about Richard—'

'No, *no*. That's not why I'm here.' She lowered her voice. 'Let's sit down. I have something to tell you, about Kees.'

Eleanor looked at her sharply, as she slumped to a chair.

'But first,' said Natalie, 'here.' She held up her whisky flask and poured a shot into the cap. 'I know you don't have a head for spirits, but now is not the time to quibble. This is medicinal.' She attempted a smile.

Eleanor looked at her, fiercely to begin with, but then her face dissolved into a small smile and she took the cap.

'Knock it all straight back,' whispered Natalie. 'It will help. I've already had one – just one.'

Eleanor sniffed the liquid, made a face, but swallowed the contents of the cap all at once. She coughed, wiped her lips with the back of her hand, nodded her head. 'I see what you mean. I suppose I feel a bit better now. What is it you have to tell me?'

Natalie took back the cap and screwed it on the flask. She slipped it into her pocket.

A few days ago, Kees told me something in confidence. Normally, I would have respected that confidence but given what has happened, given how traumatic the past few hours and days have been, and because Kees is now dead, I regard myself as released from that confidence.'

Eleanor looked at her. Her skin was not quite so *dead* as it had been. The whisky was having an effect.

'We were working in the gorge, just a few days ago when Kees told me he was homosexual.'

'What!'

'Yes. He confessed to me because, he said, he had watched me being in a minority of one in the camp, over the Ndekei trial, and he said that he wanted me to know that, although he didn't agree with my stance, he did sympathise with my solitary position.'

'But why are you telling me this now?'

'Hold on. I haven't finished.' Natalie took a deep breath. She wanted to do this slowly. 'That wasn't the whole picture. Kees also told me because he was feeling miserable and he had to talk to someone. I suppose he thought that, with us both being "outsiders", or people in a minority, I would be more sympathetic.'

'Sympathetic to what?'

'Hold on. He told me that, a day or so before,

he had received a letter from, as he put it, an older friend – an older male friend – in Amsterdam, a friend who meant a great deal to Kees, who he lived with, yet who had met someone else, he said, and who was emigrating to America, to San Francisco.'

'I still don't–'

'Eleanor, *please!* What I'm saying is that I don't think Kees' disappearance was accidental.'

Eleanor, in the act of wrapping her spectacles around her ears, stopped what she was doing.

'Yes, that's what I came to say. I think he was emotionally disturbed and that his disappearance had, at least in part, suicidal elements. He had been thrown over by his lover, he was all alone down here – doing important work, yes – but with nothing to look forward to, back at home. He was devastated.'

Eleanor, having just put on her eyeglasses, snatched them off again. 'But if you're right, that was a ghoulish way to go about it.'

'I'm not sure there's a non-ghoulish way to commit suicide but, as I told you, weeks ago, when my mother was killed there was always a doubt in my mind that she might have been suicidal too. So, in the midst of my grief at her death, I read books on suicide.' Natalie ran her tongue along her lips. 'People don't always mean to kill themselves outright. Often they put themselves in danger, at risk – they will turn on the car engine in their garage, for instance, or slit their wrists and lie in a bath of warm water – *but* they will do so in such a way, at certain times of the day when other family members, or neighbours, will interrupt what they are doing and find them. They put themselves in a situation where whether they live or die is a matter of chance and depends on whether they are found or not.'

She took out her handkerchief and wiped the sweat off her throat. 'I think that's what happened with Kees. He went off in search of his precious chert and allowed himself to stay out too long, too long in the sun, knowing it was dangerous, that he could die of dehydration or be eaten by lions or hyenas, but also knowing that we would come looking for him. With suicidal people, these calculations are always tricky. If people find you in time, they make a fuss of you, you are the centre of attention for a while and you either make a recovery or you bide your time until you feel depressed all over again.'

She put away her handkerchief. 'I'm not an expert, of course, but it seems to me that on this occasion Kees made a calculation that almost worked, but in the end didn't.'

Eleanor turned this over in her mind, not speaking for some considerable time. 'And you're telling me all this to reassure me? To lessen my feelings of guilt?'

'That comes into it, yes. I could see this morning how hard you had taken Kees' death, how you must be thinking that, after however many years it is of trouble-free digging, all of a sudden you have two deaths on your hands. For what it's worth, I don't think you can be held responsible for either death. That's why I've told you about Kees.' She wasn't going to add what Kees had said about Richard Sutton. She didn't want that

471

argument just now.

Eleanor again turned Natalie's remarks over in her mind. 'And you tell me all this, you offer me this *comfort*, I suppose you'd call it, despite our differences over Ndekei?'

'I'm not that calculating, Eleanor. At least I don't think I am. I could see how upset you were – we all could. I happened to know things that were relevant. You couldn't know what I knew, you blamed yourself more than was reasonable.' She wiped her lips with her tongue. 'I could pick on myself if I chose to – I knew what a mess Kees was in and didn't think it through, didn't anticipate he wasn't fit enough to be left on his own.'

'Now don't *you* go blaming yourself. That's ridiculous.' Eleanor reached out and put her hand on Natalie's knee. 'But thank you for telling me all of that. It has helped lift a load from my mind. Some of it, anyway.'

Eleanor was perking up, there was no doubt. She rose and moved across to the radio-telephone. 'I must talk to Jack, see what's happening. He tells me he's invited you to Lamu for Christmas, to look at the Swahili village. Are you going?'

Natalie shook her head.

'Why on earth not? Everything will be all closed up here for a couple of days. Are you afraid of flying?'

'It's not that. Christopher also invited me to Kubwa hot springs.'

'Oh dear!' sighed Eleanor. 'So you can't accept one without devastating the other.'

'I think "devastating" is putting it rather strongly. But I'm saying no to both of them.'

Eleanor pulled her chair closer to the radio-telephone. 'I should be able to say something to help you, my dear, to give you some inside information about the boys that you don't know, to help repay you for what you have just told me, and help you decide, one way or the other. But I daren't, I *daren't:* a mother can't take sides.' She smiled as she played with the dials and knobs. 'It's a good job Jock isn't alive. He'd have charmed you long before his sons did.'

As Natalie walked across the camp ground towards the refectory area, a great grey shadow swept across the row of tents and the trees where the Land Rovers were parked. Clouds. Huge white and slate-coloured balloons billowed one upon the other high in the sky, like giant sailing ships. The short rains were arriving.

Most of the others were already there when she reached the main tent and the meeting had started.

Eleanor, dressed today in navy chinos and a white shirt, was holding the draft press release in front of her. This was a business meeting to finalise the details of the press conference before they all dispersed for the Christmas break.

She was already speaking. Or rather, shouting. At Christopher.

'I cannot believe it! I repeat: *I can-not believe it!* After all this time, after weeks of delay, you have only just found out. What were you thinking? *Did you think?* Did your father and I not teach you

473

anything?' She threw her spectacles on the table in front of her. 'Words fail me.'

Natalie sat down. Puzzled, she transferred her gaze from Arnold Pryce to Jack to Daniel. Jonas had followed her in and sat next to her.

'I'm sorry,' said Christopher. 'I didn't think to ask. I never imagined–'

'You *should* have imagined. It was your job to imagine, to anticipate any likely difficulty.' Eleanor slapped the table. 'What are we going to do?'

No one answered.

Seeing Natalie and Jonas' bewilderment, Jack leaned forward and said, gently, knowing he could set his mother off again at any moment, 'The Coryndon Museum, where the press conference was to have been, has separate lavatories for blacks and whites.' He let this sink in.

Outside, rain began to fall. Natalie stared at it. Rain in Africa – this was a new experience for her.

'How did you manage to overlook something so basic?' cried Eleanor, again addressing her remarks to Christopher. 'I told you to steer clear of the main hotels, for the very reason that they are whites only.' She thrust forward her chin in the manner she had. 'The whole message of the research we do here is that mankind had its origins in this part of Africa, that the whole globe was peopled by migrants from here, that we are all *one people!*' She took a deep breath, her chest heaving. 'That is what we stand for, Christopher, and it's an important something that can't be exaggerated.'

She wiped her neck with a handkerchief. 'Think of the wars that have been fought, in the nineteenth and twentieth centuries, over nationalism, because one set of people thought that they, or their way of life, was better than others. We are all one people – that is conceivably the most important message there has ever been. We can't announce our results in a place, even a museum, where that message is contradicted in the most basic, humiliating way.' She shook her head. 'What are we going to do? I just hope this news doesn't get out – think what the press would do with it.'

'Have we lost any money?' said Jack. 'Did we have to put a deposit down?'

Christopher nodded gloomily. 'Yes, but not much.'

'Well, I don't see a problem with the press, if they find out. We just tell the truth, that we discovered, late in the day, that the museum has a racial policy we can't agree with, so we did what we did. Nairobi's got lots of buildings – cinemas, school halls, churches – it can't be difficult to find a replacement.'

He turned to his mother. 'Do you want me to–?'

'No, it's Christopher's job. He's made the mess, let him clear it up.' She turned in her seat so that she was facing Christopher. 'Do you hear? It's *your* mess, so it's *your* Christmas that is going to be spoiled. You can drive to Nairobi tomorrow morning and, whatever it takes, you will find another place for the press conference, somewhere that is available to blacks and whites

475

equally, somewhere that's easy to find, somewhere that holds enough people, somewhere with proper electricity, so we can show slides, and where the rental isn't an arm and a leg. Talk to Jack, he's on this KANU education committee, he must know about the schools and colleges, at least.'

Eleanor put her spectacles back on and picked up the papers in front of her. 'Now, let's go through our argument, make sure it's watertight, try to think of all the potential criticisms.'

Natalie looked at Christopher. He looked wretched. His mother had all but humiliated him in front of the rest of them. Yes, he had made a mistake, but was it anything more than that? Had Natalie herself been organising the venue for the press conference, would she have thought to ask if the lavatories were segregated? She supposed not. On the other hand, she told herself, she was new to Africa whereas Christopher had grown up here, so maybe Eleanor had a point.

Did Eleanor pick on Christopher more than she picked on Jack? Was Jack his mother's favourite? Natalie couldn't honestly say that Eleanor was anything other than scrupulously fair – scrupulously *hard* – on both of them.

But she couldn't help feeling a bit sorry for Christopher.

Eleanor was speaking again, as she pushed her eyeglasses back up her nose. 'The press release itself, I think, is more or less on the right lines. The right information in more or less the right order. The one change I'd like to make is to adapt a suggestion of Natalie's.'

The two women exchanged glances.

'It would be inappropriate to name our new hominid after either Richard Sutton or Kees van Schelde, and we all know there are unbeatable reasons for calling him, or her, *Homo kiharensis*.' She paused, briefly. 'But Kees did identify a new form of hand-axe – smaller, finer, sharper than what came before. With everyone's agreement, therefore, I intend to name this new culture "Scheldian". It's easy on the ear and ensures that Kees will be remembered, at least by his colleagues.'

She looked around. 'Are we agreed?'

'Well done, Eleanor, good idea,' said Jonas. 'It's the right thing to do.'

'What about Richard?' said Arnold.

In reply, Eleanor looked at Daniel. 'With your agreement, I'd like to name the gully in the gorge, where you and Russell and Richard found the knee-joint, "RSK", for "Richard Sutton's *Korongo*". That too ensures he will be remembered.' She looked around the table. 'Are we agreed?'

Natalie had a question. 'In theory I approve, wholeheartedly. But aren't you being a little bit – what's the word? – *forward*, aggressive, attaching English-language names to parts of what is, after all, a Maasai gorge? Aren't you being deliberately confrontationist?'

Eleanor nodded. 'A good point and the answer is yes, I am. We've pussy-footed around this for too long. Kenya is going to be independent soon. Black people will regain what they say is theirs. But this gorge, and what it stands for, is just as much the work of white people as black people. It is, in itself, and as I said earlier, a monument to the fact that we are all one people. So that's what I am going to add to your press release, that's the gloss I shall tack on at the end.' She took off her spectacles, and let her gaze take in the whole table. 'Since we are in this fight, we may as well punch as hard as we can. I'm not just aiming at Marongo. If we get the kind of press I'm hoping for, it will be very hard for the foundation to pull out now.'

'Okay everybody, just sit quietly while I fill her up with Avgas – we don't want to run out in mid-air, do we? – and then I'll be ready for the first group.'

Jack, Natalie, Eleanor and Arnold Pryce were standing around Jack's plane while he poured fuel into the tanks in the wings from the fortified spare cans he and Natalie had filled in Karatu. A group of about a dozen children sat on the ground next to the airstrip, their parents standing a little way off.

'Natalie,' said Jack. 'If you don't mind, I'd like you to sit in the back of the plane. If last year is anything to go by, some of the children get excited when we are in the air, they fidget like mad and don't always keep their seat belts fastened. Make sure they do, will you? Now the short rains have started, there's more cloud around and the air is less stable. If the children don't have their seat belts on and we hit some holes in the air, they could get hurt.' He smiled at her. 'Also, one or two get frightened once we have taken off and

478

they may need their hands held.'

'Okay,' he said, laying the petrol can back on the ground and screwing the lid back on the wing where the fuel pipe was. He clapped his hands. 'Who wants to go first?'

All the children raised their arms.

Jack laughed. 'Let's do it village by village. Who comes from Tukana?' Four children raised their hands and he lifted one boy off his feet and carried him to the plane. Natalie did the same with a young girl. She got in behind the girl and sat next to her. Jack filled the plane with two more children and then climbed into the cockpit himself. He started his pre-flight checks.

Arnold Pryce was busy sketching the scene and handing round his drawings to the parents.

Jack started the Comanche's engines and taxied to the end of the airstrip.

'Is everyone strapped in?' he shouted.

'Yes.' Natalie answered for the children.

'Tukana, here we come!'

The plane lurched forward and gathered speed as it raced down the strip.

'Wave!' shouted Jack and the children in the plane waved to their parents as the Comanche lifted from the ground.

Jack and Natalie made three circuits in all, each lasting about thirty minutes, as they climbed in the sky, banked and headed for one or other village, which they overflew at a low level. Each time they took in a stretch of the Sand River, where Jack knew they would see hippos and where elephants were lurking in the vegetation. He kept up a running commentary all the time,

479

pointing out aspects of the landscape that the children might otherwise miss.

One girl, Teza, was frightened by the noise of the plane and climbed on to Natalie's lap, closing her eyes. But everyone else seemed to love their time in the air and when Jack landed for the last time, two of the children went up to him, held him by the hand and led him to a log they had found while he had been flying. They made him sit on the log and then they all stood in front of him and began to sing.

Natalie stood under the wing of the plane, in the shade, watching and listening. Eleanor and Arnold Pryce had gone back to camp by now, but the children's parents were still there.

The song didn't last long and when it was over the children and their parents began to drift away. Jack came over to Natalie.

'What was the song about?' she asked.

'Oh, it was a well-known ballad in this part of the Serengeti, about a mythical land where the only inhabitants are children and all the wild animals are infants too, so there are no fights, no wars, no predators, everyone gets on. It was a nice way to say "thank you", don't you think?'

She nodded. 'Have you ever had an accident in your plane?'

'Apart from the other day, when Christopher tangled with those birds? No, I haven't. I blew a tyre on take-off once, and had to land very carefully, as slowly as possible, so the tyreless wheel didn't generate any sparks and set the fuel vapour alight. Nothing worse than that. Why?'

She shrugged. 'I think I'm getting the flying

480

bug, so I should explore the risks.'

'Birds can be a problem, if you fly into a flock of them; tiredness; incomplete maintenance. You need to know your mechanics and have faith in them. Here in Kihara we have special risks too.'

'Oh? What's that?'

He nodded towards the airstrip.

She followed his gaze.

The cheetahs were back.

'Good news and not so good news, everyone.' Eleanor sat back, her dinner half-finished. Outside the rain sluiced down, hammering on the roof of the refectory tent, rattling on the bonnets of the Land Rovers, hissing on the blackened logs of the campfire, precipitating smoke and steam and an acrid smell of burnt, wet whistling thorn. Eleanor had to raise her voice to make herself heard.

'Christopher has found us a venue for the press conference, a lecture theatre at the Royal College, which he says is earmarked to become a university after independence. So it's a suitably forward-looking institution which is *not* segregated in any way, shape or form. And it has all the facilities we need to get over our message – film screens, slide projectors, a proper microphone system. It's conveniently located and we can afford it.'

'What's the bad news?'

'Poor Christopher.' Eleanor smiled, but sadly. 'With all this rain, there was a flash flood near Ngiro. The road from Nairobi has been cut – washed away. It will be days before it is repaired and so he can't get back. I've told him to sit it out in Nairobi, to hold tight there over Christmas. He can wait in town till the press conference and spend the time making sure everything runs like clockwork. And he can make early contact with the visiting journalists.'

'I could fly up and fetch him,' said Jack. 'And take him back afterwards, so he can drive back the Land Rover.'

Eleanor shook her head. 'Don't worry, Jack. I've given him three flying lessons as a Christmas present. At Nairobi International Airport, in the private part. He'll be fine, he's got plenty to do.'

She looked round the table. 'Now, originally we were going to break for the holidays after lunch tomorrow, it being Christmas Eve. In view of the weather, however, we may as well call it a day now and start digging again after the break and after the press conference. Maxwell Sandys is coming in a plane for me tomorrow morning and we are flying up to Lake Victoria for forty-eight hours. I know Daniel's going home to see his wife and family in Nyanza. I've told the cooking staff they don't need to come in after breakfast tomorrow. Has anyone else made any plans?'

Arnold leaned forward. 'Jonas and I are going to the hot springs at Kubwa for a couple of days. Make ourselves even more beautiful.' He grinned.

'Natalie? Jack?'

Natalie was suddenly at a loss. With all the concentration necessary to prepare for the press conference, she hadn't taken on board that the camp would be quite so deserted over Christmas. She didn't know what to say.

482

'Don't worry about me or Natalie, mother. I'm going snorkelling on the reef off Lamu. Natalie's coming with me.'

Shadows

'You sit there. You can look right out to sea. India is just over the horizon.' Jack held the chair for Natalie.

'Thank you. Have you ever been to India?'

He shook his head as he sat down. 'I'm an Africa man. Doesn't it show?'

'Whenever I've been around, you've kept your tail well hidden.'

The restaurant was very small, a veranda of about eight tables of which only two others were occupied. It was lit by hurricane lamps and candles. The sea itself was the width of the beach away, inky black, collapsing on to the sand in soft slurps.

Natalie fingered the menu, a short card.

'Drink?' He ignored her last remark.

'I'd love one, but do they serve alcohol here? I thought you said that Lamu was mainly Muslim.'

'Mainly, yes, but not only. That's why I chose this hotel, if you can call it that. How many rooms did they say they had – nine?'

She nodded. 'Plus a pool, a restaurant and a shop. But the rooms are very comfortable, soft spongy beds. I'm sure I shall sleep well here.'

'What about the smell?'

'After the gorge? Oh no, it doesn't matter, doesn't even register. How many donkeys *are* there here?'

Lamu had been a surprise to Natalie in more ways than one when they had arrived. The journey up from Kihara had been enjoyable and only mildly adventurous.

'How do we avoid the storms?' She had asked that morning, as they were loading their luggage on to Jack's plane, with Mgina helping. In truth, Natalie had been rather thrown the evening before when he had announced, baldly, that she would be going with him to Lamu. But she hadn't relished being virtually alone in the camp over Christmas, especially as that was the time of year her parents had always been happiest, when their choir was busiest. And, since Christopher was marooned in Nairobi, and was not there to be upset, she had acquiesced.

'Simple,' Jack had replied. 'We leave in the morning, before the storms build up in the afternoon. If we do meet any big clouds, we go round them, or above them, not through them. In any case, I'm going to fly east to the ocean, then up the coast. The clouds tend to gather over land, especially high land. The coast, as the saying goes, should be clear.'

So it had proved, though the journey had taken closer to three and a half hours, rather than the two hours had they flown direct. During the journey she had had her first proper flying lesson. Jack had let her handle the controls, explained some of the instruments, the mysteries of air traffic control jargon, and shown her what the lines and numbers meant on the maps he kept in the plane. Natalie had practised turning the Comanche, climbing, descending, slowing down, speeding up. She had been content to watch when they had reached the coast and turned north.

They flew low, saw shoals of shark; wrecks of ships, half-hidden in the sand; clouds of white geese cruising in unison over the coral reefs. Forms of beauty, she thought, that could be seen in no other way. She *had* to learn to fly, once the trial was over. Jack had sparked something in her.

Flying at two thousand feet, a thousand feet, showed how small the world was, how everything was connected to everything else. Villages, towns, rivers, farms, factories, churches, mosques, roads. You got the bigger picture from the air, Natalie realised. In a funny way she understood that being a pilot of your own small machine, a few hundred feet up, helped you to see things politically.

They had landed on an airstrip that seemed to have an island to itself and been ferried to Lamu proper – another island – in a small skiff. Lamu had been a revelation, too. An old town dating back to the fourteenth century, its streets were too narrow for cars – none, in fact, were allowed on the island – and all transport, human or freight, was carried out by donkeys.

'I think there are about two thousand donkeys in Lamu,' said Jack. 'And all together they send out quite a smell. Ah, here's someone.' He gestured to the waitress who had just appeared. 'Two beers, please.'

She nodded and disappeared again.

He turned back to Natalie. 'Now, we haven't talked about it; I wanted to get you here in one piece first and so I'm sorry if you feel I dragooned you here, but you would have been miserable all by yourself in the camp, having to prepare your own food, make your own bed, fix your own shower. Lots of rain and mud and you'd have missed me.'

'I'm not a complete wastrel, you know. Only children learn to look after themselves in all sorts of ways.' Natalie paused. 'But yes, I'd rather be here than there.' She passed her fingers through her hair. 'Sorry if that sounds grudging. I didn't mean it like that.'

The beers arrived.

'I'll let that go,' said Jack, swallowing some beer. 'Now, ahead of tomorrow, how good a swimmer are you? The reef is not at all deep but there's one channel where the current comes in at about five knots. That's quite strong.'

'I don't know how good I am. I have only ever swum in pools when I was at school, in the North Sea, off the Lincolnshire coast, where it was so cold we never stayed in the water for very long, and in the Mediterranean, off Palestine, when I was on a dig and where it was very warm and there were no tides or currents so far as I remember. I've never even seen a reef. Is there any danger?'

'You'll be amazed by the colours of the fish, but we'll steer clear of the inlet where the current is stronger. There's no danger as such but you should avoid sea urchins. They are not scary but if you tread on one, or knock against one, their spikes are *very* painful and can break off and get under your skin. It's not life-threatening but the pain is excruciating.'

The waitress brought some salad and took their main order.

'It has to be fish,' Jack said, looking up at her. 'We'll have whatever was caught this morning. And two more beers, when we've finished these.'

He leaned forward, so that his hand was nearly touching Natalie's. 'Years and years *and years* ago, Lamu used to be a centre of the slave trade. We all know that slaves went from West Africa to America, but here they were brought down the Duldul and Tana rivers, sold at the market in Lamu, a site now occupied by a mosque, and sent north to the Middle East. That's what the prosperity of this town is – or was – based on: slaves and fishing and furniture-making. The mahogany around here is second to none.'

Jack ate some lettuce. 'Zanzibar was the main centre of slavers and Malindi. But Lamu was quite bad enough – archaeologists have discovered dungeons here, with iron shackles, and cemeteries with bodies piled up. They had obviously died on the way down-river or were so malnourished by the time they got here that they couldn't survive.'

He wiped his lips with his napkin. 'America gets a bad press over its history of slavery but the sultans of the Middle East were almost as awful. They used male slaves as soldiers or sailors in their armed forces – dangerous but possibly more interesting than being stuck on a plantation. Women were used as domestics or as sex slaves. Later, a lot were taken to Brazil. The British, who in the early nineteenth century had outlawed slavery, were intercepting the North Atlantic trade, so the Brazilians came round the Cape of Good Hope and put ashore here.'

Natalie sipped some beer. 'Have you ... have you ever been out with a black girl, a black woman?'

'Good question.' Jack nodded. 'And the answer is "no". You do see it, of course, though it's mainly older white men with younger black wives or, more likely, mistresses. In some quarters, with some people, a black mistress is all right, whereas a black wife isn't. Mistresses don't go to cocktail parties, wives do.'

He thought for a moment. 'In theory, mixed-race couples are the ideal; in practice it would be difficult. There's prejudice on both sides and there are still big cultural differences. When you see it, and as I say you *do* see it, there's obviously a very strong bond, very often a strong sexual bond, I suspect, but the couples lead solitary lives, relatively solitary anyway.'

The fish was brought. 'How about you?'

'Don't be silly; there are very few black people in Britain and those I met at Cambridge all turned out to be princes or kings from Nigeria or Ghana. The last thing they wanted was a white wife when they went back home.'

'Dominic was a good bit older than you, wasn't he? Isn't age as big a divide as race?'

She weighed this in her mind. 'No, not really. I don't think age is as fundamental a difference between people as race, though I don't want to minimise the importance of age either.'

'How was Dominic different? What was it that attracted you to him?' He grinned. 'How can I get the same effect?'

Natalie smiled. 'You could dye your hair, make it a bit greyer, that would help.' She tasted her fish. 'Well, he was good-looking of course – and you don't need much help there, either. I don't want to suggest that looks are everything, because they aren't, but good-looking people do have a head-start on the rest, don't you think? They have to follow through, of course, but that's where it starts, mostly.'

The waitress brought some slices of lemon.

'Then there was his talent. Lots of people play musical instruments but very few play them well enough to give public concerts. I loved that about him, that and the fact that he practised for several hours a day. People who read music, who play well, who spend their life in music, it's as if … as if they know some great big secret that other people don't know. Then, and maybe this was the thing that I really fell for, when he played he seemed to make love to his cello: he caressed it, he coaxed sounds out of it, he *persuaded* it to give up its secrets. When he played, when you watched him play, you could see he was absorbed by it. If you play something like Elgar's cello concerto, at times you attack the instrument, you manhandle it, while at other times you embrace it, you stroke it. You make love to it.' She blushed. 'I've said more than I should. You handle your plane a bit like that, too.'

'But he was years older than you. You haven't said anything about that.'

The waitress exchanged the empty fish plates for a bowl of fruit. 'Oranges! What a treat.' Natalie took one.

'Of course, I don't know that all older men are like Dominic was but what I liked about him was that he knew his mind. Again, it was as if he had some big secret inside him. He knew where he stood on almost everything: he had an inner *coherence*, that was it. He knew which books he liked and didn't like and why, he knew which music was good and which wasn't and why, he knew about food and diet, he took an interest in politics and though he didn't have the time to be involved, as you are, he had clear views about it. The point about coherence, if you can achieve it in your life, is that it helps you in your approach to the world, it helps you understand the world, and to slow the world down as it goes by. That's the most important gift of all, I think, because the slower life goes by, the more you can enjoy it, the more you can squeeze out of it, the more you can *relish* it, that was his word.' She sliced into her orange. 'It was his coherence that I fell for. Men my own age never have that.' She peeled the skin of the fruit away from the flesh.

'I feel out of breath just listening to you.' He grinned. 'I hate this Dominic already, how can anyone live up to such perfection?'

'Who says you have to?'

'What else impresses you? Give me some hope.'

'We could start with another beer.'

'My God, yes. Sorry about that.' He waved at the waitress. 'That's done, now what?'

'Maybe I don't want to be impressed any more. You're not Dominic, and I'm no longer the undergraduate who fell for him. I've put him behind me.'

'Have you? Are you sure?'

Natalie nodded but said nothing.

494

'Are you tired?'

She shrugged. 'I'll sleep well tonight, after a long day, being by the sea – but that's not what you meant, is it?'

Jack shook his head. 'Lamu is mainly Muslim, as I said, but there's a Christian church here, with nuns attached – a legacy of the missionary years. There's a midnight carol service tonight, a chance to sing. Are you up for it?'

'What sort of voice do you have?'

'Not bad.'

'I didn't mean that. Are you a tenor, a baritone or a bass?'

'Baritone.'

'Then the answer is yes. My father's choir in Gainsborough is always short of baritones. We'll treat the carol service as an audition. After the gorge is closed down, it will be something you can do.'

The organ could have been stronger, and more in tune, and it certainly didn't shake the ground as the one in Gainsborough did, but the small church was cute, Natalie thought, plain but with clean, pleasing lines, no waste, the kind of simple décor that threw worshippers back on themselves.

And it was full. Nuns filled the choir – maybe twenty of them. There was a smattering of white faces in the congregation but most were black and most were old.

To begin with it seemed odd to Natalie to be singing the familiar carols on the warm edges of the Indian Ocean and she held back her voice.

Not Jack. He did indeed have a very passable baritone voice and an obviously good set of lungs. He launched into each carol at full throttle and seemed to know instinctively all modulations of the choir.

Encouraged, emboldened, Natalie gradually moved her own singing up a gear till she was matching him note for note, sound for sound. It had been ages since she had had a good clear-out of her lungs, as she thought of it, and she realised she had forgotten how much she enjoyed – relished – being surrounded by singing voices just as her parents had, especially now at Christmastime. When the service ended she was more than a little disappointed.

As they walked back to the hotel, she said, 'Isn't it extraordinary how the church has dropped out of our lives so much, and so quickly? Far fewer people go to services, far more are getting married in registry offices, several of the girls I was at Cambridge with aren't even getting married, just living together.'

'Could you ever do that?'

'I don't think so, but I don't know, not really. It's one of those decisions you can't take in the abstract.'

'What's your decision on my voice? When the gorge is destroyed, do I have a job in your father's choir?' He slipped his arm in hers.

'Yes, Dr. Deacon. The vetting committee has convened and your voice passes muster.' She looked up at him. 'I'm impressed. I hope I can snorkel as well as you sing.'

'There's the reef, look, where the water is breaking over it. Think you can swim that far?'

Natalie nodded. 'We cleared our lungs last
night. I'm as ready as I'll ever be.'

The sun this morning was as fierce as ever.
They had breakfasted in a leisurely way and
strolled down to the beach wearing their swimming costumes under their jeans and shirts and
they now got ready together. Jack had brought
goggles and breathing tubes and the hotel had
rented them some flippers.

'Here,' said Jack, handing over a tube of cream.
'Put this on your legs and face and I'll do your
shoulders. You can do the same for me. You don't
feel the sun in the water but that doesn't mean it
isn't there.'

They walked down to the water's edge and for
a moment Natalie stood with just her feet in the
sea.

'You're thinking about your father, aren't you?'

'How did you know?'

'You were thinking how clear and warm and
calm this water is, how different from the North
Sea in Lincolnshire, how unlike a traditional
Christmas Day this is, and that made you think
of your father: how he's getting on, what he's
doing, if he's thinking about your mother.'

'Yes, you're right, exactly that. How did you
know?'

'Come on, it's not hard. You were miles away.
Maybe we can put a call through to him tonight,
from the hotel. You never know your luck.'

'What a good idea, Jack. Yes, please. But don't
get too sensitive all of a sudden. I've not done

this snorkelling before, or swum on a reef. I need you in pilot mode, Olympic swimmer mode, tough-guy-in-control mode.'

'I know my place.' Jack grinned. 'Now, let me fix your flippers.'

In no time they were out at sea. Natalie had never known water so warm – not so surprising, she told herself, since they were at two degrees south, as near the equator as she had ever been.

The water was clear, visibility was good but there was not much to see to begin with, just the sandy bottom of the ocean. She swam a few yards behind Jack, who seemed to know where he was going and stopped every two hundred yards or so, to rest, take a breather and ask her how she was doing. While she was quite comfortable breathing through the tube, looking down into the depths of the water, the air didn't feel quite so fresh as when they broke the surface and she breathed normally.

'Okay,' said Jack at their third break, 'we're nearly at the reef. When we reach it we'll turn left, north, and you'll begin to see the bigger, brighter-coloured fish.' He re-affixed his mask and was off.

As they reached the coral, the underwater vegetation started to grow in abundance: huge flat fans of yellow, long thin strips of blue-green, underwater bushes of brown, fields of grass-like sea-green. And then the fish began – coral fish, kingfish, wahoo, sailfish, dugong and shela. Little scarlet fish, in shoals; thin iris-coloured fish in twos and threes; great lurking marlin, violet-black and shy in the distance, schools of near-transparent fish who moved as one, jerking this way and that.

Natalie had never seen anything like it and was immediately entranced. Slowly, they worked their way up the reef, following the fish as they eased into places where the coral overhung what was below, creating caves and shadows, where they disturbed more marlin.

Every so often, Natalie broke the surface for a breather, to chew in some fresh air, as she thought of it. But she was soon back underwater, looking for species she hadn't seen before, marvelling at the sheer number of different colours. She supposed that each and every one was adapted to some niche in the marine environment but it didn't seem like that. It seemed as if it was all designed for the pleasure of human snorkellers, a vast kaleidoscopic jumble of colours and shapes, a never-ending, always-changing fashion parade. Natalie lost all sense of time.

After however long it was, Jack signalled to her to take another breather. He lifted his mask and said, 'How are you doing? Not too tired?'

'No, not all,' she replied. 'I'm loving it, all of it.'

'So the answer is: yes, you're as good at snorkelling as I am at singing. In the water you're up there with Esther Williams.'

'It's not exactly difficult.'

'You'd be surprised; some people never acquire the rhythm or don't like the underwater landscape.'

'A carol concert, and now this. They certainly take your mind off–' She was interrupted by a number of large waves, wake from a ship.

'We've been out nearly three hours.'

'We *have?*'

He nodded. 'It's just on two o'clock. From here, we'll ease back via the cliffs. When we get there, we may see some turtles. Normally they don't bother us if we don't bother them – but try not to get too close. They can snap at you if you do.' He set off again.

The cliffs, when they came to them, were skirted with bushes of brown, rubbery-looking fronds that Natalie found rather forbidding, not at all the sort of thing you would want to get caught up in.

Jack headed left, south, back towards the beach where they had left their clothes and his bag. After a moment, he turned, swam towards Natalie, and pointed back the way he had come.

She looked over to where he was pointing.

Turtles.

There were about six of them, diving and playing, one or two feeding. They were a little out to sea, and Jack motioned for Natalie to follow him, nearer in, by the underwater face of the cliff. The turtles had seen them, looking in their direction, but other than that they hadn't moved. They were really quite large, thought Natalie, and their shells reflected the underwater light in ever-changing ways. The turtles had a beauty all their own.

Now that they were swimming for home, Natalie had got slightly ahead of Jack and she looked with interest as she approached what appeared to be a cave in the cliffs. It was a dark patch, set back, with two fingers of rock stretching outwards, on either side.

As Natalie reached the first finger, and swam over it, she saw her own shadow cross the rock.

Suddenly, a large turtle was swimming rapidly towards her. He, or she, had been quietly minding its own business in the cave and must have felt trapped by Natalie's arrival, or her shadow, for it suddenly made a dash towards the other turtles, out to sea. The creature – as big as Natalie in terms of bulk – came very close and, as it did so, turned its head towards her. Fearing it would snap at her, Natalie thrashed to one side, nearer the rocks of the cliff, and in no time a bolt of sharp pain exploded in her right knee.

She had collided with the stone of the cliff and in the process landed on a sea urchin.

She cried out. Salt-water filled her mouth, she choked and jerked her head above water, snatching at her mask and snorkel. All thought of the turtle went out of her mind and she broke the surface of the water, gasping for air and clutching her knee.

Jack was with her immediately. 'I saw what happened!' he shouted. 'The turtle's gone. If you can swim to the end of the cliffs, I have some ammonia in my bag. That will help the pain. I'll go and get it.'

Natalie nodded. She was hurting too much to say anything but the end of the cliffs wasn't far off and she knew she needed to get there.

Jack had stopped snorkelling and was swimming crawl as fast as he could, the flippers helping his speed. She followed, swimming breast stroke but hardly using her right leg. If she moved her knee joint, the pain was even worse. She just let her injured leg trail in the water.

In her state, it took her ten minutes to reach the end of the cliffs and limp ashore. Although the pain was such that she just wanted to lay on the first soft sand she came to, she knew she had to reach shade for safety's sake. It was by now after three o'clock but the sun was still high in the sky. She could see Jack in the distance; he had reached the spot where they had left their belongings and he was beginning to run back towards her, carrying his bag.

There were some trees and bushes at the edge of the beach and a small patch of shade. With relief, she slumped on the sand. She looked at her knee but didn't touch it. It was impregnated with a dozen or more tiny black spikes which had broken off. She couldn't straighten her leg – it hurt too much.

Jack arrived. 'Let me look.'

She pointed.

He whistled. 'Nasty.' He took a jar from his bag and a small towel, the kind of towel they had with them in the gorge, kept in the back pocket of their trousers.

In the jar was a yellow-white liquid, transparent, which he now poured onto the towel.

'What's that?' Natalie asked.

'Liquid ammonia, ammonia dissolved in water. It helps salve the pain, with jellyfish stings and with sea urchins.'

Gently, he laid the damp towel on the flesh of her knee. Immediately she felt the pain ease.

'Ah!' she said. 'That's better, much better.'

He wetted the towel with the ammonia a second time and again laid it on her knee.

Natalie made a soft sound, somewhere between a sigh and a groan.

He wetted the towel a third time, pressed it to her knee and left it there.

'The worst of the pain is over,' he said. 'Your knee will be sore for two or three days and it will hurt to touch. In a minute I am going to use these tweezers to pull out those spikes that I can – that will help your recovery. The rest will be rejected by your body over the next two to four weeks.'

'Have you got a Ph.D. in this as well?'

'It happened to me once. Never again. It's not the sort of mistake you make twice.' Jack took the towel away. 'Kenya has a shortage of doctors, outside Nairobi. You're lucky I know what I'm doing.' He grinned. 'Now, let's see how many of these little monsters I can operate on.'

He took the tweezers and knelt in front of her.

She winced as he prodded her flesh with the tweezers. 'Are those what you pluck your eyebrows with?'

'Careful. I only have to press – just here – and you'll be in agony all over again.'

'Can't you take a joke?'

'If you can take the pain, I can take a joke.' He bent to get a closer look at Natalie's knee. 'There,' he said after a moment. 'That's one gone. Lie back if you want. This could take a while.'

Natalie lay back in the sand.

'Two.' He held up the black spike in the tweezers, then threw it away. 'Turtles apart, how did you enjoy the swim?'

'Wonderful. I've never seen such colours. Turtles apart, what a good idea this was. Thank you.'

'Three. You are not maimed for life. Your knees will regain their former glory.'

'Leave my knees alone. They have never done you any harm.'

'Four. You look very good in a bathing costume, Dr. Nelson.'

'So do you.'

'Five. Have you never tried one of these new bikini things?'

'I might have.'

'You don't have one with you, on this trip?'

'I might have.'

'Six. You could risk it tomorrow. It could be your Christmas gift to me.'

'You're easily pleased. What are you giving me?'

'It's a surprise. Seven – and I think that's it. Two others broke off and if I fiddle with them any more I'll make matters worse. But I've got about half of them out, meaning you'll have half the soreness and recover in half the time.' Jack put the tweezers in his bag. 'Think you can walk back to the hotel, or shall I send for an express donkey?'

She lifted herself up from where she'd been lying. 'How do I know I can afford a donkey until I know how much this treatment has cost?'

'True enough. I'm not cheap.'

'If I promise to wear a bikini tomorrow, will that affect the price?'

'Are you haggling with me?'

'You taught me, in Nairobi, remember?'

'And I taught you too well.'

'You haven't seen anything yet. How will this affect the price?'

She leaned forward and kissed him.

'In ... seven minutes it will no longer be Christmas Day.'

'Over there, beyond the horizon, it already isn't.'

They were sitting on the balcony that ran the length of the hotel and served both their rooms, side-by-side. They'd had dinner, strolled by the beach and now sat in wicker chairs looking out at the black nothingness of the ocean.

'Sorry you didn't get through to your father.'

'Hmmn.' Natalie sipped her whisky. 'What is your mother doing right now, do you think?'

'I don't know how to answer that. She's known Maxwell Sandys for ever, for as long as I can remember, anyway. Are they lovers – that's what you're asking, right? They must be but I've never seen any real tenderness between them. Whatever exists between them, it's locked away.' Jack looked at her. 'I don't really like talking about my mother in this way, do you mind?'

She shook her head. She had been going to tell him that she had seen Sandys enter his mother's tent, on the evening when Sandys and Jeavons had been in the camp, but she decided against it. 'What will Christopher be doing now?'

'That's not so difficult. He'll certainly have called Beth. Since we are all scattered this Christmas, she doesn't know where to contact us, as she loves to do, so he will have been in touch with

505

her and brought her up to speed. I think that today he's had the first of the flying lessons mother gave him for Christmas, so he'll have been reading some of his manuals and he will probably have gone last night for a Christmas Eve dinner at the Karibu Club – they always do something, a dinner-dance probably, with carols, black tie, the works.'

'So you're missing out.'

He looked at her. 'Am I?' He drank some of his whisky. 'Don't get me wrong, I don't enjoy the Karibu scene anywhere near as much as Christopher but I don't dismiss it. He'll have heard things last night, people will have had a few drinks and said things they might not otherwise have said. A lot of it will be trivial gossip but you never know – he may pick up valuable information. And it's good for him to be seen there. We can't afford to seem standoffish, or to look stuck-up. It will be good PR, good politics. My brother has a talent for that – better than my mother or me.'

Jack leaned over his chair and held his face very close to Natalie's. He looked at his watch. 'It is now two minutes to midnight. I think it only fair to warn you that at midnight I intend to kiss you – and not a measly peck on the cheek, either, but the real thing, a proper Hollywood-style, no-holds-barred, all-guns-blazing, fully orchestrated, fifteen-rounds affair.'

'I think I'd rather be stung by a sea urchin.'

'In that case, I won't wait.'

His mouth was on hers. He smelled of whisky. He could have shaved more closely. But he knew how to kiss, he knew how to hold her, he knew where to put his hands so she would respond.

And she was ready to respond, she wanted to respond, it had been *months* since she had responded, and her body suddenly seemed alive as it hadn't been for ages. She had all but forgotten that feeling. With Russell it had been over before it started, with Christopher there had been no spark of any kind. Natalie pressed herself against Jack and held him tight. She recalled his hands on her breasts when he had rescued her from the wildebeest in the Mara river.

There were no lights on the balcony. There was one dim street light about fifty yards away; apart from that the only illumination came from the stars.

Jack was a mass of shadows; so was she.

Natalie felt his hands moving over her. That was what she wanted and she cried out softly. But not yet. She had let Dominic make love to her on their first real evening together but that was after how many lunches and dinners, how many concerts, how many weeks?

She gripped Jack's wrist with one hand, to stop him going where he was going, but pulled him closer with her other arm kissing his neck, biting his ear with her lips.

He stopped and put his arms around her, holding her tight. He kissed her again.

Jack rolled her off the chair she was on and they slid to the floor, the wooden boards of the balcony. The smell of polish was not unpleasant and the boards were almost warm to the touch. It had been a hot day.

He lay on top of her as he kissed her again and

507

again. She felt him stir as he placed his mouth on her breast.

Her body said one thing, her mind another. She squirmed free from under him.

'Sorry,' she said after a moment.

He took her hand and kissed it. He rolled away from her and they lay, on their backs, on the warm boards, breathing heavily, then less heavily. When they were both more or less calm, he whispered, 'Let's get some sleep. We've got a big day tomorrow–'

'Oh? Why? What are we doing?'

'Absolutely nothing.'

'How many times has this bikini been in the water today?' Jack was rubbing sun lotion into Natalie's back.

'You tell me. You've been ogling me every time. *Reluquant*, the French call it.'

'I haven't been "ogling" you, that's a horrible word. I've been admiring you.'

'Nonsense. I haven't been wearing very much, I agree. I only wore it because it's Boxing Day, and you asked. But you've taken off what little I am wearing with your eyes.'

'That's a form of admiration.'

'No it isn't. Is your Swahili any better than your English?'

Jack patted her bottom. 'You're all done.' He lay down while she started on him.

'I never thought I'd be so good at doing nothing. All I've done for hours is lie on the sand, sleep and swim.'

'You'd make a good hippopotamus.'

'I'll snap at you like a turtle, if you're not careful. And I don't think I've ever been on such a beautiful beach so devoid of people.'

'And you've still got my Christmas present to come.'

'Why are you making me wait?'

'It's a test of your character.'

'You tested my character last night, on the floor of the balcony. I came through with flying colours.'

'You mean you rebuffed me.'

'You misread the situation.'

'Meaning?'

'No, no. It was a test of your character as well. You have to work it out for yourself.'

He turned over, on to his back, and pulled her to him.

'Jack! We're all lathered in sun lotion, and everyone can see.'

'Sun lotion isn't lethal and you yourself said the beach is deserted.'

He kissed her and she kissed him back. Then she turned him over again and resumed spreading sun lotion on his back.

'What time are we leaving tomorrow?'

'No hurry. Some time in the morning, so we get to Nairobi around lunchtime. We'll spend the afternoon preparing for the press conference.'

'You're done,' said Natalie, lying back down on her towel alongside Jack. 'The press conference,' she said, breathing out, 'and then the trial. This little bit of paradise will soon be over – and then the real tests of character begin.'

'I've eaten too much.' Natalie patted her stomach in the darkness.

'Dinner was only fish. You'll be hungry again at four in the morning.'

'Oh no. After all the sun and sea we've had, I'll sleep like a baby tonight. With any luck, four o'clock will pass by as silently as that ship out there.'

They were sitting on the balcony that linked their rooms, as the night before. Again, only the solitary street light and the stars offered illumination.

'Where do you think that ship is going?'

A constellation of lights on the horizon was moving slowly, right to left.

'What's the most romantic place north of here?' Natalie stretched out her legs in front of her.

'Mogadishu, Djibouti, Suez, Karachi even.'

'Suez isn't romantic, my father's been – he says it's a dump. Let's imagine Mogadishu.'

'And I've been to Mogadishu. It's more romantic here.'

'Hmmn. So what cargo is it carrying? Slaves? Wild animals for a European zoo? Are they smuggling ivory?'

'It could be ivory, if it's come from Zanzibar. That's the centre of ivory smuggling in this part of the world. More likely, it's spices – Zanzibar is Africa's leading exporter of cloves, also nutmeg and cinnamon. I don't like cinnamon, and I can take or leave–'

'I don't like those two men standing under the light, down the road.'

'What do you mean?' Jack sat up.

510

'There are two men, just beyond the light. They keep moving in and out of the shadows.'

He got to his feet and went to stand on the edge of the balcony. 'Why should two men...? It's Boxing Day, Natalie, you had too much whisky at dinner. There's a lot of unemployment in Lamu.'

She let a moment elapse as he sat down again. 'I saw them yesterday, too. They were watching us as you were administering first aid, after my encounter with that sea urchin.'

'You're making this up!'

'They were there again today, watching us on the beach. I haven't mentioned it before because I couldn't be certain it was the same two men – they were too far away, and there are a lot of men on Lamu who seem to have nothing to do. But, seeing them there again tonight, near that street lamp...'

'I can't believe it. You think they are planning to rob us?'

'That's one possibility. I can think of another.' Jack looked at her.

'Maybe they are the mysterious friends of Richard Sutton Senior.'

'No! From now on I'm going to ration your whisky consumption.'

'Maybe they've established contact with some-one on the staff at the camp in Kihara, who told them we were flying off here for Christmas. Maybe they think I was making a discreet bolt for it, stopping off here and then smuggling myself north and away, ahead of the trial.'

He shook his head. 'All this sun, it's gone to your head.'

'Look, now!' Natalie pointed. 'By the light.'

He stood up quickly. 'Yes, yes, I see now. Two men. Two shapes anyway, two shadows. But you don't know that they are the same as the men who watched you earlier today, or yesterday. I still think you are being... I can't believe Richard Sutton would go to such lengths, or have such a reach as to have you followed to Lamu.' Jack shook his head. 'It's a crazy idea. You're over-reacting.'

'You weren't there when he threatened me. You don't know, at first hand, as I do, how unpleasant, how *crude*, he can be.'

Jack sat down again. Both of them were breathing heavily. The ship, out to sea, had moved on, almost out of sight.

'Are you frightened?'

She didn't reply straight away. 'A bit.'

'I can sleep on this chair, if you want – right outside your door – if that will make you feel safer.' He moved his chair closer to hers. 'Of course, you'd be safer still if I was in the room *with* you. Think of it as my gift.' Jack grinned, lifted her hand and kissed it.

'I thought you might say that.' She put her hand on his forehead. 'I think the sun's got to you, too.' Natalie ran her fingers down his cheek. 'But as it happens, on this occasion, I agree with you.'

Wounded

'Good morning, everyone, and thank you for coming. I think we are about ready to begin, if you'd all like to sit down.'

Eleanor stood on the low stage in front of the gentle rake of seats in the main lecture hall in the Royal College in Nairobi. With her silver hair in the tightest of chignons, her crisp white shirt and her wrap-over khaki skirt, Natalie thought she looked more Parisian than ever.

The lecture hall had no windows, so it was cool. Huge saucer-shaped lights hung from black cables anchored in the wooden ceiling. A silver-white screen stood behind the stage. There were already fifty people in the room and more were still arriving.

Eleanor sat down at a long table, with micro-phones at the centre. Natalie sat on her left, Daniel on her right, with Jonas Jefferson on his right. Most of the people in the room – though by no means all – were white. Jack, Christopher and Arnold were in the front row. And in the second was Russell North.

The evening before, Natalie, Jack, Christopher, Eleanor and the rest of the team had eaten dinner together at a restaurant near the Rhodes Hotel after their meeting to discuss how the press conference should proceed. Natalie and Jack had just flown in from Lamu, Jack once again parking his Comanche where he could get a good look at the private jets on show at Nairobi International.

Christopher and his mother had stayed behind with Daniel to discuss the slides they were going to show. Arnold and Jonas had gone off in search of a late-night beer, leaving Natalie and Jack to stroll back together to the hotel. In the lobby they had bumped into Russell.

'My god,' Natalie had said. 'This is a surprise.'

Russell hadn't replied immediately. 'I'm here for the press conference,' he had said at length. 'Was anyone going to tell me? Or has my contribution been forgotten already?'

'California is twelve thousand miles from Kenya, Professor North,' said Jack. 'No one imagined you would want to make such a long journey for a two-hour press conference. But you don't need to worry, your part will get its proper due. I wrote the words myself.'

'Hmmn,' grunted Russell. He addressed himself to Natalie. 'You look more lovely than ever. Are we going to get a chance to talk?' He pointedly ignored Jack.

'Yes, of course,' said Natalie.

'When?'

There it was, the same directness, the same edge, the same stampede. Russell hadn't changed.

'Sometime tomorrow? After the conference?'

'Dinner?'

She glanced at Jack.

'Do you need his permission now?'

'Steady–' Jack put his hand on Russell's arm.

'I'm talking to *her!*' Russell shook it off.

Russell stared at her, unflinching. 'Well?'

Natalie slowly looked from Russell to Jack. 'When do we fly back to the gorge?'

'Not for a day or two, not till we have seen the press reaction to the conference.'

She had nodded, and said to Russell, 'Then I'd love to.'

'Good, let's meet here in the bar, at seven. We can have another whisky session.' He smiled but had disappeared without saying anything more.

Natalie and Jack had stood awkwardly in the lobby for a moment.

'Nightcap?' Jack had said eventually.

'No,' she replied softly. 'We all have to be at our best tomorrow, the future of the gorge may depend on it, on how we perform. Your mother said she wants me up there on the stage with her, so I'm going to bed now. I'm going to brush my hair for a couple of minutes, as I always do, and then I'm going to sleep. I want the full eight hours tonight, so I'm spick and span in the morning.'

'I get the message,' Jack had said. 'I'll have a nightcap and try to relive last night.' He kissed her on the cheek and went in to the bar as she took the stairs to her room.

When she let herself in, the overhead fan had been turned on and it was cool. She kicked off her shoes, flopped on to the bed and stared up at the whirring blades. Natalie had surprised herself on their last night in Lamu and she was still adjusting to what she had done. She couldn't explain it exactly because there had been no one reason why she had behaved as she had. Perhaps the oddest thing about the whole business is that although she had surprised herself, she hadn't really shocked herself.

Jack was the third man she had slept with.

Dominic had been the first and she always counted herself lucky that she'd had that experience. The second man had been a disaster, though it wasn't really his fault. She had accepted to go out with him on the rebound and had agreed to go to bed with him, half-convincing herself that the best way to forget Dominic would be in the oblivion of sex. Of course, the exact opposite had happened and afterwards she had felt cold and lonely and unclean.

Sex with Jack had been different again. When he had rescued her during the wildebeest stampede, and folded his hands around her breasts, it had – involuntarily – brought back the erotic times she had shared with Dominic, the afternoons in her rooms at Cambridge, hotel rooms in London, once or twice in other cities, when they had veered between tenderness and near-savagery, when her sheer greed for sensuality had exhausted her and, yes, surprised her. It was a side to Natalie that she had never expected to satisfy in the gorge and which, now that it had begun to reassert itself, she hadn't really welcomed.

But then had come the physicality and sensuality of Lamu – the swimming, the colours of the fish, the rhythmical swaying of the underwater vegetation, Jack touching the skin on her legs when he was extracting the sea-urchin spines from her knee, his frank appraisal of her body when she had worn her bikini, rubbing sun lotion over each other, the warm blackness of the hotel balcony, the warm wood, its comforting smell. Jack had not pressed himself on her before, he had not crowded her in any way but she was twenty-eight, dammit, and she had needed a man, she had needed his hands, his mouth, everything, on her, over her, around her, in her, and she had needed the release, she had needed to *be* released, to experience that release *with someone*, so she could also experience afterwards – afterwards was as important as all that went before.

Jack had not disappointed her. If he was not Dominic, his body was firmer, his muscles harder, his skin smoother, the stubble on his chin less brittle, the sounds he made were wilder. His appetite, his performance – there was no other word – had matched hers.

'Can you close the doors at the back please? That will tell latecomers we've started.' Eleanor waited while the doors were closed. Then, 'Good morning again, everyone. My name is Eleanor Deacon and I am the director of excavations at Kihara Gorge, here in Kenya. You see with me here several of my colleagues who will be introduced to you in a few moments, as we go through the story we have to tell you.'

She took off her spectacles. 'Many of you are journalists out from Britain, here on a fact-finding mission ahead of the independence conference that is to be held in London in the middle of February. My colleagues and I apologise for breaking into your busy schedule but we think our story is almost as interesting as independence and shows an important side to Kenya which, once it is a sovereign state, will set the country apart.'

She paused, to let a few latecomers find seats.

'First, a little orientation. Can we have the lights

out, please, and the first slide, Christopher.'

The lights went down and a map became visible on the screen behind the stage. It was a map of Kenya with the location of the gorge highlighted. Eleanor briefly explained the history of the gorge, its geology, its wildlife, the Maasai. Then the lights went up again.

'My late husband, Jock Deacon, and I have been excavating in Kihara for decades. Some seasons have been better than others but the reason we have asked you here today is to announce that this season, the 1961-62 season in Kihara, is the best ever. We have made half a dozen very important discoveries which, when taken together, enable us to make a major announcement today about how early man, two million years ago, first emerged here in Kenya, in the Kihara Gorge.'

Natalie, sitting on Eleanor's left, noticed how the journalists had begun to write in their notebooks. Eleanor now had their full attention.

'I will now talk you through the discoveries and what they mean. The actual objects will be available at the end, for you to inspect for yourselves, and we have prepared photographs of the discoveries, which are free for you to take away. I will describe the objects in the order in which they were discovered, so that you can get some idea of how our understanding of early man arose, which will also help convey some of the excitement of excavation.'

The lights were lowered and a slide of the knee-joint was shown.

'This was the first discovery, made by Daniel Mutumbu, seated here on my right, and by Professor Richard Sutton, of New York University, and Professor Russell North of the University of California at Berkeley, who I see is sitting in the second row this morning. The significance of this configuration of bones is that they indicate that this creature, whoever he or she was, walked upright. As you may know, the rest of the great apes walk on all fours, or else walk with their knuckles on the ground. Charles Darwin, in the nineteenth century, was the first to suggest that walking upright freed early man's hands to use and manufacture tools and it was this which became the basis of culture and eventually separated man from the other apes and set humans apart from all the other animals. We now know that this all-important process first occurred two million years ago, right here in Kenya, in Kihara Gorge. As I say, we can discuss these bones in more detail afterwards if any of you are interested.'

And so, Eleanor pressed on, introducing the jaw, the teeth and skull bones that Natalie had discovered, Natalie's shelter, Kees' hand-axes. She didn't hurry, it took a good fifty minutes before she began to wind up.

'It is an amazing story when you stop to reflect on it. Kenya, the Kihara Gorge, is the cradle of mankind. Humans first evolved right here in this part of East Africa and then spread out to populate the globe, as we see around us today. In honour of this phenomenon, this great story, this romantic idea, we are calling this new species of man's ancestor *Homo kiharenis*. The Kihara Gorge should become one of the wonders of the

521

world. To us, it already is. Thank you.'

The lights went on and a ripple of applause spread around the assembled audience.

Eleanor stood up. 'As I said, copies of the press release and photographs will be available at the back of the hall afterwards. We will now take questions. Please identify who you are and which publication you represent.'

There was a short delay before a small, balding, rather fat man stood up. 'I'm Tom Jellineck, from the *Daily Telegraph* in London. I found your presentation very interesting but I am a political reporter out here from London, so forgive me if my question is naïve. Would this early form of humanity – if I can put it that way – have been able to speak? Did he or she have language?'

'No, that's a good question,' said Eleanor, 'but we have no information on this, one way or another. If we had found the hyoid bone as part of the skull, its shape might have told us about the structure of the creature's throat, which would have enabled us to say something, but we haven't found it yet. Some people might think that, in order to construct stone tools of the kind we have found, early man would have needed language, so that parents could explain to their children what to do, but that is conjecture, indirect argument, and we have avoided speculation. I hope that helps.'

Another man stood up. 'Curtis Vallance, Reuters.' He had an American accent. 'Can you say something about these stone tools. Why is the change in style so important?'

'Yes,' said Eleanor. 'The first use of stone tools

was important because those tools enabled early man to pierce the hide of other animals. That indicates a change in diet, from one made up predominantly of vegetables to one rich in animal flesh or protein, meat. Protein, we know, aids brain development, so the use of tools increases the difference in intelligence between humans and other animals. The change to smaller tools means two things at least. One, the tools are getting more efficient and, two, they can be carried farther, they are less bulky. Early man could go looking for food, rather than have to wait till it came to him.'

Valiance nodded his thanks and scribbled in his pad.

Eleanor's gaze raked the room but before any other journalist could speak, Russell stood up. He didn't bother with who he was, but just launched into what he had to say.

'You paint a very cogent and exciting scientific picture but, speaking as a scientist myself, isn't there something rather odd about the procedure you are following, this very press conference itself, for example?' He had half-turned, so the rest of the room could hear him better. 'What I mean is: so far as I know, you haven't published any of your most recent discoveries in the scientific press, which normally would take priority. The scientific press – the scientific *community* – take a dim view of colleagues who announce their results at a jamboree like this one, so why have you gone down this route?'

Natalie was stiff with nerves; what was Russell playing at? But Eleanor kept her tone relaxed, as she said, 'I would have thought that was obvious, Professor North. A contingent of British journalists is here in Nairobi; it presents a golden opportunity for us to make known our results to a wide public and to show Kenya at its best when the eyes of the world will soon be upon her. We are of course planning scientific publication at a later date.'

Russell was still on his feet. 'So this conference has nothing to do with the upcoming trial of Mutevu Ndekei, who used to be the camp cook at Kihara and who virtually beheaded one of your team, Professor Richard Sutton? It has nothing to do with the fact that Dr. Natalie Nelson, sitting there on your left, will be the main witness against Ndekei, in a trial that will pit a white witness against a black defendant and is due to take place in the very week that the independence conference will begin in London? It has nothing to do with the fact that the Maasai tribe, who claim ownership of the gorge, have threatened to reoccupy it and destroy it if Ndekei is convicted and sentenced to hang? Are we to take it that the timing of this conference is pure coincidence?'

'Those are all–' Eleanor began, but Russell was in full stampede mode.

'Is it not true that, despite the united front you display here – today, this morning, in this lecture hall – that in fact your team is bitterly divided?' He pointed directly at Natalie. 'Is it not true that Dr. Nelson here fully intends to give evidence against Ndekei, despite the threats posed by the Maasai, but that you, Dr. Deacon, have repeatedly tried to get her to change her testimony, so

524

that the proceedings against Ndekei will be dropped, a manoeuvre that will preserve your precious gorge at any cost? Is it not true that you, Dr. Deacon, are willing to sweep the murder of a noted professor under the carpet so as to maintain your research opportunities? Isn't the whole *point* of this press conference to bolster your achievements in the gorge and to head off the Maasai? Isn't *that* why you are not following normal scientific protocol – you are trying to salvage your reputation in the face of impending disaster, that the tribal customs of Kenya will stop scientific progress in its tracks, only you can't say so for fear of being thought racist or colonialist?'

Eleanor stood up in an attempt to stem the flood, but Russell wouldn't be stemmed.

'A white man, a talented white man, a world-class scientist, was brutally murdered in a camp run by you – sliced up by a black man with a machete, a mere camp cook from the Maasai tribe, who ran off. A white woman, Dr. Natalie Nelson, was a witness. Now the murderer claims he was acting according to Maasai tradition. Where do you stand, Dr. Deacon? Should Ndekei be tried and, if convicted, hanged? Or do you think that the defence he is going to run is sufficient and relevant in today's new Kenya?'

He sat down. The stampede was over.

Natalie was sweating. There was no question but that the journalists had listened to Russell in a different way from how they had listened to Eleanor.

Natalie stared at Russell. At first he wouldn't

meet her gaze but when he did he looked at her hard, rigid, unblinking, defiant. Eleanor was deep in conversation with Daniel and with Jack, who had left his seat in the auditorium and mounted the stage. A buzz of conversation had broken out in the audience.

Finally, Eleanor stood up. 'Ladies and gentlemen,' she said and paused, to give everyone a chance to quieten down.

Jack went back to his seat.

'Ladies and gentlemen, I want you all to know that I still stand by all the comments – each and every one – that I made earlier, about the nature and importance and implications of our discoveries in Kihara Gorge. They are in my view – in *our* view–' and she motioned to the others in the stage with her, 'quite independent of other, tragic events that have taken place during the digging season. Those events have very little, if anything, to do with science, more with human folly, greed and ambition. However, since Professor North has raised the matter, entirely unexpectedly and gratuitously, I might add, since he was not invited to this press conference in the first place – though we would have had no wish to keep him away – I will now satisfy the curiosity his remarks will inevitably have aroused among you.'

And Eleanor went on to describe the murder of Richard Sutton, the reasons for it, what Natalie had witnessed, what defence Ndekei was expected to run, and why she had forced Russell North to leave the camp. And she had no choice but to speak about the Maasai threat to the gorge.

When she finished the questions came thick

and fast. 'When is this trial?'

'Is it a jury trial?'

'Who is the judge? Is he black or white?'

'What is the penalty for murder in Kenya?'

'Have tribal defences been used before in Kenya?'

'Is Ndekei in jail now? Which one?'

'Will you defend the gorge if the Maasai attack it, or occupy it? How?'

'Dr. Deacon, did you really try to get Dr. Nelson to change her testimony?'

'Maybe Dr. Nelson should answer that,' said another journalist.

Eleanor turned in her seat. 'Natalie?'

All eyes were on her. A photographer's light flashed somewhere.

'No,' said Natalie, in as deliberately flat a voice as she could muster. 'Dr. Deacon was born and bred in Kenya, I'm new here. She's been digging in the gorge for decades but she tells me this is the best season, in terms of discoveries, that there has ever been. It's natural to try to preserve something as important as Kihara. I share her enthusiasm but I saw what I saw and will say so at the trial. I have never varied in my view and all my colleagues – not just Dr. Deacon but everyone else – know that.'

Natalie wanted the morning to be over as quickly as possible and the less she said the sooner it would be.

'Tom Jellineck again. I have a question for Professor North – have I got the name right?'

Eleanor nodded.

'Professor North, you were sent away from the

camp because of your part in this ... raid on the cemetery. In the circumstances, in view of the dreadful fate that occurred to Professor Sutton, do you accept that Dr. Deacon acted responsibly, that – in effect – she saved your life?'

Russell stood up. 'Ndekei had already been captured and arrested by the time I was made to leave, so, no, I don't accept that reasoning. I don't believe anyone else would have come looking for me – an eye for an eye, so to speak, had already been achieved. I accepted because I had no choice: Dr. Deacon's authority on her digs is absolute. But I left reluctantly.'

'And is your intervention this morning motivated by revenge?' Jellineck was as dogged as Russell had been earlier.

'My intervention was motivated by the gaps in the story you were told. A man was murdered during this season's digging and, had it been left to Dr. Deacon, none of you journalists would have been any the wiser. You should ask Dr. Deacon if she is for or against Ndekei's prosecution.'

'Well, Dr. Deacon? What's the answer?'

'What I say doesn't matter. The law will take its course. What Professors Sutton and North did was in my view stupid, crass, wrong and – yes – criminal. I am white, a graduate of a British university, but I have lived and worked all my life in Kenya. I am familiar with and sometimes – sometimes, not always – sympathetic to tribal ways. Anglo-Saxon law is not the only way of organising human affairs.'

'Does that mean you are for or against the

prosecution of this cook?' Jellineck was still on his feet.

'I have said all that I want to say. But I point out that Dr. Nelson is on this platform with me today.'

There were no more questions.

Natalie's heart was racing. She noticed that Russell was sweating copiously.

'I think we have gone as far as we can for now,' said Eleanor, getting to her feet. 'Remember to pick up your photographs as you leave.'

Russell got up from his seat at the hotel bar and came towards Natalie. 'You look angry but you still look wonderful. You are more tanned than I remember you.' He leaned forward to kiss her on the cheek but she held back. 'Hmmn,' he grunted.

'I came because I promised but after your performance this morning, I can't say I'm here with any enthusiasm. Why did you say all those things?'

Russell showed her to a seat. 'They needed saying: the whole picture is important, relevant. If the press conference had been reported without mention of Richard, it would have been incomplete, wrong. Whisky?'

'Not yet, thank you. Is that why you did it? I think that reporter was right – what you did struck me as an act of spite, an attempt to sabotage what's been achieved this season.'

'Too right. That too, yes. Fights always exist on several levels, and this one is no different. I told you, the evening before I was made to leave the gorge, that I wasn't rolling over. Now you know I keep to my word.'

'How long are you going to be wounded, Russell? Will you ever get over this?'

'I'll get over it a damned sight quicker if you'll come over to my side, if you'll–'

'Russell, stop! Because I agreed to have dinner with you, doesn't mean we can just pick up where–'

'Does it mean anything, that I still feel about you the way that I do?'

Natalie shook her head. 'You're acting … you're behaving like a fossil, Russell, a fossil who has occupied the same position for years and years and has turned to stone.'

He stared at her.

'You could, if you wished, agree to be part of a team – for publication purposes anyway – a team that's made the most momentous discoveries this season, you being involved in the very first, which not only discovered the knee-joint but pointed us to the area where the other discoveries would be made. That would bring us closer together, you and me. Yet you remain stuck in your anger, your vindictiveness–'

He went to interrupt but she waved him down.

'You haven't been paying attention, all those miles away in Hollywood. The Maasai are threatening to occupy the gorge and destroy it. You know that but you overlook the fact that that means they are *still* on the warpath, so to speak. I have thought about it a lot and Eleanor was right to insist you leave–'

Again he went to interrupt; again she talked over him.

'Your career is the most important thing to you

but she was thinking of your *life*.'

'Huh! *And* the gorge–'

'No! Sending you away always risked a scene like today's – she knew that. It was more important to save your life.'

'You mean the dig couldn't afford two deaths.'

Natalie let a short pause elapse. 'As it happens, there *have* been two deaths.' She explained about Kees.

Russell shook his head and gave a low whistle. 'Poor man. Suicide. What a way to do it.' He looked up. 'But it confirms that Eleanor Deacon is losing it.'

'Russell! Kees told me that he thought Richard was homosexual. Was he? You knew him over several years, several digs. Did you know anything about that?'

Russell hesitated. 'I registered that he never had girlfriends. But no, I can't say I thought about it more than that. Very few women come on digs in Africa. Then he would go back to New York and me to Berkeley.'

'I once caught Richard and Mutevu standing very close together. Do you think ... could there have been anything between them?'

Russell stared at her. 'No! I mean, I don't know. Are you saying...?'

'I don't know what I'm saying. But you never saw anything that made you think?'

He shook his head, firmly. 'Nothing like that ever crossed my mind. And I'm not sure I like the suggestion.'

He tailed off and neither of them spoke for a moment.

531

Russell, she realised, wasn't quite as quick as he thought. If he'd really absorbed that there had been something between Richard and Ndekei, he would have realised she was telling him that the threat to himself was much diminished, and he should never have been made to leave the gorge. But since he was so belligerent, and so wrapped up in himself, Natalie was not going to help him work out what he couldn't work out for himself.

Then, 'Russell, why did you come back? Was it only for the press conference? And how did you know about it – how did you know all those details?'

Russell sipped his drink. He had reverted to vodka by the look of it.

'Richard Sutton Senior paid for me. He has a contact in the American Embassy here, who keeps him informed. We suspected the Deacons would pull some kind of stunt and so it proved–'

'Russell! It wasn't a stunt.'

'Oh no?' He looked at her and shook his head. 'Natalie, had I not intervened today, tomorrow's papers would have been full of anthropological and palaeontological details with no mention of Richard – or at least of Richard's murder.'

'There'll be more than enough time for that at the trial.'

He shook his head again. 'But by then, if the Deacons had had their way – unimpeded, you might say – the gorge would have been established as a national treasure, one of the wonders of the world, Richard's death would have been mini-mised, or side-lined altogether, an inconvenience no more. And you didn't give a straight answer today, either. She *did* try to get you to change your testimony, change your evidence, more than once.'

'I have never wavered.' Natalie said it firmly, blushing slightly, hoping he wouldn't notice.

'That's not what I said, or meant. *She* tried to get you to change your evidence. I can't forgive that.'

An appalling thought struck her. 'Are you... Would you *like* to see the gorge destroyed? If I give evidence, and say what I saw, and Ndekei is hanged, and the Maasai do what they are threatening to do, will that please you, give you satisfaction? Because you can't work in the gorge any more, do you want it spoiled for the rest of us? Is that what this is all about, Russell?'

He didn't say anything, but snatched at his drink.

'I'm right, aren't I? Richard's father, poor man, is devastated by his son's death but he wants Ndekei prosecuted and found guilty for entirely normal reasons – he wants justice for his son. But you, you want revenge, don't you? If you can't play in the gorge, you don't want anyone else to – that's it, isn't it?'

A long silence followed before Russell said, 'I can't deny it would give me some satisfaction to see the Deacons humbled. There would be a measure of justice in it, yes.'

Another long silence.

'Are you staying until the trial?'

'It was a condition of Richard Sutton Senior paying for me to come. He will be here himself, of course, nearer the time.'

'How are you going to fill in your hours? There's

533

a month to go.'

'You'd be surprised. For one thing, I'd like to talk to Marongo.'

'What? He's as likely to kill you as talk to you.'

Russell took some ice from his glass and cracked it between his teeth. 'You accuse me of being a fossil, of not appreciating how the world has changed, of being marooned in Hollywood. Don't underestimate me.' He pointed.

She followed with her eyes. Two large black men stood just outside the entrance to the bar.

'Bodyguards?'

Russell nodded.

'Have I seen them before?'

He nodded.

'In Lamu? Paid for by Richard Sutton Senior?'

He nodded again. 'So I know about you and Jack Deacon.'

'There's not a lot to know.'

'Maybe, maybe not. I don't really care. What I care about is you and me.'

Natalie ignored that. 'Why would you want to see Marongo?'

He smiled. 'Say Ndekei is convicted, say he's hanged. Marongo has political ambitions, as perhaps you know, and will make political capital whichever way the verdict goes. But I haven't been a complete fossil, Natalie. There *is* an alternative to destroying the gorge: let a new team take over. Run by me. I've been offered a full professorship at Yale. I'll be an even bigger fish next year.'

She stared at him. 'But how on earth could that work? You're the one ... you and Richard were the ones who set this whole thing in motion.'

He cracked more ice with his teeth. 'You'd be surprised how money talks, money and imagination. Sutton and I have been conferring. Maybe our interests coincide. If Ndekei is convicted and sentenced to hang, there will almost certainly be trouble, political violence, on a small scale maybe, but newsworthy. And there'll be an appeal. That will provide a focus for further trouble. Richard Sutton Senior will then intervene and say that, justice having been done with a guilty verdict, he will campaign for the commutation of the death sentence and that, as a mark of respect for his son, who committed a blunder – but no more – he wants to help the tribe. He will donate several millions to whatever causes the Maasai hold dear but only so long as they spare the gorge, which from now on will be excavated by Americans chosen by Richard Sutton Senior.'

'You'd do all that? Will it work?'

'I don't know. What I do know is that Marongo is a political animal and that Richard Sutton Senior has funded politicians and political campaigns in the past, in New York City and in Washington. He is not, shall we say, without experience – hardly wet behind the ears. I remember saying in one of my letters – one of my letters that you didn't reply to, by the way – that Sutton was a man who makes things happen and to beware. I was right and you were warned.'

Across the bar some of the British journalists were gathering, men who had been at the press conference. One or two looked in Natalie's direction but she did her best to ignore them.

535

'Russell, when Richard Sutton Senior came to the camp, with his wife, he said some very unpleasant things–'

'Yes, he's not the choirmaster-type is he?'

'That's unfair and unkind and it's not what I meant. He threatened me, he actually *boasted* about some of the unorthodox things he has done in the past, "corners get cut, toes get trodden on," and he threatened to make my life a misery if I didn't give evidence. He had me followed to Lamu, as you well know, because presumably he thought I might abscond, something that never crossed my mind.' Natalie paused. 'Are you sure, are you certain you want to be mixed up with that sort of person, that sort of rough-neck?'

'Hmmn,' growled Russell dismissively. 'All he wants from you is that you testify. Since you are going to do that there's no problem–'

'No *problem?* You've seen the lengths he'll go to, to ensure I do testify. This is a man who isn't shy of taking the law into his own hands.'

'Which, as I seem to recall, is exactly what Ndekei did.' Russell snorted. 'So we are all square there. But,' he went on as she tried to protest, 'I agree that Sutton Senior is the type who knows how to – well – cut corners, shall we say, when it's needed. But where his son is concerned there's a difference. If he can't have his son alive, then he wants his memory up there in lights – respectable, academic, professional lights – and my plan has tickled his imagination and sense of power. He didn't like Eleanor Deacon any more than I do, or her view that the gorge is more important than his son.' Russell wiped his lips with a paper napkin. 'So get used to the idea that, over the next few weeks, this whole can of worms is going to slither and slide and writhe out of control, with one of only two possible results, assuming you give evidence. One, the Maasai will destroy and reoccupy the gorge; or two, I will take over and you lot will be out in the cold – on your way, dare I say it, to becoming fossils.'

He paused, to let this sink in.

'Of course, all this doesn't necessarily apply to you. Through it all, Natalie, you say you have never wavered, about your testimony, and I have never wavered in my feelings about you. That must mean something and one of the things it means is that there's still time for you to change sides.' He leaned forward and touched her knee. 'I know you went to Lamu with Jack Deacon and you know I know. Did anything happen?'

'It's none of your business, Russell.'

'I'll take that as a yes, that you spent the night with him. Lucky him. If I hadn't been kicked out of Kihara, before he came on the scene, maybe I–'

'Russell!'

Some of the journalists looked over as she raised her voice.

'The Deacons look after each other, don't they? And now you've joined them, jumped into bed with them, metaphorically and physically–'

She slapped his face.

Now all the journalists were looking.

'Oh, Russell, stop feeling so sorry for yourself! You're behaving like a fossil all over again, stuck in one level. The world doesn't stand still–'

'It's only been a few weeks!'

'*What* has only been a few weeks?'

'Us. Our whisky sessions, listening to the baboons.'

She gasped. 'There never *was* an us! I told you that before you left. Yes, there were a few evenings of illicit whisky-drinking, a few – a very few – episodes of physical contact and maybe what? – one kiss, or was it two? All of it cut short by a piece of monumental stupidity, which was your fault. That's not enough for an "us" to be created. So you're mad to expect me to leap over to your side just because you ask. I told you all those weeks ago, during one of our fabled whisky sessions, that this season's digging would be remembered for all the wrong reasons and then along came the discoveries – the jaw, the skull, the vertebrae, Kees's hand-axes – and I forgot my own warning.'

Natalie swept her fingers through her hair. She noticed some of the journalists still looking in her direction. She ignored them.

'Then you come back again and raise all the old problems, all out of spite, envy and resentment. All caused by Richard's and your gross stupidity. And then you have the gall to invite me over to your side!'

She took a deep breath.

'Russell, what I do with Jack Deacon, or Christopher Deacon, or Eleanor Deacon should I choose to, is none of your business. You do your worst. Get into bed with that *crook*, Richard Sutton Senior, and fight the Deacons. I can't stop you. But if you do, you do it on your own, without me.'

She stood up, looking down at him.

'There was never an "us".' She touched his cheek where she had slapped him, and softened her tone. 'And there could never have been.'

Natalie turned, pushed through the scrum of journalists and left the bar.

'You know Marongo better than anyone, Jack, better than any other white person anyway. Will Russell's plan work?'

Natalie was in Jack's room at the hotel. After she had stormed out of the bar, leaving Russell with his slapped face, she had joined Eleanor, Jack, Christopher and the others, where she knew they were having dinner in the hotel coffee shop and had relayed what had occurred.

Everyone had been surprised, upset and bewildered but, because they were all in a kind of limbo, waiting for the press reaction to the conference – and Russell's intervention in it – no one seemed too prepared to get to grips with the threat he appeared to pose.

'Let's clear our fences one at a time,' said Eleanor. 'I'm tired. I need to sleep.'

'He had you followed to Lamu?' said Christopher. 'That's expensive and it shows a very determined adversary. Were you frightened?'

Natalie nodded. 'I was concerned. I wasn't certain I – we – were being followed. It seemed a bit far-fetched. But Russell confirmed it. You're right, Sutton Senior is very determined indeed.'

'A good job Jack was with you.'

She ignored that. 'What provokes me the most is: how did they *know* Jack and I were in Lamu? His contact at the American embassy couldn't have known that.'

Christopher nodded, finishing the water he was drinking. 'Sounds like he has a spy in our camp. That makes the blood go cold. You never thought of *not* giving evidence, did you? Never mentioned leaving the country?'

'No, of course not. You know that. You all know that.'

'What did you make of Lamu?' Christopher asked. 'I haven't had a chance to ask you.'

'I loved it, except for the sea urchins. A swim in the sea was a real break, a real luxury.'

'Where did you stay?'

'The Cotton House,' said Jack.

'In the rooms with the balcony?'

Natalie nodded. 'How about you? How was the Christmas Eve party at the Karibu Club?'

'Yes,' added Jack. 'Pick up any gossip?'

Christopher shook his head. 'It was all very tame. The only thing worth remarking on, the only surprise really, was that minister from Britain, you know, the one who came here.'

'Jeavons, you mean, the minister of science?'

'That's the one. Well, he was here again and deep in conversation with John Tudor.'

Jack frowned. 'They can't have had much in common: one a scientist, the other a judge.'

'Wrong,' breathed Eleanor. 'Jeavons is a *minister* of science but by training a lawyer.'

'Even so, what would they have to talk about?'

'It was Christmas Eve, for pity's sake,' said

Christopher. 'All I know is that they went at it for ages.'

Natalie decided to change the subject. 'How are the flying lessons going?'

'Well enough,' Christopher said. 'I've had no more panic attacks, if that's what you mean.'

'I didn't mean–'

He stood up. 'I'm tired too. See you tomorrow.'

'Don't say you're tired, Jack,' Natalie said, after the rest of them had departed. 'Someone needs to think this through.'

He nodded. 'Let's go to my room.' He smiled and added, 'You'll be quite safe and we'll have more privacy.'

Jack was seated now, in the chair by the chest of drawers, as Natalie lounged on the bed.

'I *did* know Marongo very well,' Jack said. 'But we haven't really been close for two or three years now. Since he's been chief, he's had to keep his distance. Yes, I'm an honorary Maasai but I'm also white – you can't hide that fact. The closer independence gets, the more political Marongo becomes.'

They had brought their whiskies with them and he swallowed some of his.

'Independence means various things and one of the things it means is change, including political change. And I can see that we may have played into Marongo's hands, with this very press conference, and in a way that plays to Russell's strengths as well.'

'What? How do you mean?'

'It's my fault, really, with this whole idea of a presentation. We'll soon see what the press makes

541

of today's events and either way we have achieved our purpose – we've made the gorge important. It will be very difficult for Marongo to destroy Kihara as it is now. That would make him and his Maasai savages. At the same time, a change of personnel could be very useful. I'm not saying it will happen, just that I can see how it would suit Marongo.'

Jack added more water to what was left of his whisky.

'As it stands now, the gorge is indelibly linked to the Deacons. My parents put it on the map, scientifically speaking; there has been a trail of scientists, journalists and politicians through here, and of course they are mainly white and they mainly came to see my father, then my mother and, if things continue, it will be Christopher, Beth and me. A change now, at independence, to a different team that is *not* the Deacons but one selected – at least tacitly – by the Maasai would associate them with whatever is discovered in the future. They would be reclaiming the gorge, but not destroying it.'

'But Russell! Of all people!' As she said this, the thought also occurred to her that Marongo knew about Ndekei and Richard. Was homosexuality a sin among the Maasai and if so did Marongo now have a personal grievance against anyone connected to Richard? Did that explain what was happening?

Jack lifted his glass to his forehead to cool it. 'Russell, or at least Richard Sutton Senior, is promising a lot of money, and politics – Marongo's main interest now – is expensive. What's more,

Marongo is a pragmatist. Richard Junior has already been killed. The Maasai have, in theory at least, been converted to Christianity. You and I know that conversion is paper-thin – they still worship their traditional gods, live in the old ways. But Marongo is the chief, his people will obey him and he knows how to wheel out Christianity when it suits him and it might suit him now, to make the most of the Christian idea of forgiveness and redemption. Think how that will play in the Western – the white – press. He, Marongo, forgives Russell, and Russell and Richard Sutton Senior redeem themselves by paying a forfeit and working in the gorge under Maasai direction.' He sighed. 'It could work.'

'I can't believe I'm hearing this!'

'I'm not saying it will happen – there's a lot of fight in the Deacons yet. But it's one scenario.'

Natalie was breathing heavily, hating what Jack was saying. 'Give me another scenario, please. Something more upbeat.'

Jack finished his whisky and refilled his glass with water. But he didn't say anything for some time.

When he did, he said quietly, 'I would very much like to make love to you again, Natalie.'

'Jack!' She coloured. 'What has that got to do with–?'

'Hear me out. I'm not about to jump on you.' He gulped his water. 'The night we spent together in Lamu was, well, it was memorable, despite those goons under the lamplight. I am not going to embarrass you by talking about the lovemaking, other than to say that the whole experience was ...

543

it sure beats finding fossils.' He grinned. 'Or flying your own plane, and I'd swap my Ph.D. for it several times over.'

He grinned again but she said, 'I still don't see what—'

'I'm getting there. I know Natalie Nelson, a bit anyway. I know who she is, what moves her, what matters to her. And I know that you agreed to spend the night with me in Lamu for a variety of complicated and simple reasons that might never come together again.'

She was listening now.

'I know some of those reasons, I can guess at others, still more are locked away inside you and are none of my business. But what I do know, Natalie, and I'm very sure of this, is that I can't let you get away. If you want an upbeat scenario – I think it's upbeat anyway – try this,' he paused. 'Marry me.'

Natalie coloured again. But she didn't say anything. Her throat was dry.

'Come and live in Africa, where there are lots of Lamus. Make it your life. Whatever happens in the gorge, there are other places to dig – the Rift valley is thousands of miles long, there are plenty of places for other discoveries to be made. Learn to fly yourself – if Christopher can do it, you can.' Jack smiled. 'Learn about African music, have your father come out here and listen to what the local tribes can do. Bring up some babies in the bush with all the wildlife and butterflies, the warmth – and the dung!' He swallowed what was left of his water. 'Let's have enough babies to start a choir.' He grinned. 'You know how I am

544

about children. How's that for a scenario?'

Silence in the room. Downstairs the British journalists were growing rowdy.

When Natalie did speak, it was to say, 'In a month or so I shall give evidence that could, if your bleak scenario proves accurate, drive the Deacons from the gorge that has been their life for decades. How would certain other Deacons feel about me *becoming* a Deacon under those circumstances?'

Jack shrugged. 'You can keep your own name if you wish. I like Natalie Nelson, it suits you. I told you that, the first time we met.'

'That wasn't so long ago. How can you be so certain of your own mind so soon?'

'You were immediately certain of seeing Ndekei.'

'Not the same thing at all.'

'Maybe not, but when you fly airplanes you have to be certain of a specific number of things – lives depend on it. That habit grows. I'm certain of what I feel for you.'

'I'm like altitude, am I? Or barometric pressure?'

He grinned. 'No, you're more like a weather pattern, a configuration, basically the same sunshine, a little cloudy at times, squally at others, the occasional growl of thunder. Help me out here, I'm not sure I can keep this up much longer.'

Another silence.

'You're right about Lamu. A weather pattern formed there, it built up – it did for me anyhow.' Natalie reached across and laid her hand on his arm. 'It was lovely. But–'

'I knew there was a "but" coming. "Buts" have peppered my life, they are up there with "howevers" and "nonethelesses". "Buts" have presaged every disappointment, ignited every set-back, begun the destruction of every hopeful scenario. I loathe "buts".'

'I won't use that word then. And I won't give you an answer tonight. I won't say no and I can't say yes either, not right now.' She thought. 'Did you really expect me to say yes this instant, to so sudden and so big a question?'

Natalie swallowed what was left of her whisky.

'What a day. I need to go to bed – I'm mentally exhausted, though I'm sure I shan't sleep.' She stood up and kissed him on the forehead. 'A choir-load of babies. That's quite a scenario, Dr. Deacon.'

Natalie had been right. Sleep wouldn't come. It was hot in the room; the overhead fan was working but not being at all effective. It had started to rain outside – the short rains had reached Nairobi. The weather in her head was changing too.

She had never hit a man before. She had never hit anyone before. She had never imagined doing so. But Russell... She didn't want to think about Russell but she couldn't avoid it. How could he conceive – plan, plot, precipitate – what he was trying to make happen? Jack and Russell were as different as could be. Jack, so far as she knew, was not at all the jealous type. But, like Jack, Russell thought politically. It was a dimension missing from her own make-up, as Jack had shown her. Natalie had been brought up to avoid jealousy and revenge but she knew, from her own un-avoidable feelings when she had been going out with Dominic and he spoke about his wife, what an unmanageable monster jealousy could be. Mgina had been right: like termites, jealousy corrodes even the strongest timber.

Jealousy might even be the very foundation on which this whole terrible scenario was built.

Natalie heard shouting in the street. What was it? Drunken revellers? A political demo? Not at this hour, surely, but that just showed how on edge she was, how much her life was determined by...

Around three, the solution came to her. It was like a flower unfolding in her brain. Something that had always been there suddenly grew bigger, more colourful, more attractive, more appealing, took on a form all its own.

She would change her story.

She would give Ndekei his freedom, Marongo his victory and the gorge a future. Natalie would say, simply, that she had had second thoughts, that in her heart she could no longer be certain that the figure she had seen that night was Ndekei. She had not seen his features, so he could have been anyone. Yes, he was wearing a white T-shirt of the kind worn by Ndekei but was he really shuffling, as she had thought? How could she tell, at that distance, in the dark?

If she changed her story Russell would be stymied and a career in the gorge was hers for the asking, even marriage to Jack.

There was the problem with Richard Sutton Senior but what, despite his threats, could he do?

Given the discoveries she had already made in the gorge – some of which she hadn't made when he had threatened her – could he really damage her?

Should she tell Richard Sutton Senior that his son was a homosexual? Did he know? If he didn't, it might make him angry, upset at the least. But the doubt that existed in her own mind, that the passions aroused by homosexuality might have been the real reason why Ndekei killed Richard, operated in both ways. In one sense, it made Ndekei *more* guilty, doubly culpable. He had his own personal private reason for killing Richard but was hiding behind tribal customs. But if that were true, the Maasai didn't deserve the chance to threaten the gorge; Ndekei's deception mustn't be allowed to succeed. Yes, he would go free, both his crimes – murder and deception – would go unpunished, but justice, in the wider sense, would be done.

The main thing was the gorge. She must learn to think politically, prioritise, compromise. She twisted and turned on the bed. The bedclothes clung to her damp skin. Maybe she could persuade Eleanor to honour Richard Sutton junior's memory much as his father planned. She hadn't pressed enough for the new species to be named in his honour. They'd announced the new name in the press conference, yes. But they hadn't gone into print yet. Maybe if she suggested it now, did a deal with Eleanor...

At four o'clock she changed her mind again. Of course she would give evidence.

Several more times that morning Natalie

changed her mind. The rain abated, the dawn came, the sun edged over the rooftops and flagpoles. She saw it all.

Fever

'I've said this before: there's good news and bad news.' Eleanor sat in her usual place at dinner. It had been two weeks since the headlines about the press conference and the associated accounts of the upcoming trial. They were now all back in the gorge digging and trying to ignore the fuss that was building up in Nairobi.

Eleanor coughed and said softly, 'I spoke at length on the radio-telephone with Harold Heath – in case you don't know, he's the editor of *Nature*. He has of course seen the reports of the press conference and is as horrified by the murder of Richard as he is intrigued and impressed by what he knows of our discoveries.' Her hands closed over her spectacles on the table in front of her. 'I couldn't resist telling him about Jonas' latest find: that we may have mankind's oldest pregnancy to report. I think he was almost as excited as I was. He is therefore willing, on this occasion, to overlook the problematic protocol issues, as he put it, and is prepared to publish our reports as usual.'

The new discovery was three days old. Jonas had discovered an ancient pelvis – at the same two million level – with an associated minuscule skull, which he was convinced was embryonic.

Eleanor smiled as she looked around the table but then grew serious. 'Now, Natalie, the bad news is that there's another attack on you in the Nairobi press, I am afraid. I haven't seen it but I was told about it by Maxwell Sandys when I spoke to him earlier, again on the radio-telephone.'

Natalie couldn't speak. She felt sick.

'What are they saying now?' said Jack. 'Anything new?'

'Well there is something new, yes, something new to me anyway, and it's distressing.' She paused and looked at Natalie with concern. 'They are saying that Natalie and Richard were lovers and so were Natalie and Russell, and that Richard was killed because of sexual jealousy, and they imply – but can't say outright – that she has, if not made up her evidence, then embellished it for personal reasons, that there is even a racist element in the fact that she is giving evidence at all. Ndekei, they are saying, has been set up.'

'How can they get away with all that?' said Jonas. 'Isn't that against the laws of libel, and contempt of court?'

'Theoretically, yes,' said Jack, leaning forward. 'The law here is based on British law. But with independence in the offing, everything is in flux and the rules are being relaxed all over the shop. Not that that's much comfort to Natalie.'

'What also bothers me,' said Eleanor, 'is how they are finding out things about camp life. Who is leaking all these details: do we have a traitor – a Judas – among us?'

Silence around the table.

Then Eleanor said, 'I'm sorry if I've upset you Natalie but I thought it better to tell you what is happening in Nairobi, what is being said, rather than have you ambushed later on, nearer the time of the trial. You're a strong person, I'm sure you can cope.'

In fact, Natalie was close to tears. Not for the first time she told herself that this was not what she had come to Africa for. She was not a racist. Or promiscuous. Given what Kees had told her about Richard, the idea of an affair with him was laughable. The press were worse than snakes. More politics.

Dinner was breaking up; there was talk of music.

'Do you want to choose tonight?' said Jack, who could see how upset Natalie was.

She shook her head, finished her water and got up. She smiled at Jack, at Eleanor and at Christopher. Then, without saying a word, she walked past the campfire towards her tent.

Natalie untied the tapes that closed the main flaps. She lit a cigarette. In the darkness, she heard voices. Were they coming from the gorge? Were the Maasai there even now, and if so what were they doing at this hour? They had been taking more and more interest in the gorge recently, as they all knew, but what could they be doing in the darkness?

'Is this a good time or a bad time?'

Jack stood over her. She hadn't heard him approach but then all manner of things were going on inside her.

'They all run into one,' she replied. 'Sit down.'

He did so and lit his own cigarette. 'You were quiet at dinner. You've been quiet a lot lately, since the press conference in fact. Events are getting to you.'

She let a pause elapse. 'You're right, but only half right.' She inhaled her cigarette smoke. 'Events *are* getting to me, yes. I am very on edge; I hate all this talk of racism and my so-called but in fact non-existent love affairs with Russell and/or Richard. I can't stop shaking, I can't sleep and I've lost most of my appetite. I'm finding it hard to concentrate on our work.'

'And my proposal didn't help, of course.' Jack crushed out what was left of his cigarette. 'I'm sorry if I'm part of the problem.'

Another pause, before she said, 'Since you mention it, Jack, I don't know whether I am going to have a clear enough mind this side of the trial to give you an answer about ... about my potential name change.'

He nodded.

'But, but you might also like to know that there's a weird weather pattern building up inside me right now, all sorts of complicated and simple emotions are swirling around in my system – clouds, squalls, more than a hint of thunder – and not a few memories, old memories, recent memories.'

He nodded, then said, 'I'm nodding as if I understand, but I don't. What are you saying? What are you trying to say?'

Natalie finished her cigarette. 'What I am saying, Dr. Deacon, is that I can't yet give you an answer on marriage. But, at the same time, I would like you to go back to your tent now, wait until everyone else has gone to bed and turned out their lights, and I then want you to sneak back here, so no one sees you, and then I'd like you to spend the night here. I want to be made love to. Don't ask any more questions. Just come back and make love to me like you did in Lamu.'

'Christopher, stop! Look, two o'clock ahead, in the tree.' Natalie's voice was high-pitched, triumphant.

Christopher brought the Land Rover to a halt. There were four of them in the vehicle. Christopher was driving, Daniel up front with him. Natalie was in the back with Aldwai, the guard. They were on their way back to the camp after the morning's digging. It was hot, the sun high and unrelenting, shadows almost absent.

'A lion,' said Natalie, silently patting herself on the back that her eyes were becoming adjusted to life in the bush. 'But why are we stopping? Don't we normally just drive on past lions?'

'Look at him,' said Christopher. 'He's emaciated and he's not moving. He may even be dead.'

'Ease forward,' said Daniel softly.

Christopher put the Land Rover into a low gear and rolled forward towards the tree.

'No sign of hyenas or vultures yet. If he's dead, he's only just died.'

'What are we doing?' said Natalie. 'Why is a dead lion so interesting?'

Daniel turned in his seat. 'There's been an outbreak of biting flies near Ngorongoro.' He inspected the lion. 'These flies suck the blood of lions, who become emaciated. They climb into trees or hyena burrows to escape the flies, but many of them die anyway. If this one's dead, we need to know. Biting flies carry diseases that badly affect horses, deer and some cattle.'

As he said this, however, the lion moved and fell out of the tree. They watched as it lay on the ground, wheezing heavily. It was certainly very thin, its ribcage showing through its pelt, parts of its body covered with bloody bare patches. As they watched, it raised itself on its front legs and began to drag itself through some bushes.

'It's lost the use of its hind legs,' breathed Christopher. 'It looks like *Stomoxys calcitrans* to me.'

'Is that the name of the fly?' said Natalie.

Daniel nodded. 'And there's no hope. The hyenas will be here soon. We need to shoot it and take it back to camp.'

'Is that necessary?' said Natalie.

Daniel turned in his seat again and reached up to the bracket where the guns were kept. 'This lion won't see out the day, Natalie. Either we kill him, quickly and painlessly, or the hyenas or wild dogs will tear him into a dozen pieces, slowly and agonisingly.'

Christopher took the other gun. 'Aldwai, keep an eye on us, will you? Natalie, stay in the Land Rover and keep all the windows closed, for now anyway. If hyenas or wild dogs come this way – and with an ailing lion it won't be long – they can be quite inquisitive.' He got out of the car.

Daniel and he moved off slowly. Aldwai followed them at a distance but stopped when he was about fifty yards from the vehicle, so he could keep an eye on Natalie, too.

It was stifling in the Land Rover. When Natalie

558

had first arrived in Kihara she had assumed she would get used to the heat. She had, but only up to a point. The midday temperatures in the gorge were just too hot for any human being to be truly comfortable and in a closed Land Rover, under full sunshine, it was worse.

But at least she had – for the most part – stopped shaking.

How her life was changing. As a young girl, as an undergraduate at Cambridge, at the beginning, she had hardly ever thought about sex. That side of her had been awakened by Dominic but for years Dominic and sex had been closely associated. She couldn't imagine having sex with anyone else: her head ruled her body – her head and her heart and her body were all one and the same entity. Not any more. Since Jack had pulled her out of the river during the wildebeest stampede, when she had enjoyed his hands on her breasts, her body had reasserted itself and no longer obeyed either her heart or her head.

Her nights were complicated affairs now. Her solitary whisky and her solitary cigarette, her close-of-day ritual, had now become instead the prelude, the calm before the storm, an aperitif, the sensual overture to a much more important main event. What would her father make of her behaviour? What would her mother have made of her behaviour? God forbid her father should ever know. What did she herself make of it? When she had first gone up to Cambridge, the idea of sleeping with someone she wasn't married to was as foreign, as strange, as unthinkable as, well, as giving evidence in a murder trial in Africa. But here she was, in Africa, being made love to by a man she'd known only a few months, in a tent, *and looking forward to it*. She couldn't say that she did what she did, or allowed to be done to her, without certain pangs of conscience, without the guilt that she was betraying some ideal her parents had for her. Nor was she oblivious to the risks. She had read, before she left for Africa, about the development of a so-called contraceptive pill in the United States but she couldn't really believe it would ever catch on. It would be wonderful if it worked but there must be side-effects, failures, problems, not least what it would do to the morals of people who – as she knew from her time at Cambridge – were much more adventurous than she.

But now, now that her body – if not yet all of her mind – had left Dominic behind, she could see that sex, if it could be divorced from what one thought one's parents would say, was, apart from anything else, a wonderful medicinal: it was like a therapeutic shower every night, that left her exhausted, but clean-spirited and clear-headed, *cleansed*. Jack was a considerate lover – at least she assumed he was, him being only the third man she had slept with.

There was invariably an air of uncertainty before Jack arrived and even after he had entered the tent. They smoked their cigarettes companionably enough and sipped their whisky. But their whispered conversation was stilted. It was only when he kissed her open mouth, when she felt his hands on her, when he pressed himself to her and she felt him harden – how erotic she found that word – only then did she feel the great tide of fire sweep through her body and all nerves, all tension, all doubt, all reticence evaporated. That was when she was most ashamed, most embarrassed at what she had become and when she found surrender exciting, irresistible.

The anticipation before and the relaxation/ exhaustion after also cleared her mind of the great confusion as to the real reason Richard had been killed. She had, she decided, sat on that confusion long enough. She would contact Maxwell Sandys and tell him what she knew.

Each night now she undressed and wore just a nightdress, the only nightdress she had brought with her, rather than her pyjamas. That had always been an unconscious act before, but now even the flimsiness of the garment was arousing. It showed that she was ready for Jack, half-naked when he arrived. That too was embarrassing, shaming and exciting all at the same time.

But – there it was again, Jack's least favourite word – good as Jack was in bed, clean and clear as she felt when it was over, she still couldn't think about marriage. He had put his proposal well, she thought. It would be lovely to learn to fly, to explore the landscape of Africa in that way. A lifetime spent in pursuit of early mankind, bringing up 'a choir' of children in such surroundings was both civilised, natural and unusual in all the right ways. And Jack adored children; he would be a good father, she was sure. But the trial, Richard's death, Russell's threats, she couldn't just dismiss those. Those bridges must be crossed before ... before she could be clear enough in her mind to give Jack an answer. What should she do? Give evidence or not, save the gorge or–

She heard a shot. Then another. Then another and she saw three hyenas break cover from the bushes ahead and scatter across the plain.

Shortly after that, Aldwai started to move back toward the Land Rover and then Christopher and Daniel appeared, both with ropes over their shoulders, pulling the dead lion behind them. The ropes were tied around the animal's hind legs, his head churning up the ground as it was dragged across the sand-soil of the plain.

As they came closer, Natalie was surprised at how large the lion was. She had never been this near to one before.

Aldwai fired his gun and two hyenas, following Christopher and Daniel, scattered again.

'Can you let down the back of the Land Rover?' Christopher shouted.

Natalie got out and went round to the rear of the vehicle, pulling out the bolts that kept the back flap in place. She let it down. When the two men reached the Land Rover, Daniel climbed up and hauled the lion's hind legs on board.

'Give me a hand here,' breathed Christopher, holding one of the animal's forelegs.

Natalie took the other one. The animal's fur certainly was mangy but it was surprising how warm the lion still was. There was a big black-red patch where it had been shot in the neck.

With Daniel pulling and Christopher and Natalie lifting, the lion was hauled on to the back of the Land Rover. It would fit in only by bending its spine. They shoved and pushed and pulled till it fitted the space. Clouds of flies were already buzzing round its bloody patch, where it had been shot. It was still stiflingly hot.

One more time Aldwai had to fire at the hyenas to keep them away.

How ugly hyenas were, thought Natalie, not for the first time. How different from the magnificence of lions – lions other than the poor creature they had manhandled into the Land Rover.

Christopher and Daniel slid back the bolts of the flap at the rear end of the vehicle and stood for a moment, resting after their exertions. Daniel went to the back seat compartment of the Land Rover and took from it a bottle of water which he handed round. They were all sweating copiously.

Christopher, looking intently at Natalie, said, 'I'd say we've earned our showers today – eh?' He smiled.

Following his gaze, she looked down at her own shirt front. The khaki was stained dark with sweat all over and clung to her breasts, so tightly that a slight bulge was prominent, where the wet cotton hugged the outline of her nipples.

'You've got tick typhus.'

'What?' Natalie, lying on her back, on her bed in her tent, was sweating but feeling a chill all at the same time. She looked up at Jonas with alarm.

'Don't worry,' he said, somewhere between a growl and a chuckle. 'It's not typhus like the nineteenth-century Charles Dickens-type variety. It's tick typhus, more like a cross between a very bad dose of 'flu and chicken pox.'

'No! Isn't that bad enough? How did I get it?'

Jonas rummaged in the bag he had brought with him. 'I should imagine it was handling that emaciated lion you brought back to camp the other day. It's been confirmed that it had biting sickness. Christopher's gone down with it, too.'

'Oh dear. What happens now?'

'Tick typhus usually lasts twelve to fifteen days. The rash on the palms of your hands is the tell-tale sign. It might spread to your arms and legs, even the soles of your feet, which is where Christopher is most affected right now. You'll feel some muscle pain and probably more than one headache.' He lifted a small brown glass bottle from his bag. 'Aureomycin, an antibiotic: take it twice a day, beginning right now, and be sure to finish the course – remember what happened to Mgina's little brother.'

Natalie nodded. 'The trial is only – what? – nineteen days away.'

'Don't worry, you'll be fine by then, trust me. But no digging in that time. Have lots of rest – you'll feel tired anyway – and keep out of the sun. Try not to sweat, that makes the rash worse. I'll tell Mgina to bring you water for a shower three times a day instead of the usual once. Shower when you have a fever, not when you feel a chill. Showers keep your skin clean and cool.'

Jonas handed her two tablets. 'Take these. No alcohol, by the way. You won't feel like doing much for the first few days and don't push your-self. Sleep as much as you can. Your body will re-cover more quickly in that way and you'll scratch yourself less.'

'Is Daniel suffering too?'

'No. Being African, he may have acquired some immunity. Or he may just have been lucky. We don't know. Now, I'll come back before dinner to see how you are. I'm just off to give Christopher his antibiotics.'

Jonas went out.

Natalie had woken up the day before with a fever and a rash on the palms of her hands. She had fought off the fever for half a day but then felt too ill to continue and collapsed in bed. Jonas had been away with Jack that day, warning the nearby tribes about the biting flies that had, in effect, killed the lion Natalie had spotted. The tribes were to be on the lookout for early signs of disease among their animals. She had been asleep when they returned and they hadn't wakened her.

This morning the rash on Natalie's hands had been much worse, she was shivering with a chill and Jonas had immediately known what was wrong.

Natalie had never been ill before and the thought of lying in bed for days on end bored her. At the same time, she had to admit, she couldn't go out into the sunshine with her rash, nor could she quite face writing papers for Eleanor and *Nature*.

She settled down, lying on her back, looking up at the roof of the tent, her hands lying on the edge of the bed where they could catch what breeze was going. There would be no late-night visits from Jack, not in the full sense anyway, while she was laid low. How could she think about sex while she was ill? she wondered. With ease, it seemed.

How she had changed – and was that natural? Had she become a freak or had she been a freak to start with and simply matured into a normal woman? Would she ever know?

Somehow she dropped off to sleep but was awakened by noises in the back tent which adjoined hers. Someone had brought water for her shower. Natalie got up and went through.

Mgina was there.

'Hello.'

'I am sorry you are not well, Miss Natalie. Dr. Jefferson says you must not shower if you feel chill.'

'No, no, don't worry, Mgina, I'm feeling sweaty.' Natalie stepped out of her damp pyjamas and stood under the shower. The water – tepid rather than hot – was very cooling as it began to evaporate on her skin. She soaped herself carefully and let the water remove the suds. The palms of her hands still itched – worse, they were still sore – but holding the soap seemed to help.

'And how are you, Mgina? How is married life? How is Endole and where is he?'

'He is looking after the cattle, Miss Natalie. With the biting sickness, all the cattle are being held close by the village.'

Natalie nodded, patting herself dry with the towel.

'And are you happy, being wife number three?'

Mgina passed across a new towel. 'This is softer, Miss Natalie, better for your rash.' As Natalie took it, she added, 'I am pregnant, Miss Natalie.'

'Oh, but that's wonderful! A new life to replace

Odnate and so soon. Is your mother pleased?'

Mgina nodded.

'As soon as I've got rid of this rash, Mgina, we must celebrate. Let me think what to do.'

'Will you be well for the trial, Miss Natalie?'

Natalie frowned. What was Mgina saying? What had she heard? Why was she so interested? It was unlike her to ask questions. Was she the leak in the camp, the link to Marongo and, even, to Richard Sutton Senior? Mgina had known Natalie and Jack were flying to Lamu at Christmas, she had helped them pack the plane. Natalie didn't want to think about it.

'Oh yes,' she replied eventually. 'Nothing has changed there.'

Mgina nodded and picked up Natalie's dirty pyjamas and left the shower tent. Natalie went back to her own quarters and lay down on the bed, naked. The twenty minutes after a shower were always the most comfortable time.

But her mind was in a swirl. Was Mgina the innocent young woman she looked, as Natalie had always thought of her, or was she something other than she seemed? Yes, she came from a different village from Ndekei but she was a Maasai; her loyalties would be the same.

Natalie would need to discuss this with Jack. He was bringing her dinner later.

How did this bloody illness change things? *Did* it change them? Was she giving evidence or was she not? How could she possibly decide while she was ill? How long could she put off her decision?

Again, despite herself, she dropped off to sleep.

Jack placed the dinner tray at the foot of Natalie's bed and kissed her head. 'Chicken,' he breathed. 'Your favourite.'

She swung her feet off the bed and sat up. She'd been ill now for more than a week and the antibiotics were beginning to kick in. Her temperature was more under control, the chills were fewer, the sweats less intense. But the rash on her hands was still pronounced and she continued to be hit by the occasional biting headache. She wasn't out of the woods yet and Jonas insisted she remain in bed.

Natalie picked up the chicken leg and chewed it. 'My appetite hasn't fully returned yet.' She replaced the leg on the plate. 'How is Christopher doing?'

'About the same as you. But he has a rash on the soles of his feet and has difficulty walking. No difficulty eating, though.'

She nibbled a potato. 'How's his mood?'

'Well, I'm sorry to say this but he's not too enamoured of you, just now. He wishes you had never spotted the damned lion, he says.'

'Why?'

'Because of being ill, he's missed his test as a pilot and because he will have been grounded for more than two weeks by the time he has fully recovered, he will have lost the number of required hours of flying time and have to start all over again. He won't now be able to get his licence for at least another month.'

She groaned. 'I couldn't know the damned lion had the wrong kind of tick.'

'I know that and, deep down, he knows that

too. He's just irritated with you, that's all.'

Natalie weighed this. Then she said, 'I suppose everyone sees you bringing me dinner every evening?'

'Yes, I suppose they do.'

'So everyone knows ... you know, about us?'

Jack crossed one leg over the other. 'They don't know everything, Natalie. They know I bring you dinner. They can read between – or beyond – the lines if they wish. But you're not the topic or focus of gossip, if that's what you're worried about. The fact that I don't visit you late at night now probably means that they think less is happening than really is or was.'

He let a silence go by as she ate more potato.

'I miss our late nights.'

She nodded. 'Me too. Christopher is not the only one who wishes I hadn't spotted the bloody lion.'

Another pause, then she raised her conversation with Mgina.

'It could be her,' said Jack. 'But then it could be anyone. The damage has been done. You will be well enough in time to give evidence. There's no point in worrying yourself silly over Mgina.'

She nodded. 'Maybe so. Any news from Nairobi?'

He didn't reply straight away, but then said, 'No.'

'You're lying!'

Yet another pause. 'Get well before you face what they're saying in Nairobi.'

She stopped eating. 'I'm not a child, Jack, and I'm on the mend. Tell me.'

He uncrossed and recrossed his legs to buy time. 'There have been demonstrations outside the prison where Ndekei is being held. There's going to be a concert in support of Ndekei on the night before the trial starts. Ndekei's wife, Atape, and his children will be paraded on stage. They will be in court.'

'So it really will be a circus?'

Jack nodded. 'I'm afraid so. The politicians have got hold of the trial. They won't let go.' He paused, then said, 'Hold on,' and went out.

He soon came back. He had two newspaper cuttings with him. 'This is a long editorial in the *East African Gazette,* a couple of days ago. It's quite interesting, thoughtful, and concludes that Kenya shouldn't go back to tribal law but that in this case – the Ndekei case – the evidence is only circumstantial and, in the wider interests of Kenya, the trial should be abandoned.'

'What?'

He nodded. 'Read it. We're lucky to have a copy because the other cutting, as you will see, is a short news report which says that the editorial in the *Gazette* was in contempt of court and the paper has been closed down.'

Natalie looked up. 'Can they do that?'

'They can and they do. One of the censors just wanted the offending article ripped out but that was judged impracticable with so many copies being printed, so all the papers were pulped and the editorial offices closed down for a week.'

'Which makes the trial even more newsworthy.'

He nodded.

'But you are still not trying to dissuade me?'

570

'I know better. We all do.'

If they knew what she knew – about Richard and Ndekei, and if it were true – what would everyone say then? she wondered. Her illness had prevented her from contacting Maxwell Sandys. How much did that matter? Would she ever know?

'Is Tudor still the judge?'

'Yes. He's coming in for some stick too.'

Natalie lay back down on the bed and put her arm behind her head. 'What would happen if I were too ill to give evidence?'

'I'm not sure. It would probably be up to the judge. He could either postpone the trial or insist the proceedings go ahead without you. Which would mean, I suppose, that the prosecution's case would collapse.' He bit his lip. 'You're not thinking of being too ill to give evidence are you?'

'Well, it wouldn't be true any more to say that I haven't wavered. This illness, this rash, has played havoc with my system. When you're sweating and scratching it's not easy to know your own mind.' She sighed. 'If Mgina *is* the...' She looked at Jack. 'I'm just exhausted the whole time.'

He nodded. 'I'm not too sure any of it matters any more anyway.'

She rolled on to her side. 'What do you mean?'

'Atape and Ndekei's children are not the only people going on stage at the concert. Marongo is going to speak. I strongly suspect he may use the opportunity to announce a deal with Russell – that avenue seems to have acquired a momentum all its own.' He took out his cigarettes. 'We have to make the most of this season because it will probably be our last in the gorge.'

Jack lit a cigarette. 'But when you are ready, if you decide you want to marry me the offer still stands.'

Eleanor tapped her water glass with her knife. The buzz of conversation over the dinner table died.

'First, I think we should all welcome back Natalie.' She turned in her seat. 'We have all missed you, my dear. How long has it been now? Two weeks? You look pale but how do you feel?'

Natalie sipped some water. 'I feel a little weak, my hands still itch now and then, but I'm hungry for the first time in days.' She smiled. 'Does that answer your question?'

'Good,' said Eleanor, turning to watch as Naiva brought in the food. She turned back. 'This is the last time we shall all be together for a while. Arnold and Jonas are staying here, during the trial, carrying on with the digging, showing the Maasai we haven't abandoned the gorge. Jack, Natalie and I will be in Nairobi. Christopher should be up and about tomorrow and will come with us. The papers for *Nature* are all written – Natalie, thank you for working while you have been rather less than one hundred per cent these past few days. I will post the papers from Nairobi, as one package. They should be in London in about a week. I have spoken again to Harold Heath and if he likes what we have written as much as he anticipates, and because of the controversial background, there will be a special edition of *Nature* devoted to the gorge.' The food had reached her and she helped herself. 'That may come late in the day for Marongo but a special edition of *Nature* is not nothing in scientific terms and Russell may find himself further out in the cold than he would like.'

Eleanor turned towards Natalie again. 'Before I forget, tomorrow night, the night before the trial starts, Jack, Christopher and I are having a family dinner – it's something we do every year at this time, to sort out family matters. So I have arranged for you to have dinner with Maxwell Sandys. I hope I did the right thing. We don't want you to be alone, the night before the trial.'

'Oh yes,' said Natalie. 'Of course. Thank you.'

'Good. We'll all fly up together in the morning, early, with Jack. Max wants to see you in the afternoon, anyway, for a final briefing. We could all meet after dinner, to see how the land lies.'

'Oh?' said Jack. 'What do you mean by that?'

Eleanor looked at Daniel. 'Daniel's going to the concert: our eyes and ears. He'll come back and tell us what Marongo had to say.'

'Hmmn,' growled Jack. 'Aren't you over-reacting? Whatever he says, nothing is going to happen immediately. Our licence doesn't run out until May, a special edition of *Nature* is a real event in scientific terms. We could still see off Russell and Richard Sutton Senior.'

'Maybe,' said Eleanor. 'Maybe so. But there are a couple of things you may not know, Jack. A Russian Jeep-type vehicle was spotted in Olinkawu the day before yesterday. I suspect there's been more gun-smuggling across the border and that some of them are destined for the Maasai.'

'But where are they getting the money?' Jack shook his head sceptically.

'That's the second thing you don't know,' growled Eleanor gloomily. 'That was the main reason Maxwell Sandys was in touch on the radio-telephone. Richard Sutton Senior arrived three days ago, and the day before yesterday he was seen meeting with Russell and Marongo. Something's going on, Jack, something political, something we don't have any control over. I'm not at all sure Sutton knows what his money is being used for but he has more than enough to buy guns.'

Natalie sat, just inside her tent, and looked out at and listened to the rain. The short rains lasted anywhere from ten minutes to an hour and a half. Nothing at all by Lincolnshire standards. The raindrops flashed and glistened and sparkled in the shine of the hurricane lamp and beat down on the roof of her tent. The smell of the acacia thorns was intensified. She found it all, for some reason, comforting.

She was still not ready to risk a whisky, but she had lit a cigarette.

How many more nights in the gorge were left to her? If she flew to Nairobi tomorrow and gave evidence as planned, and if Ndekei were convicted and then hanged, would Marongo really follow through with his threat? If the gorge were destroyed, or occupied, or a change of team were imposed, she – like the others – would become known throughout her chosen profession for this humiliating transformation of fortune, for throwing away the best season's digging ever.

If she didn't give evidence, what then? Would she be prosecuted for contempt of court or wasting police time? Would it make any difference now? Hadn't things gone too far? Despite the support of some newspapers, would Marongo take any notice? Richard Sutton Senior's money spoke louder than editorials, especially editorials that didn't see the light of day. If she could somehow face Marongo and the Maasai with Ndekei's homosexuality, would that make a difference? *Was* Ndekei homosexual? If she didn't give evidence, what would she think of herself a week from now, a month away, in the years ahead? Would Richard Sutton pursue her as he said he would? Either way, her career was almost on the rocks.

And *if* she was not giving evidence, when was she going to make up her mind? She was no nearer a decision than when she had first wavered all those weeks ago. It struck her that there were similarities between her own position and Kees van Schelde's, when he had strayed into the bush exposing himself to risks that might – or might not – kill him. The risks she faced were not mortal but they were not negligible either, not negligible professionally speaking. But, in not taking a firm decision yet, one way or the other, she was letting things ride, letting events carry on around her, in the hope that her problem would be resolved without her actually having to *do* anything herself.

Was that morally clean?

But the trial was the day after tomorrow. She would have to give evidence then, or the day after at the latest.

Or not.

Natalie was nowhere nearer a decision. She had come to the end of her cigarette. For once, it hadn't settled her. She didn't feel tired and she was still on edge. Jack wouldn't come tonight; her body was still not fully recovered. The palms of her hands still tingled.

The rain intensified.

She put out the hurricane lamp and for a few moments listened to the downpour. She loved the sound of rain.

Natalie shifted in her seat. Her skin still felt as though it was covered in a rash, though all the spots had gone.

Quietly, she undressed and, in total darkness, stepped out of her tent into the weather, completely naked. The warm raindrops pelted her skin, almost taking her breath away. Her mind wasn't settled and she was still on edge. Water ran down her cheeks, down her chest between her breasts, down her thighs, it dripped off her nose and chin and nipples. Her body was cool and clean, her skin felt free of the rash at last.

And, in the deep blackness, in the total absence of any form of light, she could see her way forward.

The Trial

'There she is! There she is!' About a dozen people, some with placards, were standing outside the court building as Natalie got out of Maxwell Sandys' car. They came towards her, jogging their placards up and down. One had a photograph of Natalie taken from one of the newspaper articles about her, and with the press headline blown up: 'WIDOW-MAKER'. Another showed a photograph of Ndekei with a rope crudely drawn around his neck, and the words: 'WHITE JUSTICE – GO HANG'.

'Widow-maker,' they chanted, 'widow-maker, *widow-maker.*'

Sandys bundled her past them and on into the courthouse. They both ran up the main stairs to the first floor and turned left into his office.

Natalie was shaking.

Sandys took her hand. 'I'm sorry about that but I thought it might help you get acclimatised, to show you what was outside the courthouse, what to expect. I'm afraid it will be even worse to-morrow.' He handed her a glass of water. 'How are you holding up?' he said. 'I gather from Eleanor that you went down with tick typhus – it never rains but it pours, eh?' He smiled grimly.

'I'm fine. I don't recommend tick typhus, but I'm fine. I gather we are having dinner together tonight and could have talked about the case then. But I'm grateful that you showed me the crowds, as mental preparation.'

He stared at her. 'Dinner? But I'm–' He stopped. 'Yes, of course, that's right. I'll come to the hotel, seven-thirty-ish. I may be a little late.'

Natalie passed a hand through her hair and nodded. 'Just talk me through what will happen and let's go from there. I'm tougher inside than I look on the outside.'

Was that true? she wondered. It had once been true but after all that had happened...

Sandys was behind his desk. He had taken off his jacket but wore a waistcoat and tie. He played with a paper knife.

'The trial starts at 10.30, as I think you know. The first morning will be taken up with the prosecution setting out our case, then the defence will do the same. Nothing too specific, no nitty gritty, but the principles of the arguments that will be used on both sides. After lunch on the first day, we – as the prosecution – will begin presenting our evidence. We have four main matters to introduce. First, the sliver of Ndekei's apron that was caught up on the thorn fence near Richard Sutton's tent. Second, the print of his wellington boot found outside the tent; and third, the boot itself, recovered by African ancillary staff at Kihara from the monkeys who were playing with it. The first two will be presented by the police who were summoned to Kihara on the morning after the murder – Frank Metcalfe and Dennis Burton – I think you met them.'

Natalie nodded. 'I remember.'

Sandys leaned forward. 'The bloody boot will just be presented as evidence. We don't have a witness to say when and where it was found,

580

because none of the locals who did find it will come to court. They are Maasai, so we never expected they would testify. For that reason, we don't know whether the judge will allow this as evidence, or whether Hilary Hall will object, since we can't prove when and where it was found. But we shall argue that it doesn't really matter where it was found, the crucial point being that it is Ndekei's boot and the blood is the same type as Richard's.' He took a breath. 'But I've decided not to introduce the watch. That's a problem, too. No Maasai will come forward to give evidence and although Eleanor could say who gave it to her, she can't say what she was told about it, why the Maasai had it in the first place, because that would all be hearsay.'

Sandys leaned forward. 'That will take up the first afternoon and maybe some of the second morning. Then we come to you. I shall lead you through your story, slowly, deliberately, allowing you to say exactly what you saw that night. I shall ask my questions in such a way that you will say what you saw several times over, so it is rubbed in. Then, when I have finished, Hilary Hall will cross-examine you. You have some idea of the line he will follow from your earlier encounter.

'He will probably begin in a friendly manner but at some point turn aggressive, trying to sow doubts in your mind, and therefore in the mind of the judge, as to what, exactly, you saw that night. He will ask how good is your eyesight and, I am afraid, whether you had been drinking, whether you were having an affair with Russell North – and/or Richard Sutton – and if either of them was with you when you saw Ndekei. All you have to do, my dear, is tell the truth, as simply as possible, and try not to get angry or riled by his questions. Remember, Hilary will be putting on an act. He will not really be angry with you, he doesn't really think you had an affair with Russell North, and of course he knows you weren't drunk. But it's his job to go through these hoops. He's just as convinced that Ndekei is guilty as we are. But that's the way the law works. If you get riled at any point, just tell yourself Hilary is acting, playing a game.'

Sandys cleaned one of his nails with the paper knife.

'And that's our case. After we have finished, Hilary will probably argue that we have no case, that all our evidence is circumstantial. Tudor will dismiss that and then the fun will begin when Ndekei is called and starts to run his defence: that he was acting according to Maasai custom. How much rope Tudor gives him is anyone's guess but I would expect very little indeed, so that either way the trial should be over by the afternoon of the second day, or the morning of the third.' He smiled at Natalie. 'It might make sense for you to leave Nairobi before the end of the trial. There's no need to expose yourself to any more unpleasantness than is absolutely necessary. And I suggest that, if you can bear it, you remain in your hotel room all day tomorrow, day one of the proceedings. Or just come down for meals. I think a low profile is called for – yes?'

Natalie nodded. Her hands were tingling again. The tick typhus just wouldn't go away.

A thought struck her. Had Jonas got the diagnosis right? Or was she more ill than she knew, more ill than Jonas knew? She felt a flush to her face. That was a fresh worry. While she was here in Nairobi, waiting to give evidence, perhaps she should see a specialist in internal medicine. Jonas was from London, after all, and not an expert in tropical diseases. But who could she turn to? Maybe Jack could help.

'I have one extra piece of information,' she said.

'Oh, yes?' replied Sandys. 'What is it?'

She told him what Kees had said about Richard Sutton being homosexual and explained about the episode in the store room. He listened intently.

'So you think Ndekei had a reason other than tribal custom to kill Richard?' Sandys had scribbled a few notes.

'I don't know. Maybe they had an argument, maybe sexual jealousy was involved. I'm guessing.'

'Hmmn,' said Sandys. 'Interesting but I don't see how we can substantiate any of it.'

'We could cross-examine him on it,' said Natalie.

'Yes, but think how that would raise the political temperature. Homosexuality is even more unpopular among blacks than it is among whites. And it would be a slur on Richard Sutton which he couldn't defend himself against.'

He put down his pen and shook his head. 'I agree that your new information may throw a very different light on the proceedings, and it certainly vitiates the defence's likely argument that you yourself were having an affair with Richard Sutton. But I don't see how we can introduce it. This man, Kees van Schelde, is dead and without testimony directly from him it's all too nebulous.' He shook his head a second time. 'I'm sorry but we simply can't go down that route. Does that upset you?'

Natalie bit her lip. 'I've been in two minds over this whole thing since Kees first revealed to me that he thought Richard was homosexual. I was going to tell you a couple of weeks ago, when you might have had time to look into it, but I fell ill.'

'I don't think that would have made any difference,' said Sandys. 'This Kees man was already dead, Richard Sutton is dead, Ndekei is the defendant – where would our evidence have come from?' He shook his head. 'It was always a non-starter, I am afraid. I'm sorry.'

Natalie shrugged. 'What was also at the back of my mind, if you said that, was a deal. I realise that all I've told you is innuendo – of course I know that. But there may be some truth to it and, if there is, Ndekei may think we know more than we do. I therefore wondered that if the defence intend to allege that I was having an affair with Richard and/or Russell, then you could ask them *not* to go that way and, in return, we wouldn't ask about Richard and Ndekei.'

A wry smile unveiled itself across Sandys' features. 'I admire your cunning, Dr. Nelson, and if you ever get bored in the gorge you will make an excellent lawyer, thinking like that. But I'm afraid the defence is allowed to fling mud, but not so the prosecution. Hilary Hall simply

584

wouldn't do a deal of that kind.'

He shook his head. 'I'm sorry, it was a valiant attempt but we can't do as you suggest, as you hope. I don't see that we can use this information in any way at all, I'm sorry.'

Sandys closed the file that was in front of him and stood up. 'Having bravely come in the front way,' he murmured, 'I think we'll spirit you out the back.'

Natalie sipped her whisky and looked at her watch. Seven thirty-eight. Maxwell Sandys had said he might be late, but how late was he going to be? She knew it was silly but she was uncomfortable, waiting in a bar, alone, even a bar in a hotel where she had her own room. People might get the wrong idea.

Not that the bar was very full at this early hour, but even so.

She was wearing her frock, the only one she had brought with her to Africa, and her wedge heels: her life-saving wedge heels that had enabled her to run away from those horrible men outside the bar when she had visited Nairobi earlier, with Jack. She and Jack were meeting up later, after his mysterious family meeting, and she was looking forward to their love-making in a proper hotel bedroom, where the beds were big and spongy and the walls were solid and sound-proof.

Natalie blushed inwardly as she thought this. Jack might say, as he often did say, that children mattered to him but sex mattered to her – oh, how it had come to matter. She had never thought she would become so ... so *demanding*, that was the word. But she couldn't help it.

She glanced at her watch again. Seven forty-one.

She looked about her. There was another couple in the bar and two women sitting together at the bar itself. They were all in dresses, one wore a hat, all were talking in low voices, so she couldn't hear what was being said. Did these other women feel about sex the way she felt about it? Were they as demanding? Did they think about it as much as she did, did they make as much noise when... She was making herself blush inwardly again.

She looked at her watch. Seven forty-three. Maxwell Sandys was really late now, verging on rude–

'Tally?'

The skin on her throat was clammy. Had she heard right? That was the name, that was the nickname her father used.

She turned and looked up at the man who was standing over her.

'Father!' she whispered. 'Oh, thank God!'

Natalie stood up. She couldn't believe it.

Her father, in a lightweight suit she hadn't seen before. Her father, stooping over her as he had done all her life. Her father with his beautiful hands, made for playing the organ. Her father, with the small piece of stubble in the cleft of his chin that he always missed when he was shaving.

He held out his hand.

She took it.

He pulled her towards him and threw his arms around her. She buried her face in his chest, smelled his smell, the smell of the house in Gains-borough: floor polish, Noah the cat, woodsmoke from the fire in his study.

They remained like that for a moment. With her head pressed sideways against his chest, she managed to murmur, 'Why are you...? When did you...?'

He took her by the shoulders, then put his hand over her mouth. 'All in good time,' he said softly. 'You wait here while I get a drink. I need a single malt.'

Natalie sat, smiling, as he went to the bar. She couldn't believe it. But there he was, her lovely father, in a lightweight suit, looking thoroughly at home in these surroundings. She found it impossible to keep a smile off her face.

Then he came and sat next to her so that their legs were touching, so they could maintain body contact.

'I'm here partly because of your director, Eleanor Deacon.'

'No! I don't believe it! I told her not to interfere. This is–'

'Hold on!' said Owen Nelson. 'Hold on. Let me tell my story. It's not easy.' He sipped his single malt. 'That's better, a lot better.' He took Natalie's hand. 'Yes, I was a very bitter man, Tally, as you may have realised. I don't know whether you knew this – maybe you did – but I blamed you for Violette's death. Not completely, of course, but your ... your affair with that cellist, it devastated your mother: a light went out inside her when you told her. You couldn't know this but she cried herself to sleep and sometimes she woke me up in the middle of the night with her sobbing. She was so *disappointed*, she felt so empty.'

He sipped more whisky.

'Anyway, when she died, I too was devastated – anyone would be – but I couldn't see straight. I blamed you, which is why I couldn't face you, why I avoided you, snubbed you, spurned you, all those horrible non-fatherly things that I did.'

She squeezed his hand. 'I understand that, I lived through it and hated it, but what I don't understand is what made you change your mind.'

'I'm coming to that.' He took out a cigarette case and offered Natalie one. She refused. She wanted to keep her hands free to hold her father. 'Three things. Three things changed my mind.' He lit his cigarette. 'You remember when you called me from Nairobi, all those weeks ago, and Mrs Bailey answered?'

Natalie nodded. She still couldn't stop smiling.

'After the exchange was over, she came back into my study where I was working, and told me I was being inhuman. That was bad enough but she added that unless I started building bridges – towards you, she meant – she would quit her job. She said she wouldn't leave me in the lurch, she would wait until I found a replacement, but that she wanted to go unless I made it up with you.'

Two couples came into the bar and he looked up before going on.

'By Christmas time, I had done nothing about anything. I have to admit that I didn't like the idea of Mrs Bailey giving me an ultimatum but then neither did I like the idea of her leaving. She and I are used to each other.' He chuckled. 'And then came all the news reports about your press conference, the one where you announced your discoveries, but also where it was revealed that you, you personally, had become a witness in a murder trial and that the case was dividing all the people on your dig.'

Owen smoked his cigarette for a moment. 'That's when I decided to write to you, to suggest that I came for the trial, to support you–'

'I never got any letter!'

'Because none was ever sent. While I was looking into the whole business, buying tickets, fixing a leave of absence with the bishop, making sure Mrs Bailey would look after Noah, deciding how to say what I wanted to say in a letter, I had this phone call – from Eleanor Deacon.'

'This is the part I don't–'

'No, Tally, no. Don't go off the deep end. I know you think she interfered, meddled, in your private affairs. That's what she said you'd say.'

'Dad! That's exactly what she did!'

'But I'm here. It worked! She convinced me not to send you a letter, that what would have the most impact on you was if I *behaved*, acted, did something and came here myself.' He crushed his cigarette out into the ashtray. 'We must have had the most expensive phone call in history – thank God she was paying – because we talked for almost half an hour. The operator kept asking if she wanted three more minutes and she kept saying, "Yes, yes, get off the line". She's very *forceful*, isn't she?'

Natalie nodded. She was angry with Eleanor for interfering but couldn't stop smiling because her father was here.

He lit another cigarette. 'Anyway, we spent a lot of time just talking about what you are all doing in the gorge. She told me about her own father, who was a missionary and who had his faith crushed; she told me about the discoveries you have made personally, what their significance is; she told me that she has written to the head of your college about how good you are.'

'She hasn't told me!'

'No. I shouldn't be telling you this, really. She says it's better if these things are anonymous, it's the way things work in Britain, but she thinks you are professor material and she wants to prepare the ground.'

Natalie was half-flattered by this news but still astounded by Eleanor's constant interference.

'Then we talked about the trial, what you saw, the threats to the gorge – which I knew about, briefly, from the reports of the press conference – and the fact that you are under a lot of pressure, from both sides, and that the trial may become a circus. She convinced me I should come for the trial, as I had been meaning to do anyway, and that to alert you in a letter would only add to the pressure. That to surprise you like this would be the best kind of support.'

Owen sipped more whisky. 'So I took her advice – and here I am.'

Natalie was still holding his hand, so she raised it to her lips and kissed his fingers. 'It's lovely, lovely. Thank you for coming.'

He disengaged his hands from Natalie's, twisted in his seat and picked up a package he had with him. 'When I talked with Eleanor Deacon, she happened to say that one of her sons has a gramophone in that gorge, so I've bought you these.' He handed her three slim brown-paper packages and kissed her cheek. 'Haydn's Trumpet Concerto, *In fermen Land*, from Wagner's *Lohengrin*, and Glinka's *Overture to Ruslan and Ludmilla*.'

Natalie took them. 'Dad, that's wonderful. Thank you.' She told him about Jack's wind-up gramophone, how they sometimes played music after dinner, with the roars of the lions and the chatter of the baboons as a backdrop.

'I'd like to hear that,' he said. 'See if I can recruit any baritones.'

Natalie laughed out loud, leaned forward and kissed him. How her fortunes had changed during the day.

They had left the gorge early that morning – Jack doing the flying, with Eleanor, Daniel, Christopher and Natalie and quite a few bags filling the plane. It had been a bumpy ride, there were plenty of short-rain storm clouds about but they had flown at only two thousand feet, so there had been some good views of the wildlife.

Christopher had been a bit distant with her in the plane, although they had sat side-by-side, behind Jack and Eleanor.

'You seem to have recovered better than I did,' he had said.

Natalie had made a face. 'I was up and about yesterday – only a day before you.'

'Maybe I would have made a quicker recovery if Jack had brought me dinner every night.'

She had ignored that. 'I still haven't got back

my appetite properly, have you?'

'Appetite for what?'

What did he mean by that? Did he mean anything? What did he know? Something was rankling with him, that much was certain.

'We can have some fish in Nairobi,' she had said, determined not to be drawn. 'Maybe that will help full recovery.'

In fact, she was less fully recovered than she let on. Besides feeling a bit sick in the plane, her hands still tingled where the rash had been – though she hadn't told Jonas because she didn't want anything to interfere with the trial.

Jack had again parked the Comanche in his favourite part of the airport, among the private jets. Natalie noticed that there were one or two more than before. The prospect of independence, she presumed, was attracting all sorts of businessmen to Kenya. Jack, she and the others were staying in the Rhodes, save for Eleanor who was lodging with Maxwell Sandys.

Her father was sipping his whisky again but looking at her more closely. 'You look pale, Tally, and a bit thin. Does that gorge really agree with you or are you as worried about the trial as Eleanor Deacon said?'

She looked around the bar. All the customers were white, the barman black. Race in Kenya, like race everywhere, was a complicated business. The newspapers in the hotel shop were full of racial news of one kind or another. South Africa was going its own brutal way, outside the Commonwealth, and in the deep south of the United States the desegregation of the universities was provoking riots and sit-ins. Adolf Eichmann was appealing against his death sentence after his trial in Israel for the murder of so many Jews.

'I *am* worried about the trial, yes, and it's wonderful of you to have come, the best news I could possibly have – Eleanor is right there. But the reason I am pale and a bit thin is that I'm just getting over a bout of tick typhus.'

'Typhus? What?'

'Don't worry!' And she told him about the lion they had killed and what had happened afterwards.

'So you see, Dad, I'm over the worst and should be as good as new very soon.'

Natalie finished her drink. 'How long do you plan to stay?'

Owen shrugged. 'My ticket is for ten days, and I can't change it. I'd like to see the gorge, if I'm allowed and welcome. Otherwise, I'll go to the coast.'

'Of course you can come to the gorge.' She held up her empty glass. 'Shall we have dinner? Eleanor played a trick on me. She said she'd arranged for me to have dinner with the prosecuting lawyer, when in fact she planned this surprise. I should have guessed something was up when Maxwell Sandys – the lawyer – looked nonplussed for a moment when I saw him this afternoon and mentioned dinner tonight. But I would never have guessed you would be here. Let's not lose a moment, and go and eat. You must be famished.'

He nodded. 'Yes, but look, I'm here to offer moral support. We'll have dinner now but after that I'll take a back seat until the trial is over.

You'll be busy and you'll be on edge. I'm here if you need me but I realise I may not see much of you until the proceedings have been and gone. How long is the trial expected to last, by the way?'

Natalie sipped her drink. The short rains had clinched it, the night before. Rain, for her, had always been associated with her father and she couldn't let him down, she decided. He would expect her to give evidence and she had let her parents down in so many ways already. In the rain at Kihara, naked, she had thought back to that day, years ago, when she and her father had swam, virtually naked on the beach at Chapel St. Leonards, when everyone else was hurrying off the sands because of the weather. A feeling of overwhelming fondness for her father had swept along Natalie's warm, wet skin and she had known what she must do.

How just it was that, at that very moment, he had been in the plane on his way to Nairobi to support her. Something was coming good in her world at last.

'Not long, not long at all. The trial will last two days, three at the most. And I don't really know how busy I shall be. There's a rally going on tonight, a rally when the local blacks will probably attack me as a white witness giving evidence against a black defendant.'

Her father shook his head. 'Your mother and I brought you up to be anything but racist, as the Church says. People here can surely see that you are not a racist?'

'Kenya will be independent soon. Race is a very

powerful political tool.'

Owen nodded. 'Yes, I realise that. I know it somewhere inside me, of course. But that it should sweep up my daughter in its crudities – that's hard. Is it getting to you? It must be.'

Natalie nodded. 'Yes it is. Of course it is.' She squeezed his hand. 'But I try not to show it and it's not all bad news, remember that. The discoveries we have made are very important – they will change the way mankind thinks of itself, and *Nature* is giving us a special edition.' She drank some whisky. 'There's also something else you don't know: Jack Deacon has asked me to marry him.'

Sipping what remained of his drink, Owen Nelson held the glass away from his lips.

'I haven't given him an answer yet – and I won't, not until the trial business is all cleared up. But, if I were to say yes, it would mean me living in Africa full-time. Not necessarily in Kihara Gorge – there are problems there that I'll tell you about over dinner – but probably somewhere very like it. How would you feel about that?'

Owen set his glass down gently. 'Part of me would feel widowed all over again, but you know me, Tally, I want what's best for you, what's best for your happiness, for your career.' He wiped his lips with his handkerchief. 'But tell me, why haven't you given Jack Deacon an answer yet? It's unlike you not to know your own mind immediately–'

'Ah! Look who's here.' Natalie moved away from her father as Eleanor and Jack appeared in the bar. She stood up. 'Is your mysterious family meeting all over?'

Eleanor smiled. 'Sorry, that was all a bit hammy, wasn't it? But the surprise worked, I hope?' She held out her hand to Owen Nelson and he took it enthusiastically.

'Oh yes, I think so.' Natalie put her arm in her father's and squeezed. She kissed his shoulder.

'It's very good of you to come to support your daughter, Mr Nelson,' said Eleanor. 'She's a very talented individual, and we've all grown very fond of her.'

'I'm pleased to hear it,' replied Owen. 'She's all I've got.'

Eleanor nodded and leaned towards him. 'Now Maxwell Sandys, the deputy attorney general, who is a friend of mine, has arranged for me to watch the trial from a special bench. Would you like to join me – Jack, Christopher and me, actually?'

'Well, yes, if that's convenient. Thank you. I was just telling Tally here that I don't want to be in the way at all. I'm here to be used by her as she wishes, and once the ordeal is over we can spend some time together.'

'Splendid. The trial tomorrow starts at 10.30. Why don't we all meet in the lobby here in the hotel at, say, 9.45 and walk over together? Is that convenient for you, Mr Nelson?'

'Fine by me. Yes.'

'Hey, are those records?' said Jack, speaking for the first time and pointing at the paper packages Owen had given his daughter. 'Yes,' said Natalie. 'Look.'

'*Ruslan and Ludmilla*,' said Jack, reading from

596

the labels. *'In fermen Land.* Isn't that from *Lohengrin?* Isn't that the one that includes the wedding march?'

'Yes, yes it does,' said Owen, looking bewildered. 'Why?'

'Oh, no reason,' said Jack, resolutely refusing to meet Natalie's eye. 'Enjoy your dinner.'

Natalie stared up at the ceiling of her room. Jack had just left and, for once, love-making had not settled either her mind or her body. Tomorrow she was giving evidence and, as today had worn on, a day of killing time for her as the court case opened, the tension inside her had mounted. She hadn't expected that: she had thought she was as well prepared as she could be, her waverings were over, her story was a simple one to tell and though there might be trouble outside the courthouse, inside the building itself all would surely be calm and orderly. Her father was here and, at dinner the evening before, all the difficulties that had passed between them had been aired and it had felt as though the two of them were starting anew. That gave her an enormous injection of inner strength. Her anger had all but disappeared.

But as the hours had dragged on today, as the heat of the sun had built up, she had grown more and more on edge. It hadn't helped that the doctor Jack had recommended, the expert in tropical diseases, was away on the coast and therefore unavailable for a consultation. So she was still a little anxious from the idea that had formed in her mind the day before, in the meeting with Maxwell Sandys, that Jonas, well meaning though he was, had got his diagnosis wrong so far as she was concerned and she was in fact more ill than he – Jonas – thought. Her skin was still blotchy, she still got a tingling in her hands where the rash had been and her headaches, instead of subsiding, were actually more frequent now than before.

It had been a difficult day in the sense that it had been a profoundly *dull* day. She knew it made sense to stay in her room at the hotel, out of sight, but she hadn't been able to read because she couldn't concentrate or relax. Jack had left her his gramophone but she hadn't been in the mood for music. Natalie had strung out breakfast and then lunch for as long as she could but the food had arrived much quicker than it might have done: the restaurant wasn't busy and it was plain that the staff wanted to tidy up and clear her plates away as soon as she had finished. She tried reading a four-day-old British newspaper that her father had brought with him but that didn't work either. And she couldn't sleep: she was slept out.

Was she going to marry Jack? She couldn't get her mind around that either, not yet. But he was involved politically, and she had found she liked that. It set him apart; apart from Dominic, even above him. She was thinking more and more about politics. Even back home, in nearby Rossington, race was an issue. Jack enlarged her mind.

At last, at long, long last, around five, he had arrived with Maxwell Sandys.

'No surprises so far,' Sandys had said, when they had been given water and were seated in chairs. 'All went more or less as I explained to you yesterday. We got through all three pieces of physical evidence today, so you are on first thing in the morning. How are you feeling? Jack said you are worried about your health.'

'Right now I'm feeling bored and looking forward to this all being over, so far as my testimony is concerned. Don't worry about my health, but thanks for asking. I'll be fine tomorrow. How is the judge?'

'Yes, I was coming to that. He seems to have turned over a new leaf – not completely new of course, he's still the same old John Tudor, but he was remarkably polite to Ndekei when he pled not guilty. When that happened, a lot of people in the public gallery cheered and Tudor immediately got going with his gavel, shouting that he would clear the court if such a thing happened again, that this was a set of proceedings that would be run fairly but firmly, according to the strictest principles of the law. We think he was warning Ndekei not to base his defence on Maasai law, that that wouldn't wash. But Tudor has been remarkably even-handed so far. He knows he's the centre of attention, and maybe all the hostile newspaper editorials have been getting to him.'

Sandys fiddled with his tie. 'Now, if today is anything to go by, there will be about three or four hundred people outside the court. Pushing through them will be quite an ordeal, my dear. There *is* a back way into the court but–'

'No, no, I'll go in the front door. I don't like what's happening as you know, but I'm not ashamed of what I'm about to do, not at all. Going in the back door would be cowardly.'

Sandys nodded. 'I thought that's what you'd say. I *hoped* it's what you'd say. If only more witnesses were like you.' He shifted in his seat. 'It's not all bad news, by the way. The newspapers have been pretty silent in the past few days, what with the *Gazette* being closed. With proceedings so near, they know they have to be careful: that they too could fall into contempt. But Edward Ongoche was in court. He is editor of the *East African Reporter* and he was telling me that they have commissioned a poll among its readers, to be run as soon as the trial is over. They asked people if tribal law should take precedence over English law and their findings are interesting. They found that their readers, who are mostly black, are divided equally. Just under fifty per cent say tribal law should take precedence and more or less the same figure say English law is better. The rest, a very few, don't know.

'Ongoche says it's a typical result in his view. Half the country realises that tribal loyalties lead to tribal grievances and rivalries and those grievances will hold the country back. When they publish their poll they are going to run an editorial attacking Marongo for exploiting Ndekei's misfortune for his own ends.' Sandys smiled at Natalie. 'It's rather late in the day for your appearance in court, my dear, but it's helpful to know that you are not quite as isolated as you may think.'

He fiddled with his tie again, which seemed too tight for his neck. 'Sutton is here by the way, and was in court, making notes furiously. He's retained a barrister to look after his interests. The man has no standing in court but I suppose it makes him feel part of the proceedings.'

Sandys had left after arranging to collect Natalie from the hotel next morning.

Jack and she had eaten dinner in her room that evening. They thought it would be bad tactics to be seen enjoying themselves in the dining room. Owen Nelson, it seemed, had got on very well with Eleanor Deacon during their time together watching the trial and the two of them were having dinner with Maxwell Sandys. Natalie was pleased for her father.

After dinner, Jack and she had lain together on her bed, and he had said, 'Would you like some music? Maybe *In fermen Land?*'

'You're not being very subtle, Dr. Deacon. I told you I wouldn't decide until after the trial.'

'Not long now.'

'No, so don't push. Also, I need to know how ill I am. If we were Americans, your marital lawyers would be asking my lawyers what the low-down on my symptoms is. Doesn't that bother you?'

'No. I don't think you're ill. You look fine to me. More than fine.'

'Hmmn. I may *look* fine, Jack, but I don't feel it. In any case, what's the hurry? Don't you like the way things are? Don't you like being where you are right now?'

Jack kissed her ear. 'I wouldn't be anywhere else in the world. I have everything I want – you, the gorge, my planes – all right here in Kenya.' He kissed her ear again.

'What about children? They are important to you.'

'Yes,' he said softly, adding a moment later, 'I'd like your babies, Natalie, if you'd like mine.'

After they had made love a second time, he had left her so that – in theory, at least – she could get some sleep before her ordeal. But sleep wouldn't come; her mind was racing, running over the questions she assumed she would be asked, how she would phrase her replies, how she could avoid being embarrassed if Hilary Hall asked about her relationships in the camp. What would *that* do to her anger? she wondered.

Although it had been her idea tonight to send Jack away immediately after their love-making, she now wished she hadn't. Normally, they lay talking and relaxing, 'coming down' from wherever they had been, as he put it. That, as much as the lovemaking itself, was important to her peace of mind.

Maybe she should ask him back. They could curl up together, like spoons in a tray, and then she would be able to sleep.

There was a tap on the door.

She was off her bed in no time, a smile on her face. Jack had had the same idea. He was sensitive like that. But when she opened the door, it wasn't Jack who stood there. It was Christopher.

'Oh,' she said. 'Oh.' All she had on was her cotton nightdress.

'I've just had a late drink with Jack,' said Christopher. 'He says he's asked you to marry him.'

Natalie caught her breath. 'Yes. Yes, he has.'

'But you didn't say yes straight away. That's

what he told me.'

She nodded. She felt naked in front of Christopher. She knew her nipples showed in outline through her nightdress.

'And if I asked you the same question, would I get the same answer?'

She stared at him. He was breathing heavily.

'I know I haven't been as forward as Jack, or Russell for that matter. I told you when we were in that cave at Ndutu how it had taken me ages to pluck up courage to suggest the excursion. But, I almost... Just because I find it difficult to show my feelings doesn't mean ... it doesn't mean I don't adore you, because I do.'

The noise from the bar below carried up to them – laughter, glasses clinking, money rattling into the till.

Natalie put her hand and arm over her chest to cover her breasts. 'I haven't given Jack an answer because, until the trial is over, I can't think straight. I'm on edge the whole time and I've got more on edge as the days have passed.' She shook her head. 'Jack's offer came out of the blue and I'm still... Even after the trial is over, I don't know when I can give him an answer.'

'Where does that leave my offer?'

'Christopher! I'm not a prize in a competition. I haven't replied to Jack's offer because I'm not even sure I want to get married right now anyway, to *anyone!* I'm touched in a way that his offer has prompted you to do what you have done, say what you have said. But...' She chewed in air, the way she had done when she had been swimming off the reef in Lamu and her knee had collided with the sea urchin. 'But although I'm not sure of my feelings for Jack, I do know that it could never work between you and me, Christopher. I loved our night in the cave and some of the game drives we have been on, the visit to the sand dunes. But that's as far as it goes, for me.' She paused, taking more deep breaths. 'I'm sorry.'

He grunted. 'If it hadn't rained when I was in Nairobi, before Christmas, if the road hadn't been cut, you would never have gone to Lamu with Jack – that's what did it, didn't it? The days you had together then. And the nights.'

'It had something to do with it, yes. But I'm sorry, Christopher, it's more complicated than that – you know it is.'

'Jack's always been luckier than me.'

Natalie shook her head. 'Luck doesn't come into it. He stood up for me, the press conference was his idea, he understood that Marongo is a political animal, he made your mother see that I wouldn't – couldn't – change my story. That set him apart from everyone else. At least, in my eyes.'

'Our mother listens to him more than she listens to the rest of us. That was always true, when we were children.'

'Really? When you both asked me away for Christmas, she refused to take sides.'

'No, no, that's not how it was! Being the oldest, the biggest, he got lots of treats before the rest of us. I was very jealous of Jack at one stage, but I got over it.'

'Tell me–' Natalie broke off and stepped back

604

as some other people went by. She didn't want to ask Christopher into her room but she didn't want the whole world to see her in her nightdress either. 'Tell me,' she repeated when they had gone. 'Jack told me a story about a fishing trip on Lake Naivasha, when you were in your teens and when he thought you had put dirt in the carburettor of the boat, out of jealousy, and that there was nearly a very nasty accident. Is that true?'

Christopher frowned. 'Did he tell you that? Jesus! I had forgotten it.' He shook his head vigorously. *Of course* it's not true. Everyone knew about Hippo Point and how dangerous hippos can be. I can't believe he told you that!'

But, Natalie noticed, Christopher was blushing. And he had begun to sweat: his forehead was shining, even in the dim light.

He shook his head again and took a step back. 'I can't believe he told you that!'

Christopher moved back towards her. 'He's poisoned you against me, hasn't he?'

'Now you're being silly. Because I don't want to marry you doesn't mean I don't like you. I do. But–'

'No! No! I know where I'm not wanted. I'm sorry I disturbed you. Good luck tomorrow.'

He turned and was gone.

An usher showed Natalie into the witness box. There were two steps up. She looked around her. The court was larger than she had expected. Most of it was polished wood – the bench where the judge sat, the benches where the lawyers sat, the witness box where she was standing. But there were two white pillars, supporting the public gallery above.

The noise from the gallery had risen as she appeared but there was no shouting.

To her right, as she faced the court, was the judge who she now came up against for the first time. John Tudor was a small, dark-haired man with a rather blueish shadow on his jaw. He wore a grey robe, with a red sash diagonally across it, and a short curly wig, almost white. He looked at her over his half-moon horn-rimmed spectacles.

Opposite the judge was Mutevu Ndekei. He was seated in the dock, also made of polished wood with a high brass rail, and he was wearing a grey, open-necked shirt with short sleeves. He looked every bit as muscular as she remembered, with big thick arms, and he towered over the guards either side of him. He looked at Natalie without expression.

From Daniel, she had learned that on the evening before the trial had started the concert in aid of Ndekei had passed off without incident. Atape and her children had been paraded on stage, Marongo had made a fiery speech but had announced no 'deal' with anyone. He was wily enough to keep Russell and Richard Sutton Senior waiting until the trial was ended. A collection had been taken at the concert for Ndekei's family and pictures of him, Atape, Tife and Natalie were all over the front pages of this morning's Nairobi newspapers.

The various lawyers – Hilary Hall, Maxwell Sandys, their respective juniors – were arrayed along the polished benches immediately in front

606

of the judge, boxes and papers on their desk-lids. Immediately behind them sat a good-looking man with a face Natalie knew but couldn't put a name to. When she looked at him he smiled back.

Over on the far wall were two benches filled with the press. They were not smiling. It was the only mixed-race part of the court, for what struck Natalie most was the fact that up in the public gallery – where she could just make out Atape, in a yellow-and-red wraparound dress – the faces were all black. In the well of the court, behind the lawyers, sat Eleanor, Jack, Christopher, Daniel and her father. Another group was made up of Richard Sutton Senior, Russell North and a barrister in a gown and wig who must be Sutton's counsel. All those faces, save for Daniel's, were white.

The usher was standing before her. 'Do you wish to take the oath or to affirm?'

'I will affirm,' said Natalie and he turned the card over so she could read from it. She knew her father would be disappointed that she had affirmed rather than taken the oath but it couldn't be helped.

She had another headache this morning, though it had only started after she and Max had fought their way through the crowds outside the court-house. What an ordeal that had been: people shouting, throwing tomatoes. She had, she thought, caught sight of the ebony walking cane carried by the man who had nearly assaulted her when she had gone walking late at night near the hotel, the evening after her first dinner with Jack.

Her hands were tingling but not badly. The

most worrying thing was her skin, which had not regained its old tone since the tick typhus. No one else knew as much as she did about her symptoms, because only she saw herself naked and in full daylight.

Jack saw her naked but not in full daylight.

She thought of the night before and blushed inwardly. What they had done with each other's naked bodies, what he had done to her with his hands, his lips, his tongue. In the hotel they had been able to make more noise than in the camp, in the tent. How erotic noise was, how liberating. How could she think about sex at a time like this? She knew by now that she could think about sex under almost any circumstances.

Maxwell Sandys rose. 'For the record, Dr. Nelson, could you please state your full name and age.'

She did so.

He then carefully took her through her story. As he had said, he asked his questions in such a way that she recounted what she had seen several times, on each occasion using different wording.

As Sandys put the questions, Natalie's eyes roamed the courtroom. It was the cleanest, coolest, most freshly painted room she had been in since she arrived in Kenya, save for the Rhodes Hotel. She had been in one or two courtrooms in Britain, once when she had acted as a character witness for an employee of her college who had been caught shoplifting, and once as a witness to a car accident. This courtroom had exactly the same feel as its British counterparts, the atmosphere being one of quiet but cold efficiency.

She understood that, and she approved of the idea that justice should be efficient. But cold? It crossed her mind then, as it had crossed her mind before, that barristers and judges – all the people who frequented the courts every day – found that the cold routine helped them in their work, but that it made them insensitive to the needs of other people who, whether as a witness, a victim, a culprit or a relative, used the courts much less often and for whom the outcome was much more important.

In the case where she had acted as a character witness, there had been little doubt that the college employee was guilty of the charges put to him. And indeed, he was convicted. But despite her appearance, and the appearance of other character witnesses, he had been given a heavy sentence – what Natalie thought was a heavy sentence anyway. The cold efficiency of the courts had chilled her that day, as she watched when the college employee had been led away to begin his sentence.

While she replied to Sandys's questions, Judge Tudor made copious notes and asked one question of his own. 'What lighting is there in the camp?'

He had a small voice to match his small stature.

Natalie had replied that there were usually a lot of hurricane lamps – two to a tent, five or six in the refectory tent, plus the light from the campfire – but that at the time she had seen Ndekei the only light was moonlight, starlight and the embers of the fire. The judge nodded and resumed his note-taking, yawning as his pen scratched across the page.

Natalie's evidence took about an hour. Then Maxwell Sandys sat down and Hilary Hall stood up.

'Dr. Nelson, I have a few questions so would you like a glass of water before proceeding?'

'Yes, please.'

Water was brought. It was a small relief to drink water that didn't smell of purification pills.

Then, 'How far is it, would you say, how far is it from where you were sitting that night to where the man you say was Mutevu Ndekei was crossing the camp?'

Hall was no less English than the judge, no less British than the courtroom itself, come to that. His voice was very mellifluous. He was tall, stringy and had a long neck. She noticed that he wore an expensive watch. His pock-marked skin was slightly incongruous. She remembered thinking that, the first time she had met him, at the deposition.

'I can't be certain exactly. Perhaps a hundred yards.'

'Would it surprise you to be told that it is exactly one hundred and forty yards?'

'I'm not very good at distances. If the distance has been measured, I accept it. And it was dark.'

'Yes, it was, wasn't it?' He paused. 'We'll come back to that.'

He brought out a large white piece of card. 'I have here a map of the camp: I mean the way the tents are laid out. Would you look at it please and tell me if you agree it is an accurate map.'

The card was handed to her.

Natalie inspected it and said, 'I can't be sure the proportions are right but, yes, the overall shape is correct.'

Hall addressed the usher. 'Please show the map to his honour and then to Sir Maxwell.'

They all waited while these manoeuvres were completed.

Natalie used the time to look to where her father was sitting. He seemed comfortable enough and, now and then, he bent his head in a huddle with Eleanor and Christopher. Her gaze fell on Richard Sutton Senior. Earlier, outside the courtroom, he had made a point of approaching her.

'So,' he said. 'You kept your promise. I'm grateful.'

Natalie nodded. 'There's nothing for you to be grateful for. I promised myself that I would give evidence, not you. It's the way I was brought up, the way I am made. There was never any need for your bullying or your famous friends in the construction business. There was never any need to have me followed. I shall give evidence today and I hope never to see you again.'

Russell had been listening to this exchange. He moved forward, towards Natalie, but she had walked on, down the corridor, turning her back on him.

Her exchange with Christopher the evening before had upset her. Not so much because she had had to face him with some harsh realities but rather because only then had she realised what jealousy had done to Christopher. She wasn't an especially jealous person herself, though she had known jealousy only too well when she had been with Dominic. But to be jealous of your brother, as Christopher was of Jack, and to have to live with it, over many years – to have your parents reinforce their preferences every so often – must have been a living hell, an ordeal she had never known. Even if your parents favoured your siblings unconsciously, well, wasn't that worse? Unconscious behaviour was in many ways more honest than conscious behaviour. Christopher must have suffered in silence for so long.

Sandys and the judge had finished looking at Hilary Hall's chart.

Hall stood up and addressed Natalie again. 'Would you agree that the camp was – is – shaped, broadly, like a large "T", in which the refectory area occupies the top left-hand branch of the "T", your tent is at the foot of the central branch, and Richard Sutton's tent was halfway along the top right-hand branch?'

'Yes, broadly speaking that's correct.'

'And the acacia fence hugs the right-hand side of the whole camp?'

'Yes.'

'Meaning that, from your tent, you could not see Richard Sutton's tent directly.'

'No, I couldn't. That's correct.'

These questions were straightforward. She answered in full voice and with confidence.

Hilary Hall had put the chart to one side and reassembled his papers in front of him. He put on his spectacles, read the paper before him, took off his spectacles and looked up at Natalie.

'And when you saw the man who you say was Mutevu Ndekei that night, he was walking from the refectory area to the top right arm of the "T"?'

'Correct.'

'How many tents are there on the right arm of the "T"?'

'Four I think.'

'There are five, I have had them counted.' Hall paused. 'Who were the other tents occupied by?'

'I think Jack Deacon, Arnold Pryce and Kees van Schelde. One was a guest tent, empty that night.'

Hall nodded. He paused. 'Five tents, three occupied: Jack Deacon was at the time in Nairobi. How do you know, then, that the figure you say was Ndekei was headed for Richard Sutton's tent?'

'I didn't, not at first. We inferred it later, in view of what happened.'

Another pause. 'You inferred it later. I see.' He laid down some papers, picked them up again. 'It was dark that night, you say; there were no hurricane lamps alight; the figure you saw was one hundred and forty yards away. At that distance, in that light – or, rather, darkness – could you see Mutevu Ndekei's features clearly?'

'There wasn't much light, no. The stars were bright, and the campfire was still alight, just. So I couldn't see Mutevu's features at all. I knew it was him because of his build, what he was wearing and how he moved.'

'She likes black flesh, that one,' someone shouted from the public gallery. 'Sexy lady!'

Tudor reached for his gavel and banged it. 'Usher!' he growled. 'Did you see who made that

613

remark? Who was it?'

The usher in the public gallery was pushing past some people and grabbed a young man, forcing him to stand up.

'This is the man, your honour,' he said.

'Eject him,' growled Tudor. 'And make sure he doesn't come back for the duration of the trial.'

He motioned Hilary Hall to sit down.

Tudor put down his pen and the gavel, and rubbed his hand over his chin. He lifted his head up. 'You people in the public gallery. This is your last warning. If there are any more interruptions, the individual making the interruption will be charged with contempt of court – an offence which carries a prison sentence, I may say – and the gallery will be cleared and closed for the entire trial.' He paused but held his gaze on the gallery. 'Do you understand? I am not bluffing! Now,' he breathed, 'all of you: *be quiet!*'

Tudor nodded to Hall and Hall stood up. He gathered his gown around him.

'Dr. Nelson, we were talking about the lack of light in the camp.' Natalie nodded. 'We'll come to Mutevu's clothes and movement in a moment, but let me go back over what you just said. You said you couldn't see Mutevu's features *at all* – is that so?'

'Yes.'

'So, you did not identify Mutevu from what you knew of his eyes, his nose, the shape of his mouth?'

'No, I–' Natalie was beginning to sweat. Above her, two large carved fans turned noiselessly.

'If you couldn't identify his features, how did

you know it was Ndekei?'

'As I told you–'

'From his clothes and his movement, is that right?'

'Yes.'

'So again, you *inferred* it was Mutevu?'

'Yes, but–'

'Let's examine his clothes and his movement. First his clothes – what was it about them that made you think it was him?'

'His white T-shirt. Mutevu's a big man, a strapping man, with a fine physique.' She paused, half-expecting another interruption from the public gallery but this time no one said anything. She went on, 'Mutevu always wore a white T-shirt, tight over his chest. That's what he had on that night.'

Hall was nodding but his features were quizzical. He frowned. 'But you have already told us that you couldn't make out his features. Strictly speaking, therefore, all you can say is that you saw *a figure* wearing a white T-shirt.'

'Yes, but one stretched tight over his chest.'

'And his movement? What was special about that?'

'He was shuffling. Mutevu has – or had – these wellington boots that he is very proud of but they are slightly too big for him and he shuffles in them. The figure I saw that night was shuffling just like Mutevu.'

'But, again, you *inferred* it was Mutevu, from the way he moved, because he shuffled. It was an *inference*.'

'If you insist, yes.'

Hall put down his papers, put away his spectacles, took out some others, picked up his papers. Pure theatre. Natalie knew that. She remembered what Sandys had said, that Hall thought Ndekei was guilty, like Sandys himself did.

'Is it not true, Dr. Nelson, is it not true that Ndekei's wellingtons went missing some time before?'

She stared at him. 'What do you mean?'

'Let me refresh your memory. Did you not yourself *find* one of Ndekei's wellingtons after it had gone missing?'

'Yes, but only one went missing – it was stolen by monkeys and I found it outside the camp a day or two later.'

'Quite so. Thank you.'

'I don't see what–'

'Thank you, Dr. Nelson. Let's leave it there, please! For now.'

Natalie took a deep breath and said nothing.

Hall paused, tapping his lips with his folded spectacles. He opened a notebook, found a particular page, read a few lines, closed the book and looked up again. Natalie was getting used to his technique now.

'Did you see this figure, this shuffling figure in a white T-shirt, carrying a weapon?'

'No.'

'This figure wasn't carrying a machete, the machete that killed Professor Sutton?'

'I didn't see one, no.'

'And when you observed this set of events, did you raise the alarm?'

'No, I – I went to bed.'

'You went to bed?'

'Yes.'

'It never occurred to you that you had just seen someone on his way to commit a crime?'

'No, I thought he was maybe visiting a woman. The very last tent in that part of the camp is a guest tent and, as I said, it was empty that night. It might have been being used for a ... well, for a meeting, a rendezvous, an affair.'

'I see.' Hall nodded. Another rigmarole with his spectacles. This time he polished them with his gown. He adjusted his wig, took out his handkerchief and wiped his lips. He put away the handkerchief.

'And how about you, Dr. Nelson, were you having an affair in the camp, with Professor Russell North maybe?'

'No, no I wasn't.' She was sweating slightly again. Her father was in court. 'That's ridiculous.'

'Is it? Is it?'

There was a commotion in the public gallery but the voices were muted. Tudor raised his gavel but the noises subsided before he could bring it down.

Hall lowered his voice, so that his tone was almost confiding. 'Is it not true that you used to sit with Professor North, late at night, drinking whisky, smoking cigarettes and talking?'

'Yes.'

'What did you talk about?'

'Our work in the gorge mainly: the excavations, what they meant.'

'Professional talk, mainly, but not only. Did you ever talk about personal matters?'

'Yes, of course, some of the time but not–'

'What sort of personal matters?'

'Our careers, our futures, our likes and dislikes. I talked about Cambridge, he talked about Australia – he is Australian.'

Where was this going?

Hall put his hand over his mouth, looked at her hard for a moment, and then took his hand away again. 'Dr. Nelson, did you ever have physical contact with Professor North?'

'Well, hardly at all really, it certainly wasn't an affair.'

He let a silence go by. 'I repeat the question: did you ever have physical contact with Professor Russell North, yes or no?'

Now it was getting tough. She forced herself to remember that Hall thought Ndekei was guilty.

She looked across to Russell. He looked back but she couldn't read his expression.

'Yes, he kissed the top of my head once, and the fingers of my hand once. But that's–'

'Thank you. That wasn't so hard, was it?' Hall gripped his gown with the fingers of his right hand. 'Had you been drinking that night?'

'One nip of whisky between the two of us.'

'You're sure it was no more than that?'

'Quite sure.'

He nodded again, took off his spectacles, wiped them again. He was, she realised, deliberately drawing this out, slowing down the whole proceedings to make what had gone on between Russell and her sound more than it was.

He placed his spectacles against his lips for a moment. 'But wasn't your whisky confiscated at one point? Was that because you were drinking too much?'

She daren't look at her father.

'Not at all, not at all. That's a horrible thing to suggest. Dr. Deacon – the director of the dig – doesn't allow alcohol on her excavations, but I–'

'Disobeyed her instructions by the sound of it.'

Sandys was on his feet. 'My Lord, Mr Hall is badgering–'

'Yes, I agree,' growled Tudor. 'Mr Hall, watch your tone, Dr Nelson is not on trial here.'

Hall half-bowed to the judge. 'I am obliged, your honour.' He paused and transferred his gaze back to Natalie.

She was sweating and upset. She knew what Hall was trying to do – sow doubts about her, her motivation, her *inferences*, the reason for those inferences. She knew he was just doing his job but she hated him. And in front of her father too. And Jack.

And now he had made her sound disobedient and therefore dishonest.

But Hall wasn't finished. 'Dr. Nelson, I want you to answer this next question very carefully. Take your time and think about your answer before giving it. Remember your affirmation at the beginning of your testimony, the equal of an oath.' He paused.

The people in the front row of the public gallery were leaning forward, their heads and their elbows showing against the shiny polish of the dark wood.

Hall rocked from one foot to the other. He put his spectacles back and looked over the lenses at

Natalie. 'Apart from Russell North, is there anyone else you have had physical contact with in the Kihara camp?'

She didn't reply but she coloured. And, as before, in Eleanor Deacon's tent, the night she had slept there, she knew she had coloured. This time, however, there was full daylight in the court, there was surely enough light for others – for her father, for Jack, for Christopher, for Eleanor Deacon herself, for the whole court – to *see* her reaction.

The skin on her throat was damp. She felt a bead of sweat trickle down between her breasts. Would anyone else notice?

She couldn't look at her father, she couldn't look at Jack, she couldn't look at the judge. But she remembered how she'd coped with Richard Sutton Junior, all those months ago, when he'd accused her of being inexperienced and how she'd faced down his father when he had expressed a wish to see the Maasai burial ground.

She looked hard at Hilary Hall, she looked hard, without blinking. *Sans clignant*, as her mother would have said, without blinking.

'I will put the question more bluntly, Dr. Nelson,' Hall was now saying, 'so there can be no misunderstanding.' He lifted his chin, taunting her. 'Apart from Russell North, is there anyone else in the Kihara camp you have had sex with?'

She gasped but tried hard to swallow it. Hall's questioning made it sound as though she had had sex with Russell North, and even made it sound as though she had had sex with more than one man in the camp. How could Hilary Hall

620

suggest such a thing? He had seen her in the deposition room; he knew she was not like that.

Sandys was looking at her and rubbing his cheek with his spectacles. Reminding her that it was all a game to defence counsel. He was telling her to relax.

She couldn't relax. Her father was here. He had come to support her, to put things right after all the unpleasantness and misunderstandings. He mustn't think that while she'd been in Africa she'd changed, grown promiscuous, loose, that her lack of faith had so transformed her that she had become a diminished woman.

Another bead of sweat ran down her neck and between her breasts. She fought the urge to wipe it away.

Then, carefully not looking at Jack, she took a deep breath.

'No,' she lied.

Another long silence, in which only the scratching of the judge's pen could be heard.

'I see,' said Hall eventually, letting an equally long silence follow to emphasise his doubt, a doubt he wanted the court to share. 'I see.'

Then his spectacles went on again. 'One more question, Dr. Nelson.' He stood up straighter. 'I put it to you that you were drinking with Professor North on the night in question. I put it to you that you saw nothing and that this story you have told was concocted the following day, after you had found what you had found: that Professor Sutton had been murdered. Your fairy tale was invented to cover up the fact that the most likely culprit in this murder was another scientist on the excavation, a rival who was jealous either of Richard Sutton's success in finding fossils and/or because you were having an affair – sex – with him. In your small, tightly knit, highly competitive community in Kihara, passions run high. And in this case passions overflowed, tragically.'

Natalie couldn't look at Hall as he said this. It was so ... so far from the truth, made her out to be so different from what she really was. Her glance raked around the rest of the court room – Tudor, Richard Sutton Senior, Eleanor, her father. As she looked at her father, her lovely father, now here with her, her mind suddenly cleared, as it had done that night in camp, when she had stood naked in the rain, being reminded of him on the beach in Lincolnshire and, in the darkness, in a flash, had seen her way forward, that she *must* give evidence.

And there was Eleanor, next to him, sitting upright, concentrating hard, almost glowing with attention. Her chignon looked as French as ever.

Natalie straightened her own stance. 'You are right about one thing, Mr Hall.'

That got his attention. That got everyone's attention. The judge stopped writing and looked over at her.

'Yes, there was – is – plenty of passion in Kihara, but not the kind you are wasting so much energy on. We are having a spectacular season there – we have excavated so many important discoveries that we debate what it all means endlessly. Normally, I live and work in Cambridge, at the university, one of the best universities in the world, a famous centre of science.' Now she met

622

Hall's eye directly. 'But I have never known intellectual passion like there is in Kihara, *mental* hard work, total involvement, complete engagement, utter dedication.' She smiled. 'If your questions are anything to go by, being a lawyer doesn't come *close* to being a palaeontologist.' She shook her head. 'So far as those passions are concerned, that determined involvement, you are profoundly mistaken or have been misled. Richard Sutton was an excellent scientist. So is Russell North. But so far as I am concerned, that's all. Sex doesn't come into it.'

'I see,' said Hall, pausing for a moment. He was thinking, tapping his spectacles on the brief in front of him. At length he raised his head. 'But at least you have admitted I was right about one thing, about the *temperature* of the passion in Kihara.' He nodded and remained standing for a few moments, so that the whole court could dwell on his last sentence.

Then he looked at the judge. 'Thank you, Your Honour, that's all,' he said softly, and sat down.

Tudor scribbled for a while, his writing once again the only sound in the room. Then he raised his head. 'Do you wish to re-examine, Sir Maxwell?'

'Just one question, your honour,' said Sandys, getting to his feet.

'Dr. Nelson, you said you didn't see Ndekei carrying a weapon. Could you see his hands, were they empty?'

'No, I mean, no, I couldn't see his hands. There was so little light that if he had been carrying a machete, for example, there was not enough light for the blade to catch it, nothing to make it shine.'

'Thank you,' said Sandys. 'You may stand down now.'

He waited while Natalie left the witness box. The usher led her to the bench where Jack and her father and the others were sitting. Jack mouthed 'Well done' and her father gave her the thumbs-up. But she looked away. She had felt half-naked in the witness box.

Sandys had turned and was watching as she sat down. Then he faced the judge again. 'That completes the case for the prosecution, your honour.'

Tudor looked at the clock. It was 12.20.

'Mr Hall?'

Hilary Hall rose and gathered up his gown in his hands. 'Your Honour, at this stage I would like to enter a plea that in this alleged crime there is no case to answer: all the evidence is circumstantial, and in view of that the charges against my client must be dismissed.'

Tudor took off his own glasses. 'Can you make your argument by lunchtime?'

'I think I can, yes.'

The judge nodded. 'Then proceed.'

Hall drank some water and put on his spectacles. He held some notes but didn't consult them. 'It's really very simple, Your Honour, and as an experienced trial judge you will be familiar, more than familiar, with the arguments I am going to employ.' He cleared his throat. 'All the evidence in this case is circumstantial, there is nothing that *directly* links my client to this crime. I will go through the elements of the prosecution's case one by one.'

He leaned on the desk-lid in front of him. 'Although the piece of Ndekei's apron that was found on the thorn hedge near the victim's tent was discovered the morning after the crime had been committed, that does not mean that it was left there during the preceding night. He worked in the camp after all, and had done for months: moving around, driving Land Rovers as well as cooking. It could have been left there well before the crime occurred and no one noticed – it is a small piece of cloth. The same argument applies to the footprint of the wellington boot found outside Professor Sutton's tent. There was no blood on it and it too could have been made at any point in the days before the crime. One might say that this is more likely than not because only one footprint was found, others having been destroyed in the days preceding. Whoever wore that boot was outside Professor Sutton's tent, yes, but not necessarily on the night in question. And the imprint, though undoubtedly of Ndekei's boot, has not been shown incontrovertibly to have been worn by him.

'The picture is further confused by the wellington boot that was found being played with by some monkeys. While it is unorthodox that no one would come to court to say where, exactly, this boot was found, we do accept the prosecution argument that the material fact is that it was Ndekei's boot with blood on it of the same group as Professor Sutton's. But this only confuses matters, because the boot found with blood on it was the *same* foot as the print found outside

Professor Sutton's tent *without* blood. Is that not more than a little odd?'

Hall shuffled more papers, drank more water.

The judge looked up at the clock.

'I come now to Dr. Nelson's evidence. As she herself said, more than once, she never saw Mutevu Ndekei's features that night. She *inferred* it was him because of what happened later, just as she *inferred* he was headed for Richard Sutton's tent because of what happened subsequently, and because of the clothes he was wearing and the way he moved – the characteristic way that he "shuffled", as she put it. At the time, she thought he was headed for an assignation with a woman, possibly in the empty tent at the end of the row. But of course that figure could have been anyone, it could have been someone looking *like* Ndekei or someone pretending to *be* Ndekei, knowing that it was Dr. Nelson's habit to sit up late, long after everyone else had gone to sleep, drinking whisky and smoking a cigarette.

'I would remind the court, Your Honour, that no murder weapon has been found and that Ndekei's boots may have been stolen days before the crucial incident and deliberately used to frame him, as the jargon goes, to cast suspicion wrongfully upon him. We know that they had been stolen – by monkeys – before and maybe that gave someone, some human, the idea to steal them again. I would remind your honour that though the blood found on the Wellington boot being played with by some monkeys was the same group as Professor Sutton's, that group – O – is shared by between forty and fifty per cent of the population. That narrows things down statistically but is hardly proves anything forensically.'

He turned towards Maxwell Sandys.

'Much has been made of the fact that Professor Sutton, together with Professor North, broke into a local Maasai burial ground, stole some ancestral bones and that Sutton was killed in an act of revenge. But here again such reasoning is pure speculation; it is all circumstantial. Not a single shred of hard evidence has been produced in this court to support such speculation. There are no witnesses to the crime, there is no confession the prosecution can produce, I repeat that no murder weapon has been found no Maasai spear, no machete, for example – which might offer some support for these wild allegations.'

He gathered up his gown again. 'As Your Honour well knows, my client – as defendant – does not have to produce rival theories about who committed this crime in order to demonstrate his innocence, but I cannot help but remark that the prosecution do not seem to have considered one very plausible alternative to their case against Mutevu Ndekei.'

He looked around the court.

'Which is that the excavation run by Dr. Eleanor Deacon was and is a close-knit group of highly ambitious, very clever people, where rivalries were and are intense, where competition is the order of the day and, it seems, where personal emotions got mixed up with professional responsibilities. That seems to me a perfect forcing ground for an explanation for this sort of murder.'

He looked about him. 'As the court has seen,

627

Dr. Nelson is a very attractive woman, very attractive indeed, and in the close confines of the excavation she was surrounded by several young men.'

He let a silence elapse before turning to the judge and saying, 'But that too, your honour, is speculation–'

'Yes, yes it is,' interjected the judge. 'And forgive me, Mr Hall, but I wish to be clear about this. Are you suggesting that someone else impersonated Mr Ndekei, or that Dr. Nelson made up her story to protect a lover who was jealous of Professor Sutton? I am confused.'

What must Richard Sutton Senior make of all this, Natalie wondered.

'I am obliged to Your Honour,' said Hall. 'But I respectfully remind the court that we in the defence are not required to make the prosecution's case for it. I merely point out some avenues of inquiry the prosecution appear to have overlooked or ignored.'

The judge nodded.

Hall continued. 'As you say, Your Honour, that is all speculation on my part and I will go no further. I simply repeat my central point: that there is no direct *physical* evidence to link my client to this crime, that everything presented in this court has been circumstantial and that, so far as motivation is concerned, no evidence at all has been presented, only conjecture.'

He paused. 'In those circumstances, I respectfully submit that any conviction based on such evidence would be unsafe, very unsafe indeed, and I refer you to *Regina v. Salter*, 1954, and *Regina v.*

McWhirter and others, 1957. It is my submission that, in the case of *Regina v. Mutevu Ndekei*, my client has no case to answer and that therefore the charges against him should be dismissed and dismissed immediately, now, this very day.'

Hall sat down.

For a moment once again, the only sound in court was the judge scribbling in his notebook with his pen. He finished, carefully screwed the top of his pen back on, put it in his inside pocket, and looked up. 'Thank you, Mr Hall.'

He looked around the court. 'Very well. I see it is now time for luncheon. I will consider your arguments over the indifferent cold meats that the court service usually provides, and will give you my decision this afternoon.'

'All rise!' barked the court usher and the judge stood up.

Everyone else did too. The attorneys nodded to Tudor, he nodded back and retired through a polished wooden door behind his chair.

'Now the fireworks start,' said Maxwell Sandys.

'How do you mean?' replied Jack.

'Hilary Hall was given a respectful hearing, very respectful by Tudor's standards, when he tried to argue there's no case to answer, but if he now attempts to mount a defence based on Maasai law, and in the process admits Ndekei killed Sutton, watch the judge go for him.'

Sandys was standing, in the well of the court, surrounded by Eleanor, Natalie, Natalie's father, Jack, Christopher and Daniel. Everyone else had gone for lunch.

'But there's something different about Tudor today, don't you think?' said Jack. 'That quip, about "indifferent cold meats" for lunch ... very unlike him. If someone else made that sort of remark, he'd see it as bringing the bench into disrepute.'

Sandys shrugged. 'That's just Tudor warming up to get nasty. He's showing his human side before his monstrous side takes over. He knows this case is high profile and he knows what his reputation is, so he wants to appear reasonable, leave no room for an appeal on procedural grounds.' He turned to Natalie. 'Now, my dear, I don't think you should stay this afternoon. It could get very stormy in the public gallery up above and outside, in the street. Ndekei might even be sentenced to hang today. Who knows when they might choose to take it out on you?'

'Oh, I don't think–' Natalie began but her father interrupted her.

'He's right, Tally.'

'In fact, unless Jack wants to stay to see the storm, he could even fly you back to the gorge this afternoon – that would be safest of all.'

Everyone looked at Jack.

He glanced at his watch. 'Let's see. There's something I have to do this afternoon – a special informal meeting of this committee I'm on to review the news that is coming out of the London independence conference, which started yesterday. That kicks off at 2.30 and shouldn't take more than an hour. So yes, I can pick Natalie up at the hotel at, say, four. That will give us time to get to the gorge before dark. What about the rest of you?'

Eleanor spoke first. 'I want to stay to the end, so does Owen and so does Daniel, just in case it turns ugly, when having a black African with us may help. Christopher is staying on anyway, to have some flying lessons, now that he is well again.' She turned to Sandys. 'You think the trial will end today?'

He shook his head. 'I can't say. It all depends on how Tudor reacts to the defence Ndekei is going to run.' Sandys paused. 'But to answer your question, Eleanor, I don't see how the trial can last beyond tomorrow morning.'

Jack nodded. 'I agree I should get Natalie out of harm's way this afternoon. I'll fly back tomorrow and collect everyone else.' He addressed his mother. 'If there's any change, you can always radio-telephone me at the camp.'

Eleanor nodded and moved towards Natalie. 'Well done, my dear; well done in the witness box, I mean. All that sex talk was quite unnecessary but you managed to remain strong and dignified *and* put that beastly barrister in his place. What would he know about intellectual passion? Incidentally, sitting with your father in court yesterday and today, we've talked a lot and he's had an interesting idea. He is, as you know, a great admirer of Teilhard de Chardin, the theologian who wanted the church to adapt to developments in palaeontology. Chardin is dead of course but your father's given me the idea to invite some religious leaders out to the gorge, people who might feel they are embarrassed by our discoveries but who might relish the chance to see at first hand what we are doing. People like Paul Tillich and

Albert Schweitzer. Having the winner of the Nobel Peace Prize visit the gorge would be a major coup, don't you think?'

Eleanor didn't wait for an answer. 'Anyway, he and I will carry on discussing it and we can all thrash out the details when we are back in the gorge.' She turned to Christopher. 'Are you going to wait with us?'

'No,' he said. 'I'm off to the airport. I've got a flying lesson this afternoon, and tomorrow and the day after that. I'll come back to Kihara then.' He patted Natalie's shoulder. 'Well done.'

'Christopher,' said Jack. 'If you're going out to the airport, could you fill my plane with juice? It will save time and Natalie and I need to get to the Kihara strip before dark.'

'Sure,' said Christopher. He kissed his mother and left.

Eleanor turned back to Sandys. 'Now, Maxwell, is there anywhere near here we can find a sandwich and a glass of water?'

'I'm ahead of you, my dear. Sandwiches and water are waiting for all of you in my office.' He turned to Natalie. 'Well done, again. Enjoy your flight back to Kihara.'

One by one they filed out of the courtroom into the corridor. As Natalie left, Richard Sutton Senior rose from the bench he was sitting on and moved in her direction. He was alone; there was no sign of Russell. That, at least, was a blessing.

She kept going but he stood directly in front of her. He looked down at her, then pulled her sleeve, forcing her to stand to one side.

He spoke softly.

'Did you and Richard–? Were you ever–?'

'No!' Natalie cried, but under her breath. Then, more softly still. 'No. Nor, whatever he may have told you, with Russell North.' She shook her head vehemently. 'No.'

She stepped around Sutton and tried to walk on but he caught her sleeve again. 'You don't understand.'

His voice had cracked and she stared at him. For once Richard Sutton Senior didn't look like a self-confident corporate lawyer. He looked like a father who had lost his son.

'For a moment there, in court, I hoped ... I dared to hope. Before he came to Africa this time, Richard told me ... he was a homosexual.'

Shouting. She was immediately awake. Shouting in the street. Not outside the hotel but some way off.

Yet another political demonstration?

As soon as Natalie had reached her hotel room, after the makeshift sandwich lunch in Maxwell Sandys' office and while she waited for Jack to collect her after his committee meeting, she had tried to digest Richard Sutton's bombshell, which confirmed after all what Kees had said. And at the same time she had worked hard to divest herself of her memories of the morning's proceedings.

Despite Sandys' warnings, and his attempts at reassurance, Hilary Hall had got under her skin. His insinuations about her sexual behaviour had made her seem loose, easy prey, the centre of a swamp of passions in Kihara, which was just so far from the truth as to be comical if it wasn't so hurtful and damaging. And that her father should have been there to be exposed to it all: how could she face him again?

Not the least of her anguish arose from the fact that she had lied in court, had perjured herself. It was the first big lie she had ever told and it sat uneasily – very uneasily – with her. Part of her, she realised, was still very naïve. Some people, she supposed, told lies of that magnitude every day of their lives, other people thought nothing of lying in court. But not her. It had been a lie she had to tell but it had exacted a price. It was one of the reasons she was drained and exhausted.

And she had fallen fast asleep, dropping off immediately.

The shouting grew louder but she couldn't make out what was being said.

She got up and moved to the window. Her room this time was at the back of the hotel and looked out on to a small square with straggly trees and at the far side a wide avenue stretched south, towards the sun. Two blocks further on she could make out a parade, placards, people dancing, shouting, singing. She still couldn't hear what the noise was all about. Were they celebrating the independence conference in far-off London? Had something happened that she didn't know about?

There was a rap on the door to her room. 'Natalie! Natalie, open up!'

She looked at her watch: twenty to three. Too early for Jack and in any case it wasn't Jack's voice.

She opened the door and then stood back as Sandys, Eleanor, Daniel and her father streamed in.

'What? What's happened? Why aren't you in court?'

'The trial's over. Tudor dismissed the charges.' Sandys undid his tie, a first. 'He agreed with Hilary Hall – there's no case to answer.' Sandys took his tie and stuffed it into his pocket. He shook his head. 'Can you believe it? All the evidence the prosecution tendered, he said, was circumstantial. Ndekei never got chance to mount his defence, to admit he killed Sutton; instead he's been freed.' Sandys went to the window of her room. 'That's the shouting you can hear – he's being carried on high through the streets, like a victorious warrior returning home.'

Natalie stared at the others one by one. 'So ... so, all the preparation, all the unpleasantness, all the threats from Richard Sutton Senior, all the energy and worry and sleepless nights have been for nothing?' She slumped on to the bed. 'How could that happen?'

Sandys wearily rubbed his hand over his face. 'I don't know. It's a very, *very* strict interpretation of the law. Our evidence was circumstantial, in that, had someone wanted to impersonate Ndekei, and done so, the evidence would have been much as we presented it. But we all knew, or thought that we knew, that Ndekei would admit the killing and claim Maasai custom as his defence. And we took our eye off the ball. Ndekei, Marongo and maybe Tshone – Hall's Maasai assistant – tricked us to do less work, less research, than we should have done. The trial didn't get that far. Tudor has been different lately but not that different. Today, however, I must say, he has interpreted the law strictly but, I am afraid, not incorrectly.'

Natalie felt as if she had been punched in the stomach. She was breathing heavily, and sweating. She leaned over and took a glass of water by the side of the bed. She looked at Sandys. 'After I left the court, Richard Sutton came up to me and asked if I'd really had sex with his son. He hoped I had, he said, because Richard Junior had confessed to being a homosexual.'

Sandys stared back at her. 'So maybe there *was* more to the murder than tribal custom.' He shook his head. 'We'll never know.'

Natalie rubbed her eyes with her hands. 'What happens now? How has Marongo reacted?'

'We don't know,' replied Eleanor, also taking a glass of water from the side of Natalie's bed. 'It's too early, though I don't expect he'll wait long until he begins to make political capital out of this.' She turned to Natalie's father. 'Why don't you go and pack, Owen, and check out of the hotel? Be ready to fly to the gorge this afternoon. Christopher's staying on in Nairobi, so there'll be room in Jack's plane for you.'

Owen nodded and made to leave the room. As he went through the doorway, however, he almost collided with Jack.

'I heard what happened,' he said, coming over to Natalie. 'Are you all right?'

'I'm fine. Shocked but fine.' She nodded and gave him a weak smile.

'A change of plan, Jack,' said Eleanor briskly. 'We're all flying back to the gorge this afternoon, now. Owen will take Christopher's place.'

'Two changes of plan,' said Jack. 'I've got to go back to this committee meeting. The news out of London is more interesting than we thought, but complicated. They started with education and science, so this committee I'm on has to consider the Kenyan response to the British proposals. It may even affect us in palaeontology. I'll give you the details in the gorge when I know more. But it means I have to stay.' He turned. 'Max, can you take my place and fly my mother and the others to the gorge? The trial's ended early, so you can't have a lot planned. You can fly yourself back tomorrow.'

Sandys looked flustered. 'Well, yes, I suppose I can. It's important to get Natalie out of Nairobi. The demonstrators might turn on the hotel if they find out where she is.'

'Good, that's settled then.' Jack handed Sandys some keys. 'All the instruments are working fine, Christopher has a lesson at the airport and will have filled the tanks.' He turned to Natalie. 'Max flies higher than me, don't forget, so your father won't get much of a view this time. But you'll get to the gorge quicker.'

'How long will your committee last?' Eleanor finished her water. 'Perhaps we should wait?'

'No, no.' Jack shook his head. 'It could go on for hours: the conference in London has turned a touch acrimonious – there are endless demonstrations – and we have a lot to get through. You need to get to Kihara well before dark – go with Max.'

He ushered them out of Natalie's room. 'You'll all have to check out, and that will take time, so get moving. Max, is your car handy?'

'Right outside. We can stop off at my house on the way to the airport, and I can pick up one or two bits and pieces.'

Natalie was emptying the one drawer in her room where she had placed some underwear. She looked at Jack as he came back in. 'Shall I stay here with you? In Nairobi, I mean?'

He shook his head.

'Don't you want me to stay?' She smiled and touched his cheek with her fingers.

'You heard what Max said, it's best for you to leave. And there would be no point, anyway – the committee might go on and on, late. And the British proposals are interesting, a real chance for us all to have an effect on the future.' Jack kissed her cheek. 'You and I will have all the time in the world in the gorge, now the ordeal is over. At least we will until Marongo does his worst.'

He lifted her hand to his lips and kissed it. 'In any case, I want you to have a clear head tonight, so you can make up your mind, one way or the other, about the big question I asked you the other day. Now is the time to bite the bullet, Dr. Nelson. Has Marongo and his brand of politics put you off Africa for ever, or...' He smiled. 'Or?' He raised his own hand. 'Don't tell me now. Tell me tomorrow.' Jack turned to the door, but swivelled back. 'You must get to the airport as soon as possible, but I'll have time tomorrow morning to buy some whisky. You must need it after what you've been through.'

He went out the door and she heard him run down the stairs to the lobby.

Fire

Natalie stared down at the landscape hundreds of feet below. The plane was at four thousand feet and still climbing. The ugly outskirts of Nairobi were just beginning to give way to farmland and areas of bush.

Sandys was still talking over the radio, she presumed to air traffic control, and she could see why. A large commercial jet was off to their left, on final approach to the airport they had just taken off from. Sandys, she had been reassured to note, was every bit as punctilious as Jack in making his pre-flight checks and had been commendably businesslike in taxiing out to the main runway – massive by Kihara standards – and lifting the Comanche into the air. As they had sped along the runway, she had caught sight of Christopher. He was running out of the departures building and waving energetically. She had waved back.

Eleanor was up front with Sandys, her father was alone in the second row with some bags and she was in the back with Daniel. There were more bags behind them.

She looked down again. There was more open bush now, dried river beds, clumps of acacia trees. She saw a line of elephants and a series of low hills, the edge of a lake. Beyond that, they passed two other dried river beds and, on a plain with savannah grass, there was a herd of zebra, running at full tilt.

They must have been close to five thousand feet now. She realised why Sandys flew so high but she preferred Jack's habit of flying lower. The zebra seemed very far away.

She tapped Daniel's knee and pointed down. 'Why are those zebra running? Is it a form of play or are they running away from something?'

He smiled. 'No, it's definitely not play. They are probably running away from wild dogs. Wild dogs seem to have a taste for zebra flesh – if they can smell zebra nearby they will ignore impala or hartebeest and seek out the zebra. It's always an interesting contest. Zebra fight back more than most animals – they kick, oh how they kick, and they bite too.'

Natalie looked down. She couldn't see any dogs. 'You don't think of wild dogs as being part of the African scene, not like lions and elephants and leopards.'

'Maybe not,' said Daniel. 'They are not very noble-looking animals, I agree, but they can't be ignored. Apart from elephants in a bad mood, they are the only animals who will attack a vehicle. I've known them bite the tyres of a Land Rover–'

He broke off as the plane lurched.

Natalie, looking down, felt the plane judder and looked across to Daniel. The plane juddered again and sank, as if it were a boat that had slid down a wave.

Natalie's heart was thumping in her chest, she gripped her seat tightly, she began to sweat.

The plane juddered again and the starboard engine stopped.

Sandys was talking – shouting – on the radio, frantically manoeuvring the controls but above the noise of the port engine. Natalie couldn't hear what he was saying.

The plane stabilised but Sandys lost height anyway. Then the plane juddered again, and again. The port engine stopped.

The Comanche immediately began to sink. Sandys tried to restart the engines but each time one or the other coughed into action and, before the propeller could complete a full turn, died.

No one else spoke as the plane began to lose height rapidly.

Natalie reached forward and gripped her father's shoulder. He put his hand on her arm.

Sandys fought with the aircraft controls to keep the nose pointing forward and down, using what height they had, and speed, to glide the plane as well as he could.

The Comanche was picking up velocity, bucking in the air. The angle of descent was deepening and the noise of the wind going by was rising to a whistle. Natalie was rigid with fear. Her knuckles were drained of blood, it hurt to swallow, it hurt to breathe.

Ahead of them was a patch of savannah, with trees beyond.

The plane lost more height. Its noise was no longer a whistle but a scream. Everyone looked forward as Sandys wrestled with the controls. He tried again to restart the engines. He failed.

There was a jolting and Natalie realised they must have lost part of the undercarriage, sheared off in the wind generated by their descent. They were now no more than two hundred feet above the landscape. Max tried one more time to start the engines. They coughed and died.

The angle of descent deepened still more. They had been gliding, now they were falling. Max fought to keep the attitude of the plane upright. One of the dead propellers on the starboard engine buckled under the pressure of air, snapped off and slapped against the side windows next to where Owen Nelson was sitting. Then it was gone.

Her father. His first time in Kenya.

Oil streamed across the wing where the propeller had broken away. It was flecked on the Comanche's windows.

At about fifty feet Max hauled back on the control stick. The flaps at the trailing edge of the wings lifted and the nose of the aircraft rose, so that it was the aircraft's wheels and belly that slammed into the ground first.

The sound of metal on rock – the screech of twisted, mangled, deformed, distended metal on stone – made a hammering noise, a booming, as if the massive gates of hell were clanging closed, a final, deadly, dead bolt, as the aircraft bounced into the air again and began to turn over.

Natalie's seat belt cut into her right thigh, her left thigh and her stomach all in rapid succession. The heads of the people in front of her jerked one way, then the other, then back again. At the same time a tide of pain exploded up Natalie's spine, spread round her lower back like a hot ring.

She heard a loud crack, snapping bone, and Eleanor's head fell to one side, nodding insanely.

The fuselage rose into the air but then the port wing scraped the ground – and sent the plane in the opposite direction causing it to drop, diagonally, on to some rocks, baking in the sun. Another hammering of metal on stone, another screeching, another mangling, yet more shards of twisted aircraft pieces. The Comanche broke almost in two and skidded down the rocks, showering sparks, turning and rolling, keening and growling, pummelled out of shape and thudding to a stop against a line of trees, when Natalie hit her head – hard – against the already misshapen metal skin of the plane, and passed out.

The first thing she heard, however long afterwards when she regained consciousness, was a cracking and a dripping sound. In the baking sun, and following the crash, the metal of the aircraft was giving off mysterious cracks and snaps like those the Land Rovers' engines gave off after they had been in use. Only much louder. She couldn't see where the dripping sound was coming from.

She was aware of the hot ring around her middle. She passed her hands over herself. No blood but she was very tender all round her hips and stomach.

Looking around her again, she still couldn't see much. Only Daniel, unconscious or dead almost on top of her, but held in place by his seat belt. Those in the front half of the plane – Eleanor, Sandys, her dear father – were out of sight, where the plane had broken and jack-knifed on hitting the rocks. She pushed Daniel. He didn't respond.

She called out. 'Hello? Hello?' It was more a croak and no one replied.

She pushed Daniel again. Still no response.

The smell of airplane fuel was everywhere and she realised that that's what the sound of dripping was: fuel leaking from the tanks which, she knew, were located in the aircraft wings.

But, where she was, she couldn't see the wings.

As she went to push Daniel off her a third time, she noticed that his legs were trapped, pinned under the bracket of what remained of the seat in front of him. She would have to crawl round him.

She made a start and unfastened her own belt. It wasn't easy. He was a big man. But somehow she managed to crawl out from under him. The small area behind the back seats was choked with luggage, four or five bags. She pushed two of them behind her, to occupy the space she herself had been sitting in and she reached upwards. The way the aircraft had fallen meant that the side of its fuselage was uppermost, so that the emergency rear door opened upwards, to the sky.

Except that when Natalie turned the handle it wouldn't budge. The shape of the fuselage had been distended and the action of the inside handle was jammed.

She was sweating now. The sound of dripping could still be heard. Did that mean there was the threat of fire?

'Hello? Hello?' Where was her father? Where was Eleanor? What had happened to Sandys?

No reply.

She was sweating. All over.

How was she going to get the emergency door

open? There was no other way out. Even if she smashed the Comanche's rear windows they were too small for her to crawl through.

The windows. Could she smash one, reach through, and open the emergency door from the outside handle?

Would that work?

She had no choice.

But what was she going to smash the window *with?* Her shoe? It was just a soft moccasin that had in any case come off. She had nothing else hard except the buckle of her belt and that wouldn't do it.

'Hello? Hello?'

No reply.

She heard the yatter of some baboons. So long as it was just baboons.

Then she noticed that the window nearest the emergency exit had a sort of clip that enabled it to be opened an inch or two at its trailing edge, to let air in when the plane was taxiing in hot weather. Jack had opened the one next to it in Ngorongoro. She reached up. It too was jammed. Or perhaps it was rusty.

She tried again.

It wouldn't budge.

She noticed it was fastened to the body of the plane by screws. If she could unwind those screws she could take off the clip and maybe reach through and turn the outside handle.

But she had no screwdriver. She pulled her belt off and tried the buckle, to see if it would fit in the groove at the top of the screws – there were three of them.

The buckle was too thick. She needed something finer. More noise from the baboons, closer now.

She looked at the pieces of luggage. One or two had plastic name tags. She tore one off.

The first one was too thick.

So was the other one.

She had a pen in her pocket but that was no good.

Suddenly, there was a deep *whoosh!* sound and the baboons barked in chorus.

She heard the flapping of flames. The airplane fuel had ignited. The smell of fuel intensified but she still couldn't see the flames.

But she knew she had to hurry. No one had come for her. She had to reach her father.

She had some coins in her pocket. They were too thick.

She looked at her watch. It was still working. It had gone five and would be dark before long.

As she looked down at her watch, she noticed the buckle on the strap. It was thin and it was metal. She took off her watch and reached up to the window.

As she did so she felt a searing pain around her middle and she swore. She was sweating all over again now and though she still couldn't see the flames, she could hear them and she was beginning to feel the heat they were radiating.

She held the watch buckle to the head of the screw. It slid into the groove. Yes! The screw itself was maybe a quarter of an inch across at its head. The buckle was closer to an inch wide. Holding her fingers near the screw, she swivelled the buckle in an anticlockwise direction.

It wouldn't budge.

She tried again. No luck.

And then suddenly the screw-head budged. It had been rusted to the surrounding metal but she had broken the crust. The screw turned easily now and soon came away.

Sweating still, she tackled the second screw. It wouldn't budge. She moved her fingers further away from the head of the screw, to give herself more leverage.

The sound of burning filled her ears. The front half of the aircraft was alight. What had happened to the people inside? There was no other sound. In her state, she didn't want to think about it.

She strained at the screw.

The buckle broke but at the same time she felt the screw give way.

When the buckle broke, she dropped it and it fell down into the depths of the aircraft, and out of reach.

The second screw was loose enough for her to be able to unwind it with her fingers.

But how would she unwind the last screw?

She felt the bracket. It was loose. She took off her belt and pushed its buckle under the bracket and yanked. The pain around her middle intensified. She yanked again.

The bracket came away from the wall of the airplane. She then threw the bracket away, took a deep breath, reached up, and pushed at the window.

It was stuck.

She pushed again, and again.

Each time she pushed, the pain at her middle worsened. But she had no choice.

She pushed again. Her eyes watered from the pain.

The window swung open. Only a few inches but enough for her to reach up again and put her hand and then her arm through the gap.

She reached round and gripped the outside handle of the emergency door. She pulled and felt the bolt slide across.

She swore again, tears caking her cheeks.

Inside the plane she manoeuvred two more pieces of luggage so that she could kneel on them. The pain around her middle slowed her down, made her sweat, made her cry, made her cry out. She bent her head and placed her shoulders next to the door. Slowly, she straightened her knees. Her back was on fire. She forced her shoulders against the door.

It was stuck.

She pushed again.

It remained stuck.

She pushed again, the sweat falling from her face in globules on to the luggage.

The heat from the flames was growing.

The emergency door flew open and a blast of hot air swept over her.

She stood up and turned.

Before her, the front half of the plane was ablaze and she stared in horror. No one could survive that raging wildfire. There was a smell of burning. With deepening despair, she realised it was the smell of roasting: of flesh, human flesh, her father's flesh, being cooked by heat. Max's flesh, Eleanor's flesh.

She daren't dwell on it, not now. She must act.

She took in her surroundings. The aircraft was on a sliding shelf of rock that ended in a line of trees that looked as though they followed the course of a dried river bed. There were baboons in the trees – but not far away, at the end of the rocks, she noticed half a dozen or so wild dogs. They were watching, waiting.

It was clear that the fire would spread to the rear half of the aircraft soon.

She dipped back down into the plane and undid Daniel's seat belt. She pushed the seat bracket that pinned his legs and pulled them free. She wrapped her arms around Daniel's chest, much as Jack had done when he rescued her from the river, and lifted him. Or she tried to. He was a big man.

As she did so, she felt him stir. He was alive.

'Come on, Daniel, we've got to hurry.'

He didn't hear. He remained slumped in his seat. There was a big bloody runnel carved in his skull.

She pulled him backward, so he was directly under the opening of the emergency door. She had decided that if she moved and rested, moved and rested, the pain was bearable, just. Tears still ran down her cheeks, into her mouth, down her neck, between her breasts. Her nose ran. She wrapped her belt under one of Daniel's armpits, led it round his neck and buckled it. It was too short to fit anywhere else. Then she climbed out of the door at the top of the aircraft, stopped for the pain to ease, and reached back in. Gripping her belt, she pulled and pulled.

The ring of pain again shot up her spine. She was forced to stop.

She was awash in sweat. The sun was sinking but the fire was still raging. How long would it take to burn all the fuel in an aircraft? A line of black smoke rose into the sky. That would surely help rescuers find the crash site – so long as daylight lasted.

Eventually, she got Daniel's head above the level of the emergency door. Now she undid her belt and used it to tie Daniel's head and neck to the hinge of the door. That meant he wouldn't slide back down, when she let go. She slid again into the aircraft. The pain still forced tears down her face. Where did so many tears come from? She gripped Daniel's legs. She shoved his torso upwards till his upper half was spilling over the ledge of the doorway.

The carpet lining at the front of the rear section of the plane had caught fire. The smell of fuel was stronger than ever.

She pushed Daniel's legs through the emergency door so he was now hanging outside the plane from the hinge where she had tied him. She climbed out and sat on the top side of the plane, breathing heavily, croaking in pain, still crying. After the briefest of pauses to recover, she undid the buckle of her belt. Daniel's feet fell on to the rocks but the rest of his body stayed slumped against the fuselage of the Comanche. Natalie slithered down to the ground herself and pulled him away. She pulled him further and laid him out on the rocks in the shadow of the wing of the plane which was standing almost upright.

The back half of the Comanche was beginning to burn now but Natalie dropped inside again. She knew what she wanted. A bottle of water. It was anybody's guess as to how long it would be before they were rescued – if the dogs didn't get them first – and she didn't want to risk dehydration the way Kees van Schelde had done.

She found the bottle, rested, and then escaped again through the emergency door.

The fire was still raging and the wild dogs had come no closer. She waited for the pain to subside, took a swig of water herself, then forced some between Daniel's lips.

She was so intent on doing this that she didn't notice that the upright wing of the plane had become loosened in its position by the fire melting the metal. Silently, it fell down on top of them both. No sooner had she noticed the shadow moving across the rock surface than she was hit on the head and, for the second time, passed out.

The flames were nibbling at Natalie's feet. Acrid black smoke was choking her lungs. Her skin was bubbling and blistering from the heat. Her hair was on fire, her nostrils clogged with the fumes of burning Avgas. The wild dogs were getting closer, she could hear their whelps and whimpers, the urgent pace of their breathing.

She kicked out at the dogs and screamed, 'No! Get away! No!'

A shadow loomed over her, two hands held her shoulders and she woke up, damp with sweat.

'You're safe, Natalie, quite safe.'

She could feel her hairline drenched with sweat. Her neck, under her arms, the backs of her knees ... all wringing wet.

She opened her eyes. She looked around, at the white room, the white walls, the white-painted lights, the white plastic blinds. The shadow standing over her materialised into a tall, thin man with grey hair.

Dominic!

No, it wasn't. 'I am David Stone, Dr. David Stone, and you are in the Oburra Clinic in Nairobi. You are not to worry. You were in a plane crash but you survived. You have some bruising, one or two internal injuries – not life-threatening, not now anyway – and a few superficial burns. But, essentially, you are beginning to mend. You were very lucky and you are not to worry. Here is someone you know.'

He stood back.

Behind him was Jack.

For some reason Natalie started to cry. There was a ring of pain around her middle.

Jack looked at the doctor.

The doctor shook his head. 'It's a normal reaction to shock.' He stepped forward with a paper cup in his hand. 'Here, drink this. It's a sedative. It will help you sleep. You need to let your body recover from what it has been through. Sleep will help.'

He forced Natalie, in the midst of her tears, to drink from the cup.

Jack pulled a chair across nearer the bed, sat down and leaned forward. He held Natalie's hand and kissed it.

For a few moments the tears continued to fall down Natalie's face into her hair, but then he realised from the regularity of her breathing that she was again sleeping.

It took another three days. She slept right through, now and then waking in a fit of horror at the nightmares she was enduring and each time Jack fetched the doctor or, when these episodes occurred during the night, the staff sister on duty. Each time Jack held her hand, told her he was there and kissed her forehead. Once or twice she wept. Always she woke in a sweat. Once or twice he left the room for an hour or more but he always came back.

Then, one morning, as he was busy reading some letters that he had with him, she said quietly, 'Jack?'

'I'm here.' He put down the letters and reached for her hand.

'What day is it?'

He told her.

'How long have I been here?'

'Almost a week.'

She took back her hand and passed them over her body, feeling her bruises, her burns – covered by bandages wrapped tightly to her skin – her scratches. She felt her face. In places it hurt to touch and she winced.

'Do you have a mirror?'

He didn't move.

'Jack!'

He brought her a round mirror with a handle.

She inspected her face – and gasped.

'They are bruises and burns, superficial. They will pass. You are still as beautiful, still as desirable, still on my list of everything I want.' He took the mirror from her. 'We will find a way to make love again, between the bruises, around the burns, avoiding what needs avoiding. Don't worry.'

She nodded but fought back tears. After a delay, she went on, 'What happened?'

'How much can you remember? You don't have to look back so soon. The doctor said–'

'I can remember the engines stopping, I can remember falling, I can remember hitting some rocks and bouncing back up into the air.' The tears began again and she shook her head. 'Your mother, my father.' Her wet cheeks glistened in the morning light. 'Max – that should have been you.'

Jack waited, just holding her hand. Minutes passed and the tears subsided.

'Tell me.'

'I think you should wait. Get stronger–'

'*Tell me.*' It was a whisper, an exhausted whisper but urgent. 'I want to know'

Jack kissed her hand. He took his time, kept his voice low.

'In some ways, and though it doesn't feel like it now, you were lucky. Max – unlike me – likes to fly high. I told you that – remember? That means he was able to put the Comanche into a glide. Had it been just you and me, flying low, we'd have had no chance. We would have fallen like a stone.' He held her hand again. 'Max tried to glide the plane down to a flat area of the savannah but you lost height too quickly and hit some rocks by a dried river bed. The aircraft split in two.'

She nodded.

'Max, my mother and your father were in the front half.' Jack paused, lowered his voice still more. 'They were either knocked unconscious or killed by the initial crash but the wings were attached to their part of the broken plane and that's where the fuel is stored. The fuel caught fire and ... and all three were burned.' He paused. 'But, since they were either dead or unconscious, they wouldn't have felt anything.'

Natalie was weeping again and Jack went out to get the doctor.

On the following day, Natalie woke up feeling just as weepy, just as ravaged, but ravenously hungry.

'That's a better sign,' said the doctor, 'a much better sign. It means a corner is being turned. Her body, if not yet her mind, is responding, recovering. Of course, it's early days, given what she's been through, but it's a start. What's her favourite food?'

Jack watched as Natalie was given some soup, two wings of chicken and some rice pudding. For the first time, she sat up in bed.

When she had finished, she pushed the tray away from her but held on to her water. 'No,' she said in a croaky voice. 'You were saying.'

Jack waited. He wouldn't be rushed. He had to get his tone just right for what was coming.

'I was saying that Maxwell Sandys, my mother and your father died in the plane crash in which Daniel and you survived.'

More tears.

First her mother, now her father. He had come to Africa because of her and now he was dead. He was dead because of her, just as her mother... Natalie had hardly seen him since he had arrived. The trial had consumed her. Now...

Her memory of events was hazy but the weight on her chest, over her heart, confirmed what she couldn't forget. Her lovely father, on his first trip to black Africa, on his way to the gorge, to explore the work of his daughter, to discuss with Eleanor his idea to bring to Kihara the world's leading theologians, was... There had been no goodbye.

'Are there any remains at all?'

Jack looked away before looking back. 'Cinders. Charred fragments. The remains of burned bones. I am having them collected.'

'Oh, Jack. This trial—'

'*Shsh.*'

'My father, Eleanor, they were getting on so well.'

He said nothing. Then, 'You're alive. You will recover. If you had been...' he shook his head and swallowed hard.

Through more tears, Natalie managed to say, 'And Daniel?'

'Is down the corridor. He had concussion like you – he hit his head badly; a few bruises and burns, but he's already up and walking, giving interviews.'

Drinking some water, she almost spilled it. 'Giving *interviews!* What do you mean? Interviews about what, and to whom?'

Jack wiped his eyes with his hand and nodded his head. 'I haven't told you the good news. You saved Daniel's life. You're a heroine. It's all over the papers here. In the photos you remind me of Grace Kelly. Well, you would do if you had fair hair. Since you are too ill, too weak to be interviewed, they are interviewing him.'

'I don't understand.'

'You don't understand because you don't remember.' Jack laid some newspapers at the foot of the bed. 'It's all in here, when you're ready. You were knocked unconscious by the plane. You crashed about three miles from a Maasai village. They saw what had happened and came to help straight away. But, since they had to travel on foot – to run, in the heat – it took them some forty minutes to reach the crash site and there was a river in the way. But they could see what was happening all the time. Others ran to the nearest telephone, though of course we knew what had happened since Max had sent out an emergency "Mayday" call.'

He drank some water himself, and handed her more paper towels to soak up the tears. He sat on the edge of the bed so he could wrap his arm around her shoulders.

'Anyway, the Maasai saw what happened. They saw you open the emergency door at the back of the plane – you must have been the first person to regain consciousness – and they saw you go back for Daniel and pull him and shove him and squeeze his enormous frame out of that small plane. Apparently, you were trying to give him some water when a wing of the aircraft fell on both of you. You were knocked on the head and both of you were unconscious when the Maasai reached you. The rest of the plane was on fire by then *and* the wing covering you and Daniel – there was airplane fuel everywhere. But the Maasai used boulders to get the wing off you and neither of you is badly burned. The flames kept the wild dogs away.'

'So the Maasai saved our lives?'

'Yes. After you had saved Daniel's life, the Maasai saved yours. The papers are making a lot of that as a symbol of the new Kenya.'

Natalie was weeping copiously again now, as grief for her father swept over her. 'I'm sorry,' she said through her tears. 'I'm acting like I'm the only one who's lost someone. You and Christopher must be devastated.'

He grunted and shook his head. 'You are the only one who's been through a plane crash. Don't worry about me – about us.' He squeezed his arm around her shoulders and then sat back in his chair.

Natalie lay for a while, sipping her water and not attempting to look at the newspapers.

Her father was dead. Dead. She was surrounded by a cold void. Now she was completely on her own.

Thank God Jack was here. He looked so vivid, so strong, so full of vim and verve, so different from the way she felt. He had enough strength for both of them, at least for now, and thank God he hadn't been piloting the plane. Her father was dead – a barren colourless nothing, somewhere she couldn't place or point to, but with Jack here she

660

wasn't all alone after all. She felt warmer when he was around. Why didn't he look more wrecked? He had lost his mother and a good friend. Was he putting on an act for her benefit? She reached out her hand for his, the comfort of his firm flesh. She longed for her body to recover enough for physical contact. Once she stopped feeling so weepy she and Jack could... There must be somewhere, between the burns and the bruises, that he could touch her... Natalie closed her eyes. How could she think of that? Her father was dead.

'What I *do* remember, Jack, is that the two engines just stopped in mid-air, one after the other.' She wiped her eyes and sniffed. 'Why, what would cause that?'

Jack waited. 'The thing I always feared would happen actually did happen.'

They looked at each other.

Natalie's waist hurt, her eyes were wet, her nose was gummy.

'You remember we parked the plane near those private jets at Nairobi International?'

She sniffed and nodded weakly.

'At lunchtime, after you'd given evidence in court, and the plan was for you and me to hurry back to Kihara, to get you out of harm's way, I asked Christopher to fill up the Comanche, to save time, since we had to get to the strip before dark.' Jack wiped his lips with the back of his hand. 'He was in a hurry, and was having his own flying lesson ... he put the wrong fuel in the plane. Jet fuel, not Avgas.'

'Jack!' More tears fell down her cheeks. 'No! *No,*' she breathed.

A long silence, as Natalie struggled to take in this news. She drifted off to sleep.

Hours later Natalie wakened. Jack was still there.

So was the cold, empty space that was now her father.

'Where's Christopher?'

'I don't know. He's disappeared.'

'He's devastated at what he did.'

'Maybe. He tried something similar before. Remember? That boat engine failure on Lake Naivasha.'

'You think this was *deliberate?* No!' The word died on her lips as she ran short of breath.

'It's crossed my mind. It should have been you and me on that plane.'

'Why? Why would he do such a thing?'

'The same reason as before, Mgina's termite in timber: jealousy. Because he thinks ... because of our trip to Lamu, me bringing you your dinners when you were ill; he thinks he's fallen in love with you like I have. He admitted as much to me the night we had a drink in the hotel, the night before you gave evidence, after I left your room, after we had... He decided that if he couldn't have you, no one could.'

Natalie sighed and shook her head. 'Jealousy wouldn't do that to someone.'

'I'm not a psychiatrist, Natalie, just a miserable palaeontologist with a brand-new Ph.D. but he's done it to me twice now. Look what jealousy did to Russell.'

He got up and prowled the room. She could see that now, today, he did look wrecked. 'My mother, your father, and Max were never meant to be on the plane. Only you and I were. The last discussion Christopher was a party to – during the lunch break in the trial, after your appearance in the witness box, before he went off for a flying lesson – was when you and I were planning to fly to the gorge, and everyone else was staying on. Only later was there a change of plan – two changes of plan, in fact, with me staying over in Nairobi, because of the committee meeting, and with Max flying everyone else back to the gorge. Christopher didn't know that.'

Natalie shook her head again, weakly. 'No, *no*,' she breathed, 'you're wrong. It was an accident, I'm sure of it.' She coughed. Even that hurt. 'As we were taking off, I saw Christopher come running out of the departures building, and waving. I waved back.' She looked up at Jack. *'He wasn't waving!* He had realised his mistake and was trying to stop us.'

'Hmmn.' Jack, by the window, shrugged. 'He tried to stop you only after he realised who was on the plane.'

'Don't say that! *Don't say that!*' She thought back to Christopher's late-night visit to her room in the hotel, when he had asked her to marry him and she had raised the subject of the boating accident on Lake Naivasha. Reminding him of that surely had nothing to do with Christopher's behaviour? She refused to believe that either.

'You must look for him, Jack. He mustn't do a Kees. He's done a dreadful thing and in some ways it will be worse for him if it *was* an accident.' She coughed again. 'You were always parking near the jets, near the jet fuel – can you honestly say you are free of all blame?'

A long silence.

Natalie tried hard to remember the look on Christopher's face as he had gestured at the Comanche as Sandys had raced the aircraft down the big runway at Nairobi International. But she'd been through too much. Those memories, nearer the crash, just wouldn't behave.

Jack prowled around the room. He'd lost his mother, poor man, but she was too weak to offer him any support. She'd make it up to him. Oh, how she'd make it up to him.

Her father was dead.

She cried herself to sleep again.

The next morning when she awakened, Jack was still there. He hadn't shaved and he hadn't changed his clothes. It didn't matter: he was there. She ate some fruit and drank some water. The ring of pain around her middle hadn't gone away. In a weak voice she said, 'We haven't talked about Ndekei, Marongo, Richard Sutton Senior, Russell North. What's happened – anything?'

'More than you could know.' He prowled the room again as he talked. 'The first thing to say is did you, by any chance, notice that Peter Jeavons was in court? He's the man who–'

'Yes, yes, of course, that's who it was. The British minister. I did notice someone whose face I couldn't put a name to. I remember thinking it was curious.'

'Curious – yes, but good for us.' Jack leaned against the window sill. 'It seems he was very taken with what he saw in the gorge and what we are achieving and trying to achieve. At the same time he was distressed by your dilemma.' Jack parted the slats of the Venetian blinds and looked out of the window again. 'You may remember that, when he was in the gorge having dinner, it was around the time my mother had received that letter from the honours committee, proposing to make her a dame, and she had refused. Remember that he tried to persuade my mother to accept the gong?'

'Yes, yes I do. But what does that have to do–?'

'I'm coming to that. The conversation at dinner gave Jeavons an idea – he's obviously a born politician. He went back to Britain and did a little research on John Tudor's family – that's right, the judge. It appears that Tudor has two brothers back in London. One is a QC and has been knighted, the other works as a private secretary in Buckingham Palace and almost certainly *will* be knighted when he retires – it goes with the job. Jeavons came back here with a message from the honours committee, which, with preparations for the independence conference in full swing, was mindful of what sort of result was to be preferred in the Ndekei trial.'

'You mean?'

'I don't know what you are thinking but Jeavons, who is a lawyer after all, went through the evidence with Tudor before the trial. That's probably what they were discussing at the Karibu Club on Christmas Eve, when Christopher saw them. And they found an acceptable way out, one that let you give your evidence but after which Ndekei was released. In return, Tudor is to be made Lord Tudor of Kilimai – that's the suburb of Nairobi where he lives – and he will retire and return to Britain grander than either of his brothers.'

She shifted her frame in bed. The pain around her middle was easier if she moved every so often. 'But that's, that's–'

'A fix, yes, and very possibly criminal.' Jack came away from the window and sat on the bed. He kissed her forehead. 'But you weren't party to the plan, you didn't know what deal the politicians were cooking, so your hands are clean. I don't expect you to like it, Dr. Nelson, but Jeavons got you off the hook with Richard Sutton. It's all tidied up and hasn't put a cloud over the independence talks. So I suggest you grin and bear it.'

'I'll bet Sutton's not grinning.'

'That's the other piece of good news. Marongo made quite a song and dance when Ndekei was acquitted – politicians always look for quick political capital – and it got quite up Sutton's nose. He saw you give evidence, he saw how you didn't wilt under cross-examination, how you insisted on your viewpoint. He liked it that you were respectful about his son in public.'

Jack lifted her hand to his cheek and rubbed his rough stubble over her skin, smiling. Get used to it, he was saying. This is the state of my beard, every morning, when you wake up.

'But he didn't like the judge's decision and he most certainly didn't like Marongo's crowing. Sutton came to Nairobi to be magnanimous and get the credit for it. In the end he had nothing to be magnanimous about. Their deal is off and he's returned to New York and won't be coming back.'

'And Russell?'

'Upstaged by Jeavons. He's gone too.'

'Jeavons has been very busy.'

'He certainly has. I got an inkling of it before. Remember I was in a long committee meeting?'

'I think so.'

'Well, we'd just had word from London that, as part of an educational–scientific collaboration between Britain and post-independence Kenya, the British – thanks to Jeavons, the science minister – were proposing a Kihara Institute of Human Origins, with a ten-year budget and for which they are quite happy to give Marongo the credit, providing he hands in his Kalashnikovs. Sutton's withdrawal left Marongo high and dry, the more so as one or two of the papers here went for him after the trial ended, saying he was more interested in politics than justice. But Jeavons' plan rescued him, politically, and after those Maasai villagers saw you pulling Daniel from the plane, a white person saving the life of a black person, Marongo has swung back to us, praising the fairness of white justice, praising you and your work, welcoming the new institute and proposing – wait for it – that my mother be buried in the gorge as a mark of respect for what she achieved.'

Jack again smiled briefly at her. 'You have to hand it to Marongo. He's as good a politician as Jeavons. The symmetry is eye-catching. What started in a burial ground, ends with one too.'

Lament

For as far as the eye could see, Maasai figures wrapped in dark red cloaks stood on the low ridges of the rolling Serengeti hills that surrounded the quartzite gash of Kihara Gorge. The late afternoon sun was still hot but not the fireball it had been earlier and there were clouds low on the horizon. Somewhere between fifteen and twenty dark-green four-wheeled vehicles were parked neatly in a row on the lip of the gorge, overlooking RSK, Richard Sutton's Korongo. A wind was beginning to stir.

In front of what looked like a small cave in the wall of the gorge stood Aldwai with his rifle. Next to him, with shovels, stood three Maasai. They had dug the grave and would fill it in later.

Two parallel lines of people stood at right angles to the wall of the gorge on either side of the grave. One was made up of Maasai elders, with Marongo at the distant end. The other line was made up of personnel from the camp, plus the minister of justice from Nairobi, who hadn't gone to the conference in London, the deputy minister of education, representatives of the university, the president of the Karibu Club, Henry Radcliffe from the Bell-Ryder Foundation, with Natalie and Jack opposite Marongo.

It was Natalie's second day out of hospital. Jack had flown her to the gorge. She knew she had to get back in a plane sooner or later. The pain around her middle was under control, with

671

drugs, but the crutches helped.

Christopher wasn't there. He hadn't been found and had not been in touch.

There were to be sandwiches and drinks back in the camp afterwards, a short reception so that those who had to fly back to Nairobi could leave before dark.

A box was brought from the Land Rover nearest the grave site. A very small box, Eleanor's remains, carried by Beth, her daughter, who had arrived from Boston. Virginia and her husband had come from Palestine. They were at Beth's side.

Maxwell Sandys was being buried in Nairobi. Owen Nelson's funeral would come later, at the church in Lincolnshire where Violette, Natalie's mother, was buried. Owen had always believed he would be reunited with his wife one day. Natalie didn't share that view but she knew that their remains belonged together. For now his were in a box, in her room, in the hotel in Nairobi. She fought back tears just thinking of them.

Beth, a beautiful, slim blonde woman, was holding up well, Natalie thought. She held herself erect, had a firm step; not a hair on her head was out of place. There could be no doubt she was Eleanor's daughter. Virginia, tall in the Deacon way, was more tearful but comforted by her husband.

As Beth and Virginia reached the lines of people, Marongo stepped forward. He gripped the staff he always held at gatherings and raised it high. At this, the Maasai began to sing. A slow, lilting melody gradually spread around the hills,

672

a vast choir of hundreds in which Marongo showed himself as having a fine voice.

Across the gorge, Natalie could see Mgina with Endole and his other wives, all singing in unison.

'Ah, I know this,' whispered Jack. 'It's a lament called *The Clouds Beneath the Sun,* and is about Ollantashante and his exploits on the battlefield, ending with his heroic death.' He gasped. 'Am I mistaken or is that Mutevu Ndekei across the gorge?'

Natalie looked to where Jack indicated.

'You're right. And Atape.'

Natalie had never heard anything so beautiful as the lament. Jack explained that it concerned a raid on the Maasai villages by another tribe, who had assembled on a windy night when their movements had been masked by the sound of whistling thorn. Ollantashante had single-handedly blocked a path up from the gorge while reinforcements had been alerted. He had himself been killed after slaying a score of the enemy.

'Marongo once asked me to translate this song into English,' whispered Jack. 'I forget most of it but not the last lines, which were very beautiful, about how, at the end of a whole day's battle, the clouds cover the sun, the wind dies, the thorn stops whistling and dies to a moan, the enemy withdraws, beaten, but the land remains:

Across the gorge, the day sinks with a hum,
A little beauty lost, a little less to come.

'That's not a literal translation of course, but it keeps to the spirit.'

Natalie began to weep. She was getting used to weeping now.

Jack took her arm and they moved out of line and stood on the other side of Beth and Virginia from Marongo.

Jack knew, as his sisters knew, that Eleanor had always wished to be buried with Jock in Nairobi. But Jack also knew – as his mother would have insisted – that Marongo's offer could not be refused. Eleanor would have approved of Jack's decision, he knew that too. Natalie realised that, politically, the burial would cement the relationship between the Maasai and the palaeontologists as nothing else would.

As the singing continued, Marongo, Beth, Virginia, Jack and Natalie approached the small hole dug in the wall of the gorge. Standing to one side was a Maasai warrior in full regalia, black and white stone jewellery, a long red cloak, a staff made from whistling thorn. As Beth and the others got close, he stepped forward and placed a toy spear on the top of the box she was carrying.

'It is their way,' said Jack. 'The spear is to help on the other side. And it means Eleanor had warrior status. She was not just an ordinary person. It's a mark of respect.'

Now Aldwai stepped forward. He raised his old rifle and fired three times into the air. A flock of birds in some nearby acacia trees scattered against the clouds beginning to cover the sun.

Beth bent down and placed the box in the hole. She pushed it further in and stood back.

The men who had dug the hole moved forward

to fill it. As they did so the singing stopped and a single voice, a fine baritone, was left to sing solo.

'That,' murmured Jack, 'is to emphasise that our journey to the other side is one that we take alone.'

Natalie, as so often before, marvelled at the simple beauty of Maasai symbolism.

As the hole was filled in and the gravediggers stood back, the soloist fell silent. Now there was just the wind.

Marongo turned and put his hand on Jack's shoulder. 'At last your kind are buried here. This land is your land as much as it is ours.' He nodded, smiled and turned away.

Natalie realised that what he had said wasn't true but that politically it was the right thing to say.

Along the hills the Maasai dispersed. In no time they were gone.

'Listen,' said Jack.

The wind had risen. The thorn was beginning to moan.

Natalie was weeping again. 'It's like the land itself is saying goodbye.'

'Look, Jack, stop, please stop.'

He braked. He and Natalie were travelling back to the camp together. Beth, Virginia and the others were in different vehicles.

They were on the plain, with a thicket of fig and acacia trees directly in front of them.

'See, it's like a replay of what we saw that other time, on the way to Karatu. In those trees, there, two giraffes, standing close, almost as if they are kissing and, between their legs, a baby giraffe, protected.'

Natalie pointed.

'Your bush eyes are better than mine now.'

They sat watching the giraffes.

'Don't you think giraffes are the most *elegant* of animals?'

She nodded. 'Graceful.'

'And they move around in twos or families, not herds, like lovers who know some great big secret. You once said that about musicians but I think it applies to giraffes as well.'

She smiled and nodded.

The giraffes seemed in no mood to hurry, occasionally looking in their direction, but not letting the infant out from under their legs.

'We should get back,' said Jack. But he made no attempt to move either and Natalie and he sat for several minutes more without speaking, just looking.

He was clean-shaven today – no stubble: he had just buried his mother. But he still looked wrecked.

The wind on the plain was still strong. The moaning of the thorn was all around them. The light was beginning to change. More clouds were moving their way. The short rains were not over.

Natalie shifted in her seat to get more comfortable. If she sat still for long, her middle started to ache.

A brace of guinea fowl moved in front of the Land Rover.

Jack leaned his head against the glass of the side window as the vehicle rocked in the wind again.

'It's time, Natalie. Time to answer my question, I mean. When I first saw you, all those weeks ago, I fell for you almost immediately – Elizabeth Taylor, Kim Novak, you put them all to one side. But I didn't show it. I thought you were so beautiful you must have someone back home, or maybe you and Christopher had something together, and you certainly were jealous of your privacy. I was slow in getting going – I always am, I call it wheelspin.'

He smiled briefly and wiped his lips with the back of his hand.

'But, *but* – that word again – after our two nights in Nairobi, after our trip to Ngorongoro, seeing you at the controls of the Comanche, with the headphones over your ears, you looked so beautiful, so alive, so *vivid* as I once told you, I knew my mind and I knew it then, instantly.'

Jack threw the empty water bottle on the back seat of the Land Rover.

'I always hoped, when I was growing up, that I would fall in love the way I fell in love with you. It was... I was happier in Lamu picking sea urchin needles out of your knee than I have ever been. And yes, I plead guilty. On Boxing Day I did ogle you in your bikini. I ogled and ogled and ogled. I had never seen someone so desirable within my reach.'

'I can't marry you, Jack.'

'*What?*' It was said faintly, as if the air had barely left his lungs. 'Please, *no*, don't say–'

'I *can't!*'

Jack was fighting for air. 'I ... I...' He shook his head. '*No!*'

She reached out and put her hand on his arm. 'You were wonderful to me in hospital. I will never forget that. And before the crash, you enlarged my life. Flying, snorkelling, I've even got a sneaking feeling for jazz.' She smiled sadly. 'And I realise with politics you've opened my eyes.' Natalie caressed his arm with her fingers.

'But there is something you don't know.' She reached up and touched his chin, forcing him to look at her. 'You don't know it because I didn't know it myself until yesterday, when Dr. Stone could leave it no longer. He had delayed telling me because he didn't think I was strong enough, strong enough physically or mentally, but since I was being discharged yesterday – discharged early so I could come to the funeral – he had no choice.'

Her lips were dry. She ran her tongue along them. 'You remember I thought I was iller than Jonas said? You recommended a doctor who was an expert in tropical diseases, someone I never got round to consulting.'

Jack nodded. He couldn't speak. He was rigid with despair.

'My hands were tingling, I had headaches all the time. I never recognised the signs and neither did you – the tick typhus misled us.' She squeezed his arm. 'I was pregnant, Jack.'

Her voice broke. 'In the crash, I lost a baby. We lost a son.'

Jack stopped breathing. The smallest of sobs escaped from his throat. He swallowed hard.

'My memory around the time of the crash is still patchy. But some of my memories are coming back and one of the things I remember is feeling a lot of pain around my middle.' She shifted again. 'A pain I still have.'

The moan of the thorn turned briefly to a whistle.

'What Dr. Stone also told me yesterday was that the ring of pain around my middle is there because, in the crash, when we bounced off those rocks and the plane turned over and landed on its side, my pelvis was broken in two places – jagged breaks that he put right in the operation when he took out the ... the dead baby.' Natalie looked away, at the vast expanse of the Serengeti. 'But he operated only after those jagged breaks had sliced into my fallopian tubes and punctured my womb ... punctured it beyond...'

Natalie's eyes were watering again. She had said enough.

She looked back to Jack. 'I can never have children.'

Jack swallowed again and looked away.

Neither of them said anything for a time, until Natalie whispered, 'What was your girlfriend's name, the one who died of leukaemia?'

Jack was looking into the distance. 'Roxanna.'

'You wouldn't marry her because she didn't want children, though she might have changed her mind had she not died. How much, how much worse would it be for you if children were an impossibility?'

When Dr. Stone had told her at first Natalie hadn't known what to do or say. His news was so unexpected, so bewildering, so *unwanted* that she had floundered as to what to feel.

679

Then it had started. It was as if a dizzying cloud of blackness had spread slowly over her. A tide of something – something scalding and chilling at the same time – had swept along her skin, like when she had shed her nightdress over her head when she was a girl.

Natalie had felt tired, exhausted, *cheated*. She was sure she would choke. She had struggled for air. She could hear her pulse drumming in her ears. Her skin was damp with sweat. She was diminished, she was less than she had been, she was tainted, less than whole, less than a person, broken, sullied and soiled. How many more awful words were there to describe how she felt?

To Jack, she managed to say, 'I told you, once, I have hardly ever given children a thought. Now I can think about them only in their absence. A door that had never been opened for me has been closed for always.'

Natalie was openly weeping now, her body wracked by rugged sobs. Spittle formed in webs at the corners of her mouth. Her tears redoubled. Her sight was a blur of shifting splinters of light.

For the second time in her life, she had been bereaved twice over, and there was now no chance of making good what had been lost. The tears rolled down her cheeks and she made no attempt to stem them. The shaking of her body rocked the Land Rover as much as the wind outside.

After a long silence, during which various waterbuck and eland crossed their line of sight in the distance, Jack leaned forward and rested his forehead on the steering wheel.

'I feel as if all the air has been let out of me, all

the blood drained away.' He sat up again and wiped his eyes with his hands. 'Nothing is going on inside me. I'm a wasteland.'

Natalie reached out again and laid her hand on his arm. 'If we got married, how long would it be before you regretted it?'

He leaned back again but said nothing.

'You were there, in the clinic, when I really needed you. We helped each other, I think. I felt warmer when you were around.' She smiled sadly. 'In Lamu I loved being ogled as much as you liked ogling. Then ... what happened happened.' She looked directly at him and her voice broke again. 'We must face it, Jack. Children matter to you – you have said it often. I saw it for myself, the day we took those boys and girls flying over their villages.'

Another long silence.

'And you've known about this for only a day?'

Natalie nodded. 'I lied about us in court. Not over this.'

She looked at him and he looked at her. He would make a good father; she had told herself that before.

He passed his hand over his face, but didn't look at her as he said, 'No one finds it odd that the urge to have children is so strong in women – why not men? The urge must exist in all men at some level. It's just that no one ever talks about it.' His fingers touched the rim of the steering wheel.

The wind still rocked the Land Rover.

'Is it some failing in me, or is it my genes doing their job, telling me they want to survive, be passed on?'

They watched in silence as some zebra ran into view and then on out of sight.

Jack went to speak again more than once, but each time subsided into silence. Finally, he said, in a whisper. 'I ... how many ways can you be bereaved? My mother, Christopher, the baby, you ... all leaving by different doors.'

An open door, she told herself silently, could be as final, as cold, as a closed one.

'Dr. Stone was wrong about you, wrong to be worried about you not having any inner strength, I mean. Daniel always said you fought your corner like a lion. Where does that ... where does it come from?'

Natalie wiped her chin with the palm of her hand. 'I must have been born with some, and my mother filled my head with *résistance*, as the French say. But your mother had a lot to do with it.' She nodded as he looked up. 'That night I shared with her in her tent, I saw her mental toughness. Whatever your father did and didn't do with all those younger women, she kept her dignity and stuck with what she was good at. It helped me ... it helped me in court, and she saw that, I think, when I managed to keep some dignity.'

To keep her dignity, Natalie had lied in court. How often had Eleanor Deacon lied – to others and herself – to keep *her* dignity, to keep her work in the gorge on the rails?

Natalie reached into her pocket for her handkerchief, wiped her eyes and cheeks, her mouth, blew her nose, looked out at the plain, the immense sky, the thorn bushes rocking and waving in the wind.

Night was not long away. Not the comforting, rainy, cosy nights of Lincolnshire but night that, here in the bush, was far more dangerous than the day.

She let another long silence go by, as more zebra moved through the acacia trees. The giraffes and the guinea fowl had disappeared.

Natalie put her arm on his. 'My bag's in the back, with my painkillers. Could you get it for me, please? My pelvis is complaining. Then we should think about putting in an appearance at the reception.'

'Of course.' He got down and went to the back of the vehicle.

Natalie looked out of the window again. The sun was now completely covered by clouds. In the distance she saw some Maasai figures in their red cloaks crossing the plain, going home.

Home. Where was that now, for her?

Natalie leaned her head against the glass of the side window and closed her wet eyes. The thorn trees were moaning – almost screaming – all around but that wasn't the sound she heard. The scream she heard came from deep within her.

Postscript

The timing given for the origins of bipedalism is correct for the years in which this book is set. Since 1962, however, the age at which early man first walked upright has been pushed further and further back. (Possibly to 4.5 million years ago, with the form of early man known as *Ardipithecus*.) For an excellent, accessible introductory account, see *Ancestral Passions: The Leakey Family and the Quest for Humankind's Beginnings*, by Virginia Morell (Simon and Schuster, 1995), one of the sources I have relied on for period and scientific detail.

Kenya was declared independent in December 1963.

Jack Deacon married Elisabeth Kilibwani in Nairobi in 1964. They had four children. He died in 1972 of testicular cancer.

Natalie Nelson married Peter Jeavons, in the House of Commons Chapel, in 1966. In 1967 she fought a parliamentary by-election for the Chapel St. Leonards constituency in Lincolnshire, winning by a comfortable margin. Three years later she was appointed a junior minister at the Foreign and Commonwealth Office with special responsibility for sub-Saharan Africa.

Christopher Deacon's body was never found.

The publishers hope that this book has given you enjoyable reading. Large Print Books are especially designed to be as easy to see and hold as possible. If you wish a complete list of our books please ask at your local library or write directly to:

Magna Large Print Books
Magna House, Long Preston,
Skipton, North Yorkshire.
BD23 4ND

This Large Print Book for the partially sighted, who cannot read normal print, is published under the auspices of

THE ULVERSCROFT FOUNDATION

THE ULVERSCROFT FOUNDATION

... we hope that you have enjoyed this Large Print Book. Please think for a moment about those people who have worse eyesight problems than you ... and are unable to even read or enjoy Large Print, without great difficulty.

You can help them by sending a donation, large or small to:

**The Ulverscroft Foundation,
1, The Green, Bradgate Road,
Anstey, Leicestershire, LE7 7FU,
England.**
or request a copy of our brochure for more details.

The Foundation will use all your help to assist those people who are handicapped by various sight problems and need special attention.

Thank you very much for your help.